PETRA

a novel

ৰৰৰ ৯৯৯

Patricia K. Gray

Pale Horse Books

Copyright © 2013 by Patricia K. Gray

Cover Design: Sally Stiles

Cover photograph of *Petra, El Khasneh*, 1842-49, a lithograph by David Roberts, courtesy of Medina Arts, Inc., Seattle WA

Grateful acknowledgment is made for permission: to reprint "Fame is a bee" from *THE POEMS OF EMILY DICKINSON: VARIORUM EDITION,* edited by Ralph W. Franklin, Cambridge, Mass.: The Belknap Press of Harvard University Press, Copyright © 1951, 1955, 1979, 1983 by the President and Fellows of Harvard College.

Grateful acknowledgment of inspiration for a phrase on page 328, "a moon like a giant sponge," derived from a poem by Christian Rose.

The Library of Congress has cataloged the Pale Horse Books edition as follows:
Gray, Patricia K.
Petra: a novel by Patricia K. Gray
p. cm.
1.Artists—Fiction. 2. Middle East—Fiction. 3. Petra—(Extinct city). 4. Travelers—Middle East—Fiction.
PS3607.R39P48 2013
2012542716

ISBN: 978-1-939917-01-0

www.palehorsebooks.com

Printed in the United States of America

For Nick, Nabil, Christian, and Sofia

Dream of a better world and follow your dream.

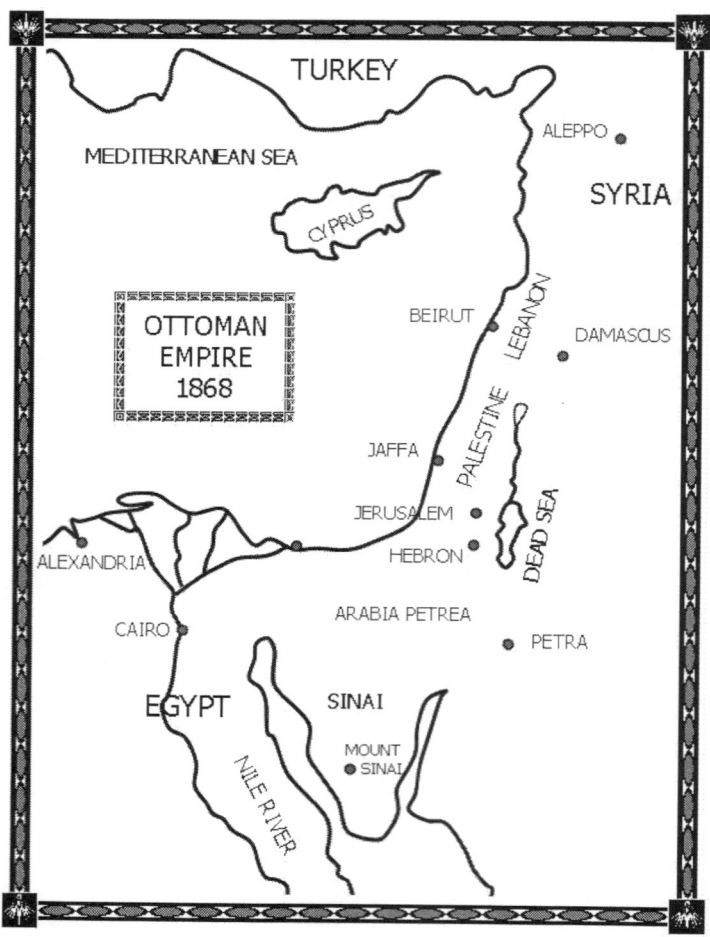

Fame is a bee.
It has a song–
It has a sting–
Ah, too, it has a wing.

Emily Dickinson

ONE

Painting is silent poetry,
and poetry is painting that speaks.
Plutarch

Paris, January 1868

The sleek black carriage clattered along the boulevard and stopped at 2 Place de l'Opera. Thomas Hudson stepped out into a light rain and sprinted toward the door of the Galerie Goupil. In those few moments, he traveled from the streets of Paris to the gates of Cairo.

Standing inside the gallery's grand salon, he turned slowly and gazed at burgundy colored walls crowded with paintings of Egypt, shimmering in the flickering light of gas lamps. The figures on the brightly painted canvases bewildered the American artist. Two dark skinned runners waving whips cleared a path for the procession of the Egyptian Pasha and his entourage. Nearby, fair skinned women, lightly dressed in diaphanous veils, danced lasciviously among soldiers in silk turbans spangled with beads and tassels. From the height of the Citadel, the conquering Napoleon astride a chestnut stallion looked down on the city of Cairo. Moving slowly through massive gates, Bedouin men, swathed in hooded kaftans against the stinging sand, steered their camels toward a vast desert.

Hudson breathed deeply, then turned to find a painting titled Slave Market. A man's hand lay on the head of a naked, shy young woman while he examined her teeth with his other hand, as if he were buying a racehorse. Beside them, another woman with a young child in her lap waited her turn before the slave dealer. The child reached down with a stick, and it seemed she might begin drawing in the sand, like Emily and John at the beach near their home. Seeing one's child sold into slavery might be as tragic as watching them die. The thought left a slick of sweat inside his shirt. Why did he torture himself, allow every child, real or imagined, to remind him of his failure as a father? If he continued on this path, no amount of brilliant painting would rescue him from oblivion.

Moving away from the exotic paintings, he found a sharp contrast in the restrained elegance of Parisian visitors mingling quietly around the gallery—the men in their black morning suits and top hats, the women in pale silk dresses with fur-trimmed coats. Others sat sedately on a red velvet banquette in the center of the room. Perhaps the slate gray January day filtering through the skylight subdued the mood; their faces registered no reaction to the paintings. It was impossible for him to know if they were shocked, pleased, or simply indifferent. He was accustomed to far more lively gatherings at his exhibits in New York.

No one appeared to be looking for him, and Hudson slipped through the crowd to examine another painting by Jacques Vesoul. Turkish soldiers guarded a pyramid of bleeding, severed heads on the doorstep of a mosque. According to the painting's title, the heads had once belonged to old and young Egyptian men identified as rebel Beys. Hudson's eyes moved up the exquisitely painted surface until he saw three more heads with bulging eyes, hung over the door by their scraggly black hair. He instinctively moved back a step and bumped into a gentleman holding opera glasses. "Pardonnez moi, Monsieur."

The Frenchman smiled at Hudson and extended his hand. "Forgive me for being late. I am Jacques Vesoul, and I have been looking forward to meeting you, Mr. Hudson."

"The pleasure is mine," Hudson said, grasping Vesoul's hand a little too tightly and for much too long. "I have been studying your fascinating interpretations of Egypt. The severed heads are quite . . . dramatic."

4

"The incident was described to me by the Sultan's aides in Constantinople. When the Mamluk Beys of Cairo rebelled against Ottoman rule in Egypt, punishment by sword was swift." Vesoul turned to look at the American artist to gauge his reaction to the violence, but Thomas Hudson's attention had shifted from bloody heads to a peaceful scene of Muhammadans in a mosque.

"It may amuse you to know, Mr. Hudson, that I used the faces of some of my more severe critics for the severed heads." Vesoul spoke with the confidence of a Parisian artist with many friends and only a few foes among the men of the press.

Hudson stiffened slightly, and his pale blue eyes widened. He had never felt quite so hostile toward his New York art critics, and he was shaken by both parts of the story.

"Come, come, Mr. Hudson. I jest with critics, but Sultans do not jest with rebels." Vesoul frowned, and his bristly eyebrows cast a shadow over deeplyset, dark eyes.

For almost an hour, the two artists conversed quietly about several paintings from Vesoul's recent travels in Egypt. Hudson frequently borrowed the Frenchman's opera glasses to examine paintings hung frame to frame and waist to high ceiling. The titles of the paintings were often vague—"An Oriental Bazaar" or "Women of the Orient," and he searched for some detail to reveal the specific place.

"What is this place you call the Orient?" Hudson asked in a whisper. "It is difficult to tell whether I am looking at the streets of Damascus or Jerusalem."

Vesoul placed his hand gently on Hudson's shoulder. "You may be looking at a combination of cities. For us, the Orient is the land between Constantinople and Alexandria, arcing like a crescent moon around the eastern Mediterranean—the center, but not the whole of the Ottoman Empire."

"And this is how it looks?"

"More or less. Why do you ask?"

"Your paintings, Monsieur Vesoul. They speak to me of violence and conquest, even the women appear conquered by the men. Is that how you think of the region?"

"*Mais oui!* The Orient has been that way since the beginning of time, Mr. Hudson. It has been conquered by Egyptians, Assyrians, Persians, Greeks, Arabs, and Ottomans, to name a few. Perhaps, it is the destiny of a crossroads where great civilizations and major religions encounter each other."

"Destiny?"

"I think so." Vesoul paused. "Already Europeans are studying their maps to divide and conquer what is left of the Ottoman Empire. As for the women, do not delude yourself, Mr. Hudson, the Orient is a man's world." He ended his comments with a small shrug.

"Divide and conquer? Are you suggesting conflict? Will there be war?" Hudson's voice rose in volume with each question.

"Conflict, perhaps, but not war." Vesoul replied.

"How can you be sure?"

"Of course, I am not sure." Now Vesoul's voice grew louder. "Who can be sure what France and England will do given any feeble excuse to slice off bits of the Ottoman Empire?"

Hudson rubbed his neck and loosened his collar. "I did not expect conflict . . .."

"*Mon Dieu*, Hudson, I did not intend to frighten you!"

Hudson noticed other visitors moving away from them, but Vesoul continued, his arms punching the air.

"We artists avoid conflict by keeping our attention on art and adventure. We experience these cultures, then translate images into glorious paintings."

Vesoul pushed Hudson gently toward a painting of a harem. "As you can see, the Orient produces in its lands, beloved of the sun, the most beautiful races, the purest types. There the human clay is less altered by civilization, more intriguing for patrons. I find . . ."

"Could we continue this discussion in a more private place, Monsieur?"

Vesoul stopped his lecture and looked around the salon before turning again to Hudson. "Do you have time to join me in our private room for coffee?"

Hudson's demeanor brightened immediately. "I would be delighted. My carriage will not arrive until six o'clock."

From a balcony above the salon, Adolphe Goupil watched the interactions between Vesoul and Hudson. He was more than idly curious about Thomas Hudson's appearance in Europe. When last in New York, Goupil was told that Hudson always rejected the idea of being represented by a European gallery or even traveling to Europe—he wanted only American influence in his art. Hudson's paintings concentrated on majestic landscapes of the natural world, with an abundance of American patriotism overflowing onto each canvas.

Goupil knew the American would be a good fish to catch for his Paris and New York galleries. If Hudson intended to paint European landscapes, interest would be especially high. Realistic images were popular among Goupil's clients, both in landscapes and Oriental scenes. He expected both Hudson and Vesoul were reluctant to refer to their work as realist painting, but that was Goupil's opinion.

The similarity of the two artists in stature and appearance impressed Goupil. Both were tall with trim figures emphasized by their erect posture—Hudson slighter taller than Vesoul. Both had classically handsome faces, receding hairlines, and large mustaches—Vesoul's a refined handlebar and Hudson's an unruly walrus style. The difference registered in their eyes. Vesoul had a fiery glint in his seal brown eyes; Hudson's blue eyes were soft and pensive. Goupil believed eyes were usually the telling feature, both in life and art.

When Goupil saw Vesoul escorting Hudson into the gallery's private room, he smiled and rose from his chair. Jacques would be at dinner, and Goupil expected to hear about Hudson's intentions later in the evening.

The private room of the Galerie Goupil reminded Hudson of athenaeum libraries in New England towns. On the left, tall arched windows flooded the interior space with light even on this cloudy afternoon. Heavy blue velvet draperies would keep out wintery nights. Well stuffed bookcases, interrupted only by doors, covered two walls, and a marble fireplace dominated the remaining wall. Above the mantle hung a painting of bearded and turbaned men lifting their hands and eyes in prayer.

"One of yours?" Hudson asked.

"Yes, of course, painted after my first visit to Cairo," Vesoul replied. "Muhammadans answer the call to prayer anywhere—in mosques, along streets, or on rooftops as you see in my painting."

Vesoul excused himself to arrange for coffee, and Hudson watched the Frenchman in his well-cut clothing cross the room with athletic grace, his dark brown hair waved in a short style that was the vogue in Paris. He admired this talented and intelligent man, felt flattered by his attention, but a bit of envy curdled his view. Both artists had achieved enormous success in their art and reputations, but the current demand for Oriental scenes had sent Vesoul's star soaring on both sides of the Atlantic, while Hudson was experiencing a waning of demand for the epic American landscape.

In the prime of his life, Hudson radiated an elegant style that spoke of stately homes and fine linen tablecloths and hid his more modest beginnings. He possessed a sharp mind and keen ambition, making him popular in New York society. Romantic women gave a second glance to his charming face—sky blue eyes and pleasingly soft mouth, his prominent eyebrows descending into lofty cheek bones and the nose of a Greek god. To his male friends, he appeared as a man of good cheer, an artist with justified confidence. He knew only an astute observer would guess he was struggling with a number of demons, especially the raging guilt following the deaths of his children

While waiting for Vesoul to return, Hudson browsed the titles of the leather bound books, mainly in French or German, until his attention settled on the massive oak table covered with maps of Egypt and Syria, including an enlarged copy of John Lewis Burckhardt's map of Petra. He was picking up the Burckhardt map when Vesoul returned to the room. "I see you share my obsession with maps, or do these belong to Monsieur Goupil?"

A slight smile crossed Vesoul's face as he shook his head. "*Non, non.* Goupil would not be interested in maps of little pecuniary value. They are part of my collection. Serious travelers are identified by the quality of maps in their baggage, *oui?*

"I agree, *Monsieur.* I always control the route of my travels." Hudson squinted to read the annotations on the Burckhardt map.

"Is the Petra Valley of interest to you, Mr. Hudson?"

"Ah, yes. Petra is my goal." Hudson replied as he raised his head, looking toward Vesoul but seeing into a farther distance. "After I saw the David Roberts lithographs and read Burckhardt's narrative, the idea of a city lost in time for over a thousand years was irresistible."

"It was not lost to the Bedouin, and I hear they are quick to remind foreigners of that fact." Vesoul moved closer to Hudson and pointed to a place on the map. "You see here, Wadi Musa?"

"You mean the dot just before the Siq?"

"*Oui, oui.* Do you know Bedouin tribes guard that area, and they may prevent you from entering Petra?"

"What? Can they do that?" Hudson dropped the map on the table. "Why? Why would they do that?"

Vesoul shrugged. "Sometimes they are angry. Who knows why. Maybe a previous traveler has offended their customs."

Hudson was aware that the suggestion of danger was usually one comma behind the word Petra. He cleared his throat quietly and asked, "Are you worried about travelers' tales of Bedouin raids and savagery?"

"Concerned, yes, but not worried. My friends tell me that with reasonable behavior, a reliable guide, and generous baksheesh, there is no problem."

Hudson nodded. "Every visitor to the Orient complains about baksheesh, but I find money speaks loudly in every language."

"*Mais, oui,*" Vesoul said with a bright smile. "It appears that we are both about to begin a journey."

"Yes, I will be following your large footsteps in the Orient after this brief visit to Paris, Monsieur Vesoul."

"We may be walking in each other's footsteps as I am leaving soon for Egypt," Vesoul added, "followed by a major expedition across the Sinai to Petra. Will this be your first time in that part of the world?"

"Yes, first on the Continent, as well. Frankly, the Old World, as we call it in America, has held less interest for me, but now I am eager to explore a very different terrain and culture."

"And will you be painting?" Vesoul's eyes narrowed a bit as he studied the American's face, waiting for a reply.

Hudson looked down and ran his fingers along the curved edge of the table. Was he ready to speak of his intentions? Was he even sure of his intentions? He and Vesoul had many American patrons in common. In the past those men had hung landscapes by Hudson in their new Fifth Avenue mansions; now they were commissioning Vesoul's exotic Oriental scenes. He valued his reputation and financial rewards and did not want either to be tarnished.

"I may paint . . . ." Hudson paused and considered again the question that needled him—would he find the inspiration to paint? He was an earnest man, motivated by ideals and the passion to translate those ideals into paint. For him, painting was not a profession, it was a calling, an irresistible desire to express the spiritual power of nature.

He tapped the table and looked directly at Vesoul. "Oriental themes are very popular in America now, as you well know. But I am a landscape artist, and I have never experienced desert terrain and ancient ruins. I will be looking to decide whether this quite different landscape has meaning for me."

Vesoul clasped his hands behind his back, straightened, and gained another inch before replying. "Goupil tells me that you and several of your colleagues in the Hudson River School have strong ideological impulses—quite unlike my own inclinations." His heavy mustache hid his grin; his shoulders relaxed as he continued. "My friends and I travel for adventure. We explore the mosques and the monuments, then rampage through the desert in pursuit of gazelles or pigeons. Incidentally, subjects for painting may arise. I think we are not so serious about our art until we return to our studios."

Hudson listened to Vesoul as he stared beyond the windows at the ghostlike shapes of buildings hovering in the mist. For him, art defined travel. Whether in Ecuador or the Arctic regions, he searched for inspiration, explored with his pencil and brush. Adventure was incidental.

" . . . and what is on your itinerary, *mon ami?*"

"Oh, yes," Hudson stammered as he regained his attention. "My main objectives are Petra and Jerusalem, but I will begin in Beirut, visiting with friends there in the American missionary community, and perhaps finding some companions for my travels among them. I have only two months for your Orient."

"So short a time for such a long journey?"

Hudson laughed. "For me it is a long time to be away from family. And your plans, *Monsieur?*"

"It will be a great and glorious caravan!" Vesoul kissed his fingertips into the air, then shuffled the maps until he found one in English. "From Paris we go to Marseilles by train, a ship from Marseilles to Alexandria, by rail to Cairo. After Cairo we take the train due east to Suez, meet the Bedouin guides and camels, and begin the most difficult part of the journey." He traced the route east with his finger. "We head south and east along the Sinai desert and through high mountains to the Monastery of St. Catharine in the great peaks of the Sinai. After a few days encampment, we descend the eastern slopes of the Sinai Mountains to Aqaba then up through Wadi Arabah into Petra."

"And you will be painting in Petra?" Hudson asked.

"Sketching, always I am sketching—people, buildings, animals, everything. Later some of them may jump into my paintings, but one cannot predict, *non?* My men and I also plan some hunting expeditions with the Bedouin in the Wadi Rum region, near Petra."

Just then the gallery assistant appeared with a tray, and the two men moved to leather armchairs in front of the fireplace. Vesoul cleared a place on a small table between them for the coffee and brandy.

The silvery clouds of the afternoon had darkened into a steely gray, and large raindrops now crashed against the wall of glass. It was a sight and sound that Hudson enjoyed, but Vesoul's assistant pulled the drapes across the windows and lit the gas lamps.

11

As the warmth of the glowing coals reached his feet, Hudson realized how chilled he had become on a wintery afternoon. Warm interiors were not a feature of Parisian structures, and the rawness affected his mood. Now, the comfort of a warm drink by a fire eased conversation for him. "About ten years ago, that Belgian art promoter held a showing of French artists of the Academy—I think at the Goupil & Son Gallery on Broadway— and it included your painting of Turkish officers and captured men in manacles moving across bare, burning sands."

"*Mais oui*," Vesoul recalled. "I called it Egyptian Recruits Crossing the Desert."

"That is the one," Hudson said. "The afternoon brilliance of the sun intensified the whiteness of the sky and the sand, and the feeling of dryness was almost suffocating." He paused, rubbing his forehead. "It was striking that the men you depicted were so diverse in facial features and costume. I felt I was seeing a broad sweep of the history and peoples of the eastern Mediterranean."

"I painted that image after my first travels in Egypt, about ten years ago," Vesoul said. "It was a happy time of youth and adventure, resulting in many pictures, more or less successful, more or less to the taste of the public. The title of the painting is, of course, ironic—as the manacles indicate, the men were enslaved, not recruited."

Hudson remembered the manacles, but had thought the men to be prisoners of war. Perhaps that was synonymous with slavery in the Ottoman Empire. "You and your French compatriots seem to have captured the Orient."

"Captured?" Vesoul frowned and his eyes narrowed. Vesoul's eyes were his dominant feature and not difficult to read. Their brown hue deepened with thought, and with excitement they moved rapidly in their orbit. There was a curious lack of precise coordination, one eye being a little heavy lidded, the other wide open.

"I hope I did not offend you, Monsieur, by my use of the word 'capture.' I meant only in the artistic sense."

"What offends me is my country's behavior, not your remark, Mr. Hudson. Ever since Napoleon's campaign of 1798, some of my countrymen have thought of Egypt in particular as our private playground. I do not identify with their economic and political aspirations, but I find the region invigorates me."

Vesoul shifted in his chair and faced Hudson directly. "I like the Orient the way it is—erupting with contradictions, endlessly fascinating, and resisting change. Alexandria is already becoming too westernized for my taste." He jabbed the fire with the poker by his chair and poured more coffee into the cups. "Enough about me. Your painting of Niagara Falls commanded a prime location at the recent Paris Exposition. I have never visited America, but I have seen a number of paintings of Niagara, and you achieved something sublime. I felt I was standing at the brink of the falls."

The compliment embarrassed Hudson, and he fumbled with his collar. He had submitted only one painting to the Exposition, but that large scale depiction of Niagara Falls epitomized everything he had to say about the power and spirituality of the American landscape. It had confirmed his early fame in America and Europe in the 1850s.

"It was a puzzle for me to assemble my sketches of the falls in my studio. As I thought about how to convey the idea of Niagara as a symbol of America's freedom and dynamism, the view from above the falls seemed right."

"How extraordinary you Americans are," Vesoul teased, "with your nationalism displayed on your chest like a medal."

"Ah, yes, we do tend to see our democratic government as the answer to man's struggle for *liberté, égalité, fraternité.*"

"*Touché, mon ami.* Here in France we are caught in an endless tennis match, hitting the ball back and forth between monarchy and republic. We speak of history and paint pictures of history, but we do not learn from history," Vesoul laughed and reached for the brandy. "Would you care for a glass of cognac?"

Hudson looked at the bottle. Was it too early for brandy? The label was impressive—never too early for such a fine bottle. He traded his coffee cup for a snifter of Courvoisier.

Vesoul talked about the rigid training in the French art academies, peppering his remarks with amusing anecdotes about drawing hands—fat, slender, stubby, hairy, dirty, broken hands.

13

Hudson spoke of his beloved teacher, Thomas Cole, a second father who marched him through pristine forests and up soaring mountains, encouraging him to express the deep spirituality of nature in his compositions, to warn Americans against the exploitation of nature.

"Goupil mentioned you traveled to South America and the Arctic as a young man," Vesoul said as if jungles and seas had appeared in Hudson's eyes. "How I envy you. I was chained by necessity to commissions in Paris. Even now, my well being depends on pleasing the public who currently want Oriental scenes. As we both know, commissions require many compromises. In French we say, '*Le client est Roi.*' "

Hudson gripped the arms of his chair as he considered the meaning of that statement, 'the client is King.' He knew that Cole would have been repelled by it. The true artist pursued his passion, not filling his pockets. Hudson wrestled with that dichotomy as he saw his prominence decline. He had assumed an independent life of acclaim and commissions would last forever. Now he confronted tempting compromises to revive his reputation and accounts.

In the midst of these disturbing thoughts, the gallery assistant appeared to ask if Hudson wanted the carriage to continue waiting. Hudson pulled out his pocket watch and saw there was little time before his dinner engagement. The two artists walked through the grand salon, and Vesoul opened the doors of Galerie Goupil to the street where the carriage waited. Afternoon rain had turned to sleet, and the steaming horses pawed at icy cobblestones reflecting the glow of the gaslights.

"*Au revoir,* Mr. Hudson. I hope for a rendezvous in Petra."

"Safe travels, *Monsieur.*" Hudson shook hands with Vesoul and closed the carriage door. The driver snapped the whip high in the air, and joined the herd of carriages heading down the boulevard.

In his dark corner of the carriage Hudson thought about the afternoon. He had been somewhat bored during his recent travels in England and France, but now he was awakening again. Was it because of Jacques Vesoul? Hudson appreciated his company, his brilliance, his caustic and witty remarks. He enjoyed watching his eyes flashing and arms turning words into gestures.

Or was his enthusiasm for Vesoul aroused by talk of painting and travel? With his stories Vesoul brought the large exhibit of French painters to life, and the paintings opened like windows revealing a vastly different world. Hudson knew that for him there was a disturbing gulf between the images that stirred his curiosity and those that created a sense of unease, even revulsion.

He had resisted the urge to ask Vesoul whether his paintings of people accurately portrayed their lives. Artists take liberties with their subjects, but he wondered when liberties became misrepresentations. Was the Frenchman revealing or inventing the Orient? Did it matter? He reminded himself that the beginnings of his journeys were often haunted by his own insecurities. For now, he needed to stay focused on his artistic goals and avoid issues that might complicate his journey. The major task at hand was to accomplish several oil paintings that would revive his reputation. Petra sat like a siren on a hidden island, waiting for a painter who could reveal her uniqueness.

The carriage swung violently in the dark night to avoid a man dressed in black who pushed a cart of coal on the slippery street. The jolt shook Hudson out of his imaginings. Black and white edges of his life leaped into focus. Perhaps he would not find landscapes with meaning. If there was no meaning, would he paint? How would he live without his art? The fingers of his right hand felt welded to the armrest; it hurt to release them.

As the carriage slowed again, he took several deep breaths and relaxed into the rhythm of the trotting horses. The darkness was occasionally interrupted by a café blazing with light, color, music. He thought about his wife, Katharine, and her yearning for the Paris of her childhood. All their dreams of seeing Paris together had to be tucked away when Tommy was born. They would not put a baby at risk after the deaths of Emily and John. The arrival of Tommy had raised Katharine out of the piercing grief, but Hudson still dragged heavy chains of guilt. Guilt measured his days into moments of sorrow and filled his nights with choking ghosts. Katharine never blamed him, and he still heard her voice urging him to travel, to paint, to find solace. Travel had always been the elixir for his spirits and the inspiration for his art.

Vesoul knew Goupil was eager to hear about Hudson's visit. After dinner with their large boisterous family, they collected cigars and cognac and moved toward the warmth of the library fireplace. Goupil was the kind of large figured, almost bald man who seemed natural with a cigar between his teeth. On the rare occasions when he temporarily removed the cigar, his booming voice resounded through the gallery workroom like a bass drum. He was a major player in the world art market and eager for news about Thomas Hudson's intentions.

"You know, Jacques," Goupil leaned forward, "Hudson is not yet represented by a gallery on the Continent. And he is still a dominant force in an American art market that is beginning to neglect American landscapes."

"*Mais, oui*, of course, I still read the critics," Vesoul said, hardly disguising the sarcasm in his tone. "I have only seen his painting of Niagara at the recent Exposition, but I expect you saw some of his South American paintings in New York."

"Yes, on several occasions. It is a strong body of work, and Hudson is a master of design and publicity."

"What do you mean?"

"I visited the Tenth Street Studio in New York City—the building where Hudson has his studio. He was exhibiting a single, quite large painting of the Andes Mountains—an extraordinary vision. I felt as if I were looking out a window in Ecuador. The unusual lighting and elaborate casing of the huge frame created an illusion of both immediacy and vastness."

Goupil paused to light his cigar. "The painting itself is a journey from the feast of botanical detail in the foreground through the geology of plains, rifts, and foothills until ascending to the snowy domes of mountains in the distance. And friends of Monsieur Hudson have written poetic brochures to guide you through the experience."

Vesoul coughed and spilled drops of his brandy. "Did that not give you some ideas for your own gallery?" Vesoul asked, wiping away the brandy drops. "Perhaps, encourage you to consider a more reasonable space to view a painting, rather than stacking them to the ceiling? Allow us to exhibit individually and charge for entrance as Hudson does? Really, Goupil, you are an amusing old hypocrite."

"Yes, yes, but the American ways are different," Goupil said. "What did you think of Hudson?"

Vesoul inhaled the seductive aroma of a hundred-year-old cognac as he swirled the liquid in the snifter. He raised it to a height where the flashes of light from the fireplace created a continuously changing color spectrum from pale gold to amber. "Hudson has a reserved temperament with occasional cracks when his sentiments leap out, and he is a good listener who absorbs ideas and replies thoughtfully. His conversation is interesting but cautious. He seems like a man who is carrying a burden that he is not ready to put down."

"What do you mean by burden?"

"It was not clear to me, but I sensed that there were heavy concerns or sorrows that reined in a more ebullient personality."

"Why is he here?" Goupil asked. "He came too late for the *Exposition Universelle.*"

"He mentioned that family matters delayed his travel. You will be surprised to hear that he is on his way to Egypt, Palestine and Syria. And you will be even more surprised to hear that he is considering painting Oriental subjects."

"*Mon dieu*, he is launching an invasion into your territory!" Goupil appeared to enjoy needling Vesoul about the increasing competition.

"We will see." Vesoul would not take up that gauntlet this late at night.

TWO

"Sighing of the waves. Cries of watchmen at night.
Lanterns. Assassins. Sun strokes."
Herman Melville, Alexandria, 1857

Marseilles to Alexandria and Beirut, January 1868

On a cold, wet January morning Thomas Hudson ascended the gangplank into the fog that had swallowed the S.S. Provence. None of the hundred or so passengers stayed on deck to wave goodbye to family members since it was impossible to see the dock. Instead, the throng of travelers noisily searched for their rooms, competing with the clanging and rumbling sounds of the ship. Hudson followed the porters with his baggage to an upper deck stateroom barely large enough for turning around without bruising elbows on the bed or washstand. At present, the porthole offered the same gray view as the walls, but eventually it would connect him with the Mediterranean Sea.

January 1868, Hudson, to his wife, Katharine in New York
My Dearest Katharine,
The passage from Marseilles to Alexandria was rough; the ship rolled and pitched terribly after the Straits of Messina, leaving travelers to cling to the deck railings or their beds. There was much whispering of seasickness which I think we all experienced, but few wanted to admit. After five days of raging winds, a perfect calm surrounded the ship as we entered the protected harbor of Alexandria under a clear night sky, with the lights of the city beautifully reflected in the bay.
The calm was brief. The SS Provence had barely dropped anchor when a low murmur became an incredible din, as dozens of rowboats overflowing

with Egyptians laid siege to our ship—desperate for the chance to carry our trunks, find our hotels, introduce us to the pleasures of the harem. Our burly captain raised his arms, blew his trumpet, and the mob began to row fiercely toward another arrival. Other more disciplined boats appeared to transfer our passengers and luggage to the docks where hotel carriages were waiting.

I am at the Peninsula & Oriental, a hotel run by the steamship company—well appointed with modern amenities and a haven from the chaos outside the door. It is near the Place des Consuls—an open space bounded by two wide boulevards, unusual in a city known for its torturously narrow and winding streets. Across from the hotel there is a central park with palm trees and splashing fountains, features designed for foreigners, but available to the public. In the afternoon happy children run through the trees in wild pursuit, playing tag or hide and seek, while their nursemaids gossip in groups. It took me back to carefree days with Emily and John at our farm.

Without you these last weeks, I felt sightless in Paris. Nothing pleased with the splendor you promised—the boulevards not so grand, the houses somewhat shabby, the opera less exciting, the exhibitions confusing, and the creme caramel not so sweet without you to smile above your spoon. I trust that you are still content with your decision to remain in New York with Tommy. I miss you every day, but understand your need to protect our child.

With all my love, Thomas

With only one full day to see Alexandria before boarding the next ship for Beirut, Hudson again mulled over the idea of giving more time to traveling in Egypt. It might be his only opportunity to be in this part of the world. Cairo and Luxor were tempting, but he had only three months and needed to keep his focus on Syria and Palestine, especially Petra. Those were the places where he envisioned the possibility of great landscape paintings.

He filled his day in Alexandria from early morning to late evening with wanderings about a city that was more international than he expected. A hotel carriage drove him to the port district. On the way he gazed open-mouthed at the flowing crowd of people and animals, screeching and braying, running and pushing. Street hawkers and donkey-boys shouted for customers; women wrapped in long blue draperies balanced burdens on their heads while dragging along strings of children; camels, asses, and horses fought for the best parts of the roads and foot walks. The driver of the carriage squeezed through these masses with the mastery of a well-oiled contortionist.

When the carriage halted near the office of the harbormaster, Hudson pushed open the door to face beggars pulling his arms, grabbing his coat, screaming for baksheesh. The driver jumped off his perch and beat back the mob, yelling, "*La, la, la, imshi, imshi.*" He pulled Hudson into the office and shut the door.

Shaking his head, Hudson said, "Welcome to the Orient!" addressing no one in particular. "What did you say to make them go away?" The driver did not speak English, but another Arab who had been watching the encounter replied, "*La* means 'no,' and *imshi* means 'go away.' You will find them useful here."

In the area of the port, flags of England, France, Germany, Russia, America, India, and China flew above sailing and steam ships. He watched while a procession of natives clad in rough tunics struggled to haul crates of manufactures from ships onto the docks, then return with bales of Egyptian long fiber cotton balanced on their heads. Men robed in galabiyas stood by with whips to hasten the circle of drudgery under a burning sun. When one of the natives tripped on a rope and dropped a bale, he felt the sting of two whips and turned on his assailants.

Fearing a fight, Hudson headed into a covered bazaar. Here, too, he found an array of nationalities and races. Negroes with skin like roasted coffee beans bargained with light brown Arabs who worked for ivory skinned Turks. They shouted at each other in Arabic—a language of robust sounds emerging from the caves of the body. Goods from the Orient, Europe, and Asia hung from tents, spilled onto tables—frankincense from Arabia; porcelain and clothing from England; a blond haired doll with china blue eyes from god knows where; glass lamps from Belgium; and fine silks from Syria and China.

Hudson picked up a carved wooden stick, about the diameter of a broom handle, but only a foot long, with what looked like a turban at one end. As he examined it, the men around him laughed and elbowed each other. One of them took the stick and placed it beside his crotch. Hudson's red face broke into a grin that pulled one side of his mouth toward his ear.

At the next tent a butcher carved the carcass of a lamb into small pieces of meat, quickly covered with flies. The sight of the offal slipping around the butcher's arm and putrid smell of rotting flesh drove him away. Losing his sense of direction, he rode a wave of humanity through a maze of stalls until the choking dust forced him out in a fit of coughing.

Hudson found himself on a winding street that emptied into a broad boulevard, deserted except for an occasional carriage. After walking about a mile under a harsh sun that quivered the landscape, he entered a quiet residential area where avenues of date palm trees shaded bright white villas beside the grand Mahmudiyah Canal. He felt delivered into a different time and place. Exhausted from the heat and noise, he sat on a low stone wall and watched the broad-beamed dahabiyas gliding through the still water, some under sail, others towed from the shore by an odd assortment of donkeys, horses, and camels harnessed together. The slender, arched masts of the boats brushed the soft blue sky. Their sails fluttered with the grace of butterflies.

The combination of architecture, water, and animals encouraged Hudson to pull out his small sketchbook and pencil. He looked at the blank pages and wondered if this simple scene should be his first sketch of the Orient—or should he look for something more grand. Why had he come to a point where he questioned every decision. Doubt dulled every action; no enthusiasm lifted his art.

Closing the sketchbook with a snap of frustration, he rose and turned toward the boulevard, then stopped and looked back at the animals towing the dahabiya. While the horses and donkeys plodded along in a steady gait, the camels appeared to resent the disgrace of pulling a boat, an unseemly burden for the ship of the desert. One of the beasts bit the flanks of the lead horse, and another dug his feet into the sand growling and bellowing against his fate. Hudson smiled at their noble rebellion against compromise.

After dinner in a quiet corner of the hotel bar, Hudson explored the nearby Muhammadan Quarter along *rue Ras el-Tin*, a safe street according to the concierge at the hotel. It was a favorite evening stroll for both visitors and locals. Shop keepers sat at the edge of the crowded street, drinking coffee with friends and beckoning strollers toward their wares.

He fingered several pieces of silver jewelry, but when the merchant pressured him, he backed away and found himself in a parade of peddlers weaving through the crowded street like circus entertainers displaying their talents. A thinly clad boy with a patched eye and scarred cheeks juggled a samovar and a stack of glasses, begging him to buy tea. A tall, black as obsidian, Nubian man whirled around him in a white linen robe covered with a collection of rainbow-colored satin shoes with turned-up toes and tiny bells. A woman, veiled head to toe, balanced small brass cages with yellow song birds, while an ancient fellow holding her elbow displayed his bag of carved wooden flutes. Hudson was tempted by the shoes until he realized that he had no idea of Katharine's foot size. All cried, "best price!" or "not too much!" Hudson kept shaking his head and politely saying, "La, la, la, imshi," the two words he now knew in Arabic. With no hope of a sale, they turned back to look for other foreigners.

Farther along, the street narrowed, then ended at a smaller crossroad that ran along the coastline. Hudson consulted his guidebook, then turned right toward the Citadel of Qaitbay. High walls concealed houses on either side of the deserted, deeply shadowed road. After walking a few minutes, he heard hoofbeats and carriage wheels scraping the roughly paved road behind him. He moved closer to the wall on his right. The carriage, already slowing, passed him, and stopped at an iron gate that swung open as a man in a white suit descended from the carriage.

Hudson guessed he was a foreigner visiting an Egyptian family. Knowing that he was not the only one moving along this lonely stretch of road reassured him.

Not far ahead the road ended at an open space around the citadel, lit only by the glow of a rising moon. Hudson appreciated the serenity of the space after the crowds on Ras el-Tin. The press of people all day tired him.

He had read that on this point, curving away from the Mediterranean Sea, the Pharos Lighthouse once stood. Now, the thick crenelated walls of a 15th century citadel loomed above him. The stone walls gave the appearance of a strongly fortified building, but no soldiers guarded the entrance or patrolled the summit where a flag snapped in the wind. On the north side, cannon in the crenels pointed toward the sea. He found a place to sit near the ramparts.

On the crisp, clear night, millions of stars lit the waters below. A light wind ruffled the waves into lacy whitecaps splashing against the shore. Hudson recalled days on the Maine coast when he sketched long into the evening until his hand felt the rhythm of the waters and the colors on his palette reflected the complex hues and luminosity of the waves. The challenge of painting storm-swept waves crashing into a rocky coast provided the first building block toward his bold idea of attempting Niagara Falls. With his left-hand fingers extended, he ticked off his waterscapes— Vermont, Maine, Ecuador, Colombia, New York . . . .

Sounds of the waves hid any noise from the two sailors who crept toward Hudson from the waterside. One grabbed him from behind—knocking off his hat, locking his arms, crushing his chest. Hudson struggled desperately against the brutal arms wrestling him into a crushing grip. He kicked back at the man's knees until the breath squeezed from his lungs ended with a sharp cry. Hudson, bent forward and gasping for breath, stared into the cruel face of the other sailor who waved a knife inches from his face. Hudson tried to push back, and the man pricked his cheek and showed him the blood. The warm blood dripping down Hudson's cheek onto his coat calmed him; he felt the knifer did not intend to kill him despite the savage look in his eyes. The men argued in a harsh sounding language unknown to Hudson, and the grip around his chest loosened slightly. He shuddered, breathing deeply until the knife wielder shoved his forearm under Hudson's chin and reached into his jacket.

A gunshot.

The man searching Hudson dropped his knife and fell to the ground, screaming and crawling. His friend released Hudson and pushed him aside, drawing his knife and scanning for the source of the shot, then grabbed his wounded friend under the armpits and dragged him in the direction of the water.

Hudson saw the dropped knife a few feet away and reached for it.

"Stop!"

Hudson squinted and saw a shadow approaching. It took a few moments for Hudson to find his voice. "I . . . , I am an American. Those thieves tried to . . . . Can you help me?"

The man was dressed in a light colored suit with a broad brimmed hat concealing his face. His pistol was pointed toward Hudson. "What are you doing here?" he asked.

"Out for a stroll after dinner . . . I expect it was foolish, but . . . ."

"Quite foolish," he said, lowering his pistol. "If I had not noticed you walking as I returned to my home, you would now be robbed and beaten."

"Or dead," Hudson added.

"No, not killed. Those men were sailors, probably Portuguese by the sound of their language; they know murdering a foreigner will lead to someone being strung up."

Hudson extended his hand as the man placed his pistol in a holster hidden by his coat. The man did not take his hand, and Hudson stammered, "Thomas Hudson . . . from New York City. I am indebted to you, sir."

"Lockwood, Charles Lockwood. We should leave. My driver is waiting for me."

Hudson kept up with Lockwood's quick stride toward the houses he had passed earlier, both men looking back occasionally to check for followers. The open carriage was not conducive to conversation, but when they arrived at Hudson's hotel, he asked, "Would you join me in the bar for a drink, Lockwood?"

"Well, I am meeting someone soon . . . , but I suppose one drink."

A waiter found them a table by the window, and the men

agreed on brandy. After settling into a chair, Lockwood reached into his pocket and brought out a leather pouch and a small paper, and Hudson waited while he tapped the tobacco into the paper, rolled the cigarette, and licked the edge. The waiter appeared with a light and two snifters of brandy.

"A toast, Mr. Lockwood, to your timely arrival and your shooting skill." Hudson raised his glass and deepened his voice. "I am most grateful."

"A lucky shot in the leg. He will be limping for a while." A smirk rounded the corner of Lockwood's mouth.

"You turned a possible disaster into simply an embarrassing moment. My first day of travel in the Orient, my only day in Alexandria, and I wander into a trap." Hudson shook his head and smiled at his companion.

Lockwood frowned and spoke like a scolding teacher. "Like in any large city, you must be careful in your wanderings at night. I live here, but I never go about alone at night."

Hudson studied the man opposite him. With his accent, he had to be an American from a southern state, and he seemed to know his way around Alexandria. His shoulder length white hair and surliness might be due to age or hardship. "May I ask what brought you to Alexandria, Lockwood?"

Lockwood hesitated as if he were choosing from a range of possible stories. "After the war of northern aggression, a number of Confederate and Union soldiers came to Egypt to modernize the army of Ismail Pasha. I still advise on munitions, but I have become more involved in business. Expect to be relocating to Beirut very soon."

"I leave for Beirut tomorrow and expect to be there several weeks before traveling in Palestine and Syria." Hudson spoke for a while about his plans, but Lockwood showed little interest in his travel or art and excused himself after draining the snifter.

"Perhaps we will meet again in Beirut, Mr. Lockwood." Lockwood nodded, but did not reply. Hudson watched the man move toward the door and thought he had never met a less congenial American.

He stared into the brown liquid which did not seem to be

calming his nerves or raising his spirits. The incident at the citadel had left him shaken. Nothing he had seen that day in Alexandria gave him reason to feel enthusiastic about painting in the Orient. An unforgiving light penetrated the day, and shadows disrupted the night. He wondered if this journey was a bad decision. So much of life was falling around his feet. He felt the pain of falling, failing. Surely bruises already stained his body. If only Katharine were here to rescue him from self-pity.

22 January 1868, Alexandria

My Dear Katharine,

After one day in Alexandria, I am eager to board the ship for Beirut this afternoon. The city strikes me as chaotic and dangerous. I expect that is the character of large port cities which are crossroads of world trade. Everywhere I wandered I found a motley assemblage of people in curious costumes. The port is thriving because of demand for the high quality Egyptian long fiber cotton. Markets are called souks or bazaars and moving among the honeycombed stalls requires a strong stomach and careful footsteps; the live animals are more numerous than the dead. Nothing in the city tempted me to open my sketchbook.

The ancient monuments, the lighthouse and library, were destroyed long ago. This afternoon I joined an Englishman to visit Cleopatra's Needles and Pompey's Column. The guide was well stuffed with history and architecture, but he was no match for the insolent Englishman who had a rude remark for every site. In the evening, I took a walk after dinner that left me with a feeling of trepidation. At the end of the day, I crawled into bed thinking that if Alexandria is typical of the Orient, it confirms your decision to remain at home with young Tommy.

As for me, now I have truly left the western world and feel the longing that a great physical distance creates. I have become so accustomed to sharing thoughts and places with you that I am constantly wondering—what would Katharine think of the veiled women or feisty camels or annoying beggars. I know what you would think of the slave market.

In two days I arrive in Beirut, and I am eager to see our friends and begin the arrangements for Petra. As always, I carry you in my mind and heart, my dearest.   *Your loving, Thomas*

Hudson posted his letter to Katharine and boarded the steamer SS Victoria, bound for Beirut with brief stops in Port Said and Jaffa. The purser greeted him at the top of the gangplank and handed him a paper assigning him to Stateroom 12. When he found the room on the lower passenger deck, he found an elderly, stout gentleman of short stature hastily unpacking a bulging leather bag worn to exhaustion.

"Excuse me, sir, but I think . . . ."

"What, what? Please, this is no time for visiting, my good man. I have much to arrange before the dinner bell rings. I hope to sit at the Captain's table so I must find my frock coat, my dress shirt, my suspenders, my Cambridge cuff links. . ." Beads of sweat arose on his furrowed brow as he bustled around the small space.

Hudson was more amused than annoyed. "I regret to inform you that you are unpacking in my stateroom, sir."

"No, no, I have my paper right here, and it clearly says Stateroom 13. And if you will look at the number on the door behind you. . . ." At that moment, Hudson moved aside, and the small brass number 12 was clearly visible.

Watching the man's reaction was like an exercise in changing the hue of skin color on a portrait. A lovely shade of rosy pink was creeping from above his shirt collar, through his cheeks and toward the shiny dome of his bald head. Hudson suggested that they simply exchange room assignments with the purser.

"How kind of you, sir, after all my rude blustering about. Without my dear wife at my side, I bungle through all these details of life. Allow me to introduce myself, David Anthony Forrest on assignment for *The Times of London*, at your service."

"I am Thomas Hudson from New York, and I am also traveling alone. Now, if you will excuse me, I will get settled, but I look forward to talking with you later."

"I am grateful to you, Mr. Hudson, and hope you will join me for a postprandial libation."

"Gladly, Mr. Forrest," he said, clearing his throat to suppress laughter at what would be pretentious language in New York.

Deciding against formal attire, Hudson dressed in a navy blue tweed suit which seemed to blend with the informality of the decorations in the first class dining room. The oak paneled room featured large paintings of nineteenth century naval battles that reminded the passengers that France and Britain were typically at war with someone in the 1800s. The Captain's table occupied half of the room and included both Hudson and Forrest, as well as several other Europeans, mostly English. Conversation circled around the construction of the canal that would link the Mediterranean with the Red Sea. The passengers were especially curious about whether they would see the canal when the SS Victoria docked in Port Said.

The elderly Captain had the appearance of a naval officer with enough savvy and skill to climb the ranks. His gray and black beard swept from ear to ear, but did not hide a jagged scar beside his nose. He seized the subject of the canal with the tenacity of an English bulldog. "The Suez project is nearing completion, and by next year the waters of the Red Sea will be flowing past the lighthouse of Port Said into the Mediterranean Sea." He paused and glared at two women across the table until they stopped whispering. "None too soon considering the financial difficulties of the canal company. It has been almost nine years of digging, and each month the grumbles are louder about poor wages for dangerous work."

A young man at the end of the table jumped up to blurt out his opinion. "It is a shocking use of slave labor. *The London Illustrated* compared the digging of the canal to the building of the pyramids—except going down instead of up. Dreadful stuff."

The Captain frowned and raised his fork, shaking it at the fellow. "Now, now, young man, the Suez Canal is a world-changing event. The cost in lives and treasure is a pittance compared to the profits to be made. Progress has its price. The factories of Europe will ship their goods to Asia in less than a month's time. Just imagine, it is currently almost four months in transit around the Cape of Good Hope. The British will regret that they did not dig this ditch. It will give the French control of a vital shortcut for the Asian trade and no doubt challenge the

British monopoly of India. Just imagine ships of the British Empire blocked from their colonies by the French Navy!"

The Captain seemed to be winding up for an evening's lecture on the British Empire when one of the ladies interrupted. "Will we be able to disembark for a visit in Port Said, Captain?"

"I think not, Lady Powell, it is no place for ladies or gentlemen, just an office building and a jumble of shacks for workers."

"What about Jaffa? I would like to see the old walled city."

The questions distracted the Captain from his lecture, and the table descended into multiple chitchats until the end-of-dinner bell sounded.

Forrest beckoned to Hudson as he exited the dining room. "Could I tempt you with that promised dollop of port to finish off the fine repast, Mr. Hudson?" Forrest was clearly eager for conversation.

"It would be my pleasure. I am interested to hear what you will be writing for *The Times*."

"Good." He rubbed his hands together. "I discovered a cozy pub on this deck near the stern." Forrest led the way, staying close to the wall as the wind picked up the waves.

Inside they found a well stocked bar and crackling fire. "Feels rather like my Fleet Street neighborhood, except for the quiet." The bartender arrived with two fluted glasses of tawny port. One was offered to Forrest for his taste and approval, before the other was set before Hudson.

"God save the Queen—from the French! The captain made it sound as if the British Empire would drown in the waters of the Suez Canal." His laughter erupted like a cough causing his wispy gray locks to leap around like spider legs.

"What do you think about the captain's claim that the French could close the canal to British ships?" Hudson asked.

"Balderdash!" Forrest chuckled. "The French know the Royal Navy could pry open any blockade with a single warship. I would wager that within a decade Britain will bring its gold and its navy and purchase a large enough share to balance the French holdings. Never underestimate the determination and power of the English merchant."

The reporter had almost finished his glass of port and now looked around for the bartender who was not at his post.

"Will your articles be about the canal?"

Forrest replied, but kept his eyes alert for the bartender. "Only indirectly. My charge is to ferret out information on the Egyptian treasury. Rumor is that it has been seriously depleted by costs of building the canal and funds demanded by the Ottoman Empire."

Hudson recalled a chat with the American ambassador in Paris. "I heard that Egypt was buying independence from the Ottomans. Is that true?"

"My sources in London tell me that a treasure chest of funds has sailed to Constantinople, but so far he has purchased only the new title of Khedive. Hardly a good investment. The dismemberment of the Ottoman Empire is being plotted in all the major capitals of Europe. The Ottomans lost Algeria to French imperialism three decades ago, and they worry that Egypt and Syria will be next on the carving plates of Britain and France."

"And America? Are the Ottomans concerned about our intentions?" Hudson asked.

"America is still considered benign, if considered at all." Forrest replied.

The door opened, and several of the ship waiters pushed in, laughing and shouting until the sight of first class passengers made them hesitate.

"Come in, come in," Forrest signaled with words and hands. "Call the bartender for your libations and remind him that we need another round."

The waiters tipped their hats, and headed for the bar stools.

"What about you, Mr. Hudson, is this a pleasure trip?"

"I hope it will be pleasurable," Hudson said, "but like you, I have a purpose. I am an artist. I paint American landscapes."

"Well, well, I am a great fan of the arts. Have your paintings been exhibited in Europe?"

"Yes, on several occasions," Hudson replied. "My work from

South America has been shown in several British galleries."

"Not so many years ago in London, there was a massive painting of the Andes. . ."

"You saw it? I believe it was at a gallery run by a German," Hudson said.

"Yes, yes. A good friend writes for the *Art-Journal*, and he was so enthusiastic about your painting that he insisted that I see it on two occasions. He wrote a very favorable review, comparing you to Turner's greatness."

"I have that article," Hudson said. "I save the reviews filled with praise, and sometimes the negative ones—to keep my head well below the clouds."

While Forrest went to look for the bartender and the bottle of port, Hudson thought back to the years when his paintings were constantly celebrated by the art press of New York. Despite what he told Vesoul about his good relations with American critics, Hudson agonized over their recent labeling of his scenes of nature as old style and repetitive. Critics feast on the new, the different. First it was the Barbizons, now the Orientalists, when they should be promoting American artists. He was distressed to see his wealthy patrons return from Europe with canvases of old men leering at nude women in Turkish baths. Their neglect of his work made him feel like a fish flung out of the water by a wave too big to ride.

Forrest returned with the bottle of port, filled both glasses, and then saw the pained look on Hudson's face. "Will you be looking for mountains to paint in the Orient?" He was trying to recall if Syria or Palestine offered a range to compare with the Andes.

"Mountains are not my only objectives. My loose itinerary includes Beirut, Jerusalem, and Petra."

"It sounds as if you are changing your focus from nature."

"I . . . I am not sure," Hudson replied. "My experience so far has been mountain and water environments . . . now I will be seeing structures of man in a desert. I suppose I will learn if that sort of nature has meaning for me."

"Meaning?"

"Of course. I cannot, I will not paint unless a landscape strikes chords of meaning for me . . . I need to feel its spirit . . . I know that sounds rather sentimental, but . . ."

"On the contrary, I find it laudable." Forrest spoke in a warm tone like a father consoling a son. "I have never heard an artist speak of the wellsprings of his art."

"I sometimes wonder if there is anything left in the spring other than ambition." Hudson tried to construct a smile.

"And so you have come here to try a different spring?"

"I expect . . . that is true."

An uncomfortable quiet was broken by Forrest knocking his fist on the table. "Well, that is a good thing. The Orient needs a man like yourself!"

"What makes you say that?"

"I have been watching the work of British and French painters in Egypt for many years. I am somewhat bothered by a tendency, particularly among the French, to portray Egyptian society as weak and decadent, perhaps vulnerable."

"What do you mean?"

"Remember, I come at this subject from a political point of view. Are you familiar with the work of Théodore Chassériau and Jacques Vesoul?"

Hudson nodded.

"They paint indolent soldiers covered with antique weapons and nude European models as exotic Egyptian women in harems. The paintings seem to demean the culture. I sound like a prudish old snob, but there is a fine line between portraying the society and exploiting the culture. I sense possible danger in people judging the Ottoman Empire by these unrepresentative images."

Hudson also had wondered about Vesoul's choices. "I have seen only two of Chassériau's paintings, but I have seen many paintings by Vesoul in New York, and most recently in Paris. I understand your criticism, and I may have similar judgments after I have experienced the Orient. For now, I am keeping my mind open and my judgments in check."

"I sincerely hope that I have not offended your artistic sensibilities, Mr. Hudson. Egypt is a complex, alluring land, full of mystery and intrigue, unintelligible to most foreigners. It is distressing for me to see it reduced to the uncommon."

Hudson glanced at his watch. "Almost midnight. I must retire now, but I have throughly enjoyed our evening. Would you like to meet for breakfast tomorrow before you leave the ship?"

"Absolutely. Perhaps I can give you some hints about Beirut and Jerusalem."

Hudson awoke to the bleating of fog horns and the warning calls of sailors. He stayed in bed until the breakfast bell and then dressed rapidly. He knocked on Forrest's door, but there was no answer so he headed up to the dining room where small round tables circled a sumptuous buffet table in the center. Forrest waved to him from a location near the windows.

"Good morning, Hudson. Not much of a view, but at least some fresh air." Forrest looked rested and rosy. "Quite a feast awaiting us."

"Appears I may need an interpreter." Other than the breads, Hudson did not recognize familiar breakfast fare.

"Reminds me of the shooting parties in Yorkshire I covered for *The Times*," he mumbled as he lurched toward the buffet, selected the largest size plate, and quickly constructed a mountain of delicacies. "You must try everything. Look at that roasted fish beside the potted shrimp and crab. Those deviled kidneys look good, and how about that spread of pickled meats? The pilau and curried beef are not to be missed, but leave room later for the strawberry fool."

Hudson's stomach rebelled at the aromas. "What is that yellowish casserole? Eggs?"

"Oh, yes!" Forrest replied. "It is called *kedgeree*, from India, quite spicy."

While the American collected breads and roasted fish, Forrest settled into his seat, stretched out his double chin, and tucked his napkin into his collar.

"Last night, you mentioned traveling to Petra," Forrest said with a noticeably more serious tone. "I understand from friends who have visited the area that it is an extraordinary sight, unlike any other place. However, I feel obliged to caution you about the Bedouin tribes near Petra. Do you know anything about them?"

The Bedouin, again. He preferred not to talk about the Bedouin, he thought, turning his spoon on the table. "I have heard a few disparaging remarks about the Bedouin way of life from travelers complaining about baksheesh, and one American traveler has written about raids and savagery." He thought back to Vesoul's advice. "A Frenchman who has traveled with Bedouin said with a good guide and ample baksheesh there should be no danger."

"Hmm," Forrest murmured. "In my experience as a traveler," he said lifting his napkin to blot his chin, "danger arises from a failure to appreciate the customs, the concerns of a society. The Bedouin are among the many tribal people of the world who, from their perspective, exist outside the scope of empires, nations, governments. It may sound simple, but in reality it is quite complex."

"I am not sure what you mean by 'outside the scope.' The Bedouin live on lands within the Ottoman Empire, is that not so?" Hudson asked.

"Yes, of course, but the Bedouin have very little concern for the authority of the Sultan, and the Sultan is wise enough to avoid acting with force in Bedouin lands. We speak of Bedouin as if they are a nation group, while in reality they are more like extended families, bound only by a few common interests."

Hudson imagined endless quarrels. "What keeps order in their lives?"

"Loyalty. A strong loyalty, first to family, and then to tribe."

"Sounds similar to our Indians in America," Hudson said. "Our attitudes about governance and private ownership of lands do not blend well with their traditions and beliefs. Unlike the Sultan's policy of avoidance, our government is beginning to use the army to enforce laws unacceptable to the Indians."

"Probably a good analogy. Here, talk of dividing the Ottoman Empire among Europeans arouses people like the Bedouin."

Hudson's eyebrows shot upward. "They know about such

matters?'"

"Steady, Hudson, I do not intend to frighten you, only to alert you," the journalist said as he signaled the waiter for more tea. "The leaders of tribes near major cities like Damascus and Aleppo probably hear rumors. The souks are humming with rumors about surveying."

"Bedouin. Souks." Hudson grumbled. "I have to concentrate on painting."

"Fair enough. But you will be painting in their society. We ignore the reasons for their possible hostility toward us . . . ."

"Hostility?" Hudson pushed back his chair and began to rise. "I know I have to be careful about painting, but what else?"

"Calm down, my good man. It is not simply what we do, but what those who look like us, act like us, have done in decades or centuries past. The Bedouin are Arabs, and Arabs have a long memory." Forrest paused to sip his tea.

"We all have long memories when it comes to injuries inflicted on us," Hudson remarked. "Why would the Bedouin view foreigners as threats?"

"At present?" Forrest paused. "They are concerned about Turkish reforms and foreign surveyors mapping their lands."

Hudson watched Forrest lick the last bit of strawberry fool coating his lips and gaze back at the buffet table. He thought about Lockwood, the American engineer and wondered if he would be involved in surveying.

"Keep in mind," Forrest added, "travelers are usually insulated from Bedouin antagonism; they are viewed as a benefit to the tribes for the guides they hire and the baksheesh they provide."

Hudson relaxed in his chair again. "So I do not need to buy myself a pistol in Beirut, Mr. Forrest?"

"No, no, in fact, I would encourage you to not carry arms. Leave that to your guide or dragoman, but choose your dragoman most carefully!"

The ship's horn was blowing in staccato notes, indicating the unloading of passengers and goods into small boats which would ferry them to the shores of Port Said.

Before Forrest walked down the gangplank, the two men exchanged addresses in the manner of people who have felt some degree of companionship in a distant land.

THREE

"If Beirut can attract the mighty line of trade and travel to her door, she will quickly take rank among the great cities of the world, if she will not, or cannot, then must she wane before some other rising queen of the East."
William M. Thomson, *The Land and the Book*, 1859

Beirut

The sea was smooth, the air pure and soft, as the ship sailed quietly into the harbor of Beirut. In the morning light, the city rested serenely between the sparkling blue Mediterranean and the noble, snowcapped Mount Lebanon. Beirut resembled a large village, far removed in space and time from the confusions of New York, London, and Paris. Thomas Hudson felt the tension of weeks of constant travel melting away like ice on a warming statue.

Nearing the shore, he had a first glimpse of Oriental style buildings climbing from the rocky coast, up the hillsides, toward ancient cedar forests. Beyond, the spine of steep mountains parallel to the Lebanese coast reached higher than he had imagined; they would combine well with classical ruins. The astonishing landscape promised new themes for paintings, and his fingers itched for his brushes. His thoughts were interrupted by the cries of sailors and dockhands preparing the ship for disembarkation.

A driver and carriage from the Bellevue Hotel in Beirut waited at the quay, and the ship steward helped Hudson negotiate the transfer of his trunks from ship to land. The driver was a cheerful fellow, bobbing his head up and down like a child's toy and speaking as if his passenger were fluent in Arabic, as they passed large gnarly rocks adorned with pigeons and red and green striped fishing boats setting out for the day's catch. The short ride along the coast delivered him to the Bellevue where he would establish a base for the time when he was not traveling. The large, airy villa converted into a hotel had been recommended by a cousin saying it offered good light for painting and splendid views of Mount Lebanon and the Mediterranean. His rooms soared from greenish marble floors to cathedral ceilings carved from stone, handsome but cold for January days and nights. There were no fireplaces or stoves, only several copper braziers filled with hot coals.

26 January 1868,
Dearest Katharine,

My home in Beirut is the Bellevue Hotel, perched high on a cliff above the Mediterranean where there are fine panoramic views of sea, shore, and sky. In the day the sea breezes warm my face and hands, but at night the winds blow cold down from the mountains, and it is freezing. Yesterday I made my way through the souk to purchase a stove and several Persian rugs to brighten and warm the hotel floors. Do not worry about the expense of the rugs; they will come home with me. I also arranged for a portable easel to be made by a local carpenter. The arrival of the rugs and stove caused some embarrassment to the hotel manager, and he appeared with apologies and additional copper braziers.

While the heat is modest, the food is truly extravagant. Last night's menu was fish soup, mutton stew with mushrooms, roast veal, cauliflower, mashed potatoes, asparagus, Bavarian cream, fine Jaffa oranges, bananas, Damascus apples, figs and dates. The table sagged with the weight of it all.

I was disappointed that neither the Blisses nor the Dodges came by to welcome me the first day. As promised, I had sent them a cable from Alexandria advising them of my arrival, and I had so looked forward to the company of friends. Today when they finally arrived I learned that the cable came on Monday, but was not delivered until Thursday! When I expressed my annoyance, Dr. Bliss laughed and said that time in the Arab world revolved around the expression 'bukra, in'shallah,' translated as, 'tomorrow, God willing.' Luckily I am here in time for a reception tomorrow night for faculty and friends of the Syrian Protestant College. I expect donations will be welcome.

No letters from you yet, but we knew there would be long delays on both ends. I trust you have received my letters from London and Paris by this time, and in another month you may have some surprises from Le Bon Marché.

All my love for you and Tommy, Thomas

The plain dining room of the Syrian Protestant College hummed with the idle chatter of receptions, and Hudson planned to make an early escape. He enjoyed talking to Dr. Bliss and his wife and then exchanged family news with the Dodges who wanted to hear about Katharine and Tommy as well as plans for their new house north of the city. They introduced him to other missionaries and faculty, but as usual he floundered in swirls of strangers. While trying to concentrate on a young missionary's woes about the college library, Hudson noticed Charles Lockwood across the room. With that mane of white hair and those droopy eyelids he was unmistakeable, and he was dressed in the same poorly tailored white suit. He occupied a far corner, surrounded by prosperous looking men who appeared attentive and amused by what the American engineer was saying. It was odd to see the man behaving in a gregarious manner.

Fairly sure that Lockwood would not seek out his company, Hudson steadily edged his way toward departure. Only a few feet from the door, he was surprised to find Lockwood at his elbow.

"Hudson! How good to see you again." Lockwood arranged a smile on his face. "I hoped to find you here."

"You did?"

"Yes, yes. Any more problems in Alexandria . . ."

"None at all." Hudson replied. "I was grateful for your help that night."

"Of course, of course. One American helping another," Lockwood said, clapping him on the shoulder.

Hudson was mystified, searching for some response to this friendly version of Lockwood. "How are your business plans?"

"Good, quite good. Just waiting for permissions." He paused for only a moment. "I do have a favor to ask you, Hudson."

"Oh. What is that?"

"Dr. Bliss mentioned that you were putting together a small

caravan for Petra, and I find myself with about a month before my work begins. I am eager to travel down that way, see Wadi Arabah and the ruins at Petra. May I join you?"

Hudson felt his body stiffening and struggled to keep his mouth from dropping. His eyes searched the air for an evasive reply. "Well, sir, my timing might not work for you."

"When do you plan to leave Beirut?"

Hudson thought quickly and responded. "Probably not for a month, maybe longer . . . ."

"Excellent! Plenty of time to organize my affairs." Lockwood was rubbing his hands together, as if an arrangement were settled.

Hudson was not so sure, but he felt indebted to the man. He stared at Lockwood who continued to talk cheerfully about Beirut and travel. He seemed to choose his words carefully as if he were picking them out of a handbook of pleasant conversation. He repeated Dr. Bliss's name several times, praising his work, giving the impression that they were good friends.

"Where are you staying, Hudson?"

"I am at the Bellevue Hotel. But . . ."

"Fine. I will stop by to discuss our travel plans." Lockwood turned and left before Hudson could say another word.

Each day around noon Hudson casually perused the newspapers in the hotel lobby, frequently glancing toward the hallway where the mail was sorted into boxes for each room. Hudson had been slightly peeved that a letter from Katharine had not arrived before he left Paris. Now he had been in Beirut almost two weeks and still no letter. He remembered emphasizing it might be the only secure mailing address until March or April when he returned to Beirut from Petra. From his days in South America, Hudson knew that news from home was unpredictable in more remote places. There were several excuses he could make for Katharine—caring for baby Tommy, moving back and forth between the farm and the city, a hard winter in New York, and of course, the unpredictability of the mail.

At least he could visualize the busy rhythms of Katharine's life. At the farm, she would be mostly alone with Tommy in their small cottage. There were only a few neighbors on nearby farms, and the town of Hudson was about five miles distant. In the city she would be staying with their dear friends, the Whites, an arrangement of great comfort to him. Katharine adored Elizabeth White. No one else had devoted so much time to nurturing her during the recent sorrows. William was President of the Boston and Albany Railroad and used his wealth to be generously supportive of the arts. Hudson considered him his best patron—he had recently commissioned two more South American scenes.

27 January 1868 William White, New York City
My Dear Mr. White,

I arrived in Beirut several days ago, relieved to unpack my trunks and thoughts among a few friends. The sailing from Alexandria to Beirut was on a most agreeable vessel with spacious staterooms and wholesome food, cooked plainly. We stopped at Port Said where the construction for the canal is well underway and should be completed in another year. The engineers would benefit from your railroad expertise as they are not planning a rail line to Cairo until the twentieth century, and that is probably a mistake. The next day we had a too brief stop at Jaffa before continuing to Beirut.

Beirut is beautifully situated at the foot of a high range of mountains, now iced with snow. The mountain sides are dotted all over with villages, churches, and convents. The American society here is very fine, especially our friends from the Protestant missionary group. No doubt you remember Reverend Daniel Bliss and Abby, as well as Reverend Stuart Dodge and his wife, Ellen, from our meeting in New York about fund raising for the Syrian Protestant College. The Dodges have introduced me to others—Cornelius Van Dyck, a scholar and physician from our Hudson River Valley, and the popular writer, William Thomson.

The College is now open in a temporary location. Bliss is the President with Dodge as Professor of Modern Languages and Van Dyck teaching medical subjects. I am learning more about their excellent work in both education and health care. Most of them speak Arabic fluently and are well integrated into the local community. You can be sure that your ample donations are bringing good results.

Now I will stop this written chatter. Off to meet with the American

Consul, Albert Johnson, to discuss my travel plans for Petra, and mail this letter before it becomes any fatter. I will be back at work on your South American scenes as soon as my easel arrives. I am determined to mail them to New York before I leave for Petra!

With regards to you and Mrs. White, Thomas Hudson

On the wall behind the desk of Consul Albert Johnson hung a framed lithograph of the 1864 Republican campaign banner for President Abraham Lincoln and Vice President Andrew Johnson. Symbols of liberty, peace, and prosperity surrounded the candidates. The only hint of the civil war raging in that year was an eagle with arrows in his talons. Hudson had noticed the lithograph before he saw the Consul, dwarfed by his oversized desk. Looking like a solemn, puny bank clerk with short, wispy black hair and a pencil-thin mustache, Johnson scrambled to his feet to greet the famous American artist.

With only a trickle of trade between America and Lebanon or Syria, Consul Johnson concentrated his professional energies on the problems or whims of American tourists. He chose to nod politely as aggrieved travelers complained about rascally guides and wily merchants. Sympathy had proved to be the best strategy and the least amount of work.

"Mr. Hudson, a pleasure to see you. I trust you had a good walk from your hotel on this unusually fine January day. Are you comfortable at the Bellevue?"

"All is well, Johnson, and if I become any more comfortable, I might lose momentum for my trip to Petra.

"Oh, you must gather your strength for Petra—weeks of excruciating travel by horse and camel through regions of Bedouin tribes hostile to foreigners. Surely, you have heard that, Mr. Hudson."

"Excruciating? Are you exaggerating?"

"Well, I definitely consider two weeks in the desert on a camel excruciating." Johnson plunked himself down on his leather chair and motioned Hudson to a roughly carved wooden chair in front of the desk. "My responsibility is to advise travelers about the backward conditions in Palestine and Syria. Americans arrive with too many illusions from books, including the Bible. Illusions leads to disappointment which leads to complaints that land on my desk."

Hudson looked at the walnut desk inlaid with iridescent mother-of-pearl. The surface was bare. "I have been warned about Petra and the Bedouin, in particular. I gather it has been an unpredictable destination since the Nabateans made it their trading base two thousand years ago. Any recent problems?" Hudson asked.

Johnson opened a drawer to his right and pulled out a thin file and placed it on the desk. Opening the file, he licked his finger and paged through the few papers.

"Yes. Here is one that might interest you. In 1859, a British artist was shot for painting in Petra." Johnson tapped on the paper with his index finger. "What do you think about that?"

Hudson placed his hand over his mouth and coughed, hiding his grin. "Actually, I know about that incident. He acted foolishly, and his leg was grazed by a bullet."

"All right, all right. This one is more serious and more recent." The Consul withdrew the top sheet and dangled it in front of Hudson.

At that distance, Hudson could only see an official seal and the French flag.

"In October of last year," Johnson read from the paper, "a dragoman escorted a French group to Wadi Rum, south of Petra. The dragoman had warned the group to stay together and to not use their guns in the wadi. On the second afternoon, Monsieur Fauré rode ahead of the group and turned into a side canyon . . ." Johnson stopped, and then said, "you know . . . the French are arrogant and tend to ignore advice."

"I think that is a harsh judgment. I only know a few Frenchmen, but they are not like that."

"Well, that is your good fortune, Mr. Hudson." He cleared his throat and continued. "Thinking that he was alone, Monsieur Fauré shot a gazelle." Johnson stopped again.

"And . . . .?"

The Consul leaned back in his chair and shook his finger at

Hudson. "You are never alone as a foreigner in the desert—the Bedouin are always watching."

Hudson was losing his patience with this tedious man. "And is it forbidden to hunt there?" He thought back to Vesoul's remarks about hunting in Wadi Rum.

"Only allowed with Bedouin guides from the local tribes."

"And did the Bedouin shoot him?" Hudson asked.

"No, no. The Bedouin took the Frenchman's horse as compensation for the gazelle and left him in the canyon. It grew dark, the man lost his way, fell into a gully, and broke his leg. His guide found him the next morning. He was lucky to survive the night."

Hudson assumed that Vesoul had the good sense and the experience to heed the advice of his guide. "I have been advised that the critical element in this trip will be hiring the very best guide or dragoman as you call them here."

"Precisely," Johnson emphasized his comment with a slight slap on the desk. "The dragoman plays the key role of guide, interpreter, provisioner, camel driver, comedian, and mediator, and it is critical to choose one with excellent credentials. Then establish your authority through a firm contract, constantly enforced." Johnson recommended a written contract and made some notes on the elements to include.

Hudson realized he had finally tapped into an area where Johnson could be useful. "What about baksheesh for the Bedouin we encounter along the way? I understand the local Bedouin typically want more than the dragoman has advised as appropriate, and without language skills, the traveler is at the mercy of both of them."

"You must have the best dragoman available and then trust him. I will send a message to the Consul in Jerusalem who will put you in touch with Mika'il El Hany—an excellent dragoman, entirely honest and with many trips to Petra with Englishmen."

"That will be much appreciated. El Hany will find us at the Hotel Mediterranean. We should arrive on February 19th."

"Have you arranged companions for the trip, Mr. Hudson?"

"Yes, just two men. One of them I believe you know—

Charles Lockwood, an American. The other is a rather quiet Englishman here for an extended visit, Professor Andrew Fowler," said Hudson.

Johnson closed the Bedouin file. "I heard Fowler preach at our church. I like his sermons, less dogmatic, more sympathetic, rather appealing to me. I understand he has traveled widely in the East."

"Yes, for more than two years, mostly in India. His brother is in the British Indian Civil Service," Hudson recalled. "Formerly a professor of ancient civilizations at Oxford, as well as an ordained minister. Nice chap, quite eager for Petra."

"Where did you meet Lockwood?" Johnson was examining his nails with an odd expression.

"I met him briefly in Alexandria. He helped me in a difficult situation. More recently, I found him here at one of Reverend Bliss' receptions to raise money for the Syrian Protestant College.

"Did he mention what brings him to Lebanon now?" Johnson asked in a slow, deliberate manner. "I thought he was working for the Egyptians."

Hudson lingered over the question. Lockwood had mentioned he was part of a British survey and map group working in Syria and Palestine. Without consulting Lockwood, Hudson did not feel at liberty to mention the survey to Johnson. "I did not ask Lockwood about his purpose in the region."

Johnson inched further. "I only ask because I received a dispatch a few days ago about a European engineering company planning to survey and map."

"Is that a problem?"

"Not as long as they have the proper permissions from the Ottoman officials."

"Hmm, permissions." Hudson thought for a moment. "Now that you mention it, Lockwood asked to join the trip because his plans had been interrupted by a delay in permissions."

In the silence that followed Hudson looked toward the glass doors leading to the balcony and coastline. He pondered the abrupt change in Johnson's personality from annoying bureaucrat to a probing civil servant.

"Well, Mr. Hudson, I expect you have found two fine companions for your caravan. If there is nothing else I can do for you, then I wish you the best of journeys." He moved around the desk to shake Hudson's hand.

Johnson stood by the window and watched Hudson striding along the sea walk. The artist was not what he expected—not a single question concerning beautiful scenery in Lebanon or Syria from a landscape painter! That was a surprise, as well as his minimal concern about safety, and then the over confidence about hazards of desert travel. A rare species among the travel genus.

He will be no match for the wily Lockwood who surely had some new scheme in mind. Surveying and mapping were not lucrative enough to draw Lockwood. It occurred to him there might be a relationship between Lockwood and the dispatch which specifically mentioned a proposal to survey the port section of Beirut and study the possibility of a road from the Mediterranean to the Euphrates. The State Department was demanding reports on any such activity—urgently. Johnson dreaded writing reports on business subjects, particularly when they were labelled urgent; but it might provide a free trip to Damascus and Baghdad. The arrival of Lockwood and a British engineer was a coincidence worth watching. If Americans were becoming involved, Washington would want endless status reports from him so they could deny any involvement if regrettable incidents arose.

He turned away from the window and paced the floor, anxiety bubbling up in him like a simmering kettle. That damn Lockwood dragged trouble behind him. He was thorny and unpredictable, and the way he tightened his mouth and hands when angry made Johnson uneasy. A friend had told him that Lockwood was capable of volcanic eruptions when he was denied what he wanted. Johnson considered the idea of cautioning Hudson about Lockwood, but reminded himself that it was not his job to pass on negative comments about fellow Americans. He had no concrete reason to raise an alarm about Lockwood.

30 January 1868 Beirut

My Dear Katharine,

A momentous day—your first letter arrived and is already worn thin as an old handkerchief. It is a relief to know that your Mother arrived to help with Tommy and keep you company in the cottage. The news that Tommy is now walking was both happy and sad. I can imagine how excited you were, and I am sad to have missed this dramatic change in his life. He is probably examining and tasting everything within his reach.

Your comment about my sister's health prompted me to write immediately to my parents. Please keep me informed. I feel so helpless at this great distance from loved ones.

The new easel arrived two days ago and is now permanent furniture beside the largest parlor window overlooking the sea—my brush dances to the rhythm of the waves lapping the rocks. I am happy to be back in the company of my paint box and canvas and feel certain that I will have ample time to finish the two small paintings of the tropics that Mr. White commissioned. Please tell him again how deeply grateful I am for his generosity in lending funds to support my extended travels.

Plans for the Petra expedition occupy my mind at present. The Consul here in Beirut has recommended a guide, or dragoman as they say here, and I will meet him in Jerusalem to make a contract. The meeting with the Consul both annoyed and amused me. He avoids work by discouraging both tourists and businessmen and conveys a sense of cultural superiority both to Arabs and Europeans. I have the feeling that he rarely strays from the relative comforts of Beirut.

An American engineer, Charles Lockwood, and an English minister and professor, Alexander Fowler, will join me for the entire trip. I met Lockwood briefly in Alexandria, and then ran into him again here at a reception. Dr. Bliss had mentioned to him that I would be traveling to Petra, and Lockwood insisted on joining the caravan, pursuing me around the room until I agreed. Given that he had helped me through a difficult incident in Alexandria, it would have been ungentlemanly to turn him down. Bit of an odd duck in his mood swings, though. In a crowd, he becomes the jovial entertainer, but one-to-one he can be prickly in his comments and manners. He is from the Virginia coastal region and speaks and looks like a Southerner with his casual posture in a crisp white suit with black tie. Even his longish, thick hair is white, as well as his sideburns. He reminds me of Mark Twain without the mustache, but his eyes are dull, not the twinkle of Twain's. His penchant is for whiskey and work. He comes with excellent credentials—a member of the United States Naval Expedition to the Jordan River and the Dead Sea in 1849. A report of that expedition is sitting on our library shelf, and I expect the section on Jerusalem might interest you.

Fowler is altogether different. Quiet, a man of cheerful disposition and thoughtful discussions. His plump, ruddy English face is framed with blond curly hair tending toward gray, and he looks like he just stepped out of a Rembrandt Peale painting, with his rumpled frock coat, shirt and stock, and usually a weskit. He teaches in the School of Ancient Civilizations at Oxford, and I plan to make him my tutor on all things Oriental, but especially concerning Petra and the Nabateans. For the last two years he has been visiting his brother's family in Calcutta and studying eastern religions in South Asia. He traveled overland between India and Beirut with an Arab scholar, staying with Bedouin tribes and learning their traditions. He is the kind of person who finds more pleasure in hearing your thoughts than in spilling out his own. In fact, I had to coax all of the above information out of him. I expect you would enjoy his company.

While Lockwood and Fowler have traveled widely in eastern lands, neither has been to Petra. Our departure is set for the middle of February. I had hoped we might start earlier, but I have been told the weather might interfere.

Meanwhile, I find Beirut much to my liking. Every fine day I walk along the rocky coast or toward the foothills of the mountains, sometimes sketching if I am alone. I think a composition of mountains, sea, and classical ruins would be an eloquent statement of the Syrian landscape.

There are many grand dwellings scattered around Beirut, and they have given me new ideas for the home we will build on Long Hill. Here, a courtyard typically lies just inside the main door. It is rather like the beating heart of the home which leads to many smaller rooms where more private life occurs. While the courtyards in Beirut are open to the sky, in our climate it could be roofed over with a large skylight above. Another appealing element is the iwan—a vaulted space, walled on three sides with the fourth side open to nature. The massive stone walls of the homes retain heat in the winter and keep out the heat of summer. I am determined to build in stone. When I return, I will show you the many sketches of features I find appealing, from the rhythmic arches of porches to ornamental motifs for windows.

Beirut is an extraordinarily beautiful town, and it is easy to understand that the missionary families are completely happy with their lives here. Their community has surrounded me with friendship, and the Blisses and Dodges remind me constantly of how much you are missed.

No one could miss you as much as I do, every hour, every day. Once the expedition to Petra begins, it will be impossible to send or receive letters, so today I have purchased a notebook where I will write letters for you to read when I return. I want you to know my thoughts as if you were beside me.

With all my love for you and our baby, Thomas

Hudson stared at the canvas on his easel with disgust. The second painting for the White commission looked more like a vase sitting in the jungle than the volcano of Cotopaxi. How foolish to be re-creating South America in a Beirut hotel. He placed his palette and paintbrush on the table, stood and stretched, then pushed open the window to a morning of warm breezes. Just beyond the rocky coast two fishermen in the stern of their boat tossed their net into the wind and water. After a few minutes of trawling, the crew took their positions and strained to pull in the heavy net, laughing as they slipped across the deck amidst the leaping, silvery fish.

That was what he needed—being out among the people of the city. He put away his paints and headed out to wander around the markets near the harbor.

The fishmongers had sold the early morning catch and now napped or smoked while they waited for the afternoon boats. Carts of meats and fruits pulled by young boys rattled into the covered portion of the market; Hudson followed and found himself assaulted by flies and a variety of pleasant and regrettable odors. The press of people in the narrow spaces between stalls moved in close formation like a tired army, carrying him along until he broke free into the center of a shop of burlap bags overflowing with grains and spices. He bumped into a bag of rice, causing a spillage to the horror of the shopkeeper, who called a child to collect every grain. He offered some coins to compensate, but the man turned his back.

Venturing into the crowd again, he was assaulted by cries of vendors directed at him. He felt a hand grab his leg and looked down to see a young woman squatting by a tray of sweets dotted with flies. He dug into his pockets for a few coins, and the woman smiled displaying her rotting teeth. The gang of children following him saw the coins and yelled 'baksheesh, baksheesh,' while shopkeepers waved trinkets and tablecloths in his face. He moved faster, weaving through what felt like clinging monkeys until he stumbled out of the market and into a street of many cafés.

He sat on a low stool beside a small table decorated with tiny mosaics, removed his hat, wiped his brow, and looked around at the other patrons, all men. Behind him, the children crept closer until the attendant shouted, shook his fist, and scattered them back into the market.

The attendant lingered beside him with a questioning look, and Hudson pointed to the glasses that sat on the adjacent table. The glass placed before him held a layer of clear amber tea, but the bottom quarter was a dark residue of largish leaves that did not look like tea. He paused, considering admonitions to be careful about eating outside the hotel, took a sip, and then drank all the mint flavored brew and asked for another. The attendant returned with the mint tea and a steaming bread resembling a doughnut covered with sesame seeds. Hudson looked up to question the order and saw the man distributing the fresh bread to every table. The aroma of the seeds created a hunger, and he tore off a bit of the top.

After the refreshment of the bread and tea, he continued along the same street which entered a quiet residential area of modest homes, each with window boxes of bright blooms. The doors hugged the sidewalks where women swept and gossiped. He would have loved to sketch the scene but did not dare pull out his pencil. After a few blocks, the street ended abruptly at the stairs to a mosque, but paths continued left and right between walls on either side. Both paths were deserted and looked the same. He headed left and soon found himself in a warren of turning and branching paths which rose and fell in disorder and dirt. The few people he passed slunk along the walls, except for a group of men who jostled him as they ran. He felt in his pocket for the card given to him by the hotel manager and decided to double back and look for a carriage, but quickly realized he had no sense of how he had come. He looked up, but the bright sun was directly overhead, giving no indication of east or west.

Hearing voices off to the distant right, he walked more quickly in that direction. The walls were now interrupted by what looked like tenement houses with banners of laundry festooning the streets, just as in New York City. More people were moving toward the now louder sounds, and Hudson thought there might be a celebration nearby. When he was finally spit out into a small square, the size and mood of the crowd frightened him. There was no turning back as entering people blocked what could have been exits. He struggled to reach a nearby building with a staircase where a few Arab men stood elevated above the chaos. One of the men took pity on him and reached down to help him rise to the top step. People continued to squeeze their way into the square, many of the men waving flags—white with a tree shape in green or brightly colored striped banners. Near the center of the square a small circle of people, all young men, faced each other, shouting and occasionally punching out at someone. The circle slowly grew larger as more men pushed their way into the skirmish. Hudson looked at the men beside him, and asked, "English?" Then louder, "English?"

The men shook their heads, but below one man shouted in English, "Christians and Druze. War," he said, pointing toward the circle. Hudson gulped back a nauseous eruption and fanned himself with his hat. The man beside him saw his distress and urged him to sit, but Hudson feared being lower than the others. He gasped for breath and observed the growing noise and agitation. Little battles broke out, and women screamed to get through the crowd. Shots rang out from two troops of mounted soldiers that rode into the square from opposite sides, trampling anyone who did not move. People were flying out of every exit as the men on horses surrounded the shrinking circle of combatants.

Hudson stepped down, but stopped when the Arab who had helped him onto the stairs seized his arm and motioned for him to stay. After the crowds had left and only the soldiers remained with the men being arrested, the Arab led him out of the square to a nearby boulevard where he found him a carriage. Hudson pulled out the hotel card which was written in English and Arabic. The driver nodded, and he jumped into the carriage. He almost forgot to thank his rescuer, who replied in Arabic, "*Ma'asalama.*" Hudson grabbed both handholds and wondered what that word meant.

7 February 1868 Beirut
Dearest Katharine,

It is five o'clock in the evening, and the sun is peacefully sliding into the Mediterranean Sea as I sip a brandy to calm my nerves. Before I continue, I assure you that I am safe and secure, back at the Hotel Bellevue, but your foolish husband blundered into another incident today. This morning I found myself bored with painting the South American scene and restless in the hotel rooms so I launched out on an exploration of the city which ended in being too close to some kind of religious conflict. The troops of the Ottoman Pasha arrived in time to prevent the fisticuffs from escalating into warfare, and a kindly Arab put me in a carriage to the hotel.

Immediately, I asked for Monsieur Lorrie, the hotel manager, because I was curious about the nature of the conflict. I explained what I had witnessed, and he interjected several "Humdillahs," and "Mon Dieus" with much frowning and head shaking. Then he spoke rapidly, in confusing stories, his hands searching the air for details. Finally I interrupted him to say I had no idea of what he was saying. Monsieur Lorrie is half-French, half-Arab—an exciting combination. He took me into his office where sitting down seemed to calm both of us.

It is a long and confusing story, but essentially, there are vicious outbreaks among the religious sects in Lebanon—Christians and Muhammadans and Druze and others—based mainly on historic animosities, but also economic issues. About eight years ago, it erupted into a full scale war with horrible massacres of men, women, and children. An Ottoman Pasha now keeps a tight rein on the communities and suppresses each incident with severe punishments.

Not something to stumble into unaware, as I did today, but no harm done, at least to me. I questioned whether I should burden you with this story, but it seems wrong to tell you only the happy and pretty stories. I will be more circumspect about my wanderings from now on—somehow I thought I would be safe in the light of day.

A letter arrived from my mother reporting that Margaret is improving from her illness slowly. They had wanted to visit with you and Tommy, but now feel it prudent to stay away for a while. My father added a brief postscript saying that Wadsworth purchased another of my paintings for his Atheneum. I am glad that he has not lost faith in me as some have. I am determined to surprise the naysayers with great paintings from the travels ahead.

We leave for Jaffa in ten days, and each morning I look for another letter from you with no success. I have taken to creating letters of the imagination which might be embarrassing for both of us!

All my Love, Thomas

FOUR

"Perched on its eternal hills, white and domed and solid, massed together and hopped with gray walls, the venerable city gleamed in the sun. So small."
Mark Twain, 1867

Beirut to Jerusalem

On a warm February afternoon, Hudson, Lockwood, and Fowler boarded a German steamer in Beirut to travel to the port of Jaffa. Hudson remained on the deck while the others went below to their staterooms. He leaned against the ship's railing, watching baggage and goods being loaded and enjoying the view of the Lebanon Mountains, freshly salted with snow. The small, scrawny porters struggled to move a dozen large wooden crates labeled Brass Lamps, Mosque of Muhammad Ali, Cairo. As they pushed and pulled on the ropes, the lamps inside the crates clanged loudly before they were dropped into the hold. The porters rolled more manageable bales of raw Lebanese silk marked for the weavers of Lyon into a storage area on deck. Woven sacks bulging with bread, vegetables, meat, and other foodstuffs for the journey were carried to the galley.

At dinner that evening, Fowler and Lockwood met for the first time. Lockwood arrived late to the table and complained about the length of his bunk. "At well over six feet, I will have to fold myself at either head or legs to fit the space," he groused.

"It must be better than a navy bunk," Hudson suggested.

"As a young man in the navy, I had no choice, but now I have a taste for more luxurious accommodations."

Fowler looked sympathetic. "It is only one night."

Lockwood continued. "This beef is overcooked, the potatoes

are soggy, and the pudding insipid. I hope this is not a forecast of the month to come." His negative remarks were emphasized by a scowl that swept across his forehead like a single dark cloud starkly modifying the atmosphere for a moment.

"The crew is German," Fowler smiled. "They are fond of stewing meats and vegetables. I rather like it for a change."

Hudson watched and listened to the conversation. Fowler was as prone to smile as Lockwood was to scowl. Fowler's cup runneth over with optimism. The cabin was not too small; it was cozy. The air was bracing, not cold and windy. When there was a problem, he posed a polite question, choosing to probe instead of complain or lecture.

Hudson shared Fowler's tendency toward cheerfulness, but when challenged or irritated, he knew he could be as intransigent as Lockwood. He recognized that Fowler and Lockwood considered him the group leader and deferred to his proposals about travel arrangements. He made it clear that he respected their depth of experience in the Orient and wanted to hear their opinions. The evening's conversation seemed strained, not the best beginning for a month of close companionship, but he thought each man had a better understanding of individual personalities by the time they said goodnight.

Hudson was awake most of the night, restlessly prowling the deck before daybreak and mulling over the kind of disturbing thoughts that penetrate darkness. This journey would be more complicated than his other travel. The cost alone was staggering, requiring him to borrow money. It must be a wise investment of money and time. Katharine understood his need to find inspiration in a vastly different landscape, and he did not want to disappoint her confidence or threaten their financial security.

In his past foreign travels, he had never needed to be concerned about potentially hostile people or complex cultures in the throes of change. In South America, he insulated himself from a local society that held little interest, simply a picturesque backdrop. The Orient already felt like a more invasive presence in his daily experiences, throbbing with a disconcerting beat which he feared could endanger his opportunity to paint.

Usually he traveled with good friends who were predictable in tough situations. Fowler impressed him as a fine and reliable man, imbued with a spirit of good will, a man of good moral character with an agile mind. His knowledge of Petra's history and other Oriental civilizations would be generously shared and valuable.

Lockwood's stormy outbursts over minor problems like beds and food were annoying, and made Hudson worry about how he would behave if a real crisis developed. The Alexandria incident had left him with a feeling of indebtedness which caused him to allow Lockwood to join his caravan without consulting others who knew him. In accepting Lockwood so quickly, he might have made a mistake.

Hudson watched the changing colors of the sky—deep blues dissolving into lighter shades at the horizon as a slowly developing sunrise crawled over the low, scalloped hills of Palestine. The light cut silhouettes into cliffs and valleys; stone houses and walls emerged from the shadows. The serenity of the early morning scene was a sweet balm for his anxious thoughts.

As he passed the pilot house for the umpteenth time, he saw the captain leaning against the starboard rail, smoking a pipe. He stopped a few feet away, looking toward the shore and pausing before he spoke softly. "A peaceful morning on land and sea . . . ."

The captain spoke without looking toward Hudson. "Yes, I never tire of this time of daybreak along the coast. But it has not been a restful night for you, Mr. Hudson. I was on duty during the night, watching your circumambulations of the deck. Was it exercise or sleeplessness?"

"A bit of both, plus anticipation," Hudson said. On the verge of a journey, he enjoyed the stage of imagination preceding reality. He felt like a young child, with eyes wide open, devouring the illustrations of *One Thousand and One Nights*. He turned to look directly at the captain. The smoke from his pipe climbed and curled with the soft breeze. It was a handsome meerschaum pipe with carvings of waves at the bottom of the bowl. The pipe, the full beard and weatherworn face under a rumpled, black peaked cap—all spoke to a rugged life at sea. "How fast are we moving?"

"About 12 knots, as we are light on passengers and freight for the run to Jaffa and Port Said," the captain replied, turning to Hudson. "Are you familiar with these modern steam ships?"

"Not really," Hudson said. "I did wonder why there are still masts and sails."

Hoffman leaned forward with a wry grin. "Soon, when we have more confidence in our engines, they will be hauled down. Less observable are the critical features—the screw propeller, compound engine, and steel hull each contributes to the vessel making its way from Beirut to Jaffa in about eleven hours."

"Yes, that is why I chose your ship, the fastest."

The captain puffed on his pipe, then said, "During the loading of the ship, I noticed that your party had an unusually large amount of baggage, including camping equipment. Where are you planning to travel from Jaffa?"

"Our first destination is Jerusalem, then on to Petra. Do you know the place, Captain?"

"Only stories from a few ambitious travelers. The structures must be extraordinary. Just imagine, classical buildings carved out of cliffs. There is also much talk of Bedouin who surround the hidden city, defending their tribal lands and rights."

Hudson paused. "I have been warned by several people of possible problems. We are simply curious travelers, no threat to the Bedouin." Hudson spoke with a firmness that belied his growing concern about traveling to a remote area known to be risky for foreigners. "What can you tell me about Jaffa, Captain Hoffman?"

"Frankly, Jaffa is one of the least desirable ports along the Mediterranean. Because there is no real harbor, we must anchor off shore which means a long, inconvenient portage of people and goods."

The high walls of the city reminded Hudson of the long siege of the city by Napoleon's troops. "Is there much of historical interest?" he asked.

"The French devastated the city and population; it is slowly rebuilding," Hoffman replied. "Even from here, you can see the minaret of the Mahmoudiya Mosque restored in this century.

One of the crew interrupted the Captain to advise him that the Duty Officer need him. "Please excuse me, Mr. Hudson. I must attend to our anchoring so that you and your friends can be ferried ashore. I wish you a good journey. Take care among the Bedouin."

18 February 1868 Beirut to Jaffa
My Dear Katharine,
At last the expedition to Jerusalem and Petra is launched. After several delays in Beirut due to stormy weather. Fowler, Lockwood and I climbed aboard the SS Salzburg yesterday afternoon, along with a fine Arabian stallion which would have stolen your heart.

I barely slept during the night, worrying about this and that, as you know I do at the beginning of travels. The three of us had our first dinner together on the ship, and Lockwood annoyed Fowler and myself with his complaining. It left me in a bad mood. Once we begin the travel to Petra we will be dependent on each other for fellowship. I have imagined long, solitary days of riding followed by good discussions around evening campfires. If Lockwood is not capable of that, I hope at least he will not spoil it.

We landed at Jaffa just after dawn. According to the captain of our steam ship, Jaffa is the main gateway for travelers to the Holy Land. The walled town sits on a rounded hill, with the waves of the Mediterranean on the west and orchards of oranges, lemons, and apricots surrounding the town on the land side. It is a curious and quaint town, but fearfully dirty. We walked along the narrow, winding streets crowded with natives and camels and quickly decided that Jaffa was picturesque only from a distance.

You will be amazed to read that we visited a group of American families from Maine attempting to farm and colonize the Holy Land. They have purchased land just outside Jaffa and built New England-style buildings for their homes and church. Like a similar group of Germans nearby, the Americans have millennial visions of preparing for the return of the Jews and the second coming of Christ. Fowler and Lockwood toured the colony and were approached by many of the unhappy colonists, some of whom were begging in the streets. Having failed at their farms and orchards, they are desperate to return to their homes in Maine.

I found a quiet spot on the front porch of what looked like a Vermont farmhouse. It offered a good coastal view of Jaffa, and I completed an oil sketch of the ancient town above the sea, with cliffs reaching up to stone walls enclosing churches, houses, and towers. More charming than the reality.

Will there be a letter in Jerusalem? That is what most occupies my mind. *Your loving Thomas*

That afternoon, Hudson engaged horses and guides for their journey to Jerusalem, with an overnight stop at the Ramleh convent of the Catholic Brothers. Along the way to the convent, Hudson stopped to sketch the vestiges of old stone terraces and fields of wild red anemones and white lilies. The sweep of nodding flower heads under a brilliant blue sky gave him a feeling of optimism, a sense of boundless inspiration lying ahead. He never knew how or if these pencil sketches would be useful, but he methodically annotated them with place names, exact colors, and sometimes weather and date.

The road from Jaffa to Jerusalem was strewn with remnants of ancient paving stones and boulders from the hillsides, slowing the horses. It was near dark when they arrived at the humble convent lit only by candles. They were greeted by three of the brothers who scurried around the kitchen and reappeared with omelets, cheese, coffee and what they called turpentine wine.

"We are never surprised by late arrivals from Jaffa," said the elderly brother who joined them at the table. "The road from Jaffa to Ramleh is in dreadful condition, and nothing will be done about it." He looked around at his hungry visitors and poured himself a glass of wine. "We were told that the Turkish Grand Vizier recently remarked that improving the road would only lead to even more visitors in Jerusalem which was already a Christian madhouse." The brother folded his hands over his bulging middle, smiled broadly, and added, "he is right, absolutely right."

In the early morning the guides were waiting, and they mounted their horses for Jerusalem. For Lockwood and Fowler, this was a return visit to the Holy City, and they chatted about places of interest. Hudson rode ahead, his anticipation of splendor propelling him toward the city of everlasting joy. The Jerusalem of his imagination was a mighty fortress, grand in aspect and glorious in meaning. It summoned memories of

Renaissance paintings and passages from the New Testament. Within its ancient stone walls, the monuments of Judaism, Christianity, and Islam proclaimed the centrality of Jerusalem for millions of believers scattered around the world. He recalled Byzantine maps which placed the city in the center of the world.

He searched the eastern horizon for his first glimpse of the shining city. Gradually the road widened and became busier with carts, animals and people, and he was shocked to find himself among unattractive modern buildings ending at Jaffa Gate, a tall, rather plain wooden gate in sand-colored stone walls.

As the group rode through the gate, they turned to the right and pulled up their horses beside the entrance to a small souk. Hudson looked disoriented

"What do you think, Hudson? Is this the Jerusalem of your dreams?"

Hudson paused to compose himself and his answer. "Frankly, I am disappointed. I expected to approach from a promontory and find the city spread below in all its splendor with the green and pleasant Judean Hills in the background."

Fowler nodded sympathetically. "Most visitors are dismayed at first glance," he said. "The western approach to Jerusalem offers no grandeur. On Sunday we will take you out St. Stephen's Gate to the Mount of Olives. No doubt, you will be inspired to pick up your pencil by the view from that . . ."

Suddenly a surge of screaming humanity appeared from every direction, descending with the determination of cawing crows on fresh carrion. Voices shouted in a babel of languages. "Come to my shop?" "Watch your horse?" "Find your hotel?" "Holy water from Jordan River?" "Piece of the True Cross?" "*Baksheesh, baksheesh.*" People reached out to grab the horses, tossing rosaries and scapulas onto the saddles. "Pay me. Pay me."

When Hudson noticed a split in the crowd, he thought they were making a path for the riders to leave. He moved his horse toward that direction, and saw a family limping toward him. They were huddled together, a mound of moving rags, faces hidden, arms deformed. Behind them, an older man lying on his back pushed himself along the stones. Several people in the crowd threw pebbles at them.

"Leprosy," Lockwood shouted. He jerked the reins of his horse, causing the horse to whinny and raise its front legs.

The frightened horse had nowhere to go, and one leg grazed the shoulder of a little girl carrying a tray of oranges. She fell under the horse, crying and rolling about to escape the hoofs of the horse.

Hudson shouted, "Stop your horse, Lockwood!"

"I am trying. Too many wretched people, too close." He lifted his whip as if to strike.

"No, Lockwood, no whip!"

One of the guides seized the whip and threw it to the ground. He jumped from his horse and grabbed the bridle of Lockwood's horse and began to rub the horse's neck. As the horse stilled, he placed his face against its nose.

The girl scooted from under the horse, standing and holding her shoulder where blood seeped through her dress. Hudson saw the fear in her tearstained face. She dropped to her knees and crawled among the crowd to collect her oranges. He started to dismount.

The guides shouted, "No! Stay on horse!"

Hudson watched helplessly, as the girl disappeared into the crowd, now retreating from the lepers. He looked again at the diseased family, standing silently at a distance. The sight of the cowering huddle, the hollow eyes, the pleading, rotting hands, hit him with the force of a blow taking his breath.

He turned to Fowler in anguish. "Could we give them some money?"

"Not now. We must leave quickly," Fowler said.

When they dismounted at the Hotel Mediterranean on a quiet street off the Via Dolorosa, Lockwood laughed and chided Hudson about the scene at the gate. "You will have to get used to the behavior of these Arabs and Jews. They are like flies on a pie."

Hudson frowned and patted the horses. He did not want an argument with the insensitive Lockwood, not here in the street. He paid the guides who were unloading their baggage from the pack horses.

Fowler appeared at his side, speaking softly. "Your reaction was natural. Only someone with a heart of stone would not be touched. I will speak to the hotel owner about sending something to the lepers."

As they walked through the courtyard of the hotel, the double door ahead opened wide with the help of two young boys, welcoming them with smiles. Entering the hotel lobby, Hudson softened into the pleasant and quiet surroundings. While they registered and arranged for dinner in the hotel dining room, the two young boys ran out to collect their baggage.

Hearing their voices, the hotel manager, Hassan, came out from a side room. "*As-Salaam Alaikum*, may peace be with you, Mr. Fowler." He remembered Fowler from his earlier visit.

"*Wa Alaikum As-salaa*m, and unto you peace, Hassan."

"*Ahlan wa-Sahlan*, welcome. It is good to see you again. And how was your brother in India?"

"Very well, and your family, Hassan?"

"My large tribe has grown to seven children since you last saw them. My wife says it is enough, but Allah provides."

"Not without your help," Fowler teased. "I want to present my American friends—Thomas Hudson from New York and Charles Lockwood from Virginia."

"It is always a pleasure to welcome Americans to my hotel." Hassan looked at each man carefully and shook hands in the western way. "One of your countrymen was here several months ago, and we still miss his good humor," said Hassan. "In the evenings, after dinner, he entertained the children with tales of frogs and riverboats that equalled Scheherazade."

"Surely that was Mr. Twain and his caravan of innocents," Hudson said. "According to the New York newspapers he amused people from Constantinople to Tangier. The rest of us Americans are dull by comparison."

"Do you have three good rooms for us, Hassan?" Fowler asked.

"Yes, of course, and I will have hot water sent to you. Please follow my sons, Hisham and Munir. And here, Mr. Hudson, I almost forgot. Two letters have arrived for you."

Hudson appeared nonchalant as he extended his hand for the letters, but Fowler noticed his step quicken as he turned and headed for the stairs. On the first floor of the hotel, Romanesque arches and vaulted ceilings in the lobby area conveyed its former glory as the chapel within a convent. The other rooms for dining and sitting were plain stone with arched windows. On the second floor, small and simply furnished guest rooms recalled the lives of the nuns. The hotel appealed to Americans and British because of its plain food and cleanliness.

In his room Hudson tore open the letter from Katharine, his hands fumbling as he smoothed the thin, translucent paper. The date of January 22 meant that it was almost a month in transit and written before she received the Alexandria letters. The long intervals exceeded the distance in his way of thinking. As usual, the pages were liberally accented with bold exclamation points marking Katharine's enthusiasm. He read it twice, filling his mind with happy pictures of Tommy and Katharine exploring spiders in their corner webs and sliding on the frozen pond. The neighboring farmer shot a deer; then his wife spent hours teaching Katharine to cook a venison stew. Friends visited frequently and gathered them up for sleigh rides through the woods. His parents were staying nearby in Claverack and came to the cottage each day to play with Tommy and give Katharine a few hours of rest. Margaret, his sister, was not well enough to travel, but her health was almost restored. All good news. Voices in the hallway announced that Fowler and Lockwood were heading to the dining room, and after another quick read, Hudson tucked Katharine's letter under his pillow. He would read the other letter from an artist friend later.

After dinner, Hudson, Lockwood, and Fowler went for an early evening walk along the top of the city walls. At this height they were sheltered from the noise and traffic of the twisting streets, and Fowler offered to help Hudson understand the layout of the city. He had just begun to talk when the call to prayer echoed from minarets throughout the city.

"What is that?" Hudson asked. "Is there a problem?" Hudson

looked down into the streets to see if people were gathering.

"It is the *adhan*, the Muhammadan call to prayer. It happens five times each day. You must have heard it in Beirut," Fowler said.

Hudson thought for a moment. "From one mosque, perhaps, but this is a little alarming."

"I find it rather lovely, reminds me of church bells."

"Do you know what it means in English, Fowler?"

"I can give you a rough translation," he said.

> *God is Greatest*
> *I bear witness that there is no God except Allah.*
> *I bear witness that Muhammad is God's Messenger*
> *Come to prayer*
> *Come to success*
> *God is Greatest*
> *There is no god except Allah.*

Hudson thought about the words. They proclaimed belief in the oneness of God, just as Christians believed. One word was confusing. "Fowler, what is meant by Come to success?"

"It is complicated, but essentially it reminds worshippers that Muhammadan precepts, like the requirement to pray, are spiritual cures for the benefit of man, not God."

Hudson had read a bit about the history of Muhammadans in Porter's *Handbook for Travellers in Syria and Palestine*, but understood little of the beliefs and practices.

"Now, where was I?" Fowler asked himself. "Oh, yes, the city layout. For better or worse, Jerusalem is divided roughly according to religion," explained Fowler. "The Muhammadan quarter in the northeastern section is just below us, and the large, open area is the *Haram ash-Sharif*, the Holy Sanctuary, with the primary Muhammadan shrines. To the south and east of the *Haram* is the Jewish quarter with the Wailing Wall and a few synagogues, and to the southwest lies the Armenian quarter with the St. James Monastery near the center. The Christian quarter is in the northwestern corner of the city. You can see the tower of the Church of the Holy Sepulchre rising above the other Christian churches and monasteries. Simple from this perspective, but a labyrinth for the traveler. Fortunately, no Minotaur."

Hudson's overall impression of the city was a jumble of low beige and gray stone buildings with pale rose-colored tile roofs, the spires of churches and minarets of the mosques poking up to provide some elevation. Only the *Haram ash-Sharif* offered an open space for several buildings in a pleasing setting of trees and fountains. He had read that this raised area had been important to Muhammadans from the very beginning of Islam. "Will we be able to visit the *Haram?*" Hudson asked.

Fowler was surprised by Hudson's interest in a Muhammadan holy place. In his experience, most Christian visitors to Jerusalem ignored all but the Biblical sites. "The *Haram* will be open to you on all days except for Friday, the Muhammadan day of prayer. I encourage you to go, take your time in observing how they gather for worship and family occasions. You may also want to visit the Wailing Wall of the Jews."

Lockwood had been quiet, but now spoke up. "Jerusalem has ten thousand years of history to keep you on your feet, Hudson. Plus, the fanatics of all major religions are amusing."

"I gather you are not a man of the Church, Mr. Lockwood," Hudson replied tartly.

"During my earlier stay in Jerusalem," Lockwood said, "I was convinced that it was not a place for serious Christians. You will decide for yourself. I readily admit I am one of those Christmas and Easter Christians."

Hudson was quiet on the walk back to the hotel. He was tired of Lockwood's abrasive remarks and lingered behind the other two. These first few days had not revealed much to like about Lockwood, but he knew he had to make the best of the situation; it would be awkward to get rid of him at this point.

In the lobby of the hotel, Hudson immediately noticed the handsomely garbed Arab man standing at the desk, speaking quietly with Hassan. He wore a long black robe edged with gold thread over a white cotton galabiya. The white kafiya covering his head emphasized the hawk-like appearance of his nose and eyes in profile.

"Good evening, Mr. Hudson, Mika'il el Hany, one of the local dragomen, is here to speak with you," Hassan said.

"Mika'il, thank you for coming," Hudson said. "Mr. Johnson in Beirut recommends you highly and promises that you have many trips to Petra under that impressive belt."

The Arab looked at his belt and at Hassan who simply shrugged.

"I'm afraid that we are too tired to begin discussions tonight, but I hope you can return tomorrow morning around nine."

"*Bukra, insha'allah.* Tomorrow, God willing." Mika'il bowed.

19 February 1868 Hudson, Jerusalem Letter to Katharine
My Dearest Katharine,
I have been wrestling with my bed for over an hour. I am either too excited or too disturbed to sleep. A letter from you was waiting at the hotel when I arrived in Jerusalem. I raced to my room and ripped it open like an addict seeking opium. I read it two, no, ten times. I smelled it, massaged it, held it to my heart. Your magic turns me into a madman. I think of our warm, safe bed and yearn for the curves of your body. Our love and closeness will survive these distances—perhaps enriched through absence if that is possible. I do know that being away from you reminds me every day, every hour of your centrality in my life; you are the sun around which revolves my life and art, my dreams and desires, all in orbit around your bright love. If others could look upon this love, they would be blinded by its brilliance. Always keep me close, my darling.

Your fresh stories of life in our Hudson Valley bring smiles to my tired face. I can imagine Tommy hunting for spiders, and my mother reading to him by the fireplace. The aroma of that venison stew may keep me awake.

Excitement also arises from, at last, being in Jerusalem. I will admit that my first reaction was one of disillusionment; Jerusalem did not unveil herself as the grand city on the mountain of my imagination. However, I have just returned from a walk along the old stone walls surrounding the old city and feel newly inspired by the sights and sounds, like a child who wants to touch and question all that comes within reach.

Our arrival in Jerusalem this afternoon was marred by incidents which continue to prey on my mind. Here, travelers are frequently harassed by merchants and beggars, and we were no exception.

The appearance of a family of lepers who live and beg near the Jaffa

Gate frightened me. Most wrap their rotting bodies to hide the sores from our eyes, but their pleading stares send arrows into the heart. I have little to offer them except money, but I will arrange for that.

Moments later Lockwood's horse was startled by the crowd and reared up. As it came down in the crowd, one of the hoofs clipped the shoulder of a little girl, and she fell to the ground. Then she risked more injury by crawling among the crowd to retrieve her oranges. I imagine she might be supporting her family with the sale of the fruit. I would have bought her oranges, but she disappeared into the crowd like a frightened lamb.

My mind keeps replaying these scenes, and I write about them to relieve my anxiety. I miss the comfort of exchanging confidences, happy and sad, with you.   *Good night, My Beloved, I feel you beside me, Your Loving Thomas*

FIVE

Jerusalem

The following morning Hudson awoke to find an arabesque pattern moving across his bedcovers as sunlight flooded through the intricate stone lattice of the windows and landed on the plain white cloth. He lay still, enjoying the painting composed by nature and changed by degrees as moving clouds filtered the sunlight. Yesterday had been a day of confused emotions, and he thought about his expectations. Usually when he traveled to a new region, he did not have distinct visual images of what he would find. In this instance, his mind had been filled from childhood with Biblical images from Renaissance paintings and nineteenth-century lithographs which created an illusion of beauty in a tranquil space. He needed to erase those earlier images implanted by religious and artistic fervor and concentrate on the present moment. He wanted his paintings of the Orient to reveal the natural and spiritual power of the landscape, not create an imaginary world.

Just then, Fowler knocked on the door. "Good morning, Hudson, time for breakfast."

"Be there in ten minutes," Hudson called, jumping out of bed and dressing quickly. He gathered notes, pencils and sketchbook and tossed them into a knapsack, along with his roll of maps.

As he took his seat at the breakfast table, Fowler was ordering an Oriental omelet, juice and coffee. Hudson seconded the order—his first choice of something beyond the continental menu. Good and ample food interested him, but he lacked an adventurous instinct at the table. "Where is Lockwood?"

"Out for a walk," Fowler replied. "He ate earlier."

When the omelets arrived, Hudson stared at his plate, shook his head with disbelief at the lump of green eggs, and took a small bite. "This is excellent—strange looking, but quite tasty. What makes it Oriental?"

"A generous dose of fresh herbs, parsley and thyme, combined with ground cumin and onion. One of my favorites," Fowler replied with a wink.

Hudson devoured the omelet and ordered another. While they ate they made plans for the day after their meeting with Mika'il. Hudson and Fowler intended to explore the city by foot. When the table was cleared, Hudson unfolded a detailed map of the Old City of Jerusalem taken from his Porter's guide. Fowler suggested they follow the Via Dolorosa from their present location in the Muhammadan quarter, then cross into the Christian quarter and begin their touring at the Church of the Holy Sepulchre. From there they could visit several other Christian churches on their way to the shops and lunch along King David Street. Lockwood returned and announced he had an appointment with the British Army engineer conducting archaeological excavations for the Palestine Exploration Fund of London.

Mika'il El Hany appeared promptly at nine o'clock. Fowler asked the waiter to bring more coffee, and Lockwood cleared the adjacent table for the bundles of maps carried by Hudson and Mika'il. The group had agreed Hudson would be their spokesman with Mika'il.

"I want an expedition that will expose us to grand natural scenery, preferably with mountainous terrain, culminating with the entrance into the valley of Petra." Hudson had read extensively about the region's geology and biblical geography and selected a map to trace his precise ideas. "I am thinking a route via Hebron, down the west side of the Dead Sea, along the mountains of Judea, through Beersheba, down to the plains of Wadi Arabah, and up to the Mountains of ash-Shara and Petra, entering the Valley of Petra through the chasm which you call the Siq." He turned to Fowler and Lockwood and added, "the Siq is a narrow, winding passageway between high cliffs that ends just in front of El Khasneh, the architectural masterpiece of the valley." He was almost breathless when he finished.

"Yes, I know the route well," Mika'il slipped his prayer beads into his pocket, "but I suggest we not try to enter Petra through the Siq."

"What? Why do you say that?"

"The Huwaitát, the local Bedouin, keep lookouts in the area of the Siq. If they are in a hostile mood, they will keep us out of the valley."

Hudson shoved his chair away from the table and stood above the group. He started to speak, then looked down at his hands gripping the back of the chair. He had a careful plan, and already an obstacle arose. From his study of maps and the Laborde lithographs, he knew sketching the spatial relationship of the Siq to El Khasneh and the geological formations of the Siq were significant for his plans. He knew that other artists, other travelers had entered Petra through the Siq and found it extraordinary, marvelous, sublime.

"What are you telling me, Mika'il?"

"*Wallahi*, really, I am talking about risk, Mr. Hudson." Mika'il was again fingering his prayer beads. "There are other, safer ways to enter the Petra Valley." He pulled the map closer to Hudson and pointed to a trail west of Petra. "This route leads us around Jebel Haroun—you call it the mountain of Aaron—to a descent into the Petra Valley. That should give us at least a day before the Huwaitát know we have arrived. Easy entrance and one less day of baksheesh."

"And can we enter the Siq from the valley side?" Hudson fixed his stare on the Arab.

"It should be safe from el Khasneh. I will take you wherever it is safe. I must protect you and avoid offending the Bedouin."

Disappointment hung from Hudson's drooping shoulders, but he nodded his agreement.

"Along the way, do you want to leave the main route for good scenery?" The dragoman pulled a tattered map from his roll and pointed out two side trails—one near the town of Beersheba in the mountain range of El Tih and the other through mountains northwest of Wadi Arabah.

Hudson smiled broadly. This was what he wanted from a guide. "Yes, I will be very interested in your suggestions, Mika'il."

For the last minutes, Lockwood had been tapping his fingers on the table impatiently, as if sending a telegraph to Hudson. "I must say I object to allowing those lying, greedy Bedouin to control our access. According to my sources, arriving through the Siq is the high point of the Petra Valley."

After a moment of silence, Mika'il spoke softly. "I do not know where you may have come across the Bedouin in your past, Mr. Lockwood. There are many tribes in Syria, Arabia, and Egypt with different customs and motives. The Huwaitát Bedouin in Petra do not fit your description. They are descendants of men who have been protecting those lands for over a thousand years. Their leaders are powerful and honest." Mika'il swept his arm in a bowing gesture and sat quietly.

Mika'il's reasoned response impressed Hudson. "I share your preference, Lockwood, but I will not jeopardize Petra for entrance by the Siq. I agree with Mika'il." Hudson turned to Fowler, who nodded with a face as calm as a cat.

Mika'il reached into the pocket of his galabiya and pulled out a contract. In the end, Hudson achieved all his requirements in a written contract with a highly reputable dragoman at a quite good price. For two hundred fifty American dollars from each person, they would have the services of Mika'il and a caravan which would gradually increase to at least twelve men, fifteen camels, three horses, three sleeping tents, and one cook tent. On leaving Petra, the large caravan would disperse. For an additional five dollars per day, Mika'il would take Hudson, Fowler, and Lockwood by horseback from Petra to Gaza, where they could board a ship for Beirut.

"It will take me three days to make arrangements." Mika'il gathered his maps as he spoke. "I need your passports to get travel permits for Petra."

Lockwood seemed agitated, scratching the side of his head and swaying from one foot to the other. "What? Why? I have never heard of travel permits here. It is ridiculous."

"The permits are a new requirement of the Turkish officials, Mr. Lockwood." Mika'il stood silently, his arm extended for the passport.

Hudson waited at the hotel door while Fowler lit his pipe. "Are you ready for a day of sightseeing my friend?. I thought we would start along the Via Dolorosa, the street that tries to follow the path Jesus took through Jerusalem toward the hill of the crucifixion."

As they walked, Fowler pointed out markings of the Stations of the Cross along the walls. "Vicious arguments break out among Christian sects about location of the sites—where He stumbled, where Veronica wiped His face. Refreshing that lack of consensus is not unique to western Christians."

Hudson thought he heard a lack of seriousness in Fowler's voice, but he was too busy keeping up with Fowler's turns along the busy twisting path to ask a question. Fowler navigated with no hesitation, until they arrived at a large, crowded, stone courtyard surrounded by religious buildings in a Romanesque style.

"And here we are my friend, the Church of the Holy Sepulchre."

"This is it? This is the supposed site of the crucifixion?"

"I know, Hudson, seems a modest structure for a momentous event in Christianity; 'tis a poor relative of the great cathedrals of Europe." Fowler shook his head sadly.

The courtyard resembled a carnival. Money changers waved currencies of the world, and tour guides shoved each other competing for customers. An elderly man carrying a stack of books shouted, "Bibles! Holy Book! English, French, German!" From booths edging the walls, sellers of holy water, olive wood crosses, scapulas, and rosaries beckoned the true believers.

Hudson dodged a few peddlers trying to keep up with Fowler's determined pace, but when a young girl tugged on his arm, he stopped. He looked into large, watery eyes on a thin, sad face streaked with dirt and tears. A little tattooed hand extended for baksheesh. As he reached into his pocket, Fowler appeared, quickly placed a coin in the child's hand and pulled Hudson forward.

"It is not wise to give to beggars in such a crowd. The horde will descend on you, the worthy and the unworthy." Fowler gestured with his pipe stem toward the line of beggars along the courtyard wall—a gang of children, women, and men searching the crowd for prey.

As they approached the open church door, a group of Orthodox priests arguing with a Turkish guard blocked the way. Dressed in elaborate, silk embroidered surplices, painted with images of the crucified Christ and wearing long beards and hooded robes, they looked alike to everyone except the Turkish guard.

"*Wallahi*, I swear, you will not bring that stove into the Church," the Turkish guard said. "Do you not remember that I caught you cooking in the Chapel of Saint Helena? You smuggle everything under those large robes, first the stove, then the meat. We Muhammadans would never do that in a mosque."

"It is part of our religious tradition," the elderly priest whined as he prodded the Turk with his crucifix.

"Then do it in your own church, in the Armenian quarter, not here. Now move away." The guard waved his sword above his head to encourage the unhappy priests to retreat quickly. He then resumed his place on a bench with several other guards who smoked pipes as long and thin as fencing sabres. Their dress identified them as Muhammadans, not Christians. They barely glanced at Fowler and Hudson who entered the vestibule and made their way just beyond the Stone of Unction

"What are those Muhammadans doing in a church?" Hudson asked.

"Shh." Fowler pulled Hudson into an alcove and whispered. "Muhammadans are the preservers of this church. Without them it would be burned to the ground every year."

"By whom?"

"The Christians," Fowler winked and pointed at the candles. "Fires and fights erupt constantly in the more secluded chapels. As you can see, there are rivulets of oil leaking from lamps, pools of melted candle wax, open braziers with charcoal—all inadequately tended by elderly monks, usually chanting or sleeping."

"And then there are the priests we just saw who want to cook their dinners." Hudson rolled his eyes.

"Every Christian sect has its encampment in here," Fowler said, "and the guards are referees to the angry disputes that erupt. They accuse each other of being scoundrels or heretics, disturb each other's prayers and services with hissing and snarling, and then grab staffs or crucifixes for a good bash. When blood is spilled, the guards move into position, clear the church and lock the door. Even the key to the church is kept by Muhammadans because the Christians could not agree on a custodian. Each day, a member of a well-known Muhammadan family appears to unlock and lock the door."

Hudson had been told by a cousin that brotherly love among the eastern Christian sects did not extend to the interior of the Holy Sepulchre. "I was somewhat prepared for the conflict, but not for this unholy din."

The bells rang out the noon hour, and a dissonant symphony of foreign tongues, chants, and instruments ascended from various chapels. "The midday rites," Fowler shouted into Hudson's ear. "Services are conducted in Latin, Greek, Turkish, Arabic, Coptic, and several other dialects, and each sect has its unique liturgy. It is best observed with eyes open and ears shut."

"Fowler, I wonder," Hudson hesitated, squinted, "do you believe this is where the crucifixion took place? Most American Protestants call it a pious fraud."

"Ah, it does not matter what we believe," said Fowler. "Faith is in the heart of the believer, and we are witnessing the devotions of true believers—they may behave slightly wild, but they venerate this site as the most significant for Christianity."

"You are right, my friend," Hudson said. "I expect I am not very tolerant when it comes to religion."

"Come, let me see if I can provide a superficial understanding of the Holy Sepulchre's various locations." Fowler guided Hudson along the shadowy passages, past shrines and vaults to small chapels with monks and worshippers singing in Greek or Arabic. Passing through a narrow door, they descended stairs partly hewn into the rock of the hill. After a few turns they reached the Chapel of Saint Helena, an elaborate structure with several altars and Byzantine columns holding up a cupola pierced by windows. A few clusters of monks with coarse brown robes and tonsured hair sat praying or reading scriptures. From the chapel, Fowler and Hudson descended farther into a roughly excavated vault. According to tradition, it was here that Helena, mother of Constantine the Great, found the three crosses, crown of thorns, and nails. A simple crucifix hung over a plain altar in front of a long row of tall candles. A monk lay prostrate on the ground before the altar.

One of the candles leaned dangerously close to falling, and Fowler moved to adjust it. The monk did not move. Hudson drew back against the wall. Seeing a man in such a state of submission bothered him.

Leaving this quiet refuge, Hudson and Fowler ascended into increasing chaos. Around them the stone building resounded with the wild cacophony of chants, organs, cymbals, and shouts of the worshippers and priests carrying crossed candles and swinging incense censers in an endless procession. Aromas of balsam, lavender, myrrh, roses, and bergamot intermingled with intoxicating effects.

They stopped beside an elevated box of sand in which lighted candles dripped into pools of wax. A crippled, elderly woman, draped in black veils and cloths, inserted a few piastres into a collection box. As she bent down to collect her candles, a priest rushing to join the procession smacked her shoulder with his crucifix. He turned his head, but did not stop as she fell against the candle stand. Hot wax splashed against her hands as she reached for a hold. The woman did not appear surprised or angry, and Fowler gently helped her to her feet. As she looked up to see her rescuer, a beatific smile warmed her face—a moment of grace shared by strangers, a singular holy experience in the Church of the Holy Sepulchre.

The crush of humanity had finally dampened Hudson's curiosity. His expression of dismay indicated that he had seen enough of eastern Christianity for the day, and Fowler suggested leaving for the bazaar.

King David Street offered the wares of the Orient in stone

shops resembling large, semicircular ovens. As they descended the stone steps that comprised the street, the fragrance of Asian spices teased their noses. Hudson stopped to enjoy their earthy colors—shades of red, orange, yellow brown, and green. The shabbiness of the shops was leavened by their colorful goods. Blue and white pottery of Jerusalem competed with brass plates from Damascus. Hebron glass in hues of amber and turquoise was shaped into useful, not decorative, items—plates and cups of all sizes. Hudson remembered the bazaar in Alexandria where most of the items seemed destined for foreigners or wealthy Arabs. Here Palestinian women were buying coarse black linen for their dresses and plain white cotton galabiyas for their husbands. He mentioned the difference to Fowler.

"Just ahead we will find a few luxury items, but you are right, Hudson, this is a more traditional market."

The street widened slightly, and on both sides, elderly men drinking coffee sat on wicker stools close to the stone walls, engrossed in their backgammon contests. They played at such a speed that an observer heard the sounds of pieces and chips more clearly than seeing the moves.

The shops in this section were larger and offered more expensive items. For smokers there were four-foot-long pipes and brass or silver hookahs. Fine Persian carpets hung beside skillful Turkish copies, and valuable antiques sat on shelves among worthless trinkets.

In a fancier store calling itself Archaeologia Arabia, Fowler silently pointed Hudson's attention to a small piece of sculpture on the shelf. While his eyes focused on the sculpture, his hand picked up several other items to examine. "What is the origin of this brass plate, *effendi?*" Fowler asked.

The merchant barely turned his head and replied, "Two hundred piastres."

"I did not ask you the price, my friend, only where it was found. The etched design resembles 15th century Damascene salvers made for the Venetian market, but it appears to be more recent work."

The merchant rose immediately, bowing slightly and

introducing himself as Tariq Aboud. "I believe you are correct about the piece. It was brought to me by a foreigner who had passed through Damascus recently. Many years ago, such early nineteenth century reproductions were common, but not now. Are you looking especially for antique brass? I have other pieces in my storeroom."

Fowler was familiar with the ubiquitous storeroom where sly merchants of antiquarian goods kept the precious items out of sight of Ottoman officials. "Brass is only one of my interests. Do you have other stone sculptures, similar to this fragment?" Fowler pointed to the sculpture that had initially drawn his attention.

The merchant drew nearer to Fowler and motioned toward Hudson. "He is with you?"

Fowler nodded, asking, "I believe the sculpture is Nabatean; is that your judgment?"

"Yes, of course, but not from Petra. It is forbidden to remove sculpture from Petra. The Bedouin patrol the valley. Men have paid with their lives . . . "

"I know of the restrictions," Fowler interrupted gently with a raised hand. "Do you have other Nabatean pieces?"

"Perhaps, but they are quite rare, and truly, this piece should not be on display. My son made a foolish mistake by putting it on the shelf." Aboud picked up the sculpture and put it under a table. "I would be most happy to take you to the storeroom."

"I will return in two days, if that is convenient," Fowler said.

"I am at your service, *Ma'asalama*. Peace be with you."

Fowler and Hudson returned to the street, continuing to descend the steps among the crowd of shoppers. At the next corner, men gathered at tables laden with lamb kebabs, musakhan chicken, hummus, pita, and glasses of hot tea. The food was cooked outside, along the street, and brought into the tented café. The aroma of baking bread drew Hudson to a sidewalk kitchen next to the café. A young girl kneaded a coarse dough and rolled it into balls about the size of an orange, then used a fat, round stick to roll it flat and thin. Her face was focused and serious until she placed two circles on a paddle held by her father. When she looked up at him, he smiled broadly and inserted the paddle and dough into a small oven where the bread puffed and browned. In two minutes it was on its way into the café, followed by Hudson and Fowler.

"What looks good to you, Hudson?

"All of it, especially that bread. Oh, and coffee, not tea." Hudson was looking at the surrounding tables covered with small dishes being shared by all.

Fowler ordered while Hudson waited for a table.

Hudson had restrained his curiosity until they were well away from the antiquities shop. "What did you really think about the sculpture fragment, Fowler?"

"I saw a few similar pieces while traveling in Arabia, and they were identified as Nabatean. I am not an expert in that period, but I would say this piece was finer, although clearly only a small part of a figure." He looked around to see if anyone was listening. "There are rumors that sculpture is being smuggled out of Petra by foreigners, perhaps even by Bedouin. The Ottoman officials are not seriously concerned, but the local Bedouin tribes are furious about the desecration of the site."

"Will you return to visit the storeroom?" Hudson asked.

"I would like to, if our schedule permits. I am not much of a buyer, but I enjoy looking. Also, I want to know what he will say to me when I am alone, without witnesses. These merchants usually cannot resist telling stories, true or false, to others who share their passion. Who knows what I might learn about Petra from him."

"Good idea. By the way, I enjoyed that little introduction to bargaining, a clever exchange as you each established your credentials." Hudson tucked away that experience for later reference.

The food arrived—plates spread with hummus drizzled with olive oil and roasted pine nuts, some kind of meat roasted on small sticks, bowls of oranges flecked with mint leaves, and the warm bread cut like slices of pie. The demitasse size cups were filled with thick black liquid, and Hudson's small sip coated his entire mouth with a smooth, pungent flavor of Arabian coffee and cardamom. There were no eating utensils or napkins, so Hudson watched Fowler for clues.

Fowler dipped a piece of bread into the hummus and looked up at Hudson. "What we have seen—people at prayer, at work—this is not what inspires your paintings?"

"No, not at all. Mind you, I do find these scenes intriguing," Hudson replied, "but I am a landscape artist, and I cannot imagine straying from that territory. Sometimes my paintings include structures and people, but such details are usually small, sometimes symbolic and primarily give a sense of scale to the natural world."

"Does that mean your painting interests in the Orient do not include the landscape of a city?" Fowler asked.

Hudson paused briefly, his pale blue eyes deepened and narrowed as they searched the distance. "I am not certain. The idea of painting Jerusalem in its natural surroundings is appealing, but I must find the view that speaks to the spirit of the place. As yet, I have not found the spirit or the view."

"Do you mean spirit in a religious sense?" Fowler asked.

"Not precisely religious." Hudson thought back to discussions among the Hudson River painters. "What I am looking for is the spirit of nature. I believe that nature has much to teach us about how to live our lives. And of course, we cannot separate nature from God."

Fowler nodded in agreement, but his furrowed brow suggested he was somewhat confused by Hudson's remarks. "Well, I would like to end today's excursion by taking you to one more religious site, the *Haram ash-Sharif* or Noble Sanctuary, the most holy site for Muhammadans outside of Arabia. You asked about it last night when we were walking the wall. I will pay this chit, Mr. Hudson, and we will be on our way—it is a short walk."

They walked along Chain Street toward the Muhammadan holy place, and Fowler spoke about Islam.

"Islam finds its roots in Judaism and Christianity. The Prophets, Jesus, and Muhammad—all revered in Islam. Jerusalem is unique because it is a Holy City for the followers of all three religions—a place where humanity meets the divine."

Hudson could not suppress a grin. "That sounds like the introduction to an Oxford lecture."

Fowler stopped, fumbling with his tie. "Oh dear, I do have a tendency to fall into teaching."

"I am only teasing you. I want to hear more."

"There is a wonderful story about Muhammad which explains why the *Haram ash-Sharif* is an essential shrine for Islam. The story comes from the Holy Qur'an. One evening, Muhammad is praying at the Kaabah in Mecca, and the angel Gabriel appears and places him on a winged stallion, al-Buraq, that takes him to a high point in Jerusalem. From there he ascends into the heavens and meets with God, Allah, who gives Muhammad a single commandment—all Muhammadans must offer prayers five times each day." Fowler paused in front of the Chain Gate, and pulled Hudson to the side so others could pass.

"That journey during a single night is considered a miracle in the Islamic tradition, and it began on Mount Moriah, the center of the *Haram ash-Sharif.*"

When they entered the gate to the *Haram*, the shrine known as the Dome of the Rock was just ahead. Hudson felt a slight dizziness as his eyes absorbed the brilliance of blue and gold shimmering in the midday sun. He could see the colors being squeezed out of tubes and blended to perfection on his palette. He would start with cobalt blue, and then follow a spectrum toward aquamarine. Gold leafing would be the only choice for the dome. The octagonal shape was striking, surmounted by a dome resting on a drum, with overall proportions that were unfamiliar, but appealing.

The racing of Hudson's mind was slowed down by Fowler's firm grip on his upper arm. "Mr. Hudson we must move out of the way. The muezzin is calling the faithful to prayer."

"Of course. I seem to have lapsed into a trance—it is an extraordinary site. Am I permitted to sketch here?"

"Over there, among the cypress trees, I think you will not offend anyone, but please do not include any people," Fowler cautioned, since the sanctuary guards might want to see what he was doing, and the inclusion of a figure could cause trouble.

Hudson sketched with the speed and confidence of a master artist, trusting his brain and hand to follow his eyes. He paid particular attention to the pleasing rhythm created by the repetition of arches on the lower facade and to the ribbon of elongated script in the blue and white tiles at the upper level of the octagon. Before he closed the sketchbook, he finished his work with notations about colors, shapes of tiles, clouds, and shadows.

When he turned to Fowler, his face was still flushed with excitement. "What is that elegant calligraphy at the top of the octagon? I assume it is some form of Arabic."

"Yes, it is Arabic in a lovely combination of language and art. The script originated in Kufa, near Baghdad, but it has become associated with architecture and art everywhere in the Islamic world. It is known as Kufic."

"Can we enter the blue mosque?"

Fowler was peering over Hudson's shoulder to get a glimpse of the sketch. "It is not a mosque, it is a shrine, the Dome of the Rock, and yes, we can enter after the time of prayer."

Muhammadans hurried from several gates, across the large paving stones, stopping at a nearby fountain to wash face, hands, and feet. Men richly garbed in embroidered kaftans over silk galabiyas walked among men covered in rags. All would stand side by side raising their eyes and hands to God with one voice of praise. "There is no God except for Allah . . . ."

During the prayer time, Hudson and Fowler walked around the *Haram ash-Sharif* looking at the Dome of the Ascension, the site where Muhammad prayed before his ascent; the Stairs of Scales of Souls, where the souls of the dead will be weighed on Judgment Day; and the Fountain of Qayt Bay, where the last stragglers completed their ablutions.

At the end of prayers, men streamed out of Al Aqsa Mosque to return to work or home. A few older men sat on the stones in the warm sunshine. Hudson approached the entrance to the Dome of the Rock, removed his shoes and socks, and entered through a double colonnade of arches and marble columns. The tiles were moist, cool on his bare feet, and he inhaled the scent of lamps burning olive oil. A steady murmur of prayers recalled the hum of nature on a summer day.

In the center of the shrine, the great sacred rock, the summit of Mount Moriah, marked the place from which Muhammad's horse leapt into the sky for the night journey. The bare, dark brown, uneven rock was about sixty feet in diameter and rose six feet above the floor, shining from the touch of many worshippers' hands. Hudson wandered beyond the four massive piers that encircled the rock and between the slender marble columns linked above by arches which supported the golden dome. The arches and walls were adorned with an abundance of mosaics—trees floating with wings and spirals of flowers springing from vases— all inlaid in ivory colored marble. Other banners of golden mosaics carried Qur'anic inscriptions around the base of the dome.

Raising his eyes even higher, he admired the manner in which the architect arranged for light to enter the space. On each of the eight sides of the octagon there were five stained glass windows set into a marble grill, sending streams of brilliantly colored light through the inner arches toward the rock. From the drum connecting the octagon with the dome, clear windows incised with verses from the Qur'an in the elegant Kufic script cast down rays of light on the enormous pillars of green and white marble. Light was nature's gift to architecture, but a wise architect had to shape its passage. Hudson felt the same was required of painters. When he was ready to leave, he found Fowler sitting outside.

"Today, I think I have found the first real spark for my artistic instincts on this journey. I deeply appreciate your bringing me here, Fowler. The shrine is magnificent, inspirational—the beginning of my conception of a great painting. Now I must see it from a distance, and I expect that the Mount of Olives might be that perfect distance."

Fowler's expression showed delight. "It sounds as if you have looked with the eye of an artist and the mind of a humanist. I have seen Christians react with disparagement or even scorn. Perhaps because the unknown makes them uncomfortable."

The men walked the short distance to the hotel in silence, lost in their individual thoughts. Their reverie ended abruptly at the doorway to the hotel where Mika'il and Lockwood were engaged in an argument.

" . . . is not necessary—those lazy Ottoman officials have nothing important to do so they bother travelers with forms and interviews." Lockwood's volume increased with every word and perspiration dampened his forehead. "I have no intention of going to their office. I am an American citizen, and they have no authority . . . ."

Several boys were nearby, mimicking and laughing at the foreigner. Lockwood reached out to strike the closest boy, and Mika'il grabbed his arm.

"I say, sir, you must restrain your temper!" Fowler stepped between Lockwood and Mika'il. "Let us go into the hotel and resolve this issue."

When they entered, Fowler signaled to Hassan to join them at a table in the deserted dining room. "It would be good to have Hassan join this conversation. Any objections?" Fowler asked. Everyone sat down in silence. "Good. We all need to hear what has caused this disagreement. Would you begin, Mr. Lockwood?"

"As I was saying, the Turks are meddlesome bureaucrats who have no authority to ask . . ."

Fowler interrupted, "I think we want to hear what the Ottoman officials did, Lockwood."

"Mika'il tells me that one of the Ottomans noticed that I was identified as a former naval officer and an engineer on my passport. He wanted to know if I was on official business. Now they are insisting that I appear at their office before granting approval for our travel to Petra. It is outrageous . . . "

"No, I think it is quite reasonable considering the pressure on the Ottomans from many directions," Hassan remarked.

"What do you mean by pressure?"

"The large influx of foreigners is causing the Ottoman officials to become alarmed and sometimes difficult," Hassan explained. "Travelers want protection from unscrupulous merchants. Merchants want protection from foreign business. European Hebrews want permission to make their home in Jerusalem. Engineers want to survey the countryside and dig under Jerusalem. So many 'wants' and so little direction from

Constantinople. The officials are afraid of making mistakes that will cost them their job or even their head." Hassan made the universal cutting-off-head gesture as he turned to Fowler.

"Mika'il, what do you have to add?"

"It is as Mr. Lockwood said. The Ottoman officials want to ask questions. They will fill out a form with the answers and add the form to the large box of papers accumulating dust in the corner. If later there is a problem, they will be able to prove they did their job. It may be a foolish request, but it must be obeyed."

"The question of concern," Hassan said, "will be whether you are planning to survey and map. The Council of the Sultan has become particularly wary of the increase in surveying by the French and British."

"Why is mapping such a problem, Hassan?" Hudson asked.

"Mapping is now considered the first hint of invasion, either by soldiers or merchants." Hassan looked toward Lockwood. "Some surveyors request permission as they are required to do, some work secretly."

Lockwood removed his hat and wiped his brow. "As I told Hudson in Beirut, I have been working with two British survey projects in Syria, but I can assure you this travel is for diversion, pleasure."

Hudson noticed that Lockwood gave the desired answer but his tone appeared insincere.

"Frankly," Lockwood continued, "I am annoyed by the requirement to appear at their office, but I will abide by the request. I don't have any languages other than English. Mika'il, would you agree to join me for the translation?"

"Yes, of course. You will be keeping the Sabbath tomorrow. Would the following morning be suitable?"

"Fine. I will meet you here at nine o'clock." Lockwood turned abruptly and left for his room.

After Lockwood left, Hassan spoke in a cautioning tone. "It has not been quiet in Jerusalem. Changes are creating confusion and suspicion. The Sultan has issued several edicts which require local Ottoman officials to perform specific functions. Instead of pretending to collect and pass on a modest amount of taxes, officials must be diligent in collecting higher taxes. Another edict allowing foreigners to buy land in Palestine has caused a local rebellion over land holdings. The edict has brought a flood of people pouring in from Russia, Greece, Austria-Hungary, Spain and North Africa. Sometimes the buyers cheat the landowners with ridiculously low bids. People who have lived here for centuries are angry with the sellers and the buyers. And the worst abuse is from swindlers who by legal means take land from people who thought they owned it."

"What does this mean for us, Hassan?" Hudson asked. "Has it affected travelers?"

"To some extent, simply because they were in the wrong place, and they looked like the bad people." Hassan's hands fluttered through the air like butterflies, and then landed in the folds of his galabiya. While he appeared to be nervous, he also seemed to be reassuring Hudson. "Travelers bring money to Jerusalem, and the Ottomans want to encourage that spending. In the areas frequented by travelers, such as the walled city, you will be safe. Most of the land being sold is beyond the walls, and in that area, you should be accompanied by guides."

Normally he did not engage in warning guests about safety. The usual tourist arrived in a group organized by a foreign company and sheltered from unpleasant incidents. These three men were moving about Jerusalem on their own. Hassan knew that Fowler was alert to cultural and social differences, but Hudson was inexperienced and Lockwood, brash. Both characteristics made them vulnerable.

Each time Hudson returned to his room, he noticed the still unopened letter from Richard Grant. It rested on his table like a leaky rowboat in a sea of troubles which he preferred to ignore. The envelope appeared to contain only a single page, but it would be crammed with disturbing news about the New York City art market. Grant was obsessed by the subject. The young artist occupied the studio next to him at the Tenth Street Studio and never hesitated to scatter his complaints about poor sales at

Hudson's feet. Last year he had signed the petition sent to Congress requesting that a heavy tax be imposed on all foreign pictures imported into our country, a foolish and offensive proposal considered amusing by European artists and Washington politicians. Hudson sliced the flap of the envelope and unfolded the paper. "Exhibit at the National Academy . . . hardly any landscape paintings hung and only one of Inness's misty canvases sold. Crowds gathered around portraits by Homer of field workers in France and Whistler's elegant women . . . Some attention to charming village scenes by Johnson and Heade's hummingbirds sipping nectar, but altogether another dismal return on efforts . . . Meanwhile, over on Broadway, Goupil's Gallery is collecting cash by the barrel for Barbizon landscapes and Egyptian street scenes!"

Hudson felt some degree of sympathy for the young man who was not without talent. His paintings of New Jersey pine barrens would have found eager buyers ten or fifteen years ago, but now they looked dated and dreary next to a lively Winslow Homer. Confronting a changing market required courage and often drastic change, and he had suggested as much to Grant. Brave talk, but he was not yet sure that he could follow his own advice. If one's entire body of work has been motivated by a desire to reveal the spiritual power of nature, how do you find meaning in painting pretty pictures?

SIX

Jerusalem

February 1868

Dearest Katharine,

Sunday in Jerusalem and no Presbyterian church for me to attend. The Protestant missionaries have failed miserably in every effort to plant their feet in Jerusalem. Instead, Lockwood and I joined Fowler and other Anglicans for Sunday service at Christ Church, near Jaffa Gate. The building was plain and blocky, resembling a large, squat tower; it was redeemed only by the handsome local stone which inhales the sun and exhales a golden glow. Inside, the size of the church overwhelmed the number in the congregation, and on a chilly morning we huddled together almost at the feet of the minister. The liturgy and chanting left me confused, and I searched in vain for some architectural feature to hold my attention.

After lunch, we rode horses out to the Mount of Olives, and there, at last, was the view of Jerusalem that made my spirits soar. From the eastern perspective at the top of the Mount, the city lies peacefully within the lap of the Judean hills. The walls of Jerusalem appear to rise miraculously out of the ground to protect the ancient city. In the foreground is the Haram ash-Sharif, the most dramatic part of the cityscape. At the focal point, the Dome of the Rock sits within the Haram like a jewel box encrusted with turquoise, diamonds, and gold. The remainder of Jerusalem stretches out to the horizon with only a few buildings registering a significant presence. Fowler has been to Jerusalem on several previous occasions, and he was able to point out places of interest. Here is where I will eventually set up my easel.

Riding back to Jerusalem at sunset, we had beautiful views of the Jordan River Valley to the east and the sun setting behind the Judean Mountains to the southwest. As we drew nearer to the city walls, a procession of women in white robes was streaming toward the Mount of Olives on a path that led to the Muhammadan cemetery. The women called out with a haunting sound, not singing or chanting, but a sound expressing loss and longing. It was a ritual with the appearance of timelessness.

Riding in the countryside always arouses my longing for you. I miss our gallops along the river, up Mount Merino, and then down to the town for tea with the Giffords before heading back to our cottage. I miss the way you bear into the wind with auburn hair flying, your habit of biting your lower lip when your horse jumps the stream, your looking back to see if I am lagging behind, your laughter when you beat me to the mount, your sweet greetings to the farmers in the fields. I miss you, my lovely Katharine, in every way.

All my love, Thomas

Hudson tucked the letter in his pocket and decided on a short stroll before dinner. Leaving the hotel courtyard, he heard his name being called.

"Mr. Hudson, please join us." Mika'il was sitting with Hassan in a café across from the hotel, each of them enjoying a hookah. "Would you like to try a pipe?"

Hudson declined and then remembered the portrait of his friend, Bayard Taylor, dressed as a Turkish bey, sitting on a plump silk cushion and smoking a hookah pipe. When Taylor traveled in the Orient, he tried everything—hookahs, Turkish baths, hasheesh—welcoming the strange and bizarre with the same abundant humor that flowed through his lectures and writings.

Hudson envied his zest. Why not, he thought. "I will take you up on that offer of a pipe, Mika'il." In an instant the hookah was in front of him, and Hassan was explaining the slow inhalation. Hudson tried a few puffs and coughed. "I am really not much of a smoker."

"*Maalesh*, never mind, Mr. Hudson," Mika'il said as he moved the hookah. "Our arrangements are almost complete. If there is no problem between the Ottoman official and Mr. Lockwood, we should be able to depart for Petra on the day after tomorrow. Does that suit you?"

"Perfectly, but I need to discuss one change with you. We want to add a night of camping on the Mount of Olives at the beginning of our expedition. Could you arrange for us to have our horses for an early morning departure to the Mount, and for your men to collect our baggage from the hotel and provide tents, dinner, and breakfast for us?"

"Of course. Do you also want a guide to remain with you for the night?"

"Probably not."

Hassan's hands began to flutter. "Excuse me, Mr. Hudson, it would be the wise choice to have a guide, a man who speaks at least a little English."

Hudson recalled Hassan's cautions about troubles outside the city walls and agreed. It was reassuring for him to see that Mika'il was not flustered by requests to modify plans. He planned to devote the entire day to preparing an oil sketch of Jerusalem. While Hudson worked, Fowler and Lockwood would ride across the plain of Rephaim, where the Philistines were routed by David, and over to Bethlehem.

Hudson crossed the street and entered the hotel. He planned to ask for hot water to bathe before dinner, but the sound of Arab music caused him to stop. One of Hassan's older sons was sitting at the main desk, playing a musical instrument which looked like a lute with a bent neck. The boy touched the strings with a soft caress, his eyes closed. The tones of the Eastern melody sang an aching sadness, resounding with disappointment or loss.

Beside him, his much younger sister tapped at a tambourine and whirled with little sense of rhythm, but a marvelous feeling of joy. She looked at her brother with admiring eyes and laughed when she made mistakes. Hudson clapped softly at the end of her spirited dance. When she saw the foreigner, she scooted under the desk and peeked around the corner. Memories of Emily swept through his mind. How she loved to play hide and seek, the bubbling up of giggles when she was found and how she flung herself into his arms. Emily would be about the age of this young girl. She would be, could be, but she was not. Why? Why did he not see the danger? Tears flooded his eyes, and he placed his hands on the desk to steady himself.

Hassan appeared at his side and whispered, "Suha is a little young for playing the riq, but I think Munir has real talent for the oud."

"Ah, is that what you call it," Hudson said as he wiped an escaping tear. "The beauty of the sound brought tears to my eyes."

"It is a very fine instrument, and Munir is learning its language."

"Was it made here in Jerusalem?"

"No, this type with the tear drop shape and light and dark wood comes only from Egypt. Are you also a musician, Mr. Hudson?"

"No, not at all. My only talent is with a brush, but occasionally I feel as if I am conducting a symphony with my brush." Hudson smiled at Munir as the song ended. "You are a fortunate man, Hassan."

"*Alhamdulillah*, thanks be to Allah."

At dinner that evening, Hudson reminded Lockwood that Mika'il would be waiting for him in the morning.

"I have not forgotten my command performance with the Ottoman bureaucracy. I plan to smother them with my Southern charm."

Fowler looked up from his plate, his cheeks rosy from several glasses of wine. "We were wondering why you were saving all that charm."

Hudson added, "Just make sure your charm does not translate into sarcasm in Arabic. The less said, the better."

Lockwood frowned and rubbed his jaw, but remained quiet.

"What will you do tomorrow, Fowler?" Hudson asked.

"The Anglican bishop invited me for breakfast with a group of British dignitaries touring in Palestine. Afterward I will return to the antiquities shop on King David Street."

"Fine. At dinner tomorrow, we can review plans for leaving Tuesday morning for the Mount of Olives."

On their morning walk to the office of the Ottoman representative, Mika'il explained to Lockwood what he expected to happen in the meeting. "It is important to keep in mind the limited power of these officials. When foreign governments were granted authority to establish consulates in Jerusalem, a number of Ottoman Capitulations were negotiated. What these mean for your situation is that as a citizen of America, you are exempt from local Ottoman legal jurisdiction."

Lockwood stopped in mid-stride and grabbed Mika'il by his arm. "If that is true, why do I need to answer their questions?"

"Please remove your hand from my arm, Mr. Lockwood. In our society, we might draw a knife in anger, but we do not touch without permission." Mika'il stood with pride gleaming in his black eyes. Lockwood moved away with some degree of embarrassment. "While the local Ottoman official has no legal power to stop you from traveling, he does have a reporting responsibility for unusual or suspicious activities of foreigners. Surveying and mapping are now considered suspicious activities."

"It is ridiculous, but I will play their game." Lockwood clasped his hands behind his back and continued walking.

The residence and office of the Ottoman representative was located in the Muhammadan quarter, a short walk from the hotel. The iron gate opened to an anteroom where two Turkish officials sat at desks on either side of a hallway that led toward a courtyard garden and beyond to the main house. Mika'il knew that the official to the right dealt with foreigners concerned about land or trade in Palestine, and he steered Lockwood toward the desk on the left where permits to travel were issued. The skinny, poorly dressed official was almost concealed by the enormous, carved wooden desk covered with stacks of rumpled papers of varying heights and glasses with moldy tea leaves. To Lockwood it seemed the pathetic little man was hiding behind his unaccomplished work.

Mika'il spoke in a low voice to Lockwood. "Do not sit until the official invites you. He is an arrogant chap who enjoys making guides and travelers suffer discomfort."

The official moved one stack of papers to the side, selected the top sheet, and studied it for an inordinate amount of time before signing it and burying it within another stack. After picking his teeth and blowing his nose, the Turk looked up to acknowledge their presence. He motioned Lockwood toward a chair, then spoke in Arabic to Mika'il, telling him that the Mutasarrif, Governor of the Ottoman Empire in Jerusalem, Omar Bey, had decided to conduct the interview of Mr. Lockwood. He would be taken to the Hall of Audience, and Mika'il would remain there.

"Mr. Lockwood speaks only English," Mika'il said.

"*Maalesh*, never mind," said the official who called the guard and gave him instructions.

Mika'il seemed puzzled about the change in the interview. "He tells me you will be interviewed by the Ottoman Mutasarrif of Jerusalem, but he does not explain the change."

Lockwood rubbed his jaw with his thumb and forefinger. "Sounds to me like they are making a mountain out of a molehill."

"What . . . ?"

Lockwood followed the guard into the courtyard. He stopped to look at the remnants of what might have been a fine garden, but now was a collection of scraggly weeds and cracked fountains protected by two antique cannons. He turned to face the main house which resembled a small Ottoman palace in the bones of the structure, but there was little meat on the bones. Tall windows flanked a double door of hammered bronze. The windows were mainly broken glass, and the exterior stone was pockmarked with bullet holes. The doors hung lopsided on their hinges but did open with the considerable efforts of two inside servants. The large hall was surmounted by a dome raised above clerestory windows, a nice feature thought Lockwood, until he noticed that the high broken windows attracted birds that flew in and out, leaving behind a messy, slippery floor. The walls at one time had been decorated with handsome Kutahya tiles in shades of blue, but only a few shards remained. The decrepit palace mirrored the decline of the empire.

The door at the far end of the hall led him to Omar Bey, who was sitting on a large, yellow leather cushion, smoking a hookah and fondling a lightly clad woman. He was a man of significant proportions in the lateral orientation. His shabby silks and damask clothing bulged with excess flesh. Above the lump of clothing was a face of enormous cheerfulness—eyes rolling with pleasure and an upturned mouth and mustache. He beckoned Lockwood forward and called for a chair, all the while laughing and teasing his concubine.

Lockwood stared at what seemed an advertisement for Turkish delight, a caricature of a Turkish high official. He had not the least idea of why this man wanted to see him.

"*Ahlan wa-Sahlan*, welcome, Mr. Lockwood. I trust you have been well treated by my staff." Omar Bey smiled facetiously and continued. "I expect you are thinking—why did this important Ottoman governor want to see me?" Omar laughed and his huge body rumbled. "Bitumen! That is what I am about and so are you. Am I right, Mr. Lockwood?"

Lockwood was startled, unable to respond. How could this man know of his interest in bitumen? Omar Bey read his face.

"Oh, Mr. Lockwood, I see I have given you big surprise! You are thinking, this Turkish Bey is even smarter than he appears." More uproarious laughter from the Governor, as he sent the woman running out of the room with a light smack of her derrière.

Lockwood recovered his wits before he spoke. "I gather that Hussain Bey is a friend of yours?"

"Oh, yes, I visit him in Constantinople quite frequently, when I escape from this boring backwater. Why, I am not able to find decent food here—you have noticed that I am wasting away?" The Governor caressed his belly with both hands.

"And what did your esteemed friend tell you of my interest in bitumen?" Lockwood asked casually, observing that Omar Bey was moving into a more serious demeanor.

"The most honorable Hussain Bey is easily confused, but he did understand that you might want to export bitumen from the Dead Sea area of the Ottoman Empire, Mr. Lockwood. Such an enterprise would need my approval before Hussain Bey presented it to the authorities at the Porte, the Council to the Sultan, as you know."

Lockwood could imagine the hands dipping into his pockets even before the bitumen was extracted. "Well, I intended to consult your eminence after my visit to Kerak . . ."

"Of course, of course, you did, Mr. Lockwood, but I wanted to alert you to the nefarious ways of the Ottoman Mutasarrif in Kerak. He is a devious scoundrel, and you would do well to avoid his extortionist habits. I have sent a message to Sheikh Zayed in Kerak, an honest and reliable man in my employ, and he is ready at any moment to assist you."

Lockwood knew there was no way to extract Omar Bey from his bitumen investigation; the man already had his fingers planted in the sticky substance. Perhaps, his contacts would be useful.

"As you must know, I am part of a caravan heading for Petra. I have no permit, firman as you call it, from your government to survey and map in the Dead Sea area, but I expect to study the terrain for feasible routes to move bitumen from the Dead Sea to the Mediterranean. I had planned to visit Kerak after Petra to identify someone who could be my agent—if there is potential for the export of bitumen."

"And where, may I ask, Mr. Lockwood, would you ship the bitumen?" Omar Bey asked.

Lockwood wanted to end the dialogue without revealing more about his plans; but the Bey was cleverly probing for economic prospects, and he did not want to antagonize him. "I have contacts in America who are considering using bitumen for paving roads if, a big if, it could be procured at a reasonable price."

"You have no bitumen mines in America?" Omar Bey asked.

"We have limited quantities of bitumen seeping to the surface above oil deposits. We call it asphalt in America. There appears to be more demand than supply at present."

The Bey clapped his hand with excitement. "Always a good situation—demand for our resources, and I am the man to make it possible for you. Will you be stopping in Hebron on your way to Petra?"

Lockwood described his rough schedule for Hebron, Petra, and Kerak. They agreed that Omar Bey would arrange for one of Sheikh Zayed's men to travel from Kerak to Hebron to make a first contact with Lockwood. Lockwood departed with much more than a travel permit.

As he made his way through the hall and courtyard to meet Mika'il, Lockwood thought about the encounter. He knew Omar Bey would be an unpredictable ally. The situation recalled an African folk tale he had heard in North Carolina about a 'Tar Baby.' He wondered if Omar Bey would be the trickster rabbit or the cunning fox.

February 1868 Jerusalem

My Dear Katharine,

Tomorrow is our last day in Jerusalem, and I will devote it to sketching and painting on the Mount of Olives. A large landscape of Jerusalem and the surrounding hills is beginning to take shape in my mind. We will camp on the Mount for our last evening before departing for Petra. I have four letters for you which I will post with the American Consul in Jerusalem.

My feelings about this city change daily as more doors are opened to its mysteries. The people, so strange at first with their multitude of tongues and costumes, become like all people—friendly or hostile, honest or dishonest. I find that exposure to so many religious sects, all with holy books and true believers, is confusing for my own certainty about doctrine. And while the past glory of Jerusalem is shrouded in present neglect, I am moved by a compelling beauty in its timeworn neighborhoods. On this journey I am trying to understand, not simply observe with my artist eye. But you can see that I am struggling. Reverend Fowler is a great help in my understanding and a jolly good companion. His religious vocation is not clear to me as he seems mostly interested in the study of religions and civilizations. He has spent many years in the Orient, Persia, and India, studying languages and cultures. I am strongly attracted to his compassionate manner toward everyone.

Lockwood is an entirely different species. I am already questioning my judgment about inviting him on this expedition. He has proved already to be a complainer about trivial matters and elusive about his objectives. He tells everyone he is on pleasure travel, but his talk of surveys for roads in Syria troubles me. We were told that the Ottoman Empire is suspicious of surveys, even when they permit them.

I have given the American Consul here in Jerusalem the rough outline of our travels—I say rough because weather will be a significant factor in our movement. If you need to contact me, it will be best to ask for White's help. He knows the Consul from his travels here, and he has contacts in this area who will search me out at whichever valley or mountain top.

My darling Katharine, I leave here with only the two letters from you, now shredded by too frequent readings. It will be three weeks at least before I am back in Beirut where I am sure there will be a full mailbag for me. Our love bridges these long distances and silences, but I have a great longing for the comfort of your touch. I miss you more than I could have imagined.

Your loving and adoring, Thomas

Hudson was writing letters at one of the desks in the lobby when Lockwood returned from his interview. Lockwood's voice was cordial as he greeted Hassan, and Hudson assumed that the interview went well. "Apparently your meeting with the Turkish official was agreeable . . ."

"Yes, it was just a formality—the kind of bureaucratic process that I often found in the Navy. He asked about my experiences with the Lynch expedition and my work in Egypt."

"Was that all?"

"He was also interested in my visit yesterday with Charles Warren of the Palestine Exploration Fund."

Hudson had read a little about Captain Warren's excavations under the city of Jerusalem and his finding old tunnels and water channels from biblical times. "I believe he has permission from Constantinople."

"Yes," Lockwood replied, "but his work near the *Haram* causes Muhammadans and Jews to complain to the Ottoman Governor. The leaders of both religions are worried he might destabilize the stone foundations or, even worse, contradict their beliefs about the meaning of the site for Muhammadans or Jews. The Ottomans should not worry. Warren is too smart to be lured into that argument."

"Did you mention your current work in Syria for the British?"

Lockwood seemed puzzled by the question. He fiddled with a brass ashtray on top of the desk, and then looked down at Hudson. "No, I did not think it relevant to pleasure travel in Petra."

Hudson stood up and shoved his fists into his pockets. "Surely, it is relevant that you are in the Ottoman Empire on a mapping survey. Did you hear what Hassan said yesterday about Ottomans being suspicious of surveys?"

Lockwood rubbed his chin, but did not reply.

"I would like your word, right now, that there will be no activity on our journey that would in any way suggest surveying or mapping."

Lockwood turned away, but Hudson saw the smirk beginning. "You have my word as an officer and a gentleman. I will see you at dinner, Hudson."

When Hudson stopped by Fowler's room after lunch, he found the Englishman sketching small figures in his journal.

"Ah, Mr. Hudson, please come in—just give me another moment to finish."

"I can come back later."

"No, please, a moment. I am eager to tell you about my afternoon with Tariq Aboud." Fowler adjusted his spectacles and added a few inscriptions to the page. "It was a remarkable experience, something out of the Arabian Nights. Do you have time for a story?"

As he pulled a chair toward the desk, Hudson bowed. "I sit like the King before Scheherazade."

"When I arrived at the shop, a German was arguing with Aboud about a package that he expected to be delivered to the shop for him. He was very disturbed when Aboud told him the package had not arrived. He began shouting and threatening the merchant, and I decided to leave. Aboud came after me and asked me to wait outside." Fowler removed his spectacles and rubbed his eyes. "I thought the episode might put a damper on our visit to his storeroom, but in a few minutes, the German left, Aboud called an assistant to watch the shop, and we headed up King David Street. A horde of morning shoppers made it difficult to follow him, but he quickly turned into a narrow, empty passage. I expected it to be the entrance to his house, but it was only the beginning of winding through the maze of the Muhammadan Quarter. The twists and turns made it impossible to keep a sense of direction, and I knew I would never find my way out alone."

"Were you worried?" Hudson asked. "You knew nothing about this merchant, or did you?"

"Actually, I asked Hassan about him and learned he was a distant cousin. Every Muhammadan in Jerusalem seems to be related." Fowler reached for the jug of water and poured a cup for Hudson and himself.

"It seemed like a long walk, perhaps because of the high stone walls on both sides, pierced only occasionally by small wooden doors. I could hear people talking, but we passed no one. I had to be careful where I put my feet as horses and donkeys also used the paths. At last, he stopped at a massive wooden door reinforced with iron filigree and rang a bell hanging to the side. Immediately a servant opened a slot in the door, recognized his master, and swung open the door.

"Before us was a courtyard, open to the sky, and two floors of balconies along rooms with many doors and windows, an Egyptian style design, very unusual for Jerusalem. In the courtyard, jasmine climbed the balcony columns, floating gently in the breeze and scenting the air. As we ascended the staircase, I asked Aboud about the design of the house.

"He explained that his mother came from Cairo and was much beloved by his father. To ease her longing for her native land, his father remodeled his ancestral home to resemble her family home in the Nasriya district of Cairo. Being a devout Muhammadan wife, she rarely left the compound; everything she loved in life was within those walls, or so he believed.

"On the second balcony, we came to a door with three different locks, and I knew we were at the Archaeologia Arabia storeroom. When Aboud unlocked the door, a servant appeared and entered silently to light the oil lamps hanging in each corner of the room and over a round table sitting on a Persian carpet. There were no windows, no entrance other than through the secured door. Otherwise, the room held four chairs and three enormous armoires from different regions of the world. To the left was a Chinese lacquered chest in cinnabar red decorated with golden dragons, winding up through a forest and rising to a mountain top. On the right stood an enormous brass and wood cupboard painted in the Tibetan style with hundreds of sitting monks surrounding a large image of a Buddha meditating under a bodhi tree. In front of us, beyond the table, Syria was represented by a cabinet of cedar wood, deeply carved in arabesques and inlaid with mother of pearl in the Damascene tradition. Without a word, Aboud opened the doors to the Syrian cabinet and stood aside."

Fowler paused at this point—either to catch his breath or to return to the moment. Sensing that memory was being summoned, Hudson waited patiently for the story to unravel. "I was dumbstruck. When I enter a museum of unbelievable treasures, I allow the art to speak for itself. Let the eyes unwrap the jewels before the questions arise.

"The first item that caught my eye was an exquisite marble amphora with handles on either side in the shape of panthers. The panthers stood on the lower ridge of the cup with their paws on the rim, looking into the interior of the cup, as if they were thirsting for its liquid. They were carved magnificently, the purplish-gray vein of the cream colored marble enhancing their beauty.

"Above the amphora sat a sculpture fragment of a woman with a Greek or Roman face, perhaps a muse, holding a mask for theater performances. It appeared to be limestone, carved very finely. The folds of drapery and strands of hair were as if the artist's tool had just left the surface. Another quite modest item on the same shelf appealed to me. It was a terracotta oil lamp, about the size of my hand. Signs of the zodiac encircled by Nabatean inscriptions decorated the surface."

"Nabatean? Do you think it came from Petra?" Hudson asked.

Fowler sipped his water before continuing. "I knew it was possible, but it could have come from other Nabatean settlements. I asked Aboud about the origin of the items, and he confirmed that the objects I mentioned were all from Petra. The amphora was not made there, probably sculpted in Constantinople, but the other items were Nabatean. He emphasized that he did not look or ask for such treasures. They were brought to him by people who felt that art was being destroyed in Petra or who steal for profit."

Hudson was not surprised by that explanation; he had heard similar justifications by people in Ecuador who pandered Inca treasures. "And what was your reaction?"

"It is a dilemma," Fowler said, shaking his head. "When people realize such objects have value, sometimes great value, they will look for them—both foreigners and Bedouin. The foreigners will take them out of the region, usually to Europe where the value will be enhanced. The Bedouin will bring them to people like Aboud who will sell them to people he trusts will not reveal the origin."

"Is there no other alternative?" Hudson asked.

"Not until there are governments or people with the money and power to protect their antiquities. In Egypt, the pashas are negotiating with the French archaeologists to keep half of the treasures in Cairo. Will that continue? Will it happen here in Palestine and Syria? It is unclear. For me, I could not in good conscience purchase these items. Of course, it is easy for me to say because I could not afford to own these items." Fowler chuckled at the schism between his conscience and his desire.

"What would happen if the Ottoman authorities learned of Aboud's collection?" Hudson asked.

"I dare say they would close their eyes. The danger lies in the removal of the objects from Petra—that is the point of contact where the local Bedouin exercise their rights and obligation to protect their heritage. Personally, I would not pick up a rock in that valley." Fowler added, emphasizing the point. "But you did not come here to talk about my visit with Aboud, did you?"

"No, but it is more fascinating than the events of my day." Hudson described Lockwood's report on the interview and his conversation with Lockwood about refraining from mapping and reports during the expedition.

"I keep thinking that Lockwood may be a complication for our travel," Hudson said. "What do you think?"

Fowler leaned back in his chair, crossing his arms, and pondering the question. "He is a bit of a prickly sort, but he adds good credentials and experience to the caravan. He is well-known in Beirut, and no one spoke ill of him. I expect he is the type of solitary man who is more comfortable on the trail than in the city. Perhaps we should not brood about his presence, but keep an eye open."

Hudson left, still doubtful about the Virginian, but he saw the logic in Fowler's approach. Fowler had a talent for being the peacemaker. Peace was what Hudson needed. He decided to walk back to the *Haram ash-Sharif* before dinner to take a last look at the exterior of the Dome of the Rock.

He arrived at the shrine before the late afternoon call to prayer and found the surrounding grounds deserted, except for the few men sweeping leaves and dust from the paving stones. It was easy for him to move quite close to the base of the shrine and examine the colors of the tiles above his head. They had mellowed from their midday shimmering appearance; now they were softer and richer in the glow of the setting sun. The earlier, strong effect of cobalt blue and aquamarine was now detailed with turquoise and indigo, an emerald green, and dabs of yellow ochre and white. It was surprising to see the enormous variety of colors and designs that had earlier blended into a blur of blue.

The calls of the muezzins echoed across the city. He turned toward the minaret beside Al Aqsa Mosque and shaded his eyes from the setting sun. The muezzin stood on the gallery of the spire, his hands directing the path of the sound, his eyes reaching for the heavens. Hudson shivered slightly, as the song of praise reverberated through his body. Worshippers brushed past him on their way to the fountains, and he moved under the branches of a cedar tree to watch them prepare for their prayers.

An elderly gentleman with a beard that reached his belt limped toward al-Kas fountain for the ritual ablutions. Hudson noticed the man's hands trembling as he removed his sandals and squatted before one of the small pipes bringing water from the interior of the fountain. He raised his gnarled hands to the water, folding the hands again and again inside of each other, then collected water in his cupped hands and rinsed his mouth and nose several times, before a complete wash of his face. After carefully folding the sleeves of his galabiya above the elbows, he washed to the elbow, first the right arm and then the left. Removing his cap, he wiped his head, hair and ears with his wet hands before sitting and scrubbing his feet up to the ankles. Finished, he replaced his cap, reached up to the rail of the fountain, and stood shakily for a brief prayer before stepping into his sandals and beginning the walk toward Al Aqsa Mosque for the afternoon prayer. A younger man appeared at his side and took his arm.

Hudson imagined it would be difficult for the old man to complete the standing, bending and prostrations involved in giving praise and offering submission to Allah. As he watched hundreds of worshippers repeat these rituals, he was struck by their humble demonstration of their belief in God—from their ritual ablutions to prostrations in prayer. Their ritual of submission to God had no parallel in the services that Hudson attended. He knew it was only symbolic, but maybe it was a necessary reminder that submission to God's will would be required, again, and again, and again.

If the death of his children was God's will, then Hudson knew he had failed in submission to his faith in God.

As he descended below Chain Gate, three men dressed in flat brown fur hats and full length black wool coats with furred collar almost ran over him. They apologized with quick nods and ran past him, turning the corner to sprint along the lower walls of the *Haram*. Hudson followed them and found himself in a small courtyard, facing a wall of large stone blocks which soared up to the level of Al Aqsa Mosque. He knew he was looking at the Wailing Wall of the Jews. Fowler had told him of this sacred place for Jews who believed this was a remnant of the Second Temple. To Hudson, it was just a wall, not grand or glorious, not sculpted or decorated, just a plain stone wall that evoked deep mysteries of worship.

There were fewer than a dozen people, and all were touching the wall—some praying, others crying. The three men who had collided with him moved toward an open space. They draped white shawls over their black coats and stood together, each with one hand on the wall and the other holding a prayer book from which they read aloud. Nearby were two men in dark suits who removed their bowler hats and touched the wall repeatedly with their foreheads. Several women, wearing long dresses and dark red shawls, stood among the men, praying and kissing the stone wall.

Everywhere Hudson turned, people prayed in this city. Touching a wall or laying a prayer rug in the market was as acceptable as a fine church or mosque or synagogue. He saw Muhammadans, Jews, and Christians worshipping and coexisting with what appeared to be tolerance for their differing beliefs. What an amazing achievement for a city that had endured wars and destruction over thousands of years, usually for religious reasons.

But none of this inspired him to pray, and that realization left a hollow feeling, a feeling he did not wish to examine.

Not far from where Hudson stood at the Wailing Wall, Lockwood and Captain Charles Warren stood above a shaft in the ground that led to tunnels below the *Haram ash-Sharif*. For his last afternoon in Jerusalem, Lockwood had arranged to explore the subterranean passages of Jerusalem with a British engineer leading the Palestine Exploration Fund. He had met Charles Warren in London through a friend serving with the Corps of Royal Engineers. Warren was spunky and amusing, undeterred by the dangers of sinking shafts into thousands of years of rubble.

As he strapped Lockwood into a harness, he joked about his reputation. "I am known as The Mole of Jerusalem. My assistant tells me my eyes are becoming smaller from burrowing in the dark." Warren squinted and laughed. "The first section is down a shaft with stairs gouged out of the rock, steep but easy. It levels out after about forty feet. Are you ready?

Lockwood looked down the stairs. They were narrow as well as steep, but he was a slim man. "Should I go first?"

"No. I will carry the lantern, you will follow. Use your arms to brace yourself against the rock. The steps are slippery."

Lockwood managed the steps even though the light from the lantern was less than desirable. Darkness reached into the small circle of light and put him on edge. After the steps, the tunnel continued sloping downward gradually, and he noticed several arches carved out of the limestone, one with modest decorations. "What was the purpose of this tunnel, Warren?"

"I am puzzling over two theories," Warren said. "I am certain that at least a portion of the tunnel and shaft relate to the city's need for additional water resources when the city was under siege. The tunnel and shaft connect with Gihon Spring which is outside the city walls; however, there is also a possibility that it was used by troops needing an unobserved passage from the barracks in the upper city to the temple area. We would need to do much excavation to be certain, and the Sultan's Governor is already becoming suspicious of our objectives."

"The Turks are suspicious of everything. Why your work?"

"Well, Mr. Lockwood, if foreigners arrived to dig under Washington, what would be the reaction of your officials?"

The next section fell into a dark hole at his feet. It was a small cleft in the rock that plunged straight down into the bowels of the earth, requiring a descent by fixed rope and boards jammed into the limestone.

"This is the access to the spring water, and now we will attach our harnesses to the ropes. Can I assume an old Navy man does not need help with knots?"

"The knots will be easy compared to the shaft. How deep is it?" Lockwood asked.

Warren heard the tension in his question. "About seventy feet. I think I mentioned that earlier."

"Yes, of course. You did. It is just that it seems endless when you are stepping into the dark."

Warren lifted the lantern over the shaft entrance, and the light fell onto Lockwood's face. "You must tell me if this is more than you expected, Mr. Lockwood. This is the point where many visitors decide they have seen enough. There is no need . . ."

"I am not frightened if that is what you mean, but I like to know what is ahead. Where do I tie into this rope?"

Warren explained how to use the rope and where the boards would provide stopping points. "I will attach the lantern to my belt. It will give enough light for you to see the boards before you reach them. Call out when you stop, and I will wait so you are not left in darkness. Any questions?"

"No. I am ready."

Warren grabbed his rope, stepped backwards and used his feet against the shaft wall to begin a slow descent, allowing Lockwood to observe his technique. Lockwood wiped his hands on his shirt and took hold of the rope. He held his breath and stepped backwards into the dark shaft, keeping his attention focused on the rope and the light. The first ten feet he dropped like a bucket banging into the sides of a well; afterward he released the rope more slowly. After a couple stops on the boards, he felt more comfortable than he had expected. Warren was almost at the bottom when Lockwood stepped on one of the boards and called out a stop. Part of the board broke away, tumbled down the shaft, and smacked Warren, causing him to slam into the rock wall and fall to the ground.

SEVEN

"We are now on holy ground. Every footfall is upon soil trodden long centuries ago by patriarch and prophet; every view the eye rests on was seen as we see it by Abraham, Isaac, and Jacob, by Samuel, David, and Solomon. The cities they built, or dwelt in, are now heaps of ruins; but the features of nature remain unchanged – the mountains, the valleys, the fountains, the rocks, are all here. It is this which gives us such a deep and lasting interest in this land."

> J. L. Porter, *Handbook for Travellers in Syria and Palestine* 1858

To Mount of Olives and Hebron

It was another restless night for Hudson. Hour after hour, he stared out of the windows, watching the crescent moon move across a midnight blue sky streaked with low clouds. Some time after it began its descent in the west, he fell asleep. The noise of the horses below his window awakened him, and he moved quickly to ready himself. As he splashed water on his face, he pictured the old man at al-Kas fountain; he might be there now, lips mumbling the verses, fingers moving his prayer beads, the kind of scene Jacques Vesoul might paint.

He dressed in the old riding clothes that would be his uniform for the caravan—brown riding pants, a soft collared flannel shirt, and thigh-length duster, topped by his pith helmet. No mirror hung in the room, but he expected he looked like a somewhat shabby country gentleman. He added his night clothes to his baggage and collected other unpacked items.

Fowler was sitting at the writing desk when Hudson walked into the lobby. "Good morning, Hudson. I am just putting the finishing touches on my epistle to my brother. I have sorely neglected my family since I left India."

"I have four letters to send via the American Consul. Will Hassan arrange for their delivery to the consulate?" Hudson asked.

"Yes, we have already discussed it," Fowler replied, "and he has our bill prepared."

Hudson did not see Lockwood in the dining area or the lobby. "Have you and Lockwood had breakfast already? Am I that slow?"

"You were long in the arms of Morpheus, Hudson." Fowler grinned and looked up from his letter writing. "I have eaten, but Lockwood has not appeared."

Hudson put his letters on the hotel desk just as Hassan came out of the back room. "Ah, Mr. Hudson, I was looking for you. Did you know that Mr. Lockwood did not return to the hotel last night?"

"What? Not at all? Not this morning?"

"No. I sent Munir to his room a few minutes ago. He is not there. The bed has not been used." Hassan looked worried and his hands were fluttering. "I thought he might have made some other arrangement with you."

"No, nothing." Hudson frowned as he turned around. "Fowler, Lockwood is not here. Apparently he did not return last . . ."

"But I am here now," Lockwood announced as he walked into the lobby, dressed in odd clothes and holding a wet bag away from his body. He handed the bag to the boy holding the door. "Has everyone had breakfast?"

"What happened to you? Where were you?" Hudson asked.

"I am famished. I need food. I will tell you in the dining room." Lockwood swaggered toward a table, and the others, including Hassan, were not far behind. He called for the waiter and ordered the full English breakfast with extra eggs and bread. Hudson seconded the order for himself.

Lockwood snapped open the napkin and placed it on his lap. He cleared his throat and began. "Yesterday afternoon I joined Captain Charles Warren for an excursion into his famous shaft below the city."

"Oh yes, of course, I know him." Hassan said. "He stayed here when he first arrived in the city last year. Nice manners, very congenial . . ."

Lockwood raised his voice above Hassan's. "All went well until the last few feet of the shaft. One of the boards inside the shaft broke lose, hit Warren, and injured his left shoulder and leg. Luckily, the lantern was not damaged." Lockwood rubbed his brow, as if the thought of being so far underground with no light still rattled him.

"Warren was able to walk, slowly, but ascending the shaft was out of the question. Instead we followed the tunnel at the base of the shaft that eventually led to an area outside the city walls near Gihon Spring. It took a good part of the night—the tunnel is too low for standing in many places, and there is a stream running through it."

"It must have been difficult for Warren with his injuries," Fowler remarked.

Lockwood stopped eating his omelet and looked up. "It was difficult, quite difficult at times. The stream water made it cold, and the air was bad. But, together we managed with Warren leaning on me. I had no desire to spend the night underground in that tunnel."

"But you did not return to the hotel?" Hassan asked.

"It was after midnight when we arrived at Warren's quarters near the Wailing Wall. He offered a bed. I was not sure the hotel would be open. For the few hours of night remaining, it was easier to bunk there. He gave me these clothes."

Hudson listened to Lockwood's story without comment. Earlier, when he heard that Lockwood had not returned to the hotel, he found himself hoping Lockwood had changed his mind about the trip. Maybe some news about his surveying business had arrived. It would have been a relief to remove what felt like a dark cloud over the caravan. On the other hand, it sounded as if Lockwood had been instrumental in resolving the crisis and getting Warren out of the tunnel and home.

"Our horses are waiting at the door, Lockwood. Will you be

ready to ride to the Mount of Olives this morning?" Hudson asked.

"Yes. I will be ready in less than an hour."

By ten o'clock, Hudson paid the bill, and their baggage was set aside for the pack horses. The three men and a guide galloped out St. Stephen's Gate toward the Mount of Olives. They rode along the outer walls of Jerusalem, past the Golden Gate, and then across the Valley of Kidron toward the Chapel of the Ascension. Here Hudson dismounted, and the guide unpacked Hudson's sketchbook and knapsack.

"Will you be comfortable here, Mr. Hudson?" Fowler asked. He looked around for other visitors or workers, but no one was in sight.

"Yes, of course. Enjoy your gallop, Gentlemen, while I enjoy my work."

Hudson planned to devote the entire day to composing a painting of Jerusalem, a painting in which nature, man, and the spiritual would be united. For several hours he walked the Mount area to consider angles and perspective. The summit of the Mount looked down on the city, and Hudson knew that several artists had chosen that spot. It was a dramatic view as the western and southern mountains were accentuated. But Hudson wanted a new, original interpretation. He envisioned a view where the perspective placed the artist only slightly above the walls of the city. The city and surroundings would appear as reaching upward to the heavens.

Moving slowly down the slope, Hudson walked west, then south to a flat area near a grove of olive trees. Beyond there, the land fell away into a small valley running west toward the city. From that point, he looked across to the southeast portion of the city where the *Haram ash-Sharif* floated above the stone walls with The Dome of the Rock at the perfect center. Hudson stood with his hands on his hips, his eyes smiling into the distance. He knew this was the place to set up his easel.

Now that the most important decision had been made, he turned his attention to the light. He had missed the early morning light for that day, but he would have another chance at sunrise tomorrow. Midday in this climate burned out color and the subtle changes in terrain, but heightened the geology, architectural motifs, the details of the cypress and olive trees that would fade in the afternoon light. He walked along the slope toward a graveyard and small monument. There on the edge of a grove of olive trees, he took a deep breath, exhaled, and settled his body into the landscape. He arranged his pencils, and opened his sketchbook for several hours of drawing.

He followed his habit of sketching from near to far, building a collection of small elements to weave into the large picture. An ancient olive tree, a few yards distant, caught his eye. Olive trees would be the primary vegetation in the painting, maybe a few cypress trees. A close study of one specimen would capture all the information he needed to create an endless variety of olive trees. With a freely moving hand and a keen sense of botany, he sketched the severely twisted trunk, interrupted with massive burls as it climbed toward the foliage. The turnings of the wood resembled entangled legs struggling for footing in the rocky soil, and swift strokes of his soft leaded pencil captured the drama.

For the foliage he switched to a harder lead, first concentrating on the large, billowy masses formed by the leaves on the upper branches and then finishing with a single branch holding slender, silvery green leaves. Satisfied with the results, Hudson added the notes that would help him months later to recall the colors, size, and location of the tree. During the next few hours he followed the same pattern of sketches and annotations, as he drew rocks, walls, a nearby shrine, and a man and donkey moving down the sloping path toward the Muhammadan cemetery.

A train of men and pack horses passed on the north side toward the top of the Mount at just the right moment to interrupt his work. He recognized them as Mika'il's men, and he was relieved as he now needed his paintbox and easel. The sun was moving to a mid-afternoon position, and it was time for oil sketches. He climbed the hill and found the men setting up tents for their evening stay. They were a rough looking group with curved, broad-bladed knives stuck in their cloth belts and ragged kafiyas covering heads and faces, but they greeted him politely. Hudson returned the greeting and began searching among the baggage for his paintbox. He found the easel and the valise that contained his supply of paperboard and canvas, but the paintbox was missing. How could it be missing? How could he be so foolish as to let it out of his sight? Anyone could have taken it. There would be no opportunity to replace the palette and tubes of paint. He looked through the baggage again. He was not a man to panic in a crisis, but he felt his heart pounding. He was angry with the men who were not even concerned with his search, but more angry with himself. He must return to the hotel.

Hudson singled out the man who seemed to be the leader of the group and tried to convey his need for a horse and guide to return to Jerusalem. His hands formed the shape of the missing box—a relatively small, flat package compared to the other baggage.

The man turned, walked to his horse, and removed a blanket from behind the saddle. He placed the blanket on the ground and unwrapped the paintbox.

Hudson smiled and nodded his thanks to the man. Mika'il had remembered and passed on his request to handle the box like an irreplaceable treasure.

At least two hours remained before twilight, enough time for several oil sketches. From his perch in the olive grove he would be able to see Fowler, Lockwood, and the guide as they returned from Bethlehem in the early evening.

Hudson found a rock that would serve as a seat and erected his easel. After removing the palette and the oil paint tubes from the box, he placed one of the canvas boards on the easel and selected a brush. It was the moment when he imagined himself a conductor raising his baton at the critical edge of decision, the final moment to observe the light and atmosphere, to know what to include and exclude, to feel the pull of the colors. The music in his mind began as he chose and mixed the colors. It rose as the brush moved across canvas like a bow moving across strings.

Hudson had no intention of painting precisely what lay

before him. His painterly instincts shaped the vision, carved out segments, and transported buildings. In the first oil sketch he placed the distant *Haram ash-Sharif* to the right of center and the nearby cemetery on a hill to the left, almost at the same level as the *Haram*. He added shades of green and yellow to the hillside and sketched in olive trees with long shadows, then gave attention to the walled city, adding the mosque and shrine, then churches and buildings in the background. He stepped back a few feet to consider his work. It was not right. The *Haram* must be the center and the Dome of the Rock at the epicenter.

He looked at the sky as he fumbled in his knapsack for another canvas board. Dark, swirling clouds were roiling in from the south, changing the atmospheric effects over the old city. The serenity of a soft blue sky was disappearing into a powerful crescendo of light and dark. With his brush flying through the air, Hudson sketched in wilder tints of rose, lavender, cream, gold, green, gray, and a single streak of blue for the mosque.

The scene before him was evaporating into darkness just as a lyrical feeling was replacing passion. He stood, stretched his arms over his head, and scanned the twilight sky, savoring the pleasure of creation. He knew he had his painting, one image on canvas, the other carved deep in his mind.

From the beginning, Hudson's art had proclaimed that inspiration could be found where the earth rose up to meet the heavens, where powerful mountains soared to a celestial sky. Nature was his gateway to understanding the divine. That evening he envisioned Jerusalem as a mountain, constructed by man, on a landscape where great prophets had struggled toward a spiritual threshold of paradise. If there were a Divine Plan, this landscape had the deepest knowledge of its history. Sitting there alone, across from famed Jerusalem, surrounded by the hills of Judea, he felt in harmony with the transcendent mysteries of the universe.

February 1868 Hudson Diary, Mount of Olives
My Dearest Katharine,
Jerusalem lays spread out before me, luminous, and silvery in her evening clothes. We are encamped on the Mount of Olives for one night before we begin

our expedition. It is quite cold, but clear and glorious with a glow of moonlight. The peacefulness of the city tonight veils a tumultuous history of sorrow and strife. Somehow Jerusalem has survived the greed, intolerance, and hubris of man for more than five millennia.

I sit here alone, shivering and wondering what lures mankind to these desert hills. It is not a land of milk and honey, but a barren wasteland testing its inhabitants, demanding every measure of determination to eke out a meager life. I suppose that anointment by God makes this land desirable, and humans labor to interpret His holy purpose.

This day on the Mount of Olives quickened my creative instincts, and I have a good set of pencil sketches and one fine oil sketch—the beginning of my effort to interpret this sacred landscape. I want to portray a glorious vision of the divine in nature, a sense of the union between God in his heavens and man in His Holy City, surrounded by the majesty of nature.

If only you were here beside me, life would be perfect. Good night, my darling Katharine, Your loving Thomas

A rainy morning was a dreary beginning for the expedition to Petra. It was difficult to leave the comfort of their warm tents, and even harder to mount their horses and head into a cold, wet wind. Mika'il met them at a crossroads below the Mount with kafiyas for protection against the rain. The three men wrapped their hats and necks in the kafiyas, imitating their Arab companions. Hudson noticed that their guide had traded his elegant black and white outfit for a brown galabiya and roughly woven brown cloak.

They passed hazy views of Bethlehem, the fields of Boaz, Rachel's Tomb, and Solomon's Pools but had no desire to linger in the rain. When the rain stopped temporarily, lunch was served—cold chicken, cold mutton, damp bread, and cold rice pudding—cold, cold, cold. A black cloud sweeping up from the southwest burst open; they remounted their horses and bent into a driving rain, slouching toward Hebron. As they approached the valley of Eshcol, the rain gave way to sunshine, and Hebron appeared, glistening white in the distance.

Hudson slowed his horse to a walk and marveled at the beauty of this noble city situated in a narrow green valley between the lower hills of Judea. Terraced vineyards and olive tree orchards climbed the rolling hillsides, and fields of grain sprouted near a stream. Mostly white buildings gave an appearance of newness to the antique town of Hebron whose name Hudson remembered from Bible school days in Hartford. The houses, shops, and mosque were clustered to form an enclosure bisected by gates where the main roads approached the town. How unlike our towns, he thought. In New England, towns were wide open and houses scattered; in Palestine, there was an obvious preference for hindering strangers.

At the south edge of the town an enclosed *Haram*, another Muhammadan sacred place, rose above the town protecting the mosque, minarets, and tombs of the patriarchs. There, in the Cave of Machpelah were the tombs of Abraham and Sarah, Isaac and Rebeccah, Jacob and Leah. Below the town on the eastern side, he saw a long swath of bright green grasses and what appeared to be grave markers. Hebron might offer some possibilities for painting.

Mika'il found an area for camping west of the town, beside the deserted remains of a stone building with several rooms. While his men built a fire and unloaded the horses, Fowler, Lockwood, and Hudson warmed their wet bodies with a run up and down the terraced vineyards and then huddled by the fire.

"Mr. Hudson, I have arranged for all of you to camp in this building. More rain is expected tonight and this farmer . . ." Mika'il was beaming with the light of his good idea and pointing to a man beside him who was welcoming them with salaams.

"Not me," Lockwood interrupted, "I prefer a tent to that filthy place. It is barely fit for animals."

Mika'il's smile dissolved, and he turned to Hudson and Fowler for their reaction.

"I, for one, will appreciate a roof over my head, Mika'il." Fowler was vigorously rubbing his hands against the chill of the air. "Will we have one of the rooms that still has a roof?"

"Certainly, come and have a look. We have put your baggage in this large room, very good, very warm and dry, a large window with shutters."

Hudson looked around at the stone walls, the earthen brazier with burning coals and decided. "This is fine for me. Could your men bring in a few large stones to raise our baggage above the earthen floor. ?

"Of course. And, Mr. Hudson," Mika'il said, reaching into his robe and drawing out a letter, "Hassan asked me to give you this letter. It arrived at the hotel this morning."

Hudson crouched near the brazier and tore open the letter from Katharine. It was a short note and did not have a date.

My Darling Thomas,

I am afraid you will be quite angry with me. I neglected, on purpose, to tell you in the letter I posted yesterday about something I did last week. Now I feel a great need to admit my omission.

You may remember my mentioning that my sister, Edith, stopped by while your parents were visiting here. She was in a desperate state, but she disguised her emotions while your father was present. Early in January, she met a man from Chicago, a banker, at the New York home of our friends, the Blakes. They attended many social events together, and she was very moody when he left New York. Now he has invited her to visit his parents in Chicago.

Of course, Edith has no money for the rail ticket or all the new clothes she will need for the calendar of social events he sent. She was reluctant to ask Aunt Mary who disapproves of all her beaus, so she asked me. I was excited for her and failed to consider our own strained finances before I asked your father for a loan of two hundred dollars. He was surprised and looked at me with one of those 'oh, my dear child' expressions, but he did give me the money with no questions asked.

Now, I am squirming in my chair because I know you have not asked your father for money since you were an art student. I plan to ask Mama for the money when she returns from France, and then I will repay your father.

Please, please forgive me.

All my love, Katharine

Hudson crumpled the letter and almost tossed it into the fire. Then he took a deep breath, smoothed the paper on his leg, and read the letter again. He could not believe it. Now his father had a fresh excuse to berate him for rejecting the family business and becoming an artist. And he felt even more pressure to produce saleable paintings based on the sketches of this journey. What could he do other than put this problem in the back of his mind, buried deeply under more immediate concerns.

An hour later, Fowler and Lockwood joined him around the brazier to discuss plans for the next day. Hudson quoted from Porter's book. "According to Porter's description, that enormous oak tree we saw in the vineyard above is known as Abraham's Oak, one of the largest trees in all of Palestine."

"Dates to the time of Abraham? Hogwash!" Lockwood said with a harsh tone, squinting his eyes in a way that linked his furry white eyebrows. Busy with cleaning and polishing his riding boots, he seemed to be relishing the warmth of the room he had rudely rejected.

"Hudson, who is this man, Porter, this according to Porter?" Lockwood asked gruffly. "You know, you should be careful about travelers who decide after a few days in a place that they are able to offer expert advice. I remember once being given the most outrageous . . ."

"Steady, Lockwood." Fowler interrupted. "Porter is the author of the only good guidebook to Palestine and Syria. Few travel here without it. I have my own copy with me."

"Well, my way is to listen and look at the foreign scene, not to rely on the written account," Lockwood mumbled.

It did not shock Hudson that Lockwood had no use for books. However, it was ironic that a man who only spoke English and barely noticed his surroundings could rely on listening and looking to interpret a foreign environment. Lockwood was not a man of thought, more like a spoiled child who blunders ahead and expects understanding for every transgression. Hudson looked at Fowler for his reaction, but Fowler sat quietly, smoking his pipe, his eyes half closed. He needed to learn from Fowler's manner of detachment.

"You can be tiresome, Lockwood," Hudson said, paging through the section of Porter's guidebook on Hebron. "Do either of you have ideas for tomorrow? We have at least one day, maybe two, to look around Hebron while Mika'il assembles supplies and pack animals." Hudson planned to sketch for part of the next day, but also walk through the town and the cemetery below.

Fowler had a small map, given to him by the bishop in Jerusalem, and he passed it around. "I am happy to wander about the streets, especially in the area surrounding the *Haram*. The two pools on the map also look interesting."

"Porter mentions the pools," Hudson added. "Says they have been a reliable source of water since King David's time, probably explains why Hebron has survived, unlike so many biblical towns."

"I will tag along if you go in the afternoon," Lockwood said.

"Why does it have to be the afternoon?"

"For the morning I have arranged with Mika'il to take my horse and one of his men to poke around the village of Beni Na'im."

"Beni what?" Fowler asked, looking up. "It is not on this map."

Lockwood picked up his boots as if to leave.

Hudson stood up, partially blocking the door. He seemed to grow in stature and strength as he confronted the man. "Why are you going there?"

"Is that any of your business?" Lockwood spoke through clenched teeth and tried to brush past Hudson.

Hudson stretched his arm across the doorway. "Yes, as leader of this caravan, I make it my business, Lockwood." The two men faced each other as rigid as rocks until Lockwood stepped back.

"Oh, it is just an old man's sentimental desire to catch a glimpse of the Dead Sea again," Lockwood replied in a tone that rang as false as the look on his face. "It is only five miles from here, up the ridge of hills to the southeast of Hebron. The guide knows the goat path up to the town, and we will be back before noon."

Hudson was still mulling over Lockwood's intention when the dinner bell sounded. How does Lockwood know about this village? Is he planning to survey or map? Why not an excursion for all of them? Would this be his pattern on the trip? Would he put the caravan at risk?

Fowler interrupted his thoughts. "I say, Hudson, look at that table. Looks like my college dining room—white linen cloth, candlesticks, china, and silverware." Out of the damp darkness, the cook and his son emerged with a steaming kettle of thick, fragrant meat and vegetable soup, along with freshly baked flat bread. The first course was followed by platters of crisp fried fish with olives, roasted poultry and potatoes, and finally a fruit pudding with coffee. To celebrate their first night on the road to Petra, Lockwood produced a small bottle of apple brandy.

The night sky was not quite clear, but as they sat around the campfire after dinner, the visible stars drew Hudson's eyes toward the heavens. Lockwood poked at the fire with a stick, stirring the embers and raising sparks. Fowler and Mika'il spoke quietly, while Hudson sipped his brandy and watched the men of the caravan settle into blankets under the open sky. It would be cold, maybe with rain or snow.

For Hudson, the day had been mostly a good beginning of the journey. The rain added drama, making the appearance of Hebron under sunlight even sweeter. Maybe there would be a sketch from that memory. This camping offered more luxury than his past expeditions, especially in the dining aspect. He was older now and appreciated the comfort.

It was a relief to be on a painting trip again. Eight years ago he had traveled to Newfoundland and Labrador, before his marriage to Katharine, before the war and the sorrows. He needed this travel to heal the wounds in his spirit. Katharine had recognized his need before he did. She watched him agonize over a nation ripped and scorched by civil war. She understood his ideals and passions were intricately tied to the promise of America, and war eroded that promise. Then as the war drew to an end, they suffered the deaths of their young children, Emily and John. Katharine had found solace in her faith and the arrival of their new baby, Tommy, but nothing relieved Hudson from his morbid state. He blamed himself for their deaths.

For too long he had remained within a hard shell, enclosing and nurturing his sorrow, but yesterday and today he felt the shell begin to crack slightly, the anguish seeping from his pores.

Sketching on the Mount of Olives pumped some excitement into his veins. He felt confident that portraying Jerusalem as a link between God, man, and nature would be a profound theme—an insight and image to revive his reputation. And something about Fowler's presence reassured him. He barely knew the man, but admired him. He felt he might draw on Fowler's wisdom and compassion.

February 1868 Hudson Diary, Hebron
My Darling Katharine,

Your note about the loan for Edith arrived today and as you guessed I was not happy about your decision. I am trying not to stew about it, and if I were there I would caution you again about our finances, but I am thousands of miles away. Of course I understand and forgive, always.

Slept well last night despite the rain and rat. The India rubber blankets on our beds protected us from the rain, but no protection from the rat. Fowler awoke to find the rat gnawing on one of his shoes. He tied the shoelaces together and hung the shoes on a ring by the door. Again to sleep, and again a gnawing sound. I struck a light, and we saw the rat sitting in one of the shoes, chewing a chunk of the leather. He scurried away, and we plugged his route of escape. No more trouble.

Awoke to another cold and windy morning with some light rain, and the news that Mika'il was nearly smothered during the night by charcoal fumes. He had spread out some of the damp blankets from the horses in his room and retired with the shutters closed and the brazier still lit. One of his men found him unconscious in his bed and dragged him out into the cold air to revive him. He told us his head ached violently, but he would be fine by the afternoon.

This morning I made a small oil sketch of a bit of Hebron and the hill beyond. The dull sky gave no effect, but I rescued the space with a few clouds. I included many modest houses built of roughly squared stones, just barely distinguished from their stony background. A few terraces with grapevines added some greenery to soften the scene. Not a great result, but it keeps my hand well oiled.

I am determined to sketch daily, using the discipline of the pencil to study this strange landscape which demands deeper insights from the artist to discover its beauty. In painting the Orient, I will need to observe and respond in an environment that is intriguing, but still alien to my emotions.

After the rain stopped, Mika'il's men built a fire for a cold, damp morning, and Hudson moved outside to enjoy the warmth and read his Porter guidebook. Hearing the noon call to prayer from Hebron, he closed the book and looked toward the town. The mosque lay out of sight, but he could imagine the muezzin standing on the high balcony of the minaret arms outstretched eyes toward the heavens. Beyond the fire, several men of the caravan laid prayer rugs on the ground and began their quiet ritual. Their bare feet looked like old brown shoes, dry and cracked, the leather-like skin breaking away from the soles. He doubted they had been able to wash. Answering the five daily calls to prayer must be difficult for them, but he expected they would do what was possible. He wondered if Mika'il answered the call.

After lunch, Mika'il arranged for Ibrahim, one of his men who spoke a few words of English, to accompany the men to the town. They entered Hebron through the south gate, near the *Haram*. Lockwood immediately insisted that Ibrahim take him to the Jewish shops, since Mika'il had told him the grapes from the vineyard were made into a local wine by the Jewish merchants.

"It appears that Mr. Lockwood's listening and looking follows a quite narrow path," Fowler said with a chuckle as he watched Lockwood stride into the bazaar behind Ibrahim.

"I wish I could share your good sense of humor. I find he increasingly gets under my skin."

Fowler placed his hand on Hudson's shoulder and pointed toward the lower portion of the *Haram*. "What can you tell me about these massive walls—according to Porter?"

Hudson threw back his head and roared with laughter at the shared joke. "In fact, Porter has a great deal to say. Let me think. He writes about the *Haram* and a cave below it where Abraham and his family may be buried, and I remember he said these twenty-foot stones forming the base of the walls are as old as Solomon's Temple in Jerusalem. Would you believe 3000 years?"

Fowler ran his hand over the pale golden stones, smoothed and shined by the touch of pilgrims over thousands of years.

"Abraham is the ancestor in common, revered by Judaism, Christianity, and Islam, and this was his city. I am humbled to be in the presence of his past."

Hudson was surprised to hear Fowler speak so emotionally. In Jerusalem, he had thought Fowler's sense of religion was more intellectual and scholarly, not one of a believer. "Why do you respond so strongly to Abraham?"

"Abraham answered the call of God without questioning. He moved his tribe across hundreds of miles to Hebron, an unknown, uninhabited place. There he began his life again, faithful to the covenant and obedient to the will of God. His life became a model for the authentic religious life because he placed his absolute faith in the direct relationship between God and man. In my way of thinking, only two other men have had the courage to respond to God's word and persuade a large following – Jesus and Muhammad."

The two men continued walking along a narrow, winding road through an area of crumbling mud-walled houses no more than stables, each with a small grain field sprouting. They saw one of the two ancient pools, solidly built with large hewn stones and brimming with winter rains, and then wandered into the bazaar where they found Ibrahim sitting outside a wine shop, absorbed in the intricate moves of a backgammon game.

"Ibrahim, where is Mister Lockwood?" Hudson asked.

He stood quickly and motioned toward the open door of the wine shop.

Fowler followed Hudson into the dim and smoky shop smelling of rancid wine. When their eyes adjusted. they were looking at Lockwood's back. He and two Arabs were sitting on low stools around a small wooden table with three small glasses, murmuring in low voices. The younger man was dressed in western clothes and appeared to be translating; the other wore Arab robes. When he looked up to see Hudson and Fowler standing inside the door, he nodded to Lockwood who glanced over his shoulder. The look of aggravation on Lockwood's face was only apparent for a moment and then dissolved into an artificial greeting.

"Hello, come in. These gentlemen have been introducing me to winemaking in the Holy Land. I bought a few bottles for our dinner. Are you ready to go back?"

Ibrahim led the men out of the north gate of Hebron for the half-mile climb to their camp. Lockwood kept up with Ibrahim, while Hudson and Fowler brought up the rear at a slower pace. Hudson's mind kept returning to the scene in the wine shop. "Fowler, did you find anything odd about Lockwood's behavior in the wine shop?"

Fowler thought for a minute and replied, "Not really about his behavior. It did strike me it was unusually lucky to find someone who could translate from Arabic to English in a small shop in Hebron."

"That occurred to me as well, but it was his expression when he turned to see us that struck me. It was a look of such hostility, as if he were angry to be found there," said Hudson.

"I missed that. I was looking at the casks of wine when we first entered. He may have been annoyed at being interrupted in his discussion about winemaking. He does have quite a fancy for wine." Fowler breathed heavily as they ascended the steeper portion.

EIGHT

Hebron

When they returned to camp, a large party of foreigners and their entourage of Arabs and animals surrounded their small encampment. The newly arrived Arabs were racing about the perimeter—unloading baggage, erecting tents, cooking food, feeding and watering animals. A cluster of Frenchmen was engaged in a loud and agitated discussion. Hudson saw Mika'il near the lazaretto, speaking with a man dressed in the style of a dragoman, and he approached them for an explanation.

"Mr. Hudson, *Alhamdulillah*, praise Allah, you have come. There was a terrible incident not far from here. An Englishman is hurt badly, and these people," Mika'il motioned toward the Frenchmen, "they are angry and frightened; their dragoman cannot speak French, and two women are in the round tent by the lazaretto taking care of the Englishman. We need to see to the man's injuries and then . . ."

Before Mika'il finished, Hudson and Fowler ran toward the tent. At that moment the tent flap was pushed aside, and a tall woman, dressed in a blue robe with black braids almost brushing the ground, emerged and stood quietly before them. Her large, cobalt blue eyes moved from Hudson to Fowler, then settled on Mika'il. She spoke rapidly, in Arabic, and Mika'il nodded his assent to each remark, then left.

"Please forgive me, gentlemen, but it is urgent that we make arrangements to transfer our friend to Jerusalem as soon as possible, and your dragoman has a better sense of this terrain than our guide, Hisham." The woman had shifted easily into the King's English. "Mr. Palmer is not mortally injured, but he is in severe pain from several broken bones and ribs."

"We are at your service, dear lady. I am Alexander Fowler from Oxford, and this is my American friend, Thomas Hudson from New York. What can we do to help? I have some minor medical skills."

"Good of you to offer. I would appreciate another opinion on my friend's injuries." She extended her hand to Fowler and then to Hudson. "I am Sitt Mezrab, from Damascus."

Fowler opened the tent flap for the woman and followed her into the tent. Hudson stood outside considering the puzzle of Sitt Mezrab. The woman's accent suggested an English origin. Her face was as lightly browned as many Arabs, but her features were European. The few wrinkles did not interfere her beauty. Her hands were very fair, and the tattooing on her wrists coincided with her simple Bedouin robe.

From inside the tent he could hear a few moans and the muffled voices of two women answering Fowler's questions. When Fowler came out of the tent, he motioned to Hudson to come with him as he walked toward their room. "It seems, at a minimum, he has a badly dislocated shoulder, broken arm and leg on the right—the leg broken in several places with a bone protruding through his calf. The wound area is quite dirty; infection could be a problem, especially with all the animals around. They are boiling water to use for cleaning the wound. I carry rather strong pain medication for emergencies."

While Fowler retrieved the medication from his baggage, Hudson looked for Lockwood. He found him sitting by the fire, just beyond the Frenchmen who continued their animated conversation. As he approached, he sensed Lockwood was eavesdropping. "Lockwood, have you had any experience with broken bones?"

"Yes. Why do you ask?"

"There is a badly injured Englishman in the new tent."

Lockwood stood and brushed off the back of his coat. "In the war I occasionally assisted the surgeons, but it was mainly holding down some poor devil while they sawed off one of his extremities. I trust that is not what we have here."

"Fowler thought you might want to take a look. The women

from their caravan are making him comfortable and clean until they can get him to Jerusalem tomorrow."

"Who is the tall Arab woman who came out of the tent?" Lockwood whispered as they neared the tent.

Hudson noted that Lockwood did not miss much, even when he appeared to be unconcerned. "Actually, I think she may be British. Bit of a mystery there."

Hours later, Matthew Palmer was asleep—the worst pain relieved by Lockwood's ability to relocate his shoulder with a rotation of the shoulder blade that was excruciating, but effective. Fowler's medicine would give him hours of sleep, perhaps until the morning when the Arabs would take turns carrying him on a makeshift litter to the German Hospital in Jerusalem. Palmer's wife, Ellen, remained in the tent with him, exhausted emotionally and physically.

The foreigners and the two dragomen were gathered around the campfire, and Sitt Mezrab and Hisham pieced the fragments of the day's events into a narrative for the English speakers.

"We were attacked this morning," Sitt Mezrab explained, "south of here, near the road to Dura. We camped there last night after leaving Hebron. Amir, my nephew, and I were riding our horses slightly ahead of the caravan, planning to hunt pigeons for the evening meal. The others were on camels with Hisham. Please, Hisham, tell them what you saw."

Hisham struggled to make himself understood, occasionally turning to Mika'il for a word. "I see one camel and rider up top of hill, not good. I hear war cry—'isswah, isswah' —many men, many camels. Before, behind."

A Frenchman with a flushed and contorted face stepped forward and shook his fist at Hisham. "*Merde*, it was a thunderous horde of demons in a tornado of dust, waving rifles and swords. I was sure they were shouting death to the infidels, and this man did nothing." He started to move toward Hisham, but was pulled back down by his compatriots.

"Calm yourself, *Monsieur*." Sitt Mezrab warned. "You would be well advised to listen so you understand your dragoman saved your skin today." She glared at the Frenchman and asked Hisham to continue.

"Raiders come around our caravan, and they are much surprised to see foreigners. Leaders argue what to do." Hisham shouted out the details. "They tell me they will take our food and camels, nothing else if no fighting."

"My nephew and I were not far ahead," Sitt Mezrab added, "and when we heard the '*isswah*,' we knew it was a camel raid. It took us less than five minutes to return at a gallop, but there was nothing to be done. We faced an overwhelming force, and very few of us had arms."

Hudson looked back and forth between Sitt Mezrab and Hisham. Seeing the distress on his face, Mika'il interrupted. "I have been leading caravans in this area for twenty years and have never heard of Bedouin attacking a small group without provocation. Hisham says they were Bedouin of the Teyáhah tribe."

"They have no honor!" Sitt Mezrab's arm shot into the air with the loud exclamation. "It is unheard of for Bedouin to raid a caravan with foreigners, but the Teyáhah . . . they are a rogue tribe. They must be desperate to attack for such a small prize— less than twenty camels."

"They did not take your horses, nor the camel of Mrs. Palmer. Why?" Hudson asked.

"A Bedouin would never push a woman from her mount." An air of pride inflected her words. "It would be a loss of face for him. The leader did not seem to be a high ranking member of his tribe, but he knew enough to not interfere with family of an Anazeh sheikh."

"And why was Mr. Palmer singled out for attack?"

"Because he did not obey the order given by Hisham and repeated by me—to get down from the camel." Sitt Mezrab looked in the direction of the Palmer's tent, lifted her head and clicked her tongue. "It was foolish and arrogant, but he would not concede, even with his wife's pleading. Being a former military officer, he just could not surrender without a fight."

"I agree with Palmer." Lockwood snapped. "Why give in to these thieves?"

"They are not thieves." She looked around the group facing her and saw the confusion in their faces. "For the Bedouin, raiding is the breath of life, a time-honored tradition. Sometimes it is sport, other times it is desperation. The intention is not to injure or kill."

"Stealing as sport?" Lockwood sneered. "They could have killed Palmer with their rough treatment. Mrs. Palmer said two Bedouin with swords dragged him down from the camel and threw him to the ground. He is an elderly man."

"I agree, it was dreadful. However, he refused to dismount, even after we warned him repeatedly." She shook her head. "If you ignore the rules, you are likely to be punished. It is no different in the West, I believe."

"Are you finding excuses for the strong brutalizing the weak?" Hudson asked.

Sitt Mezrab turned slowly to look directly at Hudson. "The Bedouin way is complicated. Life balances on a sharp edge of survival. The motive for launching a raid is usually unknown. It may be revenge for a previous raid; it may be to save the tribe from starvation. In the normal pattern of a raid, when one side knows they are losing, they give the signal for surrender and walk away until another day when they are stronger."

A pause in the conversation allowed Mika'il to step forward into the center of the group. "Now we all know the story. It is time to confirm plans for tomorrow. Hisham, what will you do?"

"My men make litter to carry Palmer. Four men carry for four hours, then change, then change again. Maybe twelve hours to Jerusalem for them by small run. They leave at sunrise. I get horses from Hebron for us. We pack and go, when ready in morning."

"And the Frenchmen, Hisham?" Sitt Mezrab asked.

The dragoman shrugged his shoulders. Hudson watched as Sitt Mezrab brought the Frenchmen into a small circle where there was much shuffling of feet, arching of eyebrows, nodding of heads, and murmurs of *"jamais, exactement, Jérusalem, rapidement, Damas, oui, oui, oui."* She returned to tell Hisham and Mika'il that the Frenchmen preferred to return to Jerusalem and Damascus.

It was late, growing cold, and the group began moving toward their tents.

As Hudson and Fowler moved toward the lazaretto, Sitt Mezrab called out to them. "Gentlemen, could I have a word with you before you retire?" She approached holding the hand of a young Arab boy.

"Of course, Madame. What can we do for you?"

"I want to introduce my nephew, Amir." The boy attempted to hide behind Sitt Mezrab, his eyes looking down, but his mouth grinning. "Come, come, Amir. Shake hands with the gentlemen."

With a tentative, limp hand and slightly bowed head, Amir greeted Hudson and Fowler without moving from his aunt's side. Soft black curls surrounded his handsome face, his bright black eyes shaded by strikingly long eyelashes.

"I have a rather presumptuous proposal to make. I might be disappointed if you turn me down, but not offended." She smiled for the first time. "Amir and I have been so eager to travel to Petra, but many obligations have prevented me from going. Now we are more than halfway there and would very much like to continue with your caravan, if it is acceptable. I wonder if the three of you would discuss my request and let me know your decision in the morning. I have already spoken with my friend, Ellen Palmer, and she is quite comfortable with my choice to leave their group."

Fowler and Hudson agreed it was something to consider. They would talk to Lockwood and speak with her again early in the morning.

Lockwood was not in his tent, so the two men waited for him to return. Hudson spoke first. "I wonder if adding a woman to the caravan will create problems, especially a foreign woman married to a Bedouin. We know almost nothing about her. She seems congenial and competent, but also very assertive. What do you think?"

"Hudson, I want to be perfectly frank with you, even though I am not a man who enjoys gossip." Fowler watched Hudson biting his lower lip. "I expect I know quite a lot about Sitt Mezrab and would be remiss in not telling you."

"Sitt is a strange name." Hudson said.

"Actually it is not her name; it is a title, something akin to 'Lady,' I believe. And that brings me to my story. Years ago, many years ago, an extraordinarily beautiful young woman by the name of Lady Anne Darby Ellington became the scandal of London. Her marriage to the much older Lord Ellington had been arranged for reasons of social status, but, let us say, her youthful and passionate nature did not blend well with the Lord's foreign policy interests. Within a few years Anne was blossoming with the child of another man. Lord Ellington overlooked that indiscretion, but when it happened again, he filed for divorce, a rather extreme measure in English society. Granting a divorce required an Act of Parliament, making both of them grist for the Fleet Street mill." Fowler paused to describe the newspapers of London.

"After that time, I paid little attention to her escapades, but she was the main course for many dinner conversations in London. There were wild affairs with kings and princes, as well as enviable marriages to a baron and count before she left the Continent. About fifteen years ago, when I first began traveling in Asia, I heard Lady Anne had married a Bedouin Sheikh from an important tribe in northern Syria. She was reported to be completely domesticated and living serenely in Damascus. I have no doubt Sitt Mezrab is our Lady Anne."

"Quite a story, Fowler. Makes that camel raid pale by comparison. So, what do you think?"

"Absolutely yes. I am quite sure she will be a fascinating companion, and what is more important, an extremely useful addition. The Mezrabi brothers are well-known, and the tribe is highly respected. It also means one of us will speak fluent Arabic which might be a great asset if there is trouble in Petra. What do you say?"

"I agree."

"Do you have any reservations about the boy, Amir?" Fowler asked.

"None at all. I am sure he is a fine lad, and he will be Sitt Mezrab's responsibility. I think we need Lockwood's agreement, but does he need to know the entire story?"

"Perhaps we should tell him she is linked to British aristocracy and leave it at that for now. Do you agree?" Fowler asked.

"Agreed. I will speak with Mika'il."

The camp began to stir before sunrise. Palmer, still groggy from the pain medication, was given more of Fowler's drug for the journey. To minimize the movement of his limbs, the men wrapped him in a blanket and roped the mummy-like figure to the litter. The first group of runners raised the litter and left, followed by the relief runners, and one of Hisham's men who spoke some English accompanying on horseback.

On his way to breakfast, Hudson passed by Sitt Mezrab's tent as she was shaking out a small red and black woven rug. "Good morning, Sitt Mezrab," he smiled broadly at she tilted her head. "We are all agreed. We would be honored to have you and Amir join the caravan."

"Really? That is splendid. Amir will be so pleased." She rolled up the small rug and tossed it into the tent. "I am having breakfast with Ellen before Hisham's caravan leaves to catch up with the litter, but perhaps we could discuss plans later, Mr. Hudson."

"Fine. Find me when you are ready."

Sitt Mezrab walked into the Palmer's tent and found her friend dozing in a camp chair. Ellen's face showed the strain of much worry and little sleep. She seemed a delicate creature with her creamy ivory skin and the blonde curls she struggled to hide under her hat and scarf, trying to avoid the desire of Arab women to touch her hair. In truth, her appearance belied the inner strength that allowed her to remain calm in her feelings about the attack and confident in the plan to get her husband to a hospital. She and Anne had sailed through harsh winds on many occasions during their long friendship. Anne sat beside Ellen and stroked her hand until her friend slowly opened her eyes. "Did you sleep last night, my dear?"

"A little . . ." Ellen replied.

"How was Matthew during the night?"

"Restless, but I don't think in pain." Ellen stretched her arms and moved her head from side to side. "He was babbling about desert castles and crusaders as if he were getting ready to launch an attack on the local Bedouin. As you well know, Matthew has a violent temper when ordered to do something—too many years of giving rather than taking orders. Yesterday was rather ridiculous, and I expect you agree."

Anne patted her hand. "Given the protocols of Bedouin raiding, which Matthew knows well, it is silly to resist once you know you are outmanned and outgunned. Leave and live to fight another day, and all that rot. As you know, I have enormous respect for most Bedouin traditions, but I view raiding as a waste of time and resources and a drain on the most vigorous men of the tribe."

"Do you worry about Medjuel?"

Anne placed her elbows on the chair arms and folded her hands. "Not about the raiding, which is left to the younger men. But I do have other worries."

"And they are?"

"Oh, Ellen," she reached for her friend's hand. "I am almost twenty years older than Medjuel and beginning to show my age. Medjuel and his brother frequently visit our tribal settlements in the outlying desert areas, and young women accompany the men to do the cooking. Lately I have heard rumors of Medjuel's wandering eye. Frankly, the trip to Petra seemed a good break to relieve my anxiety and my loneliness when he is away."

"Dear Anne, anyone can see Medjuel is absolutely devoted to you."

She smiled at the thought. "Perhaps, but I find myself worrying constantly about him. Remember when I worried about nothing? Scandals, fortunes, wars, unfaithful lovers—none of it mattered, there were constantly new men and new places. Now I am content. No, more than content. I am enthusiastic about my life in Syria, but I have few illusions." Anne looked down at her rough hands and bulging veins.

"Medjuel will stay with me because he loves me, and the tribe respects me and relies on my money. However, he will surely take another, younger wife, and it will bring me much pain."

Ellen knew this story; it had been a constant refrain from Anne. "You and Medjuel will always take care of each other, and we both know caring becomes the most essential quality. I often wish Matthew would take a lover and leave me in peace. And with that remark, I think I must mount my horse and see to the old scoundrel."

Anne walked to the horses with Ellen and helped her to mount. Ellen looked down at her friend and smiled. "Matthew and I are happy you will continue to Petra. He would have felt horribly guilty if you missed this opportunity."

"And I would never have allowed him to forget it!" Anne teased.

"Is Amir excited about continuing?" Ellen asked.

"Oh, yes, he has already made a friend. The cook's son is only a few years older than Amir."

"When we return to Damascus, we will reassure Medjuel that you and Amir are in excellent company."

"He will be furious when he hears about the incident. The Anazeh and Teyáhah are hereditary enemies." Anne had omitted that fact in her comments about raiding. "Almost every year the Teyáhah travel for more than ten days, up to the Palmyra area, to raid our animals. Last year they carried off more than four hundred head of Anazeh cattle and camels."

Ellen heard the tension in Anne's voice. "Are you concerned that Medjuel might avenge this raid?"

"There is no tribe Medjuel despises more than the Teyáhah. They lack honesty, never offer hospitality, and raid like bandits. Medjuel was already considering a revenge raid against them this spring. This incident will fire his resolve. Take care, Ellen. I will miss you in Petra."

By midmorning, Hisham led the remainder of his party out of Hebron for the ride to Jerusalem. The newly formed quartet gathered around their small dining table, waiting for Mika'il to appear with his map of southern Judea. Amir helped the cook's son bring coffee and tea to the table.

"Are you worried about the Palmers, Sitt Mezrab?" Hudson asked.

"Please, please, all of you, call me Anne," she said. "No, I would have accompanied them if I were worried. The Palmers are seasoned, fearless travelers accustomed to the unpredictability of remote destinations. They are the kind of handsome and gregarious adventurers who can enthrall a large dinner table in London with tales of man-eating tigers in Nepal, head hunters in the Congo, perilous river rapids in Ecuador. While they have never experienced such an injury, they will survive and toss it into their delicious portfolio of stories."

Settling into a chair while Anne was speaking, Mika'il heard the mention of her European name. When Hudson told him earlier that Sitt Mezrab and Amir would join the caravan and that the Sitt was an Englishwoman married to a Sheikh, Mika'il replied he knew she was not an Arab. Her Arabic was excellent, but not the guttural of a native speaker. He also mentioned he had never heard of a Bedouin married to a European woman.

Mika'il unrolled his map on the table. "Given yesterday's events I think it would be advisable to change our route to Petra to one further east from the Teyáhah lands. I have already discussed the changes with Mr. Hudson, and he agreed. It will mean skirting the area of Beersheba, then rejoining the original route near Semua. A slight, safe swing to the east as you can see, closer to the Dead Sea."

"Will we be close to the Seval River?" Lockwood asked.

"Quite close, when we are in Semua. You know the area, Mr. Lockwood?"

"Yes, from my expedition on the Dead Sea. It is a desolate region, but there is a small village near where the Seval empties into the Dead Sea. I would like to see it again."

"I would hardly call it a village, Mr. Lockwood," Mika'il said. "Just a few families collecting bitumen. Not worth a detour."

Hudson watched Lockwood scowl and rub the stubble on his jaw. The proposal from Lockwood had surfaced a little too quickly for Hudson, almost as if Lockwood had planned a detour, perhaps another of his lone excursions. The man was as cunning and quick as a cat, full of deceptions. Yesterday, after watching him sit near the Frenchmen, Hudson suspected Lockwood spoke French or at least understood it, and yet he had denied any language ability. And the scene in the Hebron wine shop still bothered him. Lockwood behaved like a loose cannon rolling around the deck of a ship.

Amir tugged at Anne's arm and whispered, "Amma, can I go to feed the horses?" Anne nodded, and the boy sprinted to the makeshift paddock.

Fowler rarely asked a question during the planning sessions, but now he raised his pipe for attention. "One more question, Mika'il. The Bedouin in Petra, are they from the Teyáhah tribe?"

"No, the Petra tribe is called Huwaitát," Mika'il said. "A large mountain range and Wadi Arabah separate the two tribes, and the Huwaitát are peaceful, not a raiding tribe. They protect Petra and earn money as guides."

"And will they be our guides?"

Mika'il nodded. "We pay them to be guides, providers of animals, and helpers. Today, I expect the first of our Huwaitát Bedouin to bring pack donkeys and a camel for the supplies I am adding from Hebron. A Huwaitát sheikh will join us in Semua with the rest of the camels."

"If there is nothing else for me," Anne said looking around the group, "I will help Amir with the horses."

"Will you be riding your horses to Petra?" Lockwood asked.

Anne clicked her tongue against her teeth, and lifted her chin in a curious gesture.

"What was that? What did you just do with your tongue?" Hudson asked.

"Oh, you mean this?" Anne asked, repeating the gesture. "It means *la*, 'no,' or 'not likely.' One of my favorite non-words in Arabic." She laughed as she watched Hudson practicing the gesture until he had the click and the lift coordinated perfectly.

"As for our horses," Anne replied, "it would be too difficult for them to be ridden in some of the terrain ahead, but they will be fine following without riders. I have arranged for one of Mika'il's men to lead Inam and Amir's horse, and I will pay for an extra camel to carry their food and water."

"Inam," repeated Fowler. "What does it mean?"

"In Arabic, Inam means 'gift'—Medjuel's finest gift to me." Anne touched her arm, fingering her gold bracelets. "No possession means as much to me as Inam. During my girlhood in Dorset, I learned about the breeding of horses from my father. Medjuel respects such knowledge so he allowed me to select the sire and the dam for my foal. She is quite the finest Arabian mare I have ever seen—you can see it in her wide-set eyes and large nostrils."

Anne, Lockwood, and Fowler continued discussing horse breeding, but Hudson slipped away for a walk on the hills. The hours passed with no sign of the Bedouin and his donkeys. Anne retired to her tent to catch up on lost sleep, and Amir helped in the kitchen tent. Hudson pulled his sketchbook out of his baggage, and Fowler and Lockwood engaged in a gymnastic routine of jumping and waving their arms until rain began to fall. Dinner was early and brief, but still an amazing variety, including a heaping tray of rice and pigeon smothered in an apricot sauce.

By evening, a cold wind blew down from the western mountains, and rain had turned to sleet. Mika'il stood at the doorstep of the lazaretto watching slivers of ice slicing the darkness. After a wasted day of waiting for the donkey man, he was eager to move the caravan the next morning. A few hours later, the sound of clanging bells wakened him. A Bedouin led a dozen belled donkeys and one camel through a veil of snow.

NINE

Atheneodorus, a philosopher and my friend, who had been to Petra, used to relate with surprise that he found many Romans and also many other strangers residing there. He observed the strangers frequently engaged in litigation, both with one another and with the natives; but the natives had never any dispute amongst themselves and lived together in perfect harmony.
Strabo. *The Geography of Strabo*, XVI.iv.21, CE 7-18

Professor Andrew Fowler

Fowler sat outside the lazaretto in the snow, reading a few pages from Strabo's *Geography*. He chuckled to himself about the idea of finding 'perfect harmony' among the Nabateans in Petra. Atheneodorus never mentioned finding perfect harmony in Athens or Rome. Glancing around the snowy vineyards, Fowler relished the harmony in this moment of his life. Here he was in the nineteenth century, on his way to Petra accompanied by his old friend, Strabo, from the first century. He imagined a cartoon his students would draw to satirize the scene—an elderly professor sitting with an ancient book beside a statue of Strabo, surrounded by sleeping students.

Students shunned classical texts. Even when given an English translation of the ancient Greek, they groaned, whined, and balked. He realized students lived mainly in the present. While he found something refreshingly Buddhist in that approach, he tried to emphasize the repeating rhythm of history in the human endeavor. For Fowler, Strabo's ancient geography sang of the interdependence of the landscape, arts, music, literature, physics, mathematics, mythology, and history—relationships that blurred in the more complicated, segmented world of the present. Using observations from India, Fowler intended to place the web of life at the center of his next courses.

After almost two years of traveling, he felt eager to resume his life as a professor at Oxford. The prospect of engaging students was again a welcome challenge. The academic calendar suited his rhythm—a time to teach, followed by a summer to travel and think. He was less confident about his personal life. During this time away from England, his wife, Mary, had been his invisible companion. Soon, he would return to the home they had shared for thirty years, and her absence would descend like the silence of the desert. He had not entered their cottage after Mary's funeral, it was too painful to consider. He had taken the train to London and Portsmouth and sailed eastward. They had planned to travel together in the Orient, Persia, and India after he retired; instead, he made the journey alone to grieve her absence.

As the rising sun spread its warmth, Fowler stood up and stretched; he removed his macintosh and placed it on the table beside him. He noticed Hudson sketching but did not interrupt. Quietly, he withdrew his pipe, tobacco, and matches from his pocket and returned to his seat. The ritual of preparing the pipe was a small meditation for Fowler. In the morning he liked to use a straight pipe, filled with an English mixture, carefully tapped and tamped into place and tested for a good draw. He was skillful at lighting the pipe, moving the lighted match in circles around the edges of the tobacco while he took deep draws, spreading the fire horizontally and vertically.

By the time Fowler had relaxed into his smoking, Hudson was standing by his side, paintbox in one hand and chair in the other hand.

"May I join you, Fowler?"

"Please do. I was watching your painting—lightning speed."

Hudson laughed. "You probably noticed it takes more time to prepare than to execute an oil sketch."

"I noticed you were completely oblivious of anything beyond the view ahead," Fowler remarked, pointing his pipe stem toward the snowy landscape of Hebron.

Hudson opened his folding chair and placed it a few feet from

Fowler. "My wife enjoys telling everyone about my private painting place—the place where my mind removes me from the world. As soon as I squeeze the first blob of paint on the palette, I am gone."

"And the colors this morning?"

"A combination of white, green, ochre, and burnt sienna, earthy colors for this unusual scene."

The night of snowfall had transformed the valley. The town was still and quiet, sleeping under a white blanket. Only the olive trees and the slender minarets of Hebron's mosque pierced the blanket.

"I say, old boy, could I have a look at the results?" Fowler asked.

Hudson reached for his paintbox and withdrew the still wet paperboard. "It is only a sketch—a study to remember the colors and terrain." Hudson had used large brushes and long strokes of color, applied liberally and blended roughly into an image of rock and weather.

Fowler examined the painting carefully. He could see only an abstraction barely hinting at subject. He wondered what Hudson saw in his mind and what would emerge in a painting. To Fowler, it seemed more a feeling than a picture. "The colors are vibrant and true, you have caught the warmth the sun has added to a chilly day. I see almost no detail. Does it come later?"

"I believe I have the detail I might need in the pencil sketches from yesterday. I doubt there will be a painting of Hebron, but sketching sharpens my understanding of this bleak terrain."

Fowler raised his eyebrows at the word 'bleak.' Maybe the artist was not finding what he had expected. The gulf between expectations and reality in desert lands tripped many a traveler. Fowler knew the landscape ahead was even more barren and forbidding.

"Have you ever traveled in deserts?" Fowler asked.

"Never. It is terra incognita for me." Hudson held the sketch at arm's length, squinting at the image, and replaced it in his paintbox. "I really had no idea of the desert when I planned this journey."

"Are you discouraged?"

"I am never discouraged, but I am surprised. In Paris, I saw the work of a Frenchman, Jacques Vesoul, who has painted the desert in Egypt and Syria. His deserts look mysterious, almost romantic. Here it is bleak, so very bleak."

Hudson looked down and scraped the snow around his feet. "I wonder if I will want to paint the desert landscape? I may have come to the wrong place for my objectives."

Fowler saw no fire in Hudson's eyes. They swam in confusion, discouragement. It had been apparent to Fowler from their first meeting that Hudson was a man bearing burdens. When he spoke of his artistic plans, it was with grave determination, not joy. When he spoke of his family, it was with a heaviness of heart. What was dragging down this man whose life seemed rich in love and talent? The only time he had seen a euphoric Hudson was on their visit to the *Haram ash-Sharif*. Something about that spot kindled a fire in the artist.

"Why did you choose to travel in the Orient, Hudson?"

Lifting his head slowly, Hudson stared silently toward the distant horizon. He wrestled with his tendency to withdraw, to lock away his feelings in an unexamined box that he strapped to his back where he considered it less noticeable. That strategy had worked well in the past, but now he was besieged by guilt and doubt and longed for resolution, the sweet scent of peacefulness. He sighed and shook his head with a rueful, tight grin. "I think I came for absolution and ambition. Those may be unwise reasons. Frankly, after decades of success in all my endeavors, I find myself adrift from my moorings."

Fowler removed his pipe. "What are the moorings in your life?"

"Family and art. You may have thought I would include religion, but art is my religion—I paint nature because I find the spiritual in nature."

Fowler moved ahead cautiously. "Do you know what has set you adrift, my friend?"

In the long pause that followed, Hudson chewed his lower lip, then inhaled slowly before he spoke. "I feel responsible for the death of my first two children. At the same time, my artistic reputation is suffering in a changing art scene. And I am ashamed to admit that sometimes I do not know which is more important to me." He turned to look directly at Fowler. "What do you think? Will I find absolution?"

Fowler puffed and watched the smoke rising like little clouds. "You will find what you seek, Hudson." He paused again as he studied Hudson's confused expression. "Is it too simple an answer? The word 'seek' is the key, you know. For me, it requires searching honestly and intensively with open mind and open heart—not easy to accomplish."

Hudson brought his hands together, making a tent with his fingers and thumbs. "I think you are suggesting I begin my search within myself."

"Yes, indeed, I would emphasize searching within," Fowler spoke gently. "But I also would say travel provides an ideal space for self-examination. I have found that travel in other cultures opens up new perspectives, new pathways to restore equilibrium. One becomes vulnerable, and being vulnerable offers space for questioning or change —sometimes both."

"I am starting to feel this seeking might be related to your recent travels."

Fowler examined the bowl of his pipe, still a bit of tobacco remaining. "Two years ago, my wife was murdered in our home by a thief who left with a few worthless items and left me with nothing of value in my life. I departed England thinking I could assuage my sorrow by visiting family in India, exploring ancient civilizations, studying Sanskrit texts, testing my physical endurance, pursuing other worthy challenges. Now I know I was simply escaping. One finds peace only by seeking within, by cultivating inner peace. A Buddhist monk in northern India helped me along this path of understanding, but I believe I could have come to my awakening by honest reflection in my Oxford study." His pipe was cold, and he knocked it against the chair leg to remove the ashes.

"I am not suggesting you return to your studio for meditation. I am saying it can be done anywhere, here or there. The only place you will find absolution is within, searching your soul for understanding and forgiveness, then opening your heart to love. Perhaps then your anxieties about ambition will resolve themselves."

Hudson sat quietly for several minutes, his head bowed. When he picked up his paintbox and stood, Fowler saw his tear stained face. "I have never had a conversation like this with a man, not even my minister. I value your friendship and concern, Fowler. You have given me much to think about. Now I must go."

As he watched him walk away, Fowler pondered Hudson's remark about his children. He was reluctant to ask, but wanted to be helpful to his new friend. He considered Hudson a friend—a man he enjoyed and respected. He gravitated toward people who thought and spoke seriously about their purposes in life. Fowler leavened his serious purposes with joyful interludes, and he imagined Hudson normally approached his life in a similar way. How to handle those times when life splinters us to the core — there lies courage.

Fowler glanced at his pocket watch and decided to take time for a second pipe before breakfast. The conversation with Hudson and the preparation of the pipe aroused lovely memories of Mary and the intimacy of their evenings together. The evening pipe signaled the time when they would exchange their thoughts about the day—thoughts about what they had read, or what they had seen on a walk, or friends they had joined for lunch. They exchanged humorous and annoying incidents, frightening or wonderful encounters, hopes and anxieties. He missed that nightly interlude more than he could believe possible.

As he relit his pipe, he heard the stirrings of the morning camp. The finishing of prayers, loading of supplies onto donkeys, preparing of breakfast—all reminders of moving toward Petra. He opened his book and again began to read:

"The capital of the Nabataeans is called Petra. It is situated on a spot which is surrounded and fortified by a smooth and level rock, which externally is abrupt and precipitous, but within there are abundant springs of water both

for domestic purposes and for watering gardens. Beyond the enclosure the country is for the most part a desert, particularly towards Judaea. Through this is the shortest road to Jericho, a journey of three or four days, and five days to the palm plantation. It is always governed by a king of the royal race. The king has a minister who is one of the Companions and is called Brother. It has excellent laws for the administration of public affairs."

Strabo. *The Geography of Strabo*, XVI.iv.21, CE 7-18

TEN

"The wandering Arabs have certainly more wit and sagacity than the people who live in towns; their heads are always clear, their spirits unimpaired by debauchery, and their minds not corrupted by slavery; and I am justified in saying that there are few nations among whom natural talents are so universally diffused as among the Bedouins."   John Lewis Burckhardt

Hebron to Semua

Hudson found Mika'il waiting to speak privately with him. "Last night around our campfire, there was much disagreement among the men. Most of them questioned why a Bedouin woman would be traveling with our group. They felt it not proper, perhaps dangerous, to include such a woman and her young Bedouin companion. They wanted me to ask her to leave."

Hudson had not anticipated this problem but quickly understood the seriousness. The men must have wondered what kind of Bedouin woman would travel with Hisham's group. They may have thought she was an outcast from her tribe or a servant of the Palmers. She had special privileges, her own horse and tent, which must have seemed odd. When it became clear she would leave Hisham's group and join our caravan, fear or even anger had replaced confusion.

"I trust you resolved the questions," Hudson said.

"I said you would decide who became a member of your party, and you would not bring danger to the caravan. I told them Sitt Mezrab is an English woman, married to an important Bedouin sheikh, and Amir is her nephew. I insisted she be treated by all with honor and respect."

"Well done, Mika'il."

Consul Johnson had been right on the mark about Mika'il's reliability as a dragoman. Hudson had previous experiences with guides who were shrewd and obsequious, qualities which made him uncomfortable. Mika'il impressed him with his solid character. From their first days together, he had negotiated his contract honestly and had handled Lockwood with courtesy but also firmness. In this instance he showed a remarkable sensitivity to foreign custom and the attitudes of his own men. Hudson felt he could rely on Mika'il's judgment in helping to resolve any troubles ahead.

He watched Mika'il and his men move swiftly to finish the packing of the donkeys. The muddy roads would slow their travel toward Semua. By the time Hudson consumed his bread stuffed with egg and a cup of tea, the caravan was departing. The horses led the way, followed by the donkeys with baggage and lastly, the camel loaded with sacks of charcoal.

As they passed the graveyard outside of Hebron, a group of Arab women in white were wailing beside a newly dug grave, oblivious to the snow and rain. The open grave sliced into the snow and the cries of the mourners caused Hudson to shiver and draw his cloak tightly.

March, 1868 Hudson Diary, Semua
Dearest Katharine,

The landscape beyond Hebron was rainy, bleak, wild, and lonely. Varieties of rock broke through the hard surface of the desert—rugged hills, mountains crusted with limestone ledges. Grass and weeds filled the interstices. Only an occasional field of sprouting grain enlivened the scene. When we left the rain behind, Mika'il selected a favorable spot for lunch.

The cook warmed our innards with a hot meal—chicken cooked over the open fire, chips of potato, and cake. The driver of the donkeys, lean as a whippet, walked around our table, looking at our repast, but Mika'il flatly refused the scraggly bearded old man even a morsel. I wondered why, but had no chance to ask. We sat around a fire of thorn bushes, grateful for the warmth as the animals were rested and watered, and the sun struggled to break through the clouds.

Two hours more brought us within sight of the village of Semua, a dreary settlement that appeared to have lost its reason for existence. Decaying brown buildings carved out of a brown hillside perched on top of a ridge pockmarked with dark brown cave openings. Only the remains of a watchtower gave a slight distinction to the scene. Winding our way across the valley and up the slopes, we saw sculptured stones with an ancient appearance. One was a piece of an ornamented cornice with a pattern of grapes and vine; another a curious basket-like ornament. They appeared to be Roman or Saracenic in origin. Closer to the village, there were very large, squared stones, some bevelled, and fragments of columns and bases. These ruins gave me some hope that Semua offered something worth painting. Fowler said that in Biblical times, it had been a prosperous town, surrounded by farmland. Now it is almost deserted, crumbling into a desiccated landscape.

A few lazing Arabs awaited our approach. The men of these towns sit in clusters, talking and smoking as if there were no work to be done. Mika'il spoke to one of the men who led him toward the watchtower. He wanted to secure a room in the tower, if one could be found dry and clean enough to be endurable. Most of us would prefer a tent to the dirty habitats of the Arabs, but it is no joke to encamp on ground soaked with water.

Mika'il returned from the room investigation with an expression more of resignation than enthusiasm. We followed him from a heap of filth outside the low arched gateway to a sea of filth over which we passed shudderingly, as we carefully picked our way from stone to stone. Then climbing a narrow flight of steps brought us into a large, arched room with several windows opening onto the valley below. The rough walls glittered with jetty soot and emitted a strong creosote odor, masking other odors. It was spacious and dry, and we congratulated Mika'il on his efforts.

As of yesterday, our group of three has grown to five. A Bedouin woman and her nephew joined us in Hebron. As you can imagine, there is much more to this story. Sitt Mezrab, or Anne as we now call her, is an English woman married to a sheikh from the Anazeh tribe of Syria. She lives part of the year in Damascus and knows several of our friends in the Beirut missionary community. Anne speaks perfect Arabic, knows the culture, and that is an advantage for us. Amir is well-behaved and independent for a boy of ten years.

Now I must get ready for dinner in our tower. Wish you were here to join us, but I have been wishing for your presence every day. I keep my eyes open for magic lamps.   All my love, your Thomas

Mika'il's men moved the baggage into the tower room and used parts of a tent to create a private space for Anne and Amir. Within an hour, a section of the room had become a dining area with another spectacle—snowy white tablecloth, French cutlery, brass candlesticks, and silver plated serving dishes beside tureens brimming with warm food. A rich vermicelli soup was followed by courses of boiled beef with turnips and rice, wild pigeons and petit pois. A pudding bright with raisins and oranges was served with coffee. Mika'il had warned them that the variety of foods would diminish as the caravan moved farther into the desert lands, but for this night the feast plumped their bellies and warmed their spirits. In the candlelit darkness, the tower became a cozy retreat. Lockwood dug into his baggage and found yet another bottle of brandy.

"Is this better than dinner in a Bedouin tent, Anne?" Lockwood asked, as he poured a small amount of brandy into each glass.

"It is quite different, but I cannot say better. Certainly there would be no brandy." Anne smiled broadly and clapped her thanks to Lockwood. "And I would not be sitting at the dinner if Bedouin men were guests. That occurs only when Medjuel and I are eating alone, and then our camels push their noses under the tent begging for scraps. It is difficult to be alone in a Bedouin camp!" Laughing, she raised her glass of brandy. "I toast all of you, my new friends, with gratitude for your good company."

The men stared at a more lighthearted Anne. Her radiant smile and teasing tone of voice had given them a glimpse of an entirely different woman—one not so burdened by her friend's accident and departure and the constant need to portray the austere Bedouin wife.

Hudson studied her face with his painterly instincts. The strength of her beauty lay in the lower part of her face—the gentle curve of her cheek, the finely sculpted lips. The color of her widely spaced eyes flowed between a clear cobalt and icy ultramarine blue, often veiling her emotions with a chilly distance. No doubt she had been gorgeous as a young girl, and despite the desert sun and time, she was still enchanting.

146

"What would we be eating in your Bedouin tent?" Hudson asked.

"*Mansef! Mansef!*" Amir shouted gleefully.

Anne smiled and thought a moment. "Yes. In your honor, we would have *mansef*. We would slaughter a sheep, roast it, and serve it on a huge platter covered with rice soaked in a yogurt sauce of raisins, almonds, onion shavings, and other bits of the lamb. You would sit on our woven carpets, and use only your right hand to tear off pieces of meat, knead the meat with rice into a ball, and pop it into your mouth."

Fowler removed his pipe and looked seriously at Amir. "Which of us would be honored with the eyes?"

Amir blushed and turned to his aunt for an answer, and Anne burst into laughter at the look on Hudson's face. "In our tribe, the tail of the sheep is also prized, so there would be something for each of you gentlemen!"

Amir's eyes opened wide at the word—tail. He tugged at Anne's arm. "Amma, what about The Tale of the Camel's Tail? Please tell it, tell it. I will do the sounds."

"Is it a Bedouin story?" The enthusiasm shone in Fowler's sparkling eyes and rosy cheeks, both enhanced by the brandy.

"The Anazehs say it is a legend from before the Qur'an was revealed to the Prophet, from the days of darkness. In those times the camel had only a stub of a tail, and she watched with envy as the horse and the donkey swished their lengthy rear extremities with shameful pride." Anne waved to Amir to begin the sounds.

"Grumph." Amir tried to look as serious as the sound.

"One day the camel stood chewing her cud and nursing her newborn calf when suddenly a small thorn bush caught fire and out of the smoke emerged a naked human child of great beauty with cocoa brown skin and long black hair, straight as a spear. The child was very thirsty. 'O, great and powerful beast, I long for your pure white milk. If you will allow me to suckle at your breast, I will grant you a wish.' "

"Gurgle?"

"The camel was not as foolish as she looked. She knew djinn came out of the smoke of a fire, and they were fearsome creatures, full of tricks. The camel chewed her cud and thought, thought and chewed her cud again, until she had an idea. 'Beautiful and sweet child, of course I will gladly share my pure white milk with you. But I fear you are cold in this harsh winter wind. Reach into my saddle bag and you will find a pretty, golden robe made out of sheep wool. After you put on the robe, please enjoy my pure white milk.' "

"Gurgle."

"The djinn felt very clever. She would have her milk and a warm robe and then escape without even granting one wish. 'Oh, great and powerful beast, you are ugly but generous, so I will give you two wishes.' The djinn removed the robe from the saddlebag and admired the softness of the wool as she wrapped it around her spindly body. Then she moved beside the calf to suck the mother camel's pure white milk. The djinn sucked greedily. When a single drop of milk splashed onto the robe, the robe turned into a golden cage, trapping the djinn. 'Oh, vile and treacherous beast, you have captured me when I meant you no harm. I am only a poor, homeless child.'

"The camel produced a ferocious grunt and snort. 'I know you are a djinn, and now you will have to grant three wishes before you are released from your cage. First, you must find enough lion tails to replace all the horrid camel stub tails in the world. Second, you must sew a lion tail on every camel from now until eternity. Third, you must address every camel as 'Oh, great and powerful beauty!' "

Now Amir grinned and said, "Ha, ha."

"The djinn rattled her golden cage in anger, but in the end, she had to agree to the three wishes. She summoned her tribe of minions with a flick of fire from the tips of her fingers and sent them north and south, east and west in search of lions. When all the lion tails were found, and all the tails were sewn into place, the djinn said, 'Oh, great and powerful beauty, you have picked a perfect tail for your species.' "

"Swish. Swish."

"The camel swished her prized tail, tickling her calf who also swished her new toy. The mother thought about all the camels of

148

the world who now could swish higher and farther than any horse or donkey. Then she spat on the golden cage and it dissolved, freeing the djinn."

"Spew. Spew."

"The djinn wiped the spit from her hair and began to spin into soaring flames. She screeched and howled, 'Oh, vain and foolish camel, I have given your species a tender and succulent tail, and now all Bedouin will be tempted to roast you over a fire for the supreme pleasure of eating your tail!' "

"Gruuuuuuumph!" Amir shouted.

"And the moral of the tale is?"

Fowler was quick to answer. "The djinn always win!"

There was much laughter and clapping, and Amir galloped around the room like a young camel.

"I can attest to the tastiness of camel tails," Fowler said. "While traveling in Afghanistan, I attended a village wedding— the kind of a wedding where, sadly, the bride's father bankrupts himself to prove his wealthy status to all his relatives and friends. A camel was slaughtered for the celebration, and every scrap of the beast was eaten by the ravenous horde, except the tail which was reserved to honor the bride's father. When the slender, slippery tail was presented to the father, he stared at the tail that had wagged his fortune and passed it to me."

Anne glanced over at Fowler with a sad smile of recognition, a familiar story of wedding extravagances ruining families. "Now the tales of the tails wag the night," she said. "Our candles have melted into warm pools, and I look forward to a warm bed. Good night gentlemen."

Amir stood beside the table, his eyes fixed on the plate of pudding sitting in front of Hudson. "Come, Amir," Hudson beckoned, "this pudding needs eating."

The boy hesitated only a moment before sliding into Hudson's lap and picking up the remaining spoon. Hudson wrapped his arms around the boy.

On Sunday morning Fowler arose early to select a Bible reading. The previous evening Hudson had asked him if he would present a brief sermon before they launched an excursion into one of the adjacent valleys. Fowler had agreed, even though he was long removed from that part of his life, having left the ministry to research and teach ancient eastern civilizations. He knew he was better suited to a life of study than one of preaching. How could he preach to others, when he was no longer certain of his beliefs? Fowler knew more about the history of religion than about faith. Abraham would be a good historical subject. They had just been in Hebron. He thumbed through Genesis looking for appropriate passages about Abraham.

When Hudson and Anne appeared for the sermon, it was still early morning. Lockwood was not in his tent or around the camp. Mika'il said he had seen Lockwood ride out earlier in an easterly direction. Anne and Hudson gathered near Fowler's tent, a quiet spot away from the clamor of the breakfast pots and pans.

"Since we are in the land of Canaan and have just visited Hebron, I thought God's message to Abraham about the Promised Land might be appropriate." Fowler was looking at Anne and Hudson, as he polished his spectacles on the crumpled sleeve of his jacket. He adjusted them on the end of his nose and opened the Bible.

"Genesis, Chapter 12, Verses 1-9:
1: Now the Lord had said unto Abraham, Get thee out of thy country, and from thy kindred, and from thy father's house, unto a land that I will show thee:

2: And I will make of thee a great nation, and I will bless thee, and make thy name great; and thou shalt be a blessing:

3: And I will bless them that bless thee, and curse him that curseth thee: and in thee shall all families of the earth be blessed.

4: So Abraham departed, as the Lord had spoken unto him; and Lot went with him: and Abraham was seventy and five years old when he departed out of Haran.

5: And Abraham took Sarah, his wife, and Lot his brother's son, and all their substance that they had gathered, and the souls that they had gotten in Haran; and they went forth to go into the land of Canaan; and into the land of Canaan they came.

6: And Abraham passed through the land unto the place of Sichem, unto the plain of Moreh. And the Canaanite was then in the land.

7: And the Lord appeared unto Abraham, and said, Unto thy seed will I give this land: and there builded he an altar unto the Lord, who appeared unto him.

8: And he removed from thence unto a mountain on the east of Bethel, and pitched his tent, having Bethel on the west, and Hai on the east: and there he builded an altar unto the Lord, and called upon the name of the Lord.

9: And Abraham journeyed, going on still toward the south."

"I often wonder what Abraham expected to find in the Promised Land." Fowler laid down his spectacles and relaxed into his camp chair. "This land of Canaan was never a land of milk and honey, never a terrain hospitable to large settlement or extensive agriculture. Its resources were few, its climate harsh. From the beginning, plague and pestilence stalked the land, and wars and disasters shook its foundations . . ."

Hudson's mind was wandering off toward a different landscape. The idea of the Promised Land had great significance for him, but it was the New Promised Land—America. He remembered as a young boy hearing ministers speak of America as a divinely ordained enterprise, planted by God in the New World. Here man would enjoy freedom, prosperity, and peace in a nature that was bountiful and spiritual. His earliest work as an artist had been inspired by the idea of the New Promised Land. He and his artist friends explored mountains, forests, and rivers for the inspiration to create paintings glowing with the wonder and spirituality of American nature. Everything fit together—art, nature, and religion.

Now the mind of the country was shifting. Nature was becoming a place to plunder. Lumbermen turning forests into wastelands. Farmers abandoning land instead of improving it. Railroads tearing up the countryside and factories belching smoke into the air and water. The great wealth of the country collecting in large piles of greed.

Where was God in that nature? Would our American

paradise become a desert like what surrounds us in Palestine, a soulless place where people struggle to survive?

"Hudson, Hudson! Are you all right?" Fowler grasped his shoulder. "We thought you were falling out your chair, my good man. Did you fall asleep with my chattering about the Promised Land?"

Hudson rearranged his body and his expression with a nervous laugh. "No, no. I was just mulling over your ideas. Quite interesting—promises and land, and man just making a muddle of it. Is it time for breakfast?"

Anne and Fowler were bewildered. Where had Hudson been for the last ten minutes?

The morning turned into afternoon. The horses had been saddled for over an hour, and still Lockwood had not returned. Hudson smacked the palm of his hand with the horsewhip. "I suggest we leave. Lockwood is clearly off on one of his solitary romps. I wish he had the courtesy to share his plans—he is such an exasperating man."

Mika'il and one of his men would guide Hudson, Fowler, Anne, and Amir on an excursion west of Semua to Wadi al-Khalil, near several ancient and present-day settlements. Since Anne and Amir were superb riders and wanted to exercise their horses, Mika'il assigned a man to be in the lead with them. They swung into their saddles and disappeared in a flurry of dust. The others would take a slower pace and stop at places of interest.

After Hudson and Fowler mounted their horses, Mika'il asked, "How were your sleeping arrangements in the tower, Mr. Hudson?"

"Dry and warm. If not for our late night visitors, it would have been perfect."

"Visitors?"

"The rampaging rats. I kept my whip at hand and made occasional cracks at them in the dark." Hudson illustrated by brandishing his whip and giving it a quick flick. The snap of the whip startled his horse, and he was off for a brief gallop.

When Fowler and Mika'il caught up, Hudson still breathed heavily from his swashbuckling episode. "The horse . . . cough, cough . . . the horse was more attentive to my whip than the rats. They seemed to think it some sort of game until I lit the lamp and charged at them."

The men rode side by side for their slow climb over the western hills. Fowler entertained Hudson by describing Lockwood's snoring which had disturbed his sleep. "I am surprised you can slumber through that symphony. He has a complexity of style rivaling Beethoven."

"I think you exaggerate . . ."

"Not a bit," said Fowler. "He begins with the wind instruments, a slowly rising, sucking in of air which increases in sound and intensity with occasional gasps until it reaches a crescendo of percussion, snorts and clicks, and then nothing. Has he strangled on the bassoon? But no, the silence signals the coming exhale. One waits with anticipation until the slow, steady hissing releases the breath with the controlled patience of a cobra, moving across the strings of a cello. I rather expected his tongue to come leaping out of his lips."

Hudson felt pleasantly relaxed. Riding with friends brought back memories of many camping trips in New England, when people from quite different backgrounds, like this group, enjoyed the camaraderie of an excursion into the countryside, laughing at inconveniences and ignoring troubles. Mika'il fit in remarkably well, not intimidated by the foreigners. Hudson wondered about his background.

At the crest of the hill, they reined in their horses for the sweeping view in every direction. Straight ahead to the west, a broad wadi cut deeply on a north to south axis. "Below is Wadi al-Khalil and beyond are El Tîh Mountains," Mika'il said.

"How does the word *wadi* translate into English, Mika'il?" Hudson asked.

"It is a stream bed, but often has no stream. The stream may only be there in the wet seasons. And sometimes a wadi, like this one, drains so many streams pouring down from mountains and hills that it becomes a raging torrent, deep and wide. The power of such water is . . . frightening." Mika'il's voice quavered.

As they descended into the wadi, Mika'il pointed out dwellings honeycombed into the sloping sides of the hills. The wretched structures were barely distinguishable from the cliffs, only squat doorways and rough-cut windows suggested a human presence. When they reached the basin of the wadi, the vast size amazed them——at least a half mile across with the length beyond view, much more impressive than what it seemed from above. The western side rose steeply into the flanks of the high mountains. On the slope of the low, round hills they had just crossed, a few valleys pointed like green arrows toward the sand colored wadi. Within each valley, low dams constructed of stone and brick helped to control flooding by catching and redirecting rain water into pools for irrigating terraced fields and watering animals. It looked a fragile system, easily destroyed by storms.

What desperate conditions for human life, Hudson thought. Occasionally, smoke issued from orifices in the ground, and he almost tripped when he realized they were walking over the roofs of underground homes. People appeared out of nowhere as word of the foreigner's arrival was shouted from hovel to hovel. They watched with squinting eyes full of suspicion, not at all friendly. Women in dirty black dresses covered most of their face with shawls. The children, barely clothed in rags, hid behind their mothers, peeking out at the strangers. The only men in the settlements, old and emaciated, leaned on staffs to stay erect. Being witness to such poverty created an eerie, painful silence. Hudson had never felt so alienated from other human beings.

"According to my grandfather's grandfather," Mika'il said, "this wadi once produced abundant crops of wheat for Bethlehem and Jerusalem. Then the climate changed over a hundred years. Each year less rain, more heat, and the land rapidly turned from farmland to desert. Now, after a hundred years, farming occurs only where the side wadis are dammed, as you can see."

The wind picked up suddenly, blowing hard from the north. Mika'il watched darkening clouds sweeping across the western peaks. Hudson could see he was agitated, frightened.

Mika'il remounted his horse and shouted at the others.

"Hurry! On your horses! We leave immediately, before the storm!"

Hudson shouted over the noise of the wind, "Not without Sitt Mezrab and Amir!"

"We go now! They are Bedouin. They will know to climb to higher ground, as we must do without delay." Even before he finished speaking, the villagers were disappearing up the hillside.

Hudson was annoyed by Mika'il's insistence. It would not be the first time he got wet in a storm, and he disliked leaving members of his group. With everyone mounted, they climbed the trail leading up the hill and saw Anne, Amir, and their guide racing from the north across a high, horizontal path which intersected with their trail.

Upon returning to camp, Hudson entered the tower and knew immediately something was wrong. One of his bags was open. The map case at the top was empty. He stepped outside and called for Mika'il.

"One of your men stole my maps. It must have happened while we were riding."

Mika'il instinctively placed his hand on the dagger he wore at his waist. "I will find out, Mr. Hudson. Be assured, your maps will be returned. Come." He signaled the guard assigned to watch the tower entrance. "Something is missing from the baggage in the tower. Which of our men entered the tower room?"

"No one, I swear by Allah," the guard replied. "All day, I sat beside the entrance to the tower. None of our men came near. Only the man with white hair entered. I saw him enter and leave the room. He left with papers in his hands."

Mika'il translated the response for Hudson. "Do you have other questions for this man?"

Hudson shook his head and thought about the possibilities. Did Lockwood leave the tower with his own papers or with the missing maps? Lockwood's baggage remained in the tower; he had seen it. As he glanced around the encampment, he did not see Lockwood. He did see the donkey driver, watching and listening. He must have understood the conversation between

155

Mika'il and the man guarding the tower. Hudson stared at the old man's wrinkled face, stony and impassive, as he moved his prayer beads steadily through his fingers. The man slowly raised his hand and pointed toward a tent almost outside the perimeter of the encampment—a tent that had not been there in the morning. Hudson and Mika'il walked to the tent, flung open the flaps, and found Lockwood sitting in the midst of maps and papers.

"Get out . . . ," Lockwood began shouting before he raised his head and saw who was standing in front of him. The scowl distorting his face faded as he fumbled for words. "I borrowed . . ."

"How dare you, Lockwood! You took the maps without my permission. I am not a fool. It looks to me that you are doing precisely what we agreed you would not do." Hudson was shaking. The veins on his temples pulsated. He had just enough presence of mind to ask Mika'il to leave before he continued. "I made it clear to you in Jerusalem—there would be no surveying, no mapping, no reports that could jeopardize the expedition." Even while Hudson was speaking, he could sense Lockwood devising a strategy.

"Whose side are you on, Hudson?"

"Sides? What are the sides here? I see only you pursuing your selfish objectives, while the rest of us are trying to enjoy a journey to Petra."

"You must not think that as a traveler you are isolated from what is happening in the Orient, Hudson."

"I do not think, I know I am isolated because I have no ulterior motives, unlike you. I came here to paint. I am not in the pay of foreign governments who are carving out empires."

"Neither am I," Lockwood shouted.

"Maybe not the government," Hudson shouted louder, "but you are working for economic interests who push governments toward exercising power for profit. The desire for colonies is an unholy alliance between the political and the economic." He took off his hat and fanned himself briskly.

"Come now, Hudson," he coaxed, "let us agree we have different visions of the world."

"I do agree, vastly different!"

Lockwood glowered. "I see an America that eventually will enter the game currently dominated by England and France. In the meantime, I intend to learn the rules and see the targets. And then I will be useful to my own country."

"How patriotic of you, Lockwood, to pursue profit, engaging in deceit and subterfuge, all for the future glory of your country."

"Listen!" Lockwood shook his index finger like a scolding minister. "Artists are players in this game that is the decline and fall of the Ottoman Empire—perhaps unwitting participants, but nevertheless involved. Think about it, Hudson. When those French artists paint pictures of cruel despots and lascivious women, what kind of story are they telling about the Orient? Is it truth or slander? Does it suggest the Orient is a place needing to be rescued by European powers?"

"Look here, Lockwood, I will not stand here and listen to you justify your work as some noble act in the context of the world stage. My concern is here, now, and my desire is to get to Petra. Frankly, I think it would be best for you to leave the expedition, but I will talk to the others." Hudson snatched the maps from the table and stomped out of the tent.

He was muttering to himself as he rapidly covered the distance to the tower and ran up the stairs. He knew he had to resolve this dilemma quickly before it contaminated the journey. He entered the room and threw the batch of maps against the wall.

"Damn that man! He will be the ruination of me! I simply cannot tolerate his arrogance, his insistence on pursuing his filthy interests, his lack of, of . . ."

" What! What is the matter?" Anne asked.

"We need to talk about Lockwood!" He smashed his fist on the table. "The man has the devil in him!"

Fowler approached Hudson and placed both hands on his shoulders. "Can you tell us what happened, my friend?"

Hudson spilled out his story, unwinding his anger, from the discovery of the maps being missing, to his accusation of Mika'il's men, to Lockwood's attempt to justify his actions. He wanted to

157

involve the others, and he wanted to be fair. He had come to a strong distrust, dislike of Lockwood and wanted, needed other perspectives.

"Frankly, I am disappointed." Fowler said. "I believe he gave you his word to stay clear of mapping and reports."

"Yes. His word as an officer and a gentleman. Obviously, he is neither; he is a mercenary of the worst sort. What do you think, Anne?"

Anne placed her clothing on the bed and hesitated before she replied. "I want to be helpful, but the dynamics of your relationship are new and confusing for me. Is Lockwood or Lockwood's work the problem for us?"

"Good question," Hudson said. "I can tolerate his arrogance, but not his work which could jeopardize this expedition. He may have permission through his business associates to work in upper Palestine and Syria, but not in the area south of Jerusalem."

For Anne's benefit, Fowler added, "When Mika'il submitted Lockwood's travel papers to the Ottoman office in Jerusalem, the official was apparently concerned about Lockwood's involvement in mapping and surveying. He required Lockwood to appear for an interview before issuing his travel permit."

"Yes, he was under suspicion by the Turks even then. After this episode, I simply don't trust the man anymore." Hudson picked up the maps and tossed them on his bed and paced the room. "I have too much invested to risk failure . . . ."

Anne spoke her mind. "If we asked him to leave, we would have to offer him a guide to return to Jerusalem, a two-day trip. Either we would have to wait four days for the guide to go and return, or remain one man short for the expedition."

"Would that be a problem?" Hudson asked.

Anne moved beside Hudson and touched his arm. "In my opinion our caravan already seems short of men employed by and loyal to Mika'il, and that means to us."

Hudson bowed his head, looking down at the floor. He did not want to consider a four day delay, and after the experience of Anne's caravan, the loss of one of Mika'il's men also seemed undesirable.

Fowler offered an idea for a truce. "If he would agree to hand over his papers and to remain with the group at all times, could you trust him on that basis?"

There was a weariness about Hudson's face, a pleading for the situation to go away so he could enjoy these days, feel the serenity he needed to sketch and paint. He sensed he would be saddled with guilt if he asked Lockwood to leave. It would haunt the remainder of his journey. Fowler had offered a reasonable solution.

"Yes, I can live with that agreement," Hudson said. "Fowler, would you mind getting Lockwood?"

Lockwood arrived with an embarrassed expression. "I apologize for taking your maps, Hudson."

Hudson listened to the bland apology with skepticism. "Do you agree to give all your papers to Fowler and stop this mapping business?"

"Yes." Lockwood slowed down his Southern drawl. "Even though most of the papers have nothing to do with mapping." He turned and left for his tent.

Hudson calmed down to the point where he realized that Anne and Fowler were stuffing clothes into their baggage. "Why are you packing?"

"Mika'il decided we should abandon the rats and move into tents. The men have set up a tent for each of us."

While Hudson got his things together, he thought about the confrontation. He did not believe Lockwood would stop mapping, just stop making it obvious, probably store it in his mind. Hudson realized this was not a major incident, just one more in a series of annoyances festering around Lockwood's presence. He wondered where Lockwood had gone while they were at Wadi al-Khalil and what he had found that required looking at his maps. Finding Lockwood in the Hebron wine shop still rankled him; the discussion seemed to have meaning beyond its appearance. Hudson worried about Ottoman officials monitoring the activities of caravans; he suspected any of the Arabs or Bedouin in the caravan, except Mika'il, might seize an opportunity to sell useful information to officials.

Any incident that jeopardized Petra simply could not be tolerated. Hudson had staked money and reputation on his artistic accomplishments in the Orient, and Petra was the jewel in the itinerary.

March 1868 Hudson Diary, Semua
My Dear Katharine,

This evening I ate dinner in my tent, away from the others. After a quarrel with Lockwood, I needed time alone. It takes me a while to let go of unpleasant events, as you know.

When Lockwood first expressed interest in joining this expedition, I thought it might be an advantage to have another American, especially a man with previous experience and current interests in the region. Now I find much that is disturbing about the man. His defense of the pursuit of empire is particularly objectionable. America will not be well served by people of his ilk. He consistently goes his own way with no concern for how it might affect the objective of the caravan. In Jerusalem he was underground with Warren, in Hebron he was probably meeting contacts, today he took off with no notice in order to map. He often appears bored or uninterested in our conversations. He does react positively to Anne. Some men are more confident with the ladies— maybe he finds us intimidating.

The next days will be difficult, covering many miles, if we are to arrive in Petra according to schedule. Fortunately, the days are becoming noticeably longer. The camels will be here in the morning, and while they will be more suited to the terrain, Mika'il tells me they will slow our progress, especially since only Anne and Amir know how to ride the beasts.

Between here and Petra, I may not need much time for sketching; much of the scenery has a sameness and sterility about it. I look about with a feeling of dismay, searching vainly for subjects—a village unusual among the similar, a stream relieving the monotony of bare earth, a forest giving proportion to hills and wadis. Instead an unmerciful desert sucks up meager moisture, wind blows away scant soil, and the people endure the will of God.

Today the only sentiment the land inspired was fear. We visited a settlement where all the people lived in caves, some underground, others in the cliffs. I was fearful about the kind of people who would crawl out of those caves. I feared what they might want from us, and then I feared that I did not care about their wants.

I find it difficult to separate the people from the landscape. As a person, I want to care about the people; as an artist, I need to concentrate my feelings on the landscape—the empty, barren desert. Fowler may have touched on part of my problem. I am viewing desert lands with an inexperienced eye. The beauty and the variety here are subtle, too subtle for my designs. I am electrified by the monumental and magnificent, not by the subtle.

The day we travel through Wadi el Yemen might offer an exception. Mika'il is certain I will be astounded by the mountains in that region. I hope he is right. Be safe my darling Katharine, Your loving Thomas

ELEVEN

"What a cruel thing is war: to separate and destroy families and friends, and mar the purest joys and happiness God has granted us in this world; to fill our hearts with hatred instead of love for our neighbors, and to devastate the fair face of this beautiful world."

General Robert E. Lee, 1862

Charles Lockwood

The mood at the dinner table was subdued. Hudson had not appeared, and Lockwood expected he was in the doghouse. After dinner Lockwood sat alone by the fire, carving at a small piece of olive wood he had found near Hebron. His initial plan was to sculpt a camel, but he had cut one of the legs too short, so now he aimed for a donkey. The quarrel about the maps still rankled him. He resented being treated like a naughty boy, scolded and punished for borrowing a few maps. The nerve of the man! His knife slipped and sliced the tip of his left thumb. He sucked the blood away to see only a superficial cut.

Hudson seemed to think Ottoman officials were tracking them day and night, watching for missteps. On the contrary, as long as taxes were collected and bribes paid, the Ottomans ignored what was happening in Syria and Palestine. It was tempting to reveal the Bey's designs to Hudson, to see his face when he learned about the Bey's greedy support of exporting bitumen. The Bey knew roads were needed for trade, and surveys were needed for roads. Lockwood felt he was almost working under the protection of the Ottomans. Hudson was like most Americans. They looked at the Ottoman Empire and envisioned Abraham and Jesus walking the hills of Palestine or sultans in exotic palaces surrounded by harems. Both illusions were just distractions from reality. Holiness and luxury were in short supply in the empire these days. In the real world, the empire resembled a warped roulette wheel at a corrupt and shabby casino—still making a pittance for the house, but slowly spinning out of control. Huge profit opportunities laid in wait for those who had the brains and the guts to get in the game.

The artists, with all their grand pretensions, annoyed him more than the tourists. Hudson seemed a decent enough man, but naive. He was a step above the Frenchies and Brits who could take a slum in Cairo and turn it into a picture pretty enough to hang in your parlor. What kind of truth was that? Regardless of what Hudson and his artist friends pretended to be, Lockwood felt their motivations were the same as his, looking for a way to make a buck in the Orient.

The fire was dying down. Lockwood shivered in his thin coat and tossed branches onto the embers until the flames sizzled.

The French and British knew the score. He had heard their intrigues. Their governments were planted in the colonial enterprise and would extend their empires by nibbling away at the edges of Ottoman territory where control was weak. Egypt thought it was on the road to independence. Balderdash. The French and their spendthrift Pashas were leading them into a quicksand of foreign debt that would bury that dream. English merchants were flocking to Oriental markets like ducks on a June bug, exporting cotton and silk to Manchester factories and selling it back as finished goods at inflated prices. Personally, he applauded this as progress toward a vigorous international market. Meanwhile, Americans wasted their time in the Orient with sightseeing in Jerusalem, painting in Petra, millennialism in Jaffa.

Old Lieutenant Lynch was a great one on the millennial idea. Lockwood laid aside his carving and poked at the fire. The burning eyes and booming voice of William Lynch had seduced him almost twenty years earlier, when he was still a country boy fresh off the hardscrabble farm of his Tidewater Virginia ancestors. He remembered how Lynch had sold the Navy on his

163

expedition to the Jordan River and the Dead Sea with talk of science and trade and signed up men like him with the promise of adventure. After a few days on the Jordan river, everyone viewed him as a religious fanatic, obsessed with the millennial idea that Jews would have to be restored to the Holy Land before the coming of the Messiah. Lockwood doubted Lynch cared much about their labors to map the Jordan River; instead he wallowed in illusions about the location of Elijah's altar or how far it was to Cana where Jesus visited the marriage feast.

Despite the scientific reports he read before the expedition, Lynch clung to the image of the Jordan as a mighty river, like the James or the Potomac, a river that tested the mettle of the Israelites crossing from the east into the Promised Land. In reality, the Jordan was more like a stream. Even small boats could not navigate the entire river. How we sweated to drag that cursed boat around and through shallow and narrow spots, only to arrive at the aptly named Dead Sea.

If the Jordan River was a joke, the Dead Sea was a nightmare, a hot, stinking miasma, sucking the life out of us. Twenty days of blazing sun on a huge body of water no one wanted to enter. It was hotter than the hinges of hell, and we were like raw meat turning on a spit without enough fresh water to drink. The huge slabs of bitumen, floating to the surface from some primeval sludge, scared the hell out of us. Jones thought they were some kind of dead monsters. The bad old days, thought Lockwood, as he picked up the olive wood to chip away at its toughness.

He saw a movement out of the corner of his left eye, and looked up to see Anne approaching. "Good evening, Miss Anne, or should I say Sitt Mezrab?"

"Anne is fine, Lockwood," she replied, smiling as she removed her shawl. "The sound of the fire lured me out of my frigid tent. May I join you?"

Lockwood moved aside on the blanket. "You are welcome. I am sitting here licking my wounds after the skirmish with Hudson."

164

Anne glanced to the left and saw the light out in Hudson's tent. "Do you understand the significance of Petra for Hudson?"

"I know he plans to paint, probably the Nabatean ruins. Anything else?"

Anne gathered her robes in her hand and sat, as Lockwood folded his knife and put the wood aside. She lowered her voice to almost a whisper. "From a remark made by Fowler, I gather Petra is the keystone in Hudson's attempt to reinvigorate his artistic reputation, a matter of great importance to him."

Lockwood jabbed his knife in the ground and jerked around to face Anne. "I am not a fool; I know what you are hinting at. Everyone thinks I am putting the caravan at risk. I am not. For reasons I will not divulge, there is no chance of Ottoman officials in Jerusalem or Petra questioning my behavior, even if it includes mapping."

"That is not Hudson's perception," Anne said.

Lockwood frowned and looked at his thumb. The bleeding had stopped. "Well, he is dead wrong."

Anne felt the door slam shut, but she had another question for Lockwood. "Do you have a gun with you?"

"Why? Are you afraid I will shoot Hudson?"

"No, of course not." Anne giggled.

Lockwood reached to the left side of his coat and felt the pistol in its holster. "Of course. I have carried a gun since the War of Northern Aggression. It became a habit, a part of my identity. I also have a couple Winchester rifles in my baggage. Why do you ask?"

"The next few days, especially in Wadi Arabah, there are excellent hunting possibilities. I expect a suggestion to hunt would be better received from a man than from a woman."

"You are a surprising woman, Anne. You appear to be a subservient Bedouin wife, but I sense a strong streak of independence. How many Bedouin wives are hunters?"

Anne laughed, shaking her head, "Not many, if any."

"Do we need Bedouin permission for hunting?"

"By then," Anne said, "the Huwaitát sheikh with the camels will have joined us. He could approve it."

"All right. I will speak to Hudson and Mika'il tomorrow. Maybe I could redeem myself by bringing in some game for dinner." Lockwood knew he had not contributed much to the caravan. He was not particularly congenial and felt awkward around a group more intelligent and sophisticated than he.

"Thank you, Lockwood."

They sat together silently, staring at the fire. When they heard voices, they looked up to see the noisy arrival of Mika'il's men, returning with more firewood. The men laughed and jostled each other while they used a small shrub to clear a space on the ground.

Anne and Lockwood listened as the men began playing a game which involved gambling, fast action, and loud cheering. "I think I know this game," Anne said. "Come along."

Lockwood rose quickly from the blanket and helped Anne to her feet. They moved to the other side of the fire to watch more closely.

The half dozen men sitting on the ground greeted them. "*As-Salaam Alaikum. Ahlan wa-Sahlan.*"

"*Shukran*, thank you." Anne replied and described the game to Lockwood. "It is simple, you need 24 stones—twelve light, twelve dark—and a flat area of ground to draw a small square with 25 spaces. Two players begin the contest. After each game, the winner continues, the loser is replaced."

"What is it called?" Lockwood asked.

"*Qirkat*. It is similar to checkers, but much more exciting. I used to play the English version with a younger, distant cousin who so hated to lose that he threw tantrums and upset the board. He became a soldier in one of the Black Watch regiments, fought in the Crimean War, and later volunteered for the Southern Cause. He was killed in the Battle of Chancellorsville—that is all the family knows."

"A terrible battle." Lockwood folded his arms across his chest and looked back at the fire. "Over 20,000 casualties, including the loss of one of our finest generals, Stonewall Jackson, shot by our own troops, a mistake in the darkness of a dark day. I was in the medical tent when they brought him for surgery and helped to hold him steady as Dr. McGuire sawed off his left arm."

"Did he survive?" Anne asked.

"For a few days. We took him to a nearby plantation where he died from pneumonia. Dr. McGuire was with him when he died. He told me that just before Jackson died, he whispered, 'Let us cross over the river, and rest under the shade of the trees.' " Lockwood paused, and Anne saw him close his eyes.

"It was a war so dreadful even God did not know which side to choose. We saw our brothers and friends and foes at the distance of a rifle. Saw the fear in their eyes, knowing it mirrored our own. Soldiers could not tell their families how awful it was; those at home could not tell soldiers how much they suffered from the war. Letters saying nothing were exchanged and treasured, simply because you held a paper touched by a loved one." Lockwood paused, rubbing his chin.

"I worked as a male nurse for Dr. McGuire after I was injured in the second year of the war and declared unfit for combat. There was no training for the medical duty. You did what you were told, or what you saw needed to be done. At the end of a day, there would be a pile of legs and arms outside the field hospital, thrown from the window nearest to the surgical table. The only thing more terrible than passing that morbid sight on the way to dinner was becoming immune to the sight. It was a relief to return to combat after six months."

Lockwood stopped. He felt the tension in his neck and twisted his head from side to side. "A year later, I stood on a hill in Richmond and saw only insanity on both sides. We no longer remembered why we were fighting; both armies were crippled by disease, death, desertion. Those of us who survived the senseless violence and inhumanity of war went home to find more death and destruction." Again he rotated his head to each side, then looked at Anne. "I am sorry. I never speak of the war. I am not sure what came over me. Good night, Anne."

She watched as Lockwood rose and walked unsteadily toward his tent.

TWELVE

"Sherif [Hazza] said that he had often heard of the tyranny of the Franks towards each other, but never thought they would have sent their countrymen to so desolate a place as this. Most of the Arabs, however, suspected that we came for gold . . ."

Captain William Francis Lynch, 1847

Semua to Wadi Arabah

At dawn Hudson stood outside his tent with a blanket wrapped around him, watching the sun breach the distant desert horizon. Nearby a terrain peppered with rocks and devoid of any living thing was sketched by the sun.

Sounds of men praying and animals stirring slowly wakened the camp. The cook's son appeared with steaming tea perfuming the air with a slightly orange and spicy scent. It was good to be alive on such a day. Only Katharine's presence could add to his feeling of contentment. They had never camped together, never shared moments like this sunrise—a time of quiet contemplation when he allowed the earth to unfold around him, instead of rushing into the business of the day. These were the moments which gave him the strength for his work, not the times of recognition and praise.

Anne moved silently to a space a few feet from Hudson and watched the man lost in reverie. "A piastre for your thoughts, Hudson."

Hudson replied without losing sight of the sunrise. "They are precious thoughts, Anne, worth much more than a piastre. I was thinking of my wife, Katharine, wishing she were here, wondering what she might say."

Anne hesitated, listening to the end of the morning prayer and thinking of Medjuel. "Each morning of camping, Medjuel repeats a Bedouin saying. Love three things: a sweet scent, a beautiful woman or man, and everything peaceful and good."

"Your Medjuel must be a wise man."

"And your Katharine, is she wise?"

Hudson moved beside Anne so they could speak quietly and not awaken the others. "She was wise in encouraging me to undertake this journey even though she would not be able to join me. We have a young son, Tommy, too young to come or leave behind."

The words hovered in the silence around them. Hudson was on the verge of telling Anne about the death of their first two children, and he felt Katharine's presence behind him, urging him to speak. She found consolation in repeating, again and again, the story of the children's deaths and the difficulty of accepting God's will. Family, friends, and ministers had helped her through that wilderness, but they could not reach him. He had not been ready to move beyond grief. Now grief possessed his spirit and art.

"Was it hard for you to leave your family, Hudson?"

"Harder than I thought it would be. I knew I would miss Katharine and Tommy, but I did not realize how much Katharine was holding me together until the distance increased. She has a quiet strength in facing every crisis, so quiet that I did not know she was carrying me and my sorrow."

Hudson took a deep breath. "Our first children, Emily and John, died two years ago in a diphtheria epidemic in New York City. I blame myself for their deaths. I selfishly wanted Katharine and the children with me in the city when they should have fled to the countryside, like other families. My selfishness caused their deaths." Hudson's head fell toward his chest; his body swayed.

"The agony," he moaned, "the terrible agony. One day they were running in the park. The next day Emily lay in bed, feverish, not wanting to eat because it hurt her throat. Our doctor arrived the next morning and pointed out the bluish tinge in her skin and her raspy breathing. When he turned toward Katharine and me, I saw a face of despair. Day and night we sat beside her bed as she coughed, then gasped and rose up struggling fitfully for the slightest breath while clutching our arms, eyes desperate for help. The terrible sound of the inhalations was followed by a frightening silence when her breathing stopped for what seemed like hours. Before she died, we learned John was also ill. In less than two weeks they were both dead, strangled by disease."

Hudson stared into the distance, his lower lip trembling, and a few tears escaping the edges of his eyes. "It was my fault, my terrible fault. In the midst of a diphtheria epidemic, I selfishly, so selfishly persuaded Katharine to stay in the city, keep the children in the city, even hired a young woman to help care for them. Unknowingly, the woman brought the disease into our home.

"Guilt later replaced the agony; terrible guilt still pounds in my head. Katharine never, never blamed me. She kept reminding me that every choice was made out of love, but I know the choice was made from pride and selfishness." He inhaled deeply to steady himself.

"Oh, Hudson," Anne sighed into the silence. "How sad, how very sad for both of you." Anne took his hand, and Hudson felt the eloquence of her gesture. She brushed a tear from his cheek and said. "At a time of great sorrow and shame, a friend comforted me, saying love will not grow in a garden of guilt. It was a great consolation for me. Come, we will walk along the ridge, and you can tell me about Katharine and Tommy."

"Oh, I thought I heard someone humming." Fowler found Lockwood behind his tent. "What are you doing?"

"What does it look like?" He replied, as he stretched his chin upward and applied soap to his neck. "Called shaving where I come from." Dressed in only trousers and an undershirt, he stood squinting into a small mirror tied to a tent rope.

"But why? I thought you were growing a beard like the rest of us." Fowler reached a hand to his own face and felt the soft stubble on his lower cheek.

"Oh . . . itching too much." He wiped the blade on the rope. "Hard to talk when you are shaving with a straight razor."

170

"Right. Sounds like the camels have arrived." Fowler meandered off toward the screeching noises.

Each Bedouin sat astride his camel with the alertness of a hawk sitting on his roost and searching the landscape for prey. Their roughly woven black robes were cinched at the waist with leather straps holding curved, broad-bladed knives or pistols. Shabby red and white kafiyas accentuated their long and narrow faces, leathery and lean to the bone, stained by the sun to a coarse brown and lined with deep furrows—a rough and solemn bunch. The leader of the Bedouin, an elderly man holding a spear, talked with Mika'il.

The camels replaced the horses which required too much water and food to survive the remainder of the travel through barren hillsides and dry wadis. At the end of each day, camels could be released; they either found water and succulent plants or managed to do without. The horses belonging to Anne and Amir would follow the caravan, the others returned to Hebron.

Mika'il counted the camels and immediately complained to the Sheikh. "I arranged for fifteen camels, four for the foreigners and one for me. The remaining ten to carry our baggage and equipment as well as provide your transportation. You did not bring enough."

"*Wallahi*, Allah is my witness." Sheikh Saud raised one of his hands above his head. "We came through rain and snow for two days, and there was much flooding in the wadis. Two men were fearful for the safety of their camels. They deserted us, went home. I swear by Allah."

The deep frown on Mika'il's face indicated his disbelief. He whispered to Hudson who had appeared at his side. "For the Bedouin, truth and lying are like water sloshing back and forth with no writing to capture it."

"You have too much baggage for these camels," Sheikh Saud whined.

"It is your problem to load all the baggage and waterskins on the camels." Mika'il turned his back on the sheikh and walked away.

Saud threw up his hands again and shouted at his men. "Sort

the equipment and baggage into seven loads."

The men owning each camel argued savagely about the distribution of the loads.

"*Wallahi*, my camel sags, and you pick out the small baggage!"

"A waterskin for every camel, I say."

"Nor for my camel, she is lame."

"Liar!"

"Take that chest out of my pile, you cheating . . . ." The shouting man drew his knife and surged forward.

Mika'il grabbed the man's arm and wrenched it backwards. For over an hour he had paced and complained about the delay. When the weight of the china chest became the final straw, he opened the chest, seized some plates and smashed them on the rocky ground. "Now is it light enough for your boys, Saud?" The startling waste frightened the camel drivers into agreement. In complete silence the men allotted the chest and remaining waterskins equally among the camels.

Hudson whispered to his dragoman, "That was nearly a disaster."

"No, not at all," Mika'il grinned, "normal behavior from Bedouin. They enjoy competition and quarrels."

"Those misshapen black bags," Hudson asked, "what are they?"

"Waterskins, for fresh water—dried skins of sheep, clean and safe. From now on, we might not find drinkable water."

Four camels were saddled for the foreigners. Amir would ride with Mika'il. The beasts growled and snapped as the sting of the camel driver's stick forced them to their knees. Anne mounted first; she was the only experienced camel rider out of the group of foreigners. In one smooth motion she mounted the saddle and was balanced for the elevation. Hudson, Fowler, and Lockwood watched intently. Anne followed the rhythm of the camel's legs, moving backward and forward in a graceful swing.

"I suppose I am next," Hudson said. He managed getting on the saddle with fine aplomb and looked for the stirrups.

"Hold onto the front and back horns, quickly before it lifts," Anne warned.

"Where are the stirrups?" Hudson felt no security about his balance as the growling camel swung backward to its fore knees, and then forward to raise its hind legs.

"Hold very tight now," Anne grimaced as Hudson wobbled.

He increased his grip for the reversing motion, as the beast moved quickly from fore knees to extended legs. With much clapping of the crowd, he took a small bow. As he watched the others mount, he realized just how ridiculous he had looked.

"Bravo, bravo," Anne cheered. "Last part of the lesson. With your camel stick, tap the right shoulder to turn right and the left for left. Finally, be alert for the dismount which is more likely to unseat one than the rising."

It was midmorning by the time the caravan departed Semua. The group moved slowly for several hours to accustom the foreigners to their mounts. They stopped for lunch and rest in a narrow wadi sheltered from a swirling wind spinning off small dust devils. During lunch the question of the number of camels came up again between Mika'il and the old sheikh. "You have too much baggage," Sheikh Saud complained, pointing to a camel struggling to rise under the weight of the waterskins.

Mika'il was furious. "You brought too few camels. The agreement was for fifteen total! Let your men carry some of the baggage."

"These Bedouin are not donkeys. They will refuse."

Mika'il approached Hudson after lunch. "The crusty old sheikh insists we engage four more camels when the two missing ones would have been sufficient. He will send a man tonight to find them."

For the remounting of his camel, Fowler leaped on with such enthusiasm that he pitched over the saddle into the dirt, sprawling awkwardly to the amusement of the Bedouin whose hard faces cracked with laughter. Amir ran to Fowler's side, helped him to his feet and dusted off his coat and trousers. The camel commented with a full-throated belch.

The afternoon ride was a long and tedious descent through unremarkable lands into a nondescript wadi, somewhat sheltered from the high winds. Sheikh Saud stuck his spear in the ground, the signal for encamping, and the dull sandy floor of the wadi was soon dotted with round white tents, bobbing in the wind.

While the Bedouin unloaded the camels and Mika'il's men collected the firewood for cooking, Hudson and his group ascended a hill to the east of the camp for a view overlooking the valley of the Dead Sea. The men felt stiff and sore from the camel ride, and they groaned as they followed the nimble Anne up the hill to where Amir was waiting. After two days of barren desert, the dark blue, choppy waters of the Dead Sea seemed a distant mirage.

"What is the depth of the sea, Lockwood?" Hudson asked.

"Our deepest sounding measured about 1200 feet."

"Does this bring back memories of your expedition?" Fowler asked. "It must have been quite an adventure."

"Not pleasant memories," he growled. "I remember our first glimpse of the north shore, littered with dead white branches and tree trunks looking like the bare bones of a thousand corpses. The wind howled like a pack of hungry wolves. Following that harbinger of doom, we spent twenty-two days suffering from sweltering heat, blistering wind, and putrid stench."

"No moments of joy?" Fowler asked.

"Occasionally, a haunting sort of beauty—herds of gazelle floating up the western bluffs, the feathery white blossoms of tamarisk bushes along the shore, an occasional glimpse of the Crusader castle at Kerak, and always, the mysterious glowing of phosphorescence in the evening."

Hudson was looking through his telescope, barely listening to Lockwood's memories. He located the castle and pointed in that direction, as he handed Anne the telescope. "Did Lynch develop any theories about how this deep cleft in the earth occurred?"

Lockwood stretched his arms forward with upturned palms. "In my right hand is the science, and in my left hand the Bible. Lynch was steeped in both versions and sometimes managed to bring them fairly close together. Based on the volcanic character of the area's rock and the deep ravine our soundings identified, Lynch speculated that the sea sunk from an extraordinary convulsion such as an earthquake, probably preceded by an eruption of fire. From that point in science, Lynch picked up the Bible and stated his belief in the Scriptural account of the destruction of the Cities of the Plain."

"A bit of a leap to get to Sodom and Gomorrah, would you say?" Fowler chuckled.

"I definitely would say," Lockwood replied, scratching his sideburns and turning his attention to the range of mountains beyond the eastern shore. "The steep mountains on the eastern side are the Mountains of Moab."

Near the base of the distant mountains, Hudson admired watercourses and undulating ridges reaching like moving fingers toward the inland sea.

"Amma, will we go down to the sea?" Amir asked.

Anne looked at Hudson, who shook his head. "Not now, Amir, but perhaps later when we are in Kerak, on our way home."

As the sun began to set, long, streaming golden rays filtered through wisps of cirrus clouds, highlighting goats and camels grazing on the hillsides. While they watched the changing sky, two young girls with a small herd of goats and several dogs appeared out of nowhere. The dogs barked furiously at the strangers. One of the girls aimed a stone that struck the ribs of the nearest cur and sent them all yelping out of sight. The girls were each carrying a newborn kid. After a few minutes of staring, especially at Amir, they showed the newborns to Anne. She knelt to speak to them and giggled as the girls played with her braids.

"I can understand some of their Arabic. They live in a nearby village where most of the dwellings are caves, but their house has mud walls. The older girl says the Bedouin call them *fellahin* and despise them because they have poor land and no camels. They are like the people we saw yesterday in the wadi beyond Semua—their life is miserable, but they do not know of any other life."

"What is that nasty pouch around the older girl's neck?" Lockwood asked as he pointed his finger at the girl.

Anne moved quickly in front of Lockwood. "Do not point or look at it." Anne spoke in a low, firm voice. "I will tell you later." Anne turned to each girl and stroked the side of her face, saying,

"*Bismallah*, blessings on you."

Walking back to camp, Anne explained the neck pouch. "It is an amulet against the *'ain*, the evil eye. If you stare at it or comment about it, her protection might be lost."

"Another black mark on my chart," Lockwood said blandly, as he moved ahead, separating himself from the others.

After dinner, a few of the Bedouin sat huddled together around the campfire, smoking their hookahs. Their camels knelt just by the men, gurgling and chewing their cuds. Anne watched the camels stretching their heads toward the fire and stoked the fire with a stick, a habit which recalled thousands of nights among the Bedouin of Syria.

"Camels crave warmth and company. When Medjuel and I are in the desert, my camel, Oudiada, will stick her nose into the tent and nuzzle my feet, a hint that she would like to come in. Of course, she is completely spoiled by my feeding her cakes of flour and goat's milk."

"My mother used to feed her camel the white flower with yellow eye," Amir said.

"Yes, I remember how she liked the taste of the camel's milk after it ate the camomile." Anne put her arm around Amir and brought him closer. A sense of times past, days that were no more, hung in the air.

Fowler thought about Anne's earlier remark concerning the Bedouin and the *fellahin*. After a few minutes, he asked, "Anne, was the village girl right? Do the Bedouin despise them?"

"Despise is too strong a word." Anne looked up with a slight frown. "It is complex; much about the Bedouin is difficult for western minds to grasp." She paused and turned away from the fire, toward Fowler. "Bedouin take pride in their courage to live a life that trades safety for freedom. Thus, they have little respect for people like the *fellahin* who hide in their hovels, wasting their lives."

"Anne, dear, that sounds like harsh criticism from someone who showed such empathy for the little girls," said Fowler.

Anne's eyes flashed with anger. "Do not patronize me, Fowler.

176

I do not blame children for their parents' mistakes. Life in these desert lands is a struggle in the best of times. One survives through fierce discipline and strong traditions. You and I come from a different world where honor is given to those who have excelled at acquiring power and property. Here, honor is earned by preserving the health and freedom of the tribe. Here honor is demonstrated by actions, not words."

Fowler was embarrassed by his careless choice of words. "Forgive me, Anne. I did not intend to give offense."

"I know, Fowler, I understand. Sometimes I am rather explosive in my defense of the Bedouin. Westerners, and sometimes Arabs, look at us as ignorant savages, wandering about the desert in search of camels to raid and wars to wage. They have no understanding of the values and traditions preserving the independence of the Bedouin. It simply looks like a mythic past interfering with their present. They would prefer the Bedouin change, settle, and stop raiding; but the Bedouin will not change according to the timetable of Europe."

"Will the Bedouin ever change, Anne?" Hudson asked.

"Good question. They will eventually change because they are surrounded by change. But they will try to find a pace of change that avoids the destruction of their society. And there will be a few who will plant their flag in the sand and stand fast until the demise of the last sheikh on a horse."

Hudson stared across the fire at the Bedouin, a poetic scene of man and beast huddled together. He quietly left the group and entered his tent. He tied open one of the flaps facing the fire and gathered his oils and a paperboard. He peered out of the small opening and began to sketch. The red and orange glow of the fire illuminated the disembodied faces of men and animals, and the sparks rose like fireflies in the black night—a peaceful vision of creatures alone in a dark, mysterious world. No one spoke; they simply shared a space. The only sound was the snap and hiss of the fire. It was an unusual scene for Hudson to paint, and he was pleased with its intensity. The figures were rough, almost crude, but captured the wildness and solitude of a desert night.

"Good morning, Mr. Hudson." Mika'il looked up from writing in his notebook. "Four additional camels arrived this morning, and all the baggage and equipment have been loaded for departure."

"No arguments?"

"Only a little quiet bargaining over the weight of the water-skins," Mika'il reported. "There is one other request . . ."

"What is it?"

"Over there." Mika'il pointed to three people standing beside a donkey, "the old man and his two children are traveling to Petra. He asked if they could accompany the caravan."

Hudson hesitated. "What does it mean for us?"

"It is not unusual for people to want the protection of being with a larger group. They ask for nothing beyond being at the rear of our caravan and sleeping near the camp."

"Fine," Hudson replied. "Strange weather today, would you say?"

"Yes," Mika'il said looking at the sky, "it is unusually still and hazy for this time of year. Maybe rain is coming. We should be leaving."

Hudson mounted his camel and moved into the place assigned to him. The caravan now stretched almost a hundred yards—ten members of Mika'il's party, the Huwaitát Sheikh, seven Bedouin, the old man and his children, twenty-two camels, three horses and a donkey. The young boy rode the donkey, while the old man and little girl walked.

As the caravan moved out of the sheltered wadi, Hudson searched in vain for some improvement in the scenery. Miles of sterile plains stretched in every direction, the distant mountains invisible in the haze. Nor did the weather improve—a cool breeze added a chill to the increasing haze. By late afternoon the strength of the wind collected sand, and the travelers wrapped their hats with kafiyas.

Mika'il watched the darkening eastern sky. When he saw the wind picking up the sandy soil and rolling it into a golden brown rope moving across the horizon, he galloped forward to halt the caravan.

"*Khamseen, khamseen, khamseen!*" His cry echoed down the line of people and animals.

Mika'il shouted directions to the Bedouin. "Four of you, there!" He pointed. "Climb on the foreigners' camels and ride in front of them! Tighten the formation, and move two by two!"

"Mika'il, you have Amir? He will be safe?" Anne saw Amir's arms wrapped tightly around Mika'il.

"Of course, Sitt Mezrab," Mika'il nodded. "He is inside my belt."

He found Hudson. "It is a sandstorm. There is no place for shelter—we must keep moving or we will be buried." Mika'il was already coughing from the sand. "Wrap your heads completely, the Bedouin will be your eyes."

Anne screamed at one of the Bedouin. "The girl, the little girl, bring her to me!" Anne started to ask about her horse, Inam, but stopped.

Hudson wrapped the kafiya around his hat, leaving a tiny slit for his left eye. By the time the Bedouin mounted in front of him, the closest camel had vanished in the swirling sand.

The light changed from a dull, cloudy glow to a yellowish-brown soup. Sand whipped eyes, nostrils, and ears exposed to its fury. Camels growled and shook their heads against the blinding, suffocating air. The shrieking of the wind soon overwhelmed human and animal sounds. The Bedouin bent their heads and plowed into the ferocity of the storm.

The noise was unbearable. Hudson was disoriented by the roaring sounds and unbalanced by blindness. He grabbed the Bedouin around the waist to keep his perch on the stubborn beast which rebelled at every step. The camel driver seemed oblivious to his grip, concentrating his effort on whipping the camel to drive it forward.

A gristly knot of fear grabbed Hudson in the gut and crept through his chest into his throat. They were lost, separated from the group, swallowed up by the desert. The camel was surely drifting. He was shaking, maybe falling. He could feel another camel bashing against his leg. When would it end? Hours? Days? How long could they survive? Why had he come to this

179

abominable place? It was disappointing, frustrating, and now dangerous. Nature had never slammed him with such ferocity. They were alone in an empty quarter of an abandoned land. He had put so much at risk to come to the Orient, and now he would be buried alive in this godforsaken land. Gradually he slipped into a state of suspended sensibility with little awareness of motion.

Some hours later, the wind fell and the sand lay in soft drifts. The storm ended as quickly as it arose. Hudson saw camels, horses, and people scattered across the now peaceful plain, slowly moving toward a central space. Mika'il and Sheikh Saud moved around the circle, counting the people and animals. The old man, his son, and the donkey were missing.

Mika'il found Anne and spoke in English. "The girl's father and brother are not with us. I would not tell her. With luck they will find our trail and follow us."

"Amir, are you well?" Anne asked.

"*Wallahi*, Amma, it was exciting, no?"

Anne lifted her chin and clicked her tongue and then asked about Inam. "Did you see my horse, Mika'il?"

"The man in charge of her wrapped her head in a kafiya and led her safely. Do not worry."

Hudson looked frantically in all directions. "We will be off the plains before dark, Mr. Hudson. I have changed the direction of the caravan to find a sheltered camp more quickly."

As they neared the foothills of the mountains, hail bounced off the ground and a cold wind bit into their clothing. It was difficult to find a protected space, and by the time the Sheikh planted his spear, it was dark. Dinner was forgotten for the comfort of a warm bed.

March 1868 Khirbet el Raul
My Darling Katharine,
The desert is not always a boring landscape. Yesterday it rose up like a mighty sword to smite us with a powerful sandstorm. I feared for our lives, but all survived.
The wind rose again during the night and whistled through the cords of the tent as it does through the rigging of a ship. I was freezing, even with all

my clothes and both blankets, but I felt safe in my canvas shell separating me from the elements—an illusion I clung to.

An old man and his boy went missing during the sandstorm, but they appeared during the night. I heard him shouting for his daughter who ran out of Anne's tent to join her family. They settled into a little hollow lying by the warmth of their donkey. How I pitied them, but Mika'il said the character of these wild people was such that it was impractical to give them food and shelter. It would create a disturbance among our men who worked for their food, and the charity would cause the recipients to make unreasonable claims. I wondered . . . .

The young girl is much tattooed with lines on her face and an ornamental pattern on her nose, suggesting they are Bedouin. Mika'il thought it strange for a Bedouin man to be traveling alone with two children and only a donkey. They may have been cast out of the tribe for a serious infraction. The old man walks each day while the boy rides the donkey. The girl is the only one of the three who carries a load. There is no whining or arguing about walking or carrying. At a very young age, she understands that most of the work of the family will fall to her. Today she rode through the khamseen with Anne and then cried herself to sleep.

In the morning it was quiet, no wind, but quite cold. I opened the tent and was startled to see we are up against the foothills of an immense range of mountains—lovely in color and form—a dove tint with silvery gray streaks coats the rocks. Chasms form large, luminous indentations on the mountain flanks.

The young girl was collecting brush for a fire. She saw me watching her and pulled her shawl across her face. I smiled and waved my hand. She stood frozen in her space, and while I could not see her mouth, I knew she did not return a smile. These desert children do not smile at foreigners. Perhaps they never smile.

The camels are also early risers. Once untethered, they begin a search for food and water. They have an amazing instinct for locating what they need and returning at the appropriate time. They are ugly and ornery, but I find them endearing in some indescribable way. Yesterday they were worth their weight in food.

Today we arrive in the Valley of El Yemen, so well advertised for splendor by Mika'il. I am ready for high dramatic effect after this vast, dreary desert.   All my Love for you and Tommy, Your Thomas

181

The day did not begin auspiciously. The cook was sick from the effects of the sandstorm, and his son dropped a pan of eggs and collapsed in tears. Anne and Amir took over the kitchen and rescued the hungry travelers with stacks of Bedouin bread stuffed with dried apricots.

The caravan began climbing the hills which had sheltered it during the night and found itself in a squall of rain and sleet. Mika'il led the foreigners ahead of the slower pack camels through the wet mist, each person looking like a pile of clothing atop a camel. On reaching the crest of the foothills, the weather cleared and they descended through a pass lined with granular rock and outcroppings of sparkling white flint.

Emerging from the pass, Hudson gazed upon the finest mountains he had found in the Orient—high peaks shouldered by curved flanks with parallel ledges which striped the surface like ribbons curving in and out to correspond with the irregularities of the slopes. As they drew nearer, the mountains became even more imposing, and Hudson expected they would enter the range through the gap directly ahead.

He was visibly disappointed when Mika'il ordered a sharp turn to the left toward more barren hills and a rocky path which presented a slow and dreary ascent. Just before they reached the highest part of the pass, the caravan halted for the foreigners to stretch their legs.

For the descent, Hudson and the others went on foot with Mika'il. It was a steep drop through a thicketed canyon until they came to an upward sweep of rock rising gradually toward the east. Mika'il motioned to Hudson to take the lead. He moved energetically toward the rock edge, then stepped back abruptly— below his feet lay a hidden wadi that cracked open the mountains of El Yemen. He gazed straight down at a floor of golden sand encircled by a cathedral of overlapping mountains.

The steep slopes of the mountains were broken into huge amphitheaters, chasms, and ravines. Precipices and ledges were seamed with tints of rose, brown, purple, gold, and white. Slopes of debris piled up in the bases of the ravines. Many strange but grand forms were cut into horizontal and vertical slices and carved by volcanic forces to resemble gothic castles. It was a scene of fearful geological convulsions, resting until the next upheaval.

Hudson opened his knapsack and flung open his sketchbook. He drew the scene roughly, then turned to move down the path.

"Mr. Hudson," Amir shouted and held up the knapsack. "You forgot your bag!"

"Please, Amir, would you carry it for me?" Hudson asked. He did not want to think about the knapsack or anything, except the need to sketch while the light was favorable. For the next hour he ran downward from view to view, with Amir at his side, quietly offering him the box of pencils at each stop.

When they reached the wadi, Hudson turned to his new assistant, "You have been a great help to me, Amir. *Shukran*, thank you."

"Ah, you speak Arabic!"

Hudson laughed and shook his head. "Not really, only a few words." He was watching the men unloading baggage, looking for his paintbox. "Say, would you like to come with me after I find my paints?"

"Yes, yes, I will tell my Amma and be back in the swish of a camel's tail."

Hudson laughed again, watching the boy zigzag through the men and baggage to find Anne. The enthusiasm of the child flooded him with joy. By the time he returned, Hudson had his paintbox in one hand and the knapsack in the other. He handed the knapsack to Amir, and together they walked up the wadi for fresh views.

They climbed to a promontory which thrust itself boldly into the valley. Now there was time and space for an oil sketch, a more studied effort. On a fresh canvas board, he sketched the outlines of the towering masses reaching high and wide, encircling him with their magnificence. He quickly prepared his palette, and added dabs of black, brown, red and yellow to the canvas— enough variation of tint to recreate the bold forms and colors. The light was failing as he held up his sketch, a mirror to the mountains and his imagination.

"What do you think, Amir? Have I captured these rocks?"

Amir looked at the painting and then at Hudson. "Capture? Do you mean if I see the mountains on the board?"

"Yes, that is exactly what I mean."

"I see those mountains, and I feel those mountains."

"Bravo, Amir. Now we must pack up these things and head to camp." On the return trip, Amir led the way. Hudson realized he had not taken a good look at the boy previously. He was small and slightly built, but moved through the rugged terrain with quick, sure strides. When he turned to look at Hudson, his dark eyes, framed by long black lashes, shone with happiness. He was quiet in a polite way, but responded enthusiastically to each question. Hudson felt happy in his company.

In camp, they found only Anne still awake. The cook's son appeared and handed them plates of lamb and rice and placed chairs by the fire. Amir sat at Hudson's feet.

"Amma, color spills from pieces of metal, and Mr. Hudson scoops it up and makes it into mountains. Do you believe it?"

Anne laughed and looked at Hudson whose eyes were brimming with tears. "Yes, I do believe that. Artists are like magicians—making something new and beautiful out of almost nothing."

An intoxicating sense of energy and confidence suffused Hudson's body. He inhaled the crisp cold air and stared into the night. The dark forms of mountains lounged up against a starry night. Leaning back in his chair, he watched a sharply etched moon open a silvery window in the sky.

Mika'il stopped by Hudson's tent in the morning since he had not appeared at breakfast. He was not there. Looking around, Mika'il saw him at a distance, walking back to camp. "Good morning, Mr. Hudson. Not enough mountains in your book yet?"

"Never enough. Wadi el Yemen is unearthly, beyond imagining, perhaps beyond my power to describe. Not only did you bring us here, but you framed the first view of the valley in a manner that was awe inspiring."

"Your expression alone tells me you are satisfied, Mr. Hudson.

Nothing quite so grand awaits us today, but I think you will be pleased with Wadi Arabah. Breakfast is on the table."

Only Amir was still at the table, and Hudson sat beside him. "Hello, Amir. Did you have a good sleep?"

Amir replied softly, not lifting his head. "I had a good sleep, but not a good wake."

"Oh? What happened with your wake?" Hudson grinned as he took a bite of his omelet.

"I was sad you left without me to help you, Mr. Hudson."

Hudson put down his fork and extended his right hand. "Take my hand in your hand, and I will make a bargain with you, Amir. Whenever there is important sketching or painting, I will ask you to be my assistant. All right?"

"Yes, please. I would very much like to help you—and to watch you. But Amma says I must not bother you."

"I think we can manage."

Fowler led Anne and Lockwood to the table. "Well, Hudson, you are the conquering hero. We have heard all about your exploits yesterday from our young friend here." Fowler nodded at Amir who glanced downward.

"But you have not seen my sketches!"

"I think we can see the sketches in your eyes and the lightness of your step," Fowler said. "It was a glorious day for all of us. I was completely knackered."

"I want to be the first to register for a lithograph of El Yemen. I expect the painting will be well beyond my resources." Lockwood congratulated Hudson with a friendly slap on the back, leaving Hudson speechless.

Anne took both of his hands and looked deeply into his eyes. "It was a joy to watch you yesterday. Such enthusiasm!"

"Ah, yes," said Hudson, "the enthusiasm rose from several sources."

The caravan rode southeast from the mountains of El Yemen through a maze of low hills and out to a high plateau covered with sharp flints, ringing like coins under the leathery feet of the camels. As they descended, Hudson looked down at the desert of

Wadi Arabah which linked the Dead Sea to the Gulf of Aqaba. The geography of this vast desert was circumscribed only by the acuity of the eye and the shape of the planet. Hudson's chest expanded as he inhaled the grandeur.

Scattered about the wadi were dozens of Bedouin goat hair tents resembling large black beetles resting in the sand. The camps were part of the Bedouin's annual migration, a place imprinted on their minds from time immemorial, a place that had not changed materially in hundreds, maybe thousands of years. How strange to live in a wilderness unmarked by permanent structures giving a date to the continuum of time. Hudson wondered how the Bedouin thought about time. Seasons were essential to their livelihood, the lunar year significant for their religion. Did people talk about their ages, about the time of their ancestors, about the beginning and ending of time?

If the map of your world was unchanged by time, did time have the same meaning? Hudson was somewhat surprised these questions were arising in his mind. He had never given much thought to how other cultures viewed their world or the universe. Truthfully, he had not given tribal cultures credit for having such thoughts. Passing near one of the tents, he could see the few possessions inside, several women cooking outside. He felt he would never have any authentic insights about their way of life.

Mika'il steered the caravan away from the camps, explaining that the coming together of several tribes occasionally erupted into violence. He stayed on a south and east course, toward the mountain range of Esh Shera in which Petra was hidden. They arrived at their campsite as the sun set, the long shadows of the day disappearing into the wadi and the last of the sun highlighting a deep rose color on the distant mountains.

That evening the temperature warmed. The caravan had left the high plateaus and hilly regions to descend into a wadi below sea level. After dinner, Hudson and his friends lingered by the campfire. Several Bedouin were nearby, eating their usual dinner of bread, dates and coffee.

Hudson studied the men carefully, thinking about a sketch for later in his tent. He turned to Anne and asked, "Why do the men throw the seed of the date over their left shoulder?"

"Superstition," Anne said as she turned to watch. "Bedouin believe each toss of a date seed adds time to their lives, but no one knows how much time."

"Time is beginning to lose all meaning for me as we go further into these ancient lands," Fowler remarked. "I have packed away my pocket watch."

"Moving through Wadi Arabah today," Hudson said, "I began to think that human time had little meaning here."

"Maybe only geologic time has meaning for this place, and recent science is certainly scrambling that picture," Lockwood said. "What do you think, Fowler, of science disproving the Biblical timeline of 7000 years of human history?"

"No worries there for Anglicans of my kind. My associates have accepted the new science about the age of our world and the probable time of creation. Where there is a parting of the ways is over the question of evolution. In that timeline, Charles Darwin has lit a ring of fire in the universities and churches of England."

Lockwood leaned forward, his face distorted by the flames. "I think Mr. Darwin has grabbed science by the tail and given it a good shake." He paused for only a moment. "Why, even the great Alexander von Humboldt looks old fashioned. How about you, Hudson? Are you disturbed by the new scientific theories about nature and humans?"

Hudson poked a stick into the heart of the fire, burning to a bright orange-red. "Humboldt was my mentor in expressing the union of nature, art, and the spiritual. For his time, he was unique in being able to connect the great laws animating and governing the universe. Now he is gone, and frankly, I am confused by the new science."

"I think I read that Darwin was greatly influenced by Humboldt; is it true?" Lockwood asked.

Lockwood's knowledge of science astonished Hudson. Maybe the man had a more serious mind than he typically displayed. "Yes, you are right. Darwin did follow Humboldt in his early studies in the conservatories and herbariums of Europe. He sailed to South America with a head full of Humboldt's exotic birds, gaudy butterflies, and weird insects."

Hudson paused. He had chosen not to read *On the Origin of Species*, but he was well versed in the theory. "I have much admiration for Darwin's work, and I know change is inescapable in science. New theories will arise, but, even if true, we may or may not be able to integrate them into our thinking." Hudson rose from his chair, shivering slightly as he steadied himself. "Personally, I cannot accept a nature rising out of disorder, struggle, competition. For me, Darwin's ideas about the origin of species present a soulless nature, 'red in tooth and claw,' as someone said. That nature erodes the basic premises of my art. I can more easily abandon science than the spirituality of nature essential to my art."

Fowler took a slow, deep draw on his pipe before he joined in. "I do not see evolution as an assault on religion, but rather as a new and better understanding of a God who constructed the laws of the universe and then allowed nature to unfold in all its beautiful, awful, and admirable variety."

A long silence hung in the air, each person probably thinking about Fowler's description—an approach keeping God in the equation.

Anne offered an ending. "I wonder if this new science may present us with a God who is even more majestic than our previous conceptions. A God challenging man to survive not in a serene promised land, but in chaos."

With a mischievous grin, Fowler asked, "How did we get from pocket watches to chaos?"

During a night when the sky was ablaze with lightning, and thunder bounced off the mountains, Hudson slept fitfully. He dreamed of a mad scientist running through a jungle, collecting tropical animals, chanting spells, and changing snakes and birds into camels and gazelles, shouting, "Evolve, evolve!" He awoke laughing about a gazelle shedding the green feathers of a parrot. He enjoyed the laughter. Only two days ago, he had spent hours berating himself for the decision to travel here, and now he was happy with his friends and the mountains—and the feathered gazelle.

7 March 1868, Wadi Arabah

Dearest Katharine,

Almost three months have passed since we said goodbye at the dock in New York, and at least another month will pass before I return. When I left, four months seemed like a few turns of the calendar, now it feels like an entire calendar. I feel your absence constantly, long desperately to see your face, yearn for your touch. The thought of walking down our country path—arm in arm, the gray-white sycamores stretching their white branches into a blue sky, the last, lacy edges of snow creeping toward the woods, the soft clicking of the red branch canes, the silvery river winding toward the city—it makes me weep. I have vowed to myself—no more journeys without Katharine.

You would have enjoyed this journey, perhaps even more than I. I am so obsessed by the desire to accomplish wonderful paintings that sometimes I neglect to value what is not paintable—friendships, exchanges of ideas, each day's surprises, even the annoyances and disappointments make me feel alive. You would savor all of it, every day. Now, with Anne's arrival in our group, you would have a soulmate, a woman you would charm and enjoy. She is much older than you, about twenty years I would guess, and has more experience with the varieties of life than anyone I know. Can you imagine beginning in the palaces of Europe and ending in the tents of Syria?

El Yemen was even more than Mika'il promised. A sublime hidden valley within a cathedral of peaks, grandly monumental after days and days of little to paint. Strangely, the day also awakened strong emotions of releasing my guilt. I can only think the company and admiration of young Amr, led me to that new place.

Last night we wandered into a discussion of Humboldt and Darwin, and you will be relieved to know I maintained a calm, rational approach to this delicate topic for me. My artistic philosophy, my ambition in painting, is so intimately linked to Humboldt's concepts of the natural world. For me, it is not simply an academic theory to banter about for a few hours and then walk away. It is the very core of my being. As for Darwin, I do not reject his science, I simply join the ostriches by putting my head in the sand. At the end, Anne suggested the new science might be leading to a God challenging man to survive not in a serene promised land, but in chaos. I wonder what you would think of that idea . . .

My mind is full of questions for you, my darling, my heart overflowing with love, Your lonely husband, Thomas

Hudson shook out his night clothes and stuffed them into an empty corner of his bag. The smell of his clothing no longer bothered him, but loose dirt weighed down the bag. He pushed the bag outside and saw Mika'il waiting for him.

"Good morning, Mika'il. What wonders do you have for our last day before Petra?"

"Nothing of great note today," said Mika'il, "but I think it would be a good day for our Bedouin to see you sketching. We could stop at several places, get them used to the idea before Petra.

"Excellent," Hudson smiled and rubbed his hands together. "Will I be able to sketch the camels?"

"*Ma'lum,* of course." Seeing Hudson in such a fine mood, Mika'il decided to make a personal request. "Mr. Hudson, I respectfully ask if you would make two sketches of me?"

"What! What did you say?"

Mika'il stepped back. "Maybe only one sketch?"

"Oh, no, easily two sketches. Of course. I am willing to violate the taboo if you are. What do you have in mind?"

"I would like one sketch to show me angry and the other to show me peaceful. Could you do it?" Mika'il asked.

"Angry, like when you broke the plates, Mika'il?"

He blushed into a reddish-brown complexion, then nodded.

"In the afternoon, Mika'il, before dark, in my tent."

Mika'il bowed, turned to leave, and found Lockwood at his back.

"Just the two people I need," Lockwood said. "I would like to spend a few hours hunting for desert pigeon—the same birds the men often bring in the evening to the cook. Anne would also like to shoot."

"Do you have guns?" Hudson asked.

"Anne and I both have rifles in our baggage." Lockwood saw Hudson's eyebrows shoot up. "But we would like to borrow shotguns for shooting birds, and we need a couple of guides to get us to wherever we are camping tonight. You are welcome to join us, Hudson."

"My sport today is sketching. What do you think, Mika'il? Will Sheikh Saud allow it?"

"Shooting pigeons, yes—shooting anything else, no. I have guns they can use. It would be wise," he added, "for you to wear a robe over your clothes and for Anne to keep her head covered. Just in case other Bedouin are in the area."

"Fine, perhaps Fowler will join us," Lockwood said.

When Lockwood left, Mika'il said, "I will send two of my best men with them. On camels, their ability to hunt will be limited, even if they are excellent shooters."

Hudson remembered his bargain with Amir. After he dug his sketching materials out of his bag, he spoke to Anne about her plans for her nephew. Amir would stay with Hudson and the caravan.

The entire group started together and split about an hour into the day. Anne, Lockwood, and Fowler would scout the edges of Wadi Arabah for pigeons, while Hudson, Amir, and the rest of the caravan headed southeast to the passes and wadis leading toward Petra.

For Hudson, the morning was wasted in dreary, dreary hills. He tried to sketch while riding but was not pleased with the results. Relief from boredom arrived during their lunch stop at an oasis surrounded by coarse grasses and dwarf palms. There, Hudson pulled out his larger sketchpad, and immediately Amir was at his elbow.

He sat quietly as the artist sketched several camels eating, drinking, and resting at the pools. After a few minutes, Amir picked up a small stick and began to draw a camel in the sandy soil. The boy barely looked at the animal, scratching a precise outline of the camel alive in his mind. In trying to add details, he damaged the outline and erased the camel with a swipe of his hand. As he began again with a larger outline, Hudson passed him his pocket sketchbook and a pencil.

Amir looked at the white sheet of paper for a long time before placing the tip of the pencil on the page. Then he studied the camel he had chosen, held his breath, and set the pencil in slow motion. There would be no erasing. He looked up at Hudson after completing the outline, and grinned when Hudson signaled his approval. Amir then furrowed his brow in imitation of the artist and plotted the details. Several of the Bedouin came close to see what they were doing, but they showed no reaction other than curiosity.

Out of the corner of his eye, Hudson watched every stroke and remembered the excitement of the simple act of creation for no apparent purpose—the pure joy of seeing something outside and expressing it from within. Whether the boy had talent or not was immaterial. Enthusiasm leaped in the flutter of his eyes, and that was enough to release a soaring feeling in Hudson, causing him to wonder about the nature of affection. Amir offered a lightness lifting him above his worries.

After lunch Amir wandered away, while Hudson and Mika'il rested and chatted about the days ahead. Hudson watched the boy climb up and around a pile of rocks near the larger oasis. The boy waved, signaling him to come. As Hudson approached the rocks, Amir put his finger to his lips and Hudson moved quietly. In a small hollow formed by the boulders, an extraordinary bird with black and white wings and a crown of golden feathers was pecking at the soil with its long, slender black beak. Amir and Hudson pressed their bodies against the warm rocks, hiding from the busy bird who soon turned from eating to fluttering in a sand bath. When the bird sensed the humans, it laid back its crown feathers and soared into the sky with an 'oop-oop-oop.' Amir laughed, flapping his arms and singing, "oop-oop-oopy."

"What is that funny fellow, Amir?"

"It is my favorite! A hoopoe! Sometimes it catches a large insect, like a locust, and beats it against the ground before sucking out its insides. You must see that one day!" Amir seemed delighted to be teaching Hudson something of value.

When they arrived at their evening camp, Amir ran off to care for the horses. Hudson prepared his easel and palette for oil sketches and called Mika'il to his tent. Mika'il appeared in the finely woven white cotton galabiya and kafiya, the clothes he had worn in Jerusalem. He decided the poses. For the peaceful sketch he stood directly facing Hudson, arms at his sides, in his right hand his camel stick pointed at the ground. For the angry sketch, Mika'il turned his head into profile, drew his dagger and held it forward in a threatening manner. Hudson enhanced the angry sketch by changing the white galabiya to black and adding a red and gray striped robe. It took less than an hour to complete both sketches, and Mika'il stood as straight and still as a column. While the sketches were rough in appearance for Hudson, they were fine portraits in Mika'il's eyes, and he bowed with gratitude for the results.

"Mr. Hudson, there is something bothering me, but I am not sure it is appropriate for me to say."

"What is it Mika'il?

"It is about Mr. Lockwood. Remember when I went with him to the office of the Ottoman officials in Jerusalem?"

"Yes. I remember, about the travel permit."

"I thought he would be questioned by the official who usually issues the permits. Instead, he was taken to the Office of Omar Bey, Mutasarrif, Governor of the Ottoman Empire in Jerusalem. That was most unusual."

"You did not tell me at the time?" Hudson asked.

"No, because there did not seem to be a problem. The permit was given. But later in Hebron, I heard a strange report from Ibrahim, the man who accompanied you to the village. He said Mr. Lockwood knew the name of the wine shop he wanted to visit. When they arrived, two men were waiting for Lockwood, and Ibrahim was told to wait outside. One of the men was the Bedouin sheikh of Kerak. I do not know if any of this is important for you, but after the map problem with Mr. Lockwood, it bothered me."

"Thank you, Mika'il. It was right for you to tell me, and I also have no idea if it is important."

The dragoman turned to leave, and was opening the tent flap when Hudson said, "One question . . ."

"Yes, Mr. Hudson.

"The other day in Wadi el Khalil, when the storm arose—you contradicted my wish to stay until Anne and Amir returned. Why were you so frightened?"

Mika'il shuffled his feet nervously, hung his head, and seemed insecure for the first time.

"Are you afraid of storms, Mika'il?" Hudson asked. "It is no shame."

"Yes, there is shame." He raised his eyes, not proud and confident as usual, instead darting around the small tent. "I am not familiar with all the rivers and side wadis feeding into Wadi al-Khalil, but I know the danger of early spring floods. I do fear those storms."

"What is it? Can you tell me?"

Mika'il lowered his head again, searching for an answer in the dirt at his feet. "I will tell you, Mr. Hudson, so you will know that only something terrible can frighten your guide.

"It was back in the time I lived with my family, my parents and a younger brother and baby sister. In those years we were still among our Bedouin tribe. Spring was my favorite season of the year, the time when the mother camels gave birth. When the camel calves were safely delivered and began nursing, it was a time of tribal celebration.

"One year we stayed behind in our winter camping wadi after other families left for the celebration because one of our female camels had not yet given birth. On the third morning, we awoke to her birthing pains, and I ran to help my father.

"During the birth I heard a rumbling noise, probably thunder in the distance. The rains had been heavy and long in that spring. Within minutes the rumble became a roar coming towards us from the narrow western end of the wadi, at the high mountains. My father left the birthing camel, screaming at me to get the family to higher ground, and he rushed to pull the other camels and sheep up the steep slope. I saw the water surging into the wadi as I ran down to the tent yelling for my mother. My mother would not listen. She said the water would remain around her ankles, her knees. Clinging to the tent post, she held baby Aliya, and Kassim's arms were wrapped around her waist. She did not trust my pleas to leave the tent, climb to safety—I was so young. Suddenly, the roar of the thundering waves drowned my voice. I tried to grab my brother, but he would not let go of my mother. I watched in horror as a mountain of water raged and crashed on us."

Mika'il stopped waving his arms frantically and became quiet, sweat dripping into his beard. "I never saw them again. I was tossed up to the side of the wadi by the waves and climbed into a tree, lashing myself to a limb. All night, it stormed. The next morning I walked to where our tent had stood. Nothing remained, not a scrap. The floodwaters had scoured the valley clean of any sign of life. It was long ago. I have another life now, away from my Bedouin roots." Mika'il put his hand on the knife in his belt and stood proudly. "Never again will I allow myself to be at the mercy of nature."

Hudson held out his hand to Mika'il. "I understand your fear, my friend. There is no shame."

Hudson suggested the sketches remain in his tent to dry until the next day. Later in the night, Hudson made copies to give to Katharine.

The hunting party was not immediately successful.

"It has been hours, and we have not taken a shot," Lockwood groused. "I am beginning to think Mika'il sent us on a wild goose chase."

"Goose? There are no geese here, my good man!" Fowler was driving his camel with new enthusiasm. That morning the camel driver had displayed increased confidence in Fowler's ability to ride by tossing him the rope serving as a rein and giving the beast a slap. He was afloat on the ship of the desert without a tugboat.

"It is an expression, Fowler," said Lockwood. "A wild goose chase is a search for something you cannot find."

Anne was laughing at both of them—Lockwood with his silly suspicion and Fowler with his proud as a peacock riding.

"Patience, Lockwood, this is normal for desert hunting. The pigeons fly close to the ground, and they are well camouflaged. The men tell me they know the places to go and afternoon will be the best time."

"I think we should stop for lunch and revive ourselves." Fowler was always ready to eat, and these desert picnics were feasts compared to his usual fare as a traveler.

The camels were tied to stakes in the ground to prevent them from wandering, and Mika'il's men unwrapped the food.

Suddenly, Lockwood jumped up, waving his arms, smacking his legs, and turning in circles.

"What in heaven's name! What are you doing, Lockwood?"

"These damn bugs, bees or something . . ." He looked at an insect in his hand. "They have been . . ." he smacked another one on his cheek, "AFTER ME ALL DAY!"

"Not bothering the rest of us," Fowler remarked. "Might have something to do with the lotion you use after shaving. Who are you trying to impress with that scent?"

". . . for my rash," Lockwood mumbled.

In the afternoon, shadows of loose clouds moved across the desert floor, making it easier to see the desert pigeons. Lockwood and Anne found plenty of targets, and Fowler cruised serenely on his camel. In less than an hour they had a string of birds that would provide a good dinner for the entire camp.

Fowler salivated at the sight of the pigeons. "There will be fine eating tonight. Bravo, ye mighty hunters!"

"Lockwood, I believe you made every shot count. Have you hunted in the desert before today?" Anne asked.

"No. My only other experience in a desert was with the Lynch expedition in the area of the Dead Sea, but Lieutenant Lynch's rule was 'no hunting and no drinking.' Certainly took the fun out of a young man's life."

"Medjuel and I frequently take visitors who are excellent hunters into the desert. Usually they are quite frustrated by not being able to see the game, particularly the fowl which are so well camouflaged. It can take days to develop the eyes of a desert hunter, but you quickly locked onto the prey. You shot most of the birds on the string. You should feel proud."

"Thank you, Anne." Lockwood lowered his head as he spoke and walked past her toward his camel.

Anne was frowning as she turned to Fowler. "His habit of abruptly ending a conversation annoys me. Even when it is about something he knows and appears to enjoy, he seems to feel a right to drop the ball and depart."

"I read it as insecurity, embarrassment." Fowler spoke quietly. "He seems unable to take advantage of people reaching out to him. Bit of a loner."

Anne nodded, a wry smile replacing her frown. "I can feel Medjuel at my elbow, warning me about trying to solve everyone's problems." Camp was almost an hour away, and she dropped back in the line of camels to close her eyes and think about Medjuel.

THIRTEEN

". . . You have made it quite clear that you are disappointed with my decision to marry a Bedouin and remain in Syria. Time and time again, I have made careless choices based on titles or treasure or other trifles. Now at my ripe age of forty, a man who is gallant, honorable, and brave brings me a love that is simple and true, a love that tames my wilder instincts. Within his Bedouin tribe I am more fulfilled with love and labor than I have ever experienced. Dear Mother, you and England are well rid of this nomad . . ."

Letter from Anne to her mother in England

Anne Darby Mezrab

Anne swayed with the soothing rhythm of her camel's stride while her mind roamed another terrain. In straddling two cultures, she often imagined herself a lawyer for both the prosecution and defense. With Europeans if she criticized the Bedouin, she felt guilty; if she explained the reason for an idea or custom, she felt apologetic. Among the Bedouin, if she advanced European ideas, they often appeared envious or suspicious. Despite the potential conflict, she persevered in both directions—loyalty to the tribe and friendships with foreigners.

It was invigorating for Anne to occasionally immerse herself in western society, and being able to join Hudson's group for the caravan to Petra was a stroke of luck after the disaster with the Palmers. She had left Damascus knowing it was an ideal time to engage in an absorbing journey. The rumors of a beautiful, nubile Bedouin girl following Medjuel's camp had caused Anne to want some distance from her husband. Medjuel had been unusually faithful for a Bedouin sheikh and younger husband, but if a dalliance or second marriage occurred, she would be expected to accept it gracefully. Given her own youthful escapades, nothing Medjuel did would be even mildly shocking.

At age sixty, Anne barely recognized the lithe and careless girl of her youth. She had fluttered around the courts of Europe, leaving wounded lovers and delicious scandals in a flurry of publicity. It was quite easy for her to escape censure with the privileges of an aristocratic family and the grace of a fair face. All trespasses were forgiven, all injuries excused, at least for a while.

Her marriage to Lord Ellington at age eighteen accentuated her callow behavior. She was ripe with desire, begging for ballrooms and royal hunts. But her brilliant husband pursued foreign policy rather than passions. While he argued in the House of Lords, Anne wrote romantic poetry, then tumbled into bed with her cousin and bore his child. Lord Ellington graciously acknowledged the boy as his son; he did not, however, look kindly on her dalliance with the Austrian ambassador, Prince Felix Schwarzenberg. Their well-dissected affair sold stacks of newspapers and entertained many London dinner parties, but Ellington was not amused and divorced her with the blessings of Parliament.

Felix was her Lord Byron, albeit with a mustache and German accent. He proved himself a vain and false lover, and after two years and two children, Felix abandoned her in Paris. It was the beginning of her long pattern of investing love based solely on passion, instead of allowing affection and reason to be part of the accounting.

By the time she left Paris for Munich in 1830, her English son and her son in Paris were both dead from illnesses, and she callously left her daughter to be raised by an aunt. It was an unforgivable choice which reminded her that she did not deserve to have the pleasure of children. For almost twenty years she changed lovers and titles the way other women changed bonnets—a Bavarian king, a Prussian Baron, an Italian painter, a Greek count—some lovers, some marriages.

Anne's musings were interrupted by her camel kneeling for dismount in their camp. The ride had ended, but a memory still begged for attention. She moved toward the campfire to be alone.

Anne reached around her neck and felt the gold locket containing a few blond curls. The locket and chain were a warm, constant presence, something to touch, rarely open. Inside was a portrait of a face Anne knew better than her own.

"Is that your amulet, Anne?" Hudson asked gently.

Anne turned to find Hudson beside her warming his hands by the fire. "Perhaps it is. I have never thought of it in quite that way, but it does give me a feeling of comfort."

"Something from Medjuel, or is it presumptuous to ask?"

"Oh, no, it is not from Medjuel." She paused, silently remembering how deeply Hudson was affected by the death of his children.

"But the locket may have led me to Medjuel." Anne's misty eyes turned back to the flames of the fire.

Hudson watched her quietly.

"Before I traveled to Syria, I was married to a Greek Count; we had a son, Leonidas. From the beginning, Leonidas nestled into my arms and heart, and motherly love at last winged its way into my life. He was the warm sun of Greece, reflecting his beauty and joy on my days. He was the full moon of my darkest nights of loss and failure. At last a love, consuming my passion, returning my adoration. For six years his happy face and curious fingers stirred wonder into my life."

Anne lifted her head, and Hudson saw her face glowing with the memory of a child's love. He moved closer but did not speak.

"On a summer day, twenty years ago, while vacationing on the island of Corfu, my precious son fell from a balcony to his death, right before my eyes. My world was shattered. Why had I entrusted him to a careless nursemaid? I wanted to kill myself. I felt alone, with no meaning in my life. Sorrow and guilt were unrelenting. In the end, one survives, but never forgets. I bought the locket to hold his portrait and a few strands of his hair. The remembering is what saved me. At first, one remembers only what is lost by death. Eventually one remembers what was gained from life, however brief."

Hudson reached for Anne's hands and looked into eyes mirroring his sympathy. He saw her gift of understanding and knew only people who have borne the terrible death of children can offer that quiet knowing of pain. No need to speak further of the sorrow.

"Anne, you mentioned that Leonidas may have led you to Medjuel?"

Anne smiled, happy to talk about how Medjuel rescued her from the darkness. "For several years, I drifted in a dreadful sea of despair and finally landed on the shores of Syria. When I began my traveling in the spring of 1853, I was still a Victorian lady wearing a fur trimmed jacket over a green satin riding habit. By that summer, I was on a camel, following Medjuel's caravan to the desert ruins of Palmyra, dressed in a simple cotton shift with a cloak, much as I wear today, a white cotton kafiya, and an earlier pair of these yellow boots with pointed toes." She lifted her blue robe to her ankle for Hudson to see the shoes.

He had seen the lemony leather shoes on many occasions, and laughed at her tapping foot. "And Medjuel? What was he wearing?"

"Medjuel was much more handsomely attired as a Sheikh of the Anazeh tribe. He wore a striped galabiya under a scarlet cloak with a dark orange kafiya, and a wide sash wound and knotted around his waist to hold a cluster of knives and pistols, quite ferocious. I remember he was very proud of his red boots." Anne giggled at her fifteen year old memory of their first adventure together.

"If you come to Damascus to visit us, you will see our portraits painted in just this kind of clothing, hanging in the public sitting room. The only difference is I wear a long, sheer black veil, and my arms are slightly forward in what I call 'the subservient woman's pose.' It occurred to me that the German artist who painted the portrait may have viewed me in that way. Medjuel found it an amusing idea." Anne did not mention the other portrait of her hanging in their bedroom for Medjuel's enjoyment. It depicted Anne when she was a seventeen year old coquette with tendrils of curls escaping in every direction and a come-hither look in her eyes.

"Anne, I have another question. It is about Amir . . ." Hudson paused, "did something happen to his mother?"

Anne looked surprised. "Has he talked about his mother?"

"No, not at all," Hudson replied. "But when the two of you mentioned her the other day, it was in the past tense. And occasionally, a deep sadness appears in his face."

"Hudson, he is like you—healing from a tragic loss. His mother died in childbirth about six months ago, and his father is so bereaved that he is neglecting his children. Amir is the eldest son and feels especially wounded by his father's sorrow. You have given him a happiness missing for many months."

Hudson felt a rush of blood in his chest. "I expect we have helped each other."

The cook's son enlisted the help of Amir and all of Mika'il's men to decapitate, pluck, and gut the pigeons, readying them for the fire. After much grumbling and a little jesting about women's work, the pigeons were strung on long, sturdy sticks and hoisted above the open fire, the men taking turns at holding the two ends of the four sticks, and slowly turning the birds to a brown crustiness. While the pigeons roasted, the cook rattled large copper pans of dough, rolled the dough into balls, flattened them, and fried the circles on a dry stove.

Lockwood's skill had made it possible for everyone to put aside their usual meal of coarse bread and dates and partake of a feast announced by the aroma of roasting pigeons seeping through the campground like a fog of hasheesh. The prospect of roasted meat improved moods, and the Bedouin and Mika'il's men mingled more than usual. After the evening prayer, the trays of pigeons and bread were presented to the entire camp. Each member of the caravan found a place around the fire, eating Bedouin style, their fingers dripping with the juices of the game soaking into the bread. The two guides for the hunt entertained the gathering with descriptions of Lockwood's shooting prowess, repeatedly turning to signal their approval to Lockwood by shaking their guns in the air. Translations were shouted around the circle, creating an interlude of camaraderie. For his part, Lockwood seemed both embarrassed and pleased by the attention.

Fowler turned to Lockwood, wiped his mouth with his neckerchief and said, "You have earned the respect of the Huwaitát today."

Lockwood shifted slightly and gave a quick nod, but did not respond.

"For the Bedouin," Anne said, "hunting is both sport and necessity. The marksman who does not waste ammunition or leave an animal wounded gains honor in the tribe. I propose a toast to Lockwood." Anne raised her water cup and was joined by the others.

As the food disappeared, the gathering splintered into small clusters, and Hudson's group moved to their usual table for coffee. Fowler leaned back in his chair and removed his pipe. "It all seems very romantic—riding off into desert sunsets, hunting game on camels, feasts around a campfire, tents with carpets and coffee pots, traveling from summer camps to winter homes . . . "

Anne interrupted his fantasy with a sharp response. "Try to avoid romanticizing the Bedouin life, Fowler. Foreigners often make that mistake when they see my life which hardly reveals the Bedouin experience."

"Steady, Anne," replied Fowler. "I was teasing you. I imagine you walk a confusing path between eastern and western traditions. How do you describe your life to your foreign friends?"

Anne lowered her head and smoothed out the folds of her soiled blue robe. It was a familiar question, and on each occasion she chose between the fanciful or candid description, depending on who was asking and what was expected. "I could spin out a tale of Bedouin chivalry and hospitality, but I will offer you the least embellished story." Anne paused, raised her head, and looked at Fowler. "As you must know, Fowler, Bedouin tribes and even subtribes vary enormously. Each tribe adjusts its manner and livelihood to their particular landscape, desert or mountains, wadis or oases. Most will be herders, a few will farm or trade, some become guides."

"Do you mean guides for foreigners?" Hudson asked.

"Not only foreign travelers," Anne replied. "For centuries the

Bedouin have guided the traders moving east and west between the great markets of Asia and Europe. Caravans of valuable commodities need guides who can find the safest route and provide protection when trouble occurs."

"And when trouble occurs among tribes?" Lockwood asked.

"Sheikhs mediate disputes, in the tribe or beyond the tribe. It is convenient but not easy when generations live together in a cluster of family tents with a communal kitchen. Inevitably there are arguments and sometimes physical attacks over work, property, women. I expect we all know the mixed blessings of living among a large extended family."

"My granny used to say family gatherings were sweeter than pecan pie and crazier than bed bugs." Lockwood roared with laughter, slapping his thigh and shaking his head. "Sorry, Anne."

Hudson's right hand was tapping the table lightly. He was bursting with questions for Anne. "What is your tribe? Where do they live? How do they survive?"

A broad smile covered Anne's face. "So many questions, Hudson, but I am pleased the first question was not about how many wives the Bedouin have!"

When the laughter died down and more coffee poured, Anne continued. "Medjuel and I are part of the Sba'a, a subtribe within the Anazeh, a major tribe in northern Syria. Because of our breeding skills, we are known as 'people of the horse.' The leader of the Sba'a is Muhammad el Mezrab, a man who had the courage to approve my marriage to his brother when tradition argued against it. My husband, Medjuel, is likely to become the next leader. Medjuel is a wise and fair man in his dealings with me and the tribe.

"The Sba'a live most of the year in the badiyah which means the open country; it is not exactly desert, but it is a wild and unforgiving place, offering little for human sustenance. Our grazing herds find barely enough in years of good rainfall. Our badiyah is between Homs and Baghdad. With our camels, sheep, and goats we scrape together a meager life, protecting caravans, trading camels or goats for food, and scavenging the desert for the few useful animals and plants. In the summer the tribe moves to

Hama or Homs to be near the markets for our animals."

Anne paused and glanced at the faces around her. Hudson and Fowler had attentive expressions. Lockwood seemed to be asleep. Anne admired Hudson, enjoyed Fowler, and puzzled over Lockwood. It was a combination that resulted in intriguing company.

Hudson had not finished with his questions. "Anne, I hope I will not offend you, but before I began this travel I read several books by English and American authors who never failed to complain about Bedouin. Are Bedouin who interact with travelers as greedy and aggressive as many foreigners suggest?"

Anne was quick to reply. "The interaction between Bedouin and travelers is rarely without conflict. It is a question of expectations. The travelers expect the subservient Bedouin who will defer to all their unrealistic desires. As for the Bedouin, their encounters with outsiders have rarely led them to expect anything other than small recompense for their services and abuse of their customs and lands." Anne paused and shook her head. "Sorry. That was rather defensive, but I think it is common among people living on the edge of survival to be either aggressive or obsequious—which is worse?"

"And why do you think that is true, Anne?" Hudson asked.

"Vulnerability," Anne replied without hesitation. "Day after day, they live with hunger, illness, the extremes of heat and cold, constant quarreling and fighting among families and tribes, loss of animals and crops. Blood feuds descend through generations. Revenge becomes an annual event like the spring camel fair. Foreigners, on the contrary, appear to have easy lives, abundant resources, and tightly closed purses."

"Do Bedouin ever leave the tribe?' Hudson asked. "Do they ever choose a more predictable way of living?"

"Very few," Anne replied, shaking her head. "It seems the logical answer to us, but for most Bedouin the freedom of their life is more important than comfort and greater certainty."

Fowler phrased his question very carefully. "Has it been difficult to adjust to a woman's life in a Bedouin tent?"

Anne expected that question. It usually arose from her

women visitors. "Medjuel has accepted my need for an independence unknown among Bedouin women. I love and respect him so I adopt the dress, customs, and manners of the tribe in most, but not all, situations. When we are together within the tribe, I assume some of the traditional woman's role of taking care of my husband so that he will not lose face. I prepare his hookah pipe and even wash his feet at the end of the day. Other women cook his meal and milk his camels. When we are alone in Damascus, my girl servant takes on these duties. I honor and obey him in public among foreigners, but Medjuel knows my precise tolerances and never pushes beyond those levels. The compromises are often difficult, even demeaning, but without them we would have lost each other in a desert of differences."

"Anne, that hardly sounds like a fulfilling life for someone with your background," Hudson said. "Washing feet sounds more like a servant than a wife."

"My mother washed my father's feet every day." Amir's voice came out of the darkness. He sat cross-legged on the sand, beyond the circle of light around the table. "My mother sang to him as she poured the water on his legs and sometimes splashed it on his face."

Anne closed her eyes and covered her mouth with her hands. Fowler intervened quickly. "Amir, come and join us."

"Will I come, Amma?" he asked.

"*Ma'lum*, of course, Amir." Anne signaled him toward her lap and kissed his forehead.

"And the other Bedouin women?" Fowler asked. "How do they view you?"

"I am not entirely sure," Anne replied. "At first, I was ignored. Then Amir's mother, Yasmin, became my friend."

"My mother loved Amma so much," Amir said. "She taught Amma many things—how to dye her hair black, how to make coffee, how to milk a camel. It was funny when Amma squirted the milk in her eye."

Anne hugged the boy. "Of course, wives of sheikhs enjoy certain privileges. The life of the typical Bedouin woman is intolerable—long days of backbreaking work and neglected needs. I would not, could not, tolerate their suffering and neglect. My time with the tribe is limited by design. I move between our homes in Damascus and Homs."

"My father says Amma helps our tribe in many ways," Amir said.

Anne seemed pleased to hear that Amir had been told about her role in the family. "Over the years I have found ways to be useful in the tribe. The Sba'a are often guides for Palmyra, just as the Huwaitát are for Petra, and my language skills are useful for guiding. Because I learned to care for horses in my youth, Medjuel trusts me to be involved in the breeding, conditioning, and doctoring of the Sba'a horses. I have learned traditional cures from other women, and I add my slight knowledge of western medicine to be helpful to the women and children. The children need education, the lambs need help in birthing, Medjuel often talks to me about tribal problems—there is much important work to be done."

"What do you do for pleasure?" Lockwood sounded as if he had found nothing appealing in the description of her life.

Anne restrained a laugh. "Pleasure? My entire life is pleasure. We probably arrange our pleasures much as you do. We entertain family and friends in our tent or in our homes, trading information about the tribes and learning what is happening in the world. There are no concert halls or art galleries, but we frequently invite musicians and dancers to entertain at our parties. Our greatest pleasure is to escape to the desert, alone or with a small retinue. It is a time for camel racing, hunting, falconry, and running the salukis." Anne stopped. "Do you know the saluki breed? Amazingly smart and fast dogs. They can outrun even a gazelle, then block its escape until hunters are close enough to shoot. I have a pair—Mumkin and Mish Mumkin, 'possible' and 'impossible.' If they were here, they would be pawing and whining for those pigeon bones."

"If the bones were tossed," Amir added, "Mumkin would snarl, and Mish Mumkin would stay back until he finished. Mumkin is the male, and men eat first!"

"Amir is right," Anne said, as she looked at the faces of the men at the table.

"I know all of this sounds strange to you, but it is a life I have learned to value, even with the compromises, the strangeness and unpredictability." She paused and looked toward the sky. "At night in the emptiness of the desert, with Medjuel beside me and the dogs at my feet, I find an inner stillness, so elusive in life, so essential for my happiness. There I sleep the sleep I delight in, under the broad, brilliant canopy of heaven. Look around you. Is this not a divine pleasure?"

The stillness of the desert surrounded the travelers. Above, the crescent moon hung uncertainly in a cloud bewildered sky. The stars appeared and disappeared like the blinking of a lighthouse lamp.

"Do you ever miss your life in England?" Fowler asked quietly.

Anne sighed and hugged Amir, keeping her eyes to the night sky where the Milky Way laid a path into the universe. She remembered a favorite midnight blue ball gown, swirling in layers of tulle embedded with silver sequins. She was amazed to find that distant memory, summoned from long ago. "No, honestly, I do not. Here I am more fulfilled with love and labor than I have ever experienced. At last, I am using my desire for freedom and adventure to accomplish deeds which give me a feeling of pride." When she turned to look at her friends, there was a gentleness in her smile that did not hide the determination in her eyes.

FOURTEEN

"Whatever preference I might give in general to the European character, yet I was soon obliged to acknowledge, on seeing the Bedouins, that, with all their faults, they were one of the noblest nations with which I ever had an opportunity of becoming acquainted."　　　John Lewis Burckhardt

Wadi Arabah to Petra

The Bedouin had eaten well, and sleep came easily with the comfort of a full stomach and a warm night. Beside a fire smoldering with its last embers, a few of the younger men smoked and played qirkat, and Amir squeezed into the group. Mika'il, a roll of maps tucked under his arm, passed by them on the way to the table. "Put more wood on the fire," he said. The men looked up, waved, but did not move toward the wood pile.

Hudson was watching the scene and wondering if Mika'il would insist they tend the fire. It was difficult to divert young men from entertainment, and these lads had few moments of relaxation. When their elders were around, tasks and errands kept them on their feet—prepare the food, mind the camels, fetch water, fill the waterskins, fix the hookah pipe, guard the camp, get my blanket. Tonight had offered a rare interlude of good food followed by a measure of fun, and Mika'il simply shook his head and continued walking.

"Mr. Hudson it is late. Should we hold the maps until the morning?" he asked.

"No, no. Plenty of time before bed. Unroll them here." Hudson moved the lantern on the table to make room for the maps. "I am eager to see tomorrow's route."

Mika'il handed the large scale map of Wadi Arabah to

Hudson. Anne, Fowler, and Lockwood stood for a better view. "For the past few days, we have moved south along the western ridge above Wadi Arabah. Today, we descended here, near Wadi Ghamr and crossed this section of Wadi Arabah. Tomorrow we head south toward the Mountains of ash-Shara. Petra sits hidden within that range. These markings indicate the interlocking hills which complicate entry into the ancient city."

Fowler looked up over his spectacles at Hudson and raised a finger. "Does the map indicate the location of Aaron's tomb?"

"Yes." Hudson pointed to a peak slightly southwest of Petra. "Here, on Jebel Haroun, the mountain of Aaron—and that is the question to be decided. Can you explain, Mika'il?"

"Due to the difficult terrain," Mika'il pointed to the map and the mountains surrounding the Petra Valley on the northwest, "it is best to travel farther south before we head east. That route takes us near Jebel Haroun so it would be only a short diversion from the main caravan route for those wanting to see the tomb and view from the mountain."

"From what I read," Hudson added, "the view will be more remarkable than the tomb—and our last chance on this journey to experience a high peak."

"Will the camels be able to ascend Jebel Haroun?" Fowler asked.

"No, there is one section too steep for the camels," Mika'il said.

"Maybe too steep for me?" Fowler asked, removing his spectacles.

"You should be fine," Mika'il said. "There is a zigzag path on the steep part, good for walkers, but too tight for camels. The camels will take you to the pass. The old man with the donkey will accompany you and guard the camels. From there, it is a climb of about one thousand feet, including the steep section."

Everyone opted in favor of Jebel Haroun, and Mika'il laid a more detailed map on the table. "After descending from the peak, you will move through Wadi Saba'ra, ascend to a divide, then descend through Wadi Thughra." He traced the route with his finger.

Anne pushed the lantern closer to the map.

"You will enter the Petra Valley just beyond the mountain of Umm al-Biyara, and then it is a short distance to our camp."

"Can you point out the camp location, Mika'il?"

"If no other party has taken the grassy area near this western edge of the Petra Valley, we will be next to these ruins." He pointed to the Qasr al-Bint. "We should arrive about two hours before you. Our camp will be visible as you round the base of Umm al-Biyara."

"More questions?"

"Have you organized the celebration?" Anne laughed as she raised her arms in a twisting, seductive manner and jangled her bracelets.

Hudson sat opposite Lockwood and noticed him staring at Anne, seemingly entranced by her gesture. Anne was no longer a young woman, but she was alluring in the ways of a worldly and wise woman. He wondered if Lockwood was falling under her spell.

"Mika'il? A special dinner, music?"

"Perhaps a *mansef*, the Bedouin feast? I will ask the Huwaitát about music."

"Perfect," Anne clapped.

Lockwood sat, peeling melted wax from the lantern candle and rolling it into small spheres which he stacked like cannon balls. "I still think we should assert ourselves and enter through the Siq." He looked up at a wall of strained faces. "Bedouin have no reason to be hostile toward us, and we have a Huwaitát sheikh in our caravan."

Fowler replied calmly to Lockwood's persistence. "Remember the Huwaitát tribe are not the only tribe around the Siq area. Here is a thought about Bedouin hostility—in the first decades after Burckhardt discovered . . ."

"I object!" Anne said as her index finger shot into the air.

"To what?"

"Burckhardt did not discover Petra," Anne insisted. "It was never lost . . . at least not to the Bedouin," she grinned.

"I sit corrected," Fowler chuckled. "Now where was I . . .?

Oh, yes, after Burckhardt slipped into Petra," he paused and winked at Anne, "a few dozen foreigners traveled here, a few scribbled their names in the tombs, but no real harm done. In recent years the number of travelers has increased considerably, and Petra has become a double-edged sword for the Huwaitát."

Lockwood sneered and moved his chair back slightly. "Sounds like another camel load of excuses for Bedouin bad behavior."

"Not everyone thinks as you do." Anne grumbled. "Please continue, Fowler."

"A double-edged sword swings two ways. For the Bedouin, Petra has become a silver purse filled by travelers like us who are willing to pay a handsome price for the privilege of being here." Fowler paused to relight his pipe, but no smoke arose. He laid it aside and continued.

"However, the risks arriving with foreigners are significant. For example, not everyone arrives with benign intentions. Two weeks ago in Jerusalem I saw artifacts taken from Petra by foreigners or Arabs or even Bedouin. But certainly not by Huwaitát Bedouin or with their permission. For the Huwaitát, Petra remains sacred space, not to be profaned, and it is their tribal duty to protect that valley." Fowler picked up his pipe and knocked out the dregs, and then carefully looked from face to face. "We should all be aware the Huwaitát may judge us based on actions of foreigners who have preceded us."

"Good point, Fowler." Anne said. "If Medjuel were here, he would add that the behavior and ideas of foreigners—individuals and governments—often offend or threaten the Bedouin. As I mentioned before, our leaders know change is inevitable, and some change is desirable, but they must find their own way toward change, at their own pace." Anne stood up, yawning and drawing her robe against the chill of the night air.

"And lastly, because my bed calls, living in these lands, I constantly remind myself that I am still a foreigner with limited understanding of the perspective of these societies. We Europeans and Americans often speak with the wisdom of freedom and democracy, but frequently act with violence and greed. The Huwaitát may not have newspapers and books to remind them of the foreigner's behavior, but they have memories stretching back for centuries. Good night, my friends; I am off to dream about Petra."

Hudson watched as Anne, and then Fowler, headed to their tents. Only he and Lockwood remained. He picked up a stick and spread out the dead fire, thinking about what Fowler and Anne said about freedom, values, change. What do any of us know about another society's values, or even the spectrum of American values? He thought it unfortunate, perhaps dangerous, that the Ottoman Empire failed to rein in the pursuit of colonies. People like Lockwood had a minor part in the drama, but the major actors were powerful Europeans, sucking marrow out of the bones of an old, indebted, and shrinking Ottoman Empire.

"What do you think, Lockwood, about the double edged sword?"

"I think there are plenty of swords, with damn sharp edges. But I also think there is a lot of fancy talk that is purely and simply out of touch with the world today." He placed his folded arms on the edge of the table. "I am a plain man with plain talk who believes you cannot stop progress."

"And progress requires drastic changes?" Hudson asked.

"Usually. Empires rise and fall. These days in London and Paris the Ottoman Empire is called the 'sick man of Europe.' Sick is a generous word—it is dying. England is the new empire. France will challenge her where possible, and Germany will not be far behind, but England will win in this century. She has the economic and military might."

"You plan to benefit, I gather."

"Frankly, I want to be in the game, and I will play for any side that pays," Lockwood said, slapping the table and sending one of the glasses to the ground. "The antiquities, the tribes—all that is peripheral, insignificant compared to the prizes to be won. Does that shock you?"

Hudson rearranged his thoughts before he spoke. "Yes, indeed. We are both Americans, but we obviously live in different worlds. I have friends in the business world who might applaud your remarks. Make no mistake, I am a good businessman and expect to get a fair price for my efforts as an artist. However, I can say, in good conscience, I do not desire to gain at the expense of other lives and societies." Even as the words spilled out of his mouth, Hudson knew he was posturing.

Lockwood looked at Hudson, moved his head forward with a sly smile, and snapped with the sureness of a crocodile. "Who buys your paintings? Professors and ministers? Or, are they sold to the robber barons of New York City, laying down railroad tracks with Chinese coolies and hiring children for twelve-hour days in their mills? It is a tough old world, Hudson."

Hudson had no immediate reply. He would not enter an argument with Lockwood about ethical versus immoral business actions. He stared straight into Lockwood's face until he could no longer tolerate his sneering manner, then turned away.

Hudson groaned when he saw the sliver of light through the tent opening. Sitting up, he stretched his arms above his head, and inhaled the cool air surrounding him in his warm bed. Pushing the bedcovers aside, he reached to peek out the tent flaps and caught sight of the finest sky since Jerusalem. Toward the east, a splash of egg yolk colored light lay under layers of royal blue and navy. Hudson rubbed his hands together, warming his fingers with the thought of sketching. All the optimism of earlier years flooded into his mind that morning, readying him for the grandeur of a city carved from the natural world. He believed that finding and painting the spirit of Petra's landscape would restore his confidence, his reputation as an artist. He grasped these thoughts with the power of a hawk seizing its prey.

"Good morning, Fowler," Hudson greeted his friend, who as usual was reading outside his tent." Would you like tea if I can find it?""

"Yes, indeed, and a good morning to you." Fowler glanced up from his reading. "Looks as if the weather gods are smiling at us, Hudson." Thomas Hudson whistled as he walked toward the kitchen tent where he found the cook's son boiling water for tea. Not far away two Muhammadans stood on their prayer rugs with their hands raising up to the sky, reciting their morning prayers.

He savored the morning and evening times of day when the light crept in and out, changing the landscape dramatically. It felt like a daily eclipse, revealing and concealing the earth. He thought about his farm north of New York City and the sunrises over the Taconics, sunsets beyond the Catskills. He almost wept as he thought about Katharine and Tommy sleeping in their cozy cottage, waking to a late winter morning, Katharine stoking the fire in the kitchen stove and toasting bread for their breakfast. In a few weeks the fields would be greening in the Hudson Valley, and he would be with his family.

As he moved a chair next to Fowler, he noticed the peculiar book in his lap. It was almost as fat as it was long and wide because of a variety of insertions stuffed into the pages. "Is your book falling apart?"

"This shabby volume?" Fowler patted the open pages. "It is my Book of Wonders—all the ideas I collect for wondering. It began as *The Histories of Herodotus*, and then I added excerpts of early texts and drawings of the bizarre and beautiful, maps of remote places, lists of mountains to climb and rivers to walk along, grand and insignificant temples and palaces to visit, the customs of ordinary and elusive people—all the wondrous elements of a grand journey." Fowler looked lovingly at the leather bound volume, falling apart in his hands. "It has been my most reliable and entertaining companion over the last two years of travel."

"And your friend, Strabo? He lives in those pages?"

"Oh, yes, Strabo informs me about geography on an almost daily basis. He thinks geography is the great determinant of the human condition. Would you agree, Hudson?"

"Determinant? I am not sure about that, Fowler. For our times, Humboldt would counter with the interdependence between man and the earth."

"Yesterday, Anne remarked about landscape affecting the character of the Bedouin. Do you recall?" Fowler asked.

"Yes. It struck me as quite important." Hudson said.

"It caused me to think back to Strabo's theories. For him, it was not enough for the geographer to simply draw maps; he must suggest why and how places existed. He felt it was through natural features—mountains, rivers, seas, oceans—that we gain a clear idea of nations, cities, and peoples." Fowler paused and looked at the bowl of his pipe.

"In other words, societies have advantages and disadvantages, some from nature, some from human effort. But the geographer knows nature is the more permanent of the two determinants. The human design will change or disappear. And then something else clicked for me. The Bedouin's sense of freedom arises from being more dependent on the natural world than on the world of human design."

"Quite contrary to our societies' ideas about freedom," Hudson said.

"Yes, we tend to believe freedom arises out of political systems, and nature must adjust to man. I wonder who will be proven right?"

Fowler turned again to his book. "This morning I have been reading about God's curse on Idumea, the name of this land before the Nabateans arrived."

"A curse? Now we have to deal with a curse? Do tell me."

"I would be delighted." He cleared his throat. "These bits are from Isaiah 34:7-15, King James version, 1611."

"And the unicorns shall come down with them, and the bullocks with the bulls; and their land shall be soaked with blood, and their dust made fat with fatness. For it is the day of the LORD'S vengeance, and the year of recompenses for the controversy of Zion. And the streams thereof shall be turned into pitch, and the dust thereof into brimstone, and the land thereof shall become burning pitch. It shall not be quenched night nor day; the smoke thereof shall go up for ever: from generation to generation it shall lie waste; none shall pass through it for ever and ever. But the cormorant and the bittern shall possess it; the owl also and the raven shall dwell in it: and He shall stretch out upon it the line of confusion, and the stones of emptiness. They shall call the nobles thereof to the kingdom, but none shall be there, and all her princes shall be nothing. And thorns shall come up in her palaces, nettles and brambles in the fortresses thereof: and it shall be an habitation of dragons, and a court for owls. The wild beasts of the desert shall also meet with the wild

beasts of the island, and the satyr shall cry to his fellow; the screech owl also shall rest there, and find for herself a place of rest. There shall the great owl make her nest, and lay, and hatch, and gather under her shadow: there shall the vultures also be gathered, every one with her mate."

Fowler peered over his spectacles at Hudson. "Sounds like there will be quite a crowd waiting for us in Petra."

"Do you think those birds are the minions of the Bedouin?" Hudson asked. "Will they reveal our presence to the lords of the Huwaitát? Hark! Do you hear the cries of the wild beasts?" Hudson stopped to listen. The soft purring of mourning doves in an acacia tree was the only sound. Fowler chuckled himself into a fit of laughter, almost causing the cook's son to upset the cups of tea.

Within the hour, the camp bustled toward departure. The foreigners' camels waited with their loads, mysterious musings written on their faces.

Amir was arguing with Anne about the trip to Jebel Haroun. "I want to go with the Bedouin. It is more fun for me." Amir pouted and stamped his foot. "My father told me to stay with the Bedouin, if possible."

"Amir, are you telling the truth?" Anne held Amir's shoulder and lifted his chin.

"*Maleesh*, never mind. He wants me to be a man, a Bedouin man."

Anne masked her smile. "Well, that part I believe. All right, but you must stay close to Mika'il. Promise me, Amir."

Amir stood straight and put his hand to his heart. "I promise."

Mika'il started Hudson's group on their camels, following the old man and donkey, even before the tents were down. With the detour to Jebel Haroun, they had a longer day ahead than the rest of the caravan, and Mika'il assumed Hudson wanted to sketch on the approach into Petra, further lengthening their day. Before Hudson mounted his camel, Mika'il reminded him of the approximate locations of Snake Monument and the Umayyad caravanserai, places that might interest the group while they were descending Wadi Thughra.

Anne's camel stayed close to the donkey as their path corkscrewed through an ancient fault pointing toward Jebel Haroun. The camel nudged the donkey, trying to get ahead, and bellowed when Anne jerked its head back. A moment later, the camel bared its teeth and nipped the left flank of the donkey. The raspy braying of the donkey irritated the camel who answered with deep growls until the old man shouted and charged ahead to protect his donkey.

During the ascent Hudson was happily distracted by a newly intriguing landscape with miniature pleasures tucked around the twisting path. Orange lizards baked on warm stones, and pencil thin snakes slithered away from the camel's feet. In crevices along the cliffs, clusters of pink flowers rose above olive gray foliage, and song birds twittered from their perches. The landscape quickened with signs of life, the hand of God reaching into a desolate landscape. In the Americas, he saw the hand of God everywhere—in the architecture of mountains soaring mightily close to the heavens, in volcanoes rumbling and erupting with fires of destruction, in waterfalls and rivers healing the lands, and in valleys and forests nurturing human life. The voice of God resounded in those sublime places. Here the voice spoke as softly as an old man whispering his prayers.

Following the old man and donkey, they edged along a path cut from an overhanging cliff and came upon a scene of light brown sandstone pinnacles capped with a layer of white limestone. One more turn deposited them at the pass where they dismounted and tied the camel ropes to outcroppings of rocks. Looking due east, they gazed upon a tremendous canyon. The view was almost as grand as the Yemen Valley, but quite different. Yemen was a flat, broad valley with pyramidal mountains floating just above the sand like solitary islands. Here, knobby peaks rose above gorges lined with shrubbery and jagged rocks of dark purple and brown hues. Sculpted precipices plunged into ravines beyond the reach of light. In the distance were several ranges of oddly folded mountains, resembling stacked loaves of braided bread.

Fowler stared nervously at the steep cliff below his feet. "This precipitous drop, I trust, is not our route to Petra."

"No. Not to my taste either," Hudson replied. "Our path down begins where the camels are tied, and it appears on the map to be a quite gradual descent to Wadi Saba'ra. But first we head up the trail on the left to Jebel Haroun."

They stopped for a quick lunch, and Lockwood again brought up the subject of access to Petra. "We are on the brink of entering Petra, and it seems to me we should have a backup plan in case we are stopped by the Bedouin. Maybe it is my military training. I typically have an alternate plan."

"In case you did not listen, Lockwood," Anne said, "Mika'il and the caravan will arrive in Petra hours ahead of us. They will be setting up the tents in the valley without any foreigners along to cause concerns. I expect he was delighted when we decided on Jebel Haroun. By the time we arrive at Petra, it will be twilight, and we will be almost invisible until the morning. Quite brilliant, yes?"

Hudson watched Lockwood react favorably to Anne's reasoning. He knew if he had made the same remarks, Lockwood would have found some flaw. Anne had a noticeably calming effect on the feisty man.

A short trudge up a gradually rising track and several sets of steps hacked out of the mountainside led to the plain white mosque on the summit which marked the tomb of Aaron, known as Haroun to Muhammadans. The topography of their journey was spread before them on this living map. Curving around them on the north, east, and south was the wilderness of ash-Shara, an ancient mountain chain of craggy walls. To the west, they looked down to the basin of Wadi Arabah where they had camped the previous night, and across to the jagged ridges of Tîh, and the faintly blue hills of Palestine. To the northeast, Lockwood spotted a sculptured rock form on the face of a distant, lower peak. Hudson took out his telescope.

"I think it is the temple known as the Monastery. Burckhardt had it on his map, but did not reach it. Have a look, Fowler."

Handing the telescope to Fowler, Hudson pulled his small sketchbook out of his pocket.

"Yes," Fowler agreed. "I remember it from the Roberts lithograph; He called it El Deir. Quite similar to El Khasneh, perhaps a little less elaborate in decoration."

When they returned to the pass, the old man reported that Mika'il and the caravan had passed through about an hour earlier. While the others mounted their camels, Hudson dusted off a geometric carving in the yellowish sandstone. It was a face, outlined in a rectangular block, quite flat except for the heavy eyebrows over eyelids linked to the nose and a prominent mouth. He made a quick sketch and almost finished it when suddenly the old man was jumping out of his sandals, waving his arms, and shouting at Anne in Arabic.

"He says making a picture is unsafe; we will be fired at."

Hudson stopped his sketch and looked around. No one for miles, but fear drained and contorted the old man's face. He had assumed a great responsibility in guiding them for the day and had behaved well. Hudson put the sketchbook in his pocket and mounted the camel.

Their descent took them abruptly away from high, hard, jagged mountains toward rounded, soft sandstone hills where slashes of rose colored rock leaped out of dark cliffs. Below them Wadi Saba'ra spread into a wide valley with active streams and crop plantings near black Bedouin tents. After days of seeing little or no vegetation, a small olive grove seemed to Hudson as refreshing as a forest. The wadi narrowed as it rose toward its northern end; caves and rough tombs carved out of the cliffs became more visible. The almost horizontal growth of cedar trees suggested strong north winds roaring down the valley, but that day the air was still. As they ascended the northern end of the wadi they came to a narrow divide where any rain runoff from the high mountains spilled either south to Wadi Saba'ra or north to Wadi Thughra and Petra.

From the high point, Hudson looked down at a jumble of boulders to the right and straight ahead at a ravine like a deep knife cut through wet clay. After the pastoral appearance of Wadi Saba'ra, the wildness of Thughra surprised him. "According to Mika'il, we have two choices for descending Wadi Thughra. There is a track on our left that hugs the western cliff above the ravine for about two miles before moving toward the center where the wadi starts to flatten."

"The track looks easy for camels. Must be how Mika'il's group went," Fowler said.

Lockwood searched the right side of the wadi with Hudson's telescope. "The boulders beside the eastern cliff appeal to me."

"There is no defined path through the boulders," Hudson explained, "but Mika'il said it was not difficult to make one's way to the Snake Monument, near the end of the boulders."

"I would like very much to see the snake rising up from the rock," Anne said.

"It sounds like a good adventure to me, and we have about four hours until twilight. It is only three miles down Thughra to the camp." Hudson looked at the others for their reaction.

"Sounds good to me," Fowler said. "But the dear old camels?"

"Mika'il said we could send the camels down the track with the old man and donkey. The man would wait at the caravanserai, near where the track crosses the ravine." Hudson pointed to the location of the caravanserai on the map.

Lockwood peered at the small mark. "Is it a building?"

"Yes. One of the many structures built centuries ago from Constantinople to Kabul to lodge travelers and trade goods," Fowler explained. "The Nabateans used them to keep the riffraff, strangers and traders, out of the main part of Petra."

Anne translated Hudson's plan for the old man who had been told of this possibility by Mika'il. "*Ya, Sitt*. First, I take the camels to a stream for water. Then I wait at caravanserai. *Ma'asalama*."

Hudson and Lockwood scouted the boulders before settling on a starting point. The enormous egg-shaped rocks were stacked and balanced into a labyrinthine maze that invited going astray. Lockwood offered to lead, and the others stayed close behind as they squeezed and crawled through the gaps. It only seemed dangerous when they glanced backwards at what they had just navigated. The sunlight bounced off the upper reaches of the eastern cliff, making it possible to keep their direction fairly steady. Within an hour they were near the cliff and could see a sculpture rising slightly above the boulders. They continued the descent toward what they thought was Snake Monument until the height of the boulders blocked their sight line, then decided to climb a section of the cliff jutting into the wadi for a better view.

After a bit of wandering toward the cliff, Anne looked up and saw the snake emerging out of a huge block of stone. "Snake above!" She shouted and pointed at the head of a reptile resting on its coils.

"What do you suppose it represents, Fowler?" Hudson asked.

"Snake figures are not unusual for the Nabateans, I gather. But this sculpture in this place has never been understood. It could have been an altar for sacrifice or a warning for people entering from this direction . . ."

Before Fowler finished, there was a rumbling from the cliff above them and an avalanche of rocks tumbled in their direction. The rocks hit the ground just ahead of them, throwing up a cloud of dust and pebbles. Looking upward, they saw young boys rolling large rocks toward the cliff edge. They were rooted to the ground by disbelief. When larger rocks were pushed over the edge, the cliffside shook, dislodging more rocks that roared down the precipice. Lockwood grabbed Anne's arm and ran toward a small cave. Hudson and Fowler headed in the other direction but too slowly. Fowler's leg was struck by one of the rocks, and he fell to the ground. Dodging some moving rocks, Hudson was immediately beside him.

Anne left the cave and leaped up on a flat rock, screaming at the boys. "*Khalas hela, khalas hela, khalas!* Stop it immediately!" At the sound of the command in Arabic, they stopped, turned, and disappeared.

Fowler raised his torn pants leg, already bloodied, trying to see the extent of the injury. Hudson stood beside him and scanned the cliff for further activity until Anne and Lockwood arrived.

"Only a surface scratch, no need to bother." Fowler had barely looked at the wound before he tried to cover it again.

"Nonsense, Fowler. Let me see." Anne gently slipped the pant leg up. The area of the wound was bloody, dirty, and slightly swollen. She pressed softly near the cut to allow her to see the depth of the wound. "More than a scratch, but not terribly deep. A little antiseptic and good bandages should do it—all of which I have in my baggage. We need to get you up to see if you can put weight on the leg without pain."

Lockwood and Hudson raised Fowler to his feet. As he shifted his weight to the injured leg, he winced. He looked up at Anne through his dusty spectacles and said, "Not too bad."

Hudson shook his head with a wry grin. "Anne, Lockwood and I can be Fowler's crutches to keep the weight off the leg. That might slow the bleeding and control the swelling."

In less than half an hour they made their way to the caravanserai where the old man was dozing in the late afternoon sun, the donkey beside him and the camels tied to a stone obelisk by the road.

The caravanserai was a partially roofed building, offering protection and a relatively clean place to sit. There was a stream nearby, and Anne suggested they get water to clean the dirt from around the wound. Hudson and Lockwood placed Fowler on the broad ledge around the inside perimeter.

Anne left, intending to wake the old man and send him for water. Instead, she saw a crowd of Bedouin women and children running toward her. When they saw Anne, they stopped and began ululating, the high-pitched wailing sound so familiar among Bedouin at times of sorrow and celebration. It always unnerved her—too awful for lamenting, too shrill and constant to create a celebratory mood.

Out of the corner of her eye Anne saw a movement. One of the older boys picked up a rock and reached back as if to throw it. Anne pointed at him, and the women turned to look. It was a moment that changed the confrontation.

Anne spoke. "*Bi'smi'llah al Rahmán al Rahím*. In the name of

God, most Gracious, most Compassionate."

Silence. No movement. Finally a woman holding the hand of a young boy stepped forward and addressed Anne. "I want my son to see your men."

"What does your son want from these men?" Anne looked at the frightened boy. "Why did your boys try to hurt us with rocks? You might have killed us."

The woman snarled. "You speak of killing? My first son lies in our tent, now two weeks. He is almost dead. *Wallahi*, there must be revenge!"

"No, no. It was not us. We came today, only today, in peace." Anne pleaded. "Come, come with me and bring your son. There is some mistake." Anne beckoned the woman to come.

The young boy was shy, uneasy, and Anne urged him to take her hand. The three walked into the caravanserai, and Anne motioned to Hudson and Lockwood to step aside. The boy looked first at Fowler, then at the other men. He shook his head, and spoke softly to his mother. "No, not them."

"You are sure, Jamal?"

"Sure."

Anne followed as the mother and child backed out of the door. Outside the woman bent and whispered to her son. He lowered his head and moved behind his mother, holding onto her long black sleeve. He repeated again and again, "No, no, I did not. I was with Faisal."

When the woman raised her arm, Anne feared she would strike the boy and moved forward instinctively. Anne looked into a haggard face, worn and wrinkled before its time, a few tears pooling in her eyes.

"Let me help you, *ukhti*, my sister. What happened to your elder son?"

The woman seemed confused by Anne's appearance and language. She whispered a few words to her son and pushed him forward.

"*As-salaam Alaikum, ya Sitt.*"

"*Wa Alaikum As-salaam*, Jamal."

A little saliva curled out of the edges of his mouth as he

spoke. "I did not throw rocks against you. Those boys with rocks are friends of my brother, Faisal. Those boys are angry because Faisal was shot. They did not want to hurt you, only stop you so I could see you."

Anne turned to the boy's mother. "I am from the Anazeh tribe in Syria, and I know about healing. Will you let me see Faisal?"

The woman replied quickly, "Yes, yes, but we must go fast, before the men return with the goats. His father will not like it."

Anne went inside the caravanserai to explain what she would do. "Hudson, I would suggest you put Fowler on the donkey, get on your camel and let the old man ride Fowler's camel. Get down to camp and attend to Fowler's cut. Mika'il must have a medical kit, or ask Amir to find the one in my baggage. Lockwood, would you wait here for me?"

As the two women and the boy walked up the trail toward the cluster of Bedouin tents, the group of women and children watching the drama began to split apart, opening a path. The women, dressed in dusty black robes with heads covered, were quiet now, the only sound being a shuffling as the little children pushed each other for a better view. Anne saw scowling, quizzical, and blank faces as she followed Jamal and his mother.

Jamal ran into the tent to the pallet where his brother lay sleeping. Anne was close behind, and she watched Jamal kneel, touch his brother's cheek, and begin whispering in his ear. Jamal motioned for Anne to sit beside him. "Faisal hears you, but he cannot speak."

"*As-salaam Alaikum*, Faisal. My name is Sitt Mezrab, and I am from the Anazeh tribe in Syria. Do you know it?"

Faisal blinked his eyes twice. Jamal clapped with excitement. "That means yes, yes. He understands, ya Sitt."

Anne swallowed the tightness in her throat. "Faisal, I would like to see where you were hurt. I want to see if it is healing."

Faisal now appeared afraid. He looked from his brother who nodded, to his mother who sat stroking his hair. "It will not hurt you, Faisal, you will not feel pain," his mother said. "It will be like the turning each hour to keep you from sweating."

Jamal explained how they moved Faisal. Anne moved to the far side of the pallet, and then she saw the man sitting in the shadowy corner of the tent. She was startled and looked at the mother.

"Do not be afraid; he is my elderly grandfather. He is not aware of us."

After Faisal was turned on his stomach, his mother removed the rags serving as bandages. Anne noticed the rags were clean, probably changed frequently. The wound was almost an inch in diameter at the center of the back in the upper spine, about three or four inches from the base of the skull. Since she had not seen an exit wound on Faisal's upper body, she knew the bullet was still inside. The wound was healing well. There was no sign of infection or unusual swelling. Faisal would be paralyzed forever from below his neck. She looked around at the ragged walls of the tent that would be his living tomb. The grandfather was saying prayers, moving his beads swiftly through his gnarled fingers.

She hesitated before asking the next question. "How did this happen?"

The mother shook her head, crying and moaning, and pointed to Jamal.

"I cannot tell you. My father says not to speak of it. It is for Huwaitát only."

A tragic scene swept through Anne's mind. Someone shot a child in the back. A child. A child running away. He was running away. He would never run again. All the air was sucked out of her. It was hard to find a breath. She had forgotten to breathe. She gasped, and her hands reached out to stroke Faisal's legs. She buried her head between her arms, still massaging his legs, and wept. What could she do? Nothing would help this boy. It was heartbreaking to know her only contribution could be a few coins. She reached inside her robe to retrieve a small leather purse and handed it to the mother. *"Ma'asalama, ukhti."*

When Anne walked into the caravanserai, Lockwood handed her a cup of tea. "One of the Bedouin women brought the tea for us."

Anne placed the tea on the ledge. She turned to Lockwood and asked, "Would you hold me, tightly, as if you were keeping my body from falling apart?"

Lockwood encircled her limp body in his arms and drew her close. She turned her head and slid it against his shoulder. Time elapsed with no sound or movement. Lockwood felt Anne's body gaining strength.

Without moving, she spoke. "Thank you, Lockwood.

"Are you all right, Anne?"

"I think so," she said, stepping back from him. "And it is time to leave, to get to camp. When we are all together, I will tell you a tragic story. Right now, I need to be quiet."

They rode down the track following the stream bed. Both sides of the cliffs were riddled with caves and tombs, scattered up the rock like seabird nests. A little way ahead they saw small tombs with simple geometric designs cut into the cliffs. They were little more than caves with a decorative door frame carved into the surface of the rock. At a lower level the tombs were ornamented with Assyrian and Egyptian designs. As the riders drew closer to the valley, the tombs became more elaborate and larger.

The track now became a worn road weaving down a shadowy passage between sandstone banks just above the stream bed. It would be a dangerous route in the rainy season. Time had worn the exposed rock into rhythmic waves, the softer rock wearing away and leaving a deep, rippled appearance. Anne reached out to touch the warm, grainy surface of the soft yellow and dove-grey rock.

Around the next bend the road opened onto the ancient city of Petra. The riders pulled up their horses and stopped. Below them the valley of Petra glowed with soft colors—amber, topaz, burnt orange, pale red, topaz, deep blues and purples. Cliffs ascended hundreds of feet to create walls interrupted by wadis sweeping down from the nearby hills. Streams from the wadis and cliffs nurtured small green spaces. Along the fortress-like walls, structures of grand and modest design climbed above each other, the silent remains of a civilization which had carved homes, temples, and tombs in a naturally fortified refuge.

Anne broke the silence. "How extraordinary. I am close to weeping . . . ."

Lockwood reached over and placed his hand on Anne's arm. He pointed to horses and riders kicking up clouds of dust on a track below. They heard the voices of Hudson and Mika'il, calling to them.

Anne greeted the men with questions. "How is Fowler? How deep the wound? Did the bleeding stop? Did you find antiseptic? How about bandages?" Reassured about Fowler's condition, Anne looked over Hudson's shoulder. "How glorious to come upon Petra as the sun is setting." Her face relaxed into a broad smile. "The colors are divine. The structures blend so well into their environment, it is difficult to separate the individual buildings. They nestle together with the pride of posh townhouses in London."

Hudson turned his horse toward the last rays of soft light, catching and weaving the colors of the tombs on the eastern cliff. He handed his telescope to Anne and pointed to the northeast. "The slanting sun has gilded the facades of those tombs. Just look at the one with the Corinthian columns! I believe they are the Royal Tombs. I have great plans for them." Hudson was overwhelmed by the images of paintings coming from every direction, like an army of djinni floating out of magic lamps.

The light was fading and they still had a couple hundred feet of descent to get to the camp. Anne handed the telescope to Lockwood and pointed toward the Qasr al-Bint temple, patting his hand and smiling sweetly. He could see their familiar round white tents planted in a small field of green. Their caravan was safely settled in the valley. He laughed and bowed slightly as he returned the telescope to Hudson.

FIFTEEN

"Oh, Signore, we have come into a world where everything is made of chocolate, ham, curry powder and salmon."
Chef of the English painter, Edward Lear, 1858

Petra

Fowler hobbled toward Qasr al-Bint, using Amir's shoulder as if he were a walking stick. Easing himself down to a chair, he lifted his bandaged leg onto a slice of column that had fallen from the temple.

Would you like tea, Mr. Fowler?" Amir asked. "Amma says a cup of tea is the best medicine."

"Yes, please, Amir. You know, your Amma is a very clever woman." The boy grinned and ran off to the cook tent.

Every few minutes, he looked up to the point where the road spilled out of Wadi Thughra, looking for Anne and Lockwood. The sun inched toward the mountains, and he reached for his pipe. It needed a good cleaning, but those tools were in his tent. By the time Amir returned with the steaming cup of mint scented tea, he had filled and lit the pipe.

Amir sat on the ground beside him, legs folded and crossed like a little monk. "Mr. Fowler, are you worried about Amma and Mr. Lockwood?"

Fowler patted the boy's shoulder. The tightly woven cloth of his tunic felt soft and fine, not at all like Jamal's rough tunic. "Not really, I am sure your Amma knows where to find us."

Around him, men continued erecting tents, arranging the kitchen, and collecting branches for campfires. The cook

229

supervised the slaughtering of the sheep for the *mansef*, while his son picked hulls and stones out of ten pounds of rice. There was nothing to do but wait for the others.

Amir smoothed the sand in front of him and began drawing the portico of the temple to their right. The boy appeared to be attuned to every sight and sound, and while Fowler was commenting on his temple sketch, Amir pointed toward a faint column of dust near the road.

"I feared you had been captured by the Bedouin women to be sold as slaves," Fowler chuckled. "Come and tell me your story." Fowler beckoned them toward the nearby chairs.

Mika'il placed his right hand on his chest as he looked directly at Amir. Anne noticed the gesture of gratitude, then knelt by Fowler to examine the bandage. It was new cloth, tied tightly enough to have stopped the flow of blood. "How did you clean the wound, Mika'il?"

"I rinsed it many times with a little salt in boiled water. It is what we do. The wound is large, but not deep."

"Fine, perfectly fine. You have done well." Anne brushed away some sand which had blown onto Fowler's lower leg. "In the morning we can repeat the cleaning and add a new bandage." Anne gave Fowler a kiss on the cheek before standing and asking, "Any pain?"

Fowler was grinning, pleased but embarrassed by the attention. "Not much, and I consider the subject closed. Now, I want to hear about the scene of the crime."

Anne moved one of the chairs closer to the fire and sat facing the group. "In fact, there was a crime, a much worse crime than the rolling of the rocks." Anne paused and studied the tattoos on her wrists. "I am thinking about where to begin."

Lockwood was becoming impatient. "Why did the Bedouin boys attack us with rocks? Why not begin there?"

Anne spoke very slowly. "That was the beginning for us, but it was not the beginning for them."

"Bedouin boys threw rocks at you, Amma?" Amir asked in a puzzled voice.

"Yes, Amir, it did happen. I want you to listen quietly so you will understand. Will you do that?"

"Yes, *Amma*, but . . ."

"No buts."

Hudson leaned forward in his chair. "Are you sure you want to talk about this tonight? It could wait for the morning, Anne."

"No, it should not wait. I know only a part of the story, but I want all of you, including Mika'il and Amir, to know that the Huwaitát are in the midst of a crisis."

The men looked at each other. Hudson and Fowler turned to Anne with expressions of confusion; Lockwood looked annoyed.

She had their attention. "About two weeks ago, the older brother of the boy you saw at the caravanserai was shot in the back. I am guessing he was running away from someone he did not . . ."

"Was it a Bedouin?" Hudson asked.

"They did not say. I expect Jamal knows . . . knows much more, but he has been told by his father to be quiet about the shooting." Anne twisted the bracelets on her wrists as she spoke. "I saw the boy in their family tent. He is paralyzed from the neck down, and he does not speak. The bullet lodged in the upper spine."

"How terrible, how very terrible," Fowler murmured. "And the wound, Anne?"

"Appears to be healing well—no signs of infection." Anne spoke of Faisal, locked into his body, communicating only with his eyes. She described his brother, Jamal, staying by his side, searching for any sign of improvement and encouraging him in small ways; his mother hovering over him, touching him, stroking him, and turning him with care. "The men of the family only care about revenge," Anne said, "but the tent is a refuge of abiding love and faith in the will of Allah."

"Does the family know who is responsible?"

Anne shook her head and sighed. "I think not. As I mentioned, the boy's father has forbidden the mother and son, or anyone, to say anything about the shooting."

Lockwood unleashed his temper. "And we were attacked

because they want to punish everyone?"

"The boys who rolled the rocks off the cliff intended to stop us, not hurt us," Anne kept her voice calm, but she did not hide her irritation with Lockwood.

"How do you know . . . ?"

"Lockwood," Hudson shouted, "you would do well to listen with your ears, not your mouth!"

Lockwood's eyes flashed with anger, but he remained quiet.

Anne explained what Jamal had told her. "The Huwaitát want to stop everyone who comes into the valley until Jamal can identify the shooter. For some reason, they believe the shooter will return."

"So, Jamal saw the shooter—he was with his brother when it happened. How terrible," Fowler moaned, massaging his temple.

"What does this mean for us, Mika'il?" Hudson was tapping the table with his fingers. Are we safe because Jamal has seen all of us and said we were not responsible?" Hudson hoped it was the logical result.

"Based on what we know, I believe you are safe." Mika'il stood up, placed his hand on his dagger and continued. "It may be part of a blood feud among the Bedouin, but I need to know more. There are many Huwaitát among us—Sheikh Saud and most of his camel drivers. I will question them tonight. By now they may have heard rumors."

"Rumors . . . oh, yes, there will be rumors," Lockwood smirked. "The Bedouin turn molehills into mountains! I will not let their nonsense interfere with my plans!"

Hudson exploded. "Your plans, my plans, everyone's plans will be affected! Listen here, Lockwood, until we know we are safe in this valley, there will be no plans, no risks."

Lockwood stood with his mouth open. No one moved. "I apologize, Hudson." He kicked at the dirt. "I spoke carelessly."

Hudson nodded and walked away.

The dinner bell rang, and Anne excused herself, taking Amir's hand and heading for a wash. Lockwood and Mika'il were leaving and Fowler piped up. "Has everyone forgotten about me? Here I sit, injured and ignored after the Battle of Wadi Thughra."

The two men lifted Fowler to his feet and helped him to his seat at the table.

The table was bare—no cloth, no china, no silverware.

"Where . . .?" Lockwood began.

"Shh," Anne motioned him to the chair beside her.

When everyone settled into their seats, Mika'il raised his arm. The cook's son banged on a pot with a wooden spoon, and led a parade from the kitchen. Behind him, two men were holding either side of an enormous tray, followed by another man balancing a basket with wine bottles and glasses, and lastly came the cook proudly carrying a plate stacked with bread. Mika'il stood up, and the men covered the table with the tray.

"Bravo, bravo! *Mabrouk! Mansef!*" Anne cheered. Everyone clapped and whistled. Amir ran to get the small table from their tent for the bread and wine.

Fowler surprised them by asking to say grace. "Oh, great gods of the Nabateans—*Dushara and al-Kutba, Allat and al-Uzza*—we thank thee for allowing us to enter your sanctuary and ask for your divine protection."

"Judging by today, we may need some divine intervention," Hudson said.

Lockwood began pouring wine and passing glasses. "A little for Amir?" he asked Anne.

"Oh, no, no. His father would be furious with me."

Hudson stood and proposed a toast. "It is fitting to raise a glass to the memory of kings and queens whose tombs surround us. According to Fowler, the Nabatean royals drank wild honey and water, but we celebrate with this humble wine!"

"Hear, hear."

"Bottoms up."

"*Allah yaafeek.*"

"Now what do we do?" Hudson asked.

Anne passed the bread, and then asked Amir, "Are you ready to show them?"

He grinned and plunged his fingers into the rice mixture, bringing up a smallish amount, just enough to roll into a ball that

233

would fit comfortably into his mouth. Amir held out his palm to show the ball and then popped it into his mouth. Hudson was amazed he could form such a perfect ball with only his right hand.

"I hope you noticed, right hand only! It is forbidden to use the left hand." Anne warned.

"And if we make a mess of it?"

"Just stuff it into your mouth," Anne giggled. "No one important is watching."

"What is in this, Mika'il? Or should we ask?"

"Roasted sheep meat combined with rice and a sauce made from yogurt, meat juices, apricots, almonds, onions, and spices." Mika'il paused. "No eyeballs tonight."

After a few tentative forays, everyone joined the plunging, ignoring their greasy hands and faces. They leaned farther and farther over the tray as they learned how to keep the drops and drippings out of their laps. Only Fowler had the patience to accomplish a well-formed ball. At the end, with stomachs more than full, a huge mound of *mansef* remained.

"Mr. Hudson, can we give this to the men?" Mika'il asked.

"Of course, is it enough?"

"The cook made extra rice to add to make enough. Thank you." Mika'il bowed and left to arrange for the food to be removed.

"I wonder if this dinner would measure up for the Nabateans?" Anne was licking her fingers, then wiping her hands on the towel she passed around.

"My Greek friend, Strabo," Fowler said with an impish glint in his eyes, "described Nabatean parties. Would you like to hear?" Seeing the nodding heads, he sent Amir to his tent to collect the Book of Wonders and his spectacles.

"Thank you, Amir." Fowler rubbed the spectacles on his sleeve and hooked them around his ears. "Now let me see . . . . Yes, here it is, in the *Geographica*, chapter 16:

"The Nabataeans are a sensible people, and are so much inclined to acquire possessions that they publicly fine anyone who has diminished his

possessions and also confer honours on anyone who has increased them. Since they have but few slaves, they are served by their kinsfolk for the most part, or by one another, or by themselves; so that the custom extends even to their kings.

They prepare common meals together in groups of thirteen persons; and they have two girl singers for each banquet. The king holds many drinking bouts in magnificent style, but no one drinks more than eleven cupfuls, each time using a different golden cup. The king is so democratic that, in addition to serving himself, he sometimes even serves the rest himself in his turn. He often renders an account of his kingship in the popular assembly; and sometimes his mode of life is examined. Their homes, through the use of stone, are costly; but, on account of peace, the cities are not walled. Most of the country is well supplied with fruits except the olive; they use sesame oil instead. The sheep are white-fleeced and the oxen are large, but the country produces no horses. Camels afford the service they require instead of horses. They go out without tunics, with girdles about their loins, and with slippers on their feet — even the kings, though in their case the colour is purple."

"Sounds very democratic," Hudson laughed.

"Perhaps," Fowler said. "I do think it curious that the king permitted the conduct of his personal life to be reviewed." He paused while he reached in his pocket to retrieve his pipe and tobacco. "I think we know more than enough about our royals. For example, did you know . . . ."

As he listened to Fowler's melodious voice, Hudson gazed around the valley he had so longed to reach. The tombs were invisible below a midnight blue sky, but the temple of Qasr al-Bint cast a dark shadow toward the camp. He heard the faint warbles of night birds nesting in the cliffs and the echoing howls of distant jackals. He imagined another time when the sounds of trade caravans and marching soldiers clattered along the stone road. In this place, time between then and now seeped into the sand. People still gathered around a campfire to keep back the darkness, as they had from time beyond memory. The heartbeat of enduring humanity kept a steady rhythm in the midst of the rise and fall of great civilizations. Hudson closed his eyes for a moment and etched the memory in his mind.

When Hudson opened his eyes again, Fowler was filling his

pipe. It seemed to Hudson that Fowler enjoyed the ritual of filling, tamping and lighting as much as the smoking of the pipe. Perhaps, it was an antechamber to his thoughts.

"When are you going to spin out the tale of how the Nabateans found the money to create this fabulous city?" Anne asked, as she held up her glass for more wine.

"An unlikely, but true, story in only two words—world trade." Fowler mumbled as he lit his pipe.

"Hogwash!"" Lockwood laughed and looked around, but no one was even smiling. "You would have us believe a hidden valley in a remote corner of Syria would attract sufficient trade to become this city?"

Fowler was accustomed to the unripe Oxford student who lived to challenge his professor. He removed his pipe and pointed the stem at Lockwood. "You, Mr. Lockwood, have an unfortunate tendency to pounce before pondering." He said it with a chuckle and a merry wink.

"Try to imagine the region in the centuries before Christ. The Biblical Kingdom of Idumea or Edom was now Arabia Petraea, inhabited by Nabateans from Arabia. These Nabateans abandoned the nomadic life of their ancestors in favor of a settled community in Petra, an ideal landscape. The mountains offered them security from attack, and water was abundant from springs and rain. They terraced, irrigated, and farmed their lands to support their city and nearby towns. And they knew they had located themselves along an ancient and profitable trade route from south Arabia to the Mediterranean. Maybe you can guess what moved through here for centuries as highly profitable trade items."

Hudson looked at Anne and Lockwood who shook their heads. "Mr. Porter reports frankincense and myrrh," he said.

"Ah, Hudson, to the front of the class for you! The wise men followed a centuries old trail in bringing aromatics to the Nativity of Christ. Frankincense and myrrh for incense, perfumery, and fumigation were in great demand throughout the region, and they moved by land and sea from Arabia to Aqaba, then to Petra for taxing, trading, and shipping onward to Gaza, Alexandria,

Damascus, Tyre, Rhodes, Antioch, and Constantinople. In London, we would call the Nabateans 'middlemen.' Eventually the merchants of Petra would see spices, pearls, cinnabar, and silk traveling west from China and India, and payment being returned to the east in coin, semiprecious stones, ceramics, and bronze objects. Trade—always the lifeblood of great empires." Fowler looked around at his friends. "I can be an impossible bore when I get launched on historical subjects."

"Nonsense, it is fascinating. I will be following you around tomorrow like a puppy dog, nibbling every crumb of knowledge you drop." Anne seemed quite pleased to be tutored by an Oxford don.

Lockwood also listened carefully, fidgeting until he could question Fowler. "When I was in Kerak at the time of the Lynch expedition, I heard that the Nabateans exported large quantities of bitumen from the eastern part of the Dead Sea to Egypt. Have you come across such a trade in your reading, Fowler?"

"Yes, quite so. Strabo and other historians write of the use of bitumen in Egypt for embalming and sealing coffins, and for mortar or waterproofing boats."

"I suppose I am the only one here who has no idea what bitumen is?" Anne said.

"Basically, a mineral," Lockwood said. "It results from organisms living in water that die and become buried in a lake or ocean or under rock. Over thousands of years the heat and pressure of the earth transform the organisms into bitumen or petroleum. The Romans called it asphaltum. On the Lynch expedition we found shiny black pebbles of bitumen along the shore and lumps floating on the surface of the Dead Sea. The Arab boatmen sold it in the markets of Kerak."

"Do you have an interest in bitumen, Lockwood?" Hudson thought back to Mika'il's remark about Lockwood meeting the Sheikh of Kerak in Hebron.

"I know it is in great demand for paving roads," he replied curtly and turned to Fowler. "What happened to the Nabateans and their trade empire?"

"The Romans happened," Fowler replied. "Appeared on the

237

Petra doorstep in the first century AD." By around 100 AD, they took control of the city and gradually moved trade routes farther north. In the next few hundred years, the Roman Empire fell, earthquakes damaged Petra, and by the 8th century the valley was almost completely deserted and . . . ."

"Could you speak a little louder, Fowler?" Lockwood asked. "It is hard to hear above the noise of those Bedouin."

Anne laughed. "That is not noise; it is chanting."

Hudson stood up to watch. He noticed the number of Bedouin in the camp was larger than usual. Anne listened for a few minutes and decided to move closer to the festivities. When Mika'il saw her approach, he had his men unroll a large striped carpet near the fire. Fowler and Hudson joined her. Lockwood drifted away from the group.

The Bedouin performers stood or sat in concentric circles on the windward side of the fire. The drummers sat in the center keeping a steady two-step beat. Around them the singers formed two facing groups, chanting a call and response—bowing, swaying, and clapping to the rhythm. Beyond the chanters, a group of swordsmen and riflemen stood until the music increased in volume, and then they moved round the circle in a slow, deliberate step, whirling and keeping time with the drums and chanting. As the frenzy of the music increased, they shouted, leaped, and waved their swords and rifles in the air.

Hudson was transfixed by the ceremony; it seemed more ritual than entertainment. It throbbed with an affirmation of identity and continuity. All the Bedouin men joined in, and each knew their role and timing. The sounds of drums, singing, and shouting resounded through the valley with the intensity of a call to battle. Hudson found the spectacle hypnotic and frightening. As uneasiness turned into tension, and he excused himself. When he reached his tent, the sounds were still thumping in his chest.

The clear light of the moon and the desire to escape the noise tempted Lockwood to walk farther into the valley than he intended. He passed the theater and was now in a narrow ravine which he believed led to El Khasneh and the Siq. The passage was warmer than the valley, the rock still holding the warmth of the sun, but it was darker, with only indirect light from the moon. He moved slowly, feeling, but not seeing stones in the path. He whistled a tune which bounced off the high walls.

A faint noise, he stopped. Pebbles moving. Ahead or behind? He looked quickly in both directions. Was someone stalking him? He saw no one, but he felt a presence. There was no place to hide or escape within the rock walls, and he could only move forward or backward. Not a good place to be. There! A shadow! Was it a person, a tree? He eased his pistol out of the holster and turned slowly in a circle. Nothing. He was angry at himself for walking into a trap. He wanted to call out but could think of nothing in Arabic. What was the greeting the Anne used? "*As-salaam Alaikum. As-salaam Alaikum,*" Lockwood shouted into the darkness.

Now a sharp scrape of movement ahead of him, and Lockwood turned toward the noise. The silhouetted figure of a large man in robes moved into the path. The man was a Bedouin, and he held a rifle, pointed at Lockwood. Both men stood still and silent. Lockwood shuddered at the thought of his indefensible position. He was alone; the man before him was likely to have friends nearby. A slight nausea accompanied the chills slithering down his spine. He slowly returned his pistol to its holster, and then the Bedouin lifted the barrel of his rifle with several jabs upward in a clear signal to go back. Lockwood raised his arms and walked backwards slowly for a few yards; then he turned and moved swiftly toward the valley. As he emerged from the passage, he caught a glimpse of another Bedouin, standing guard against the cliff wall. Lockwood kept his eyes straight ahead and strode vigorously toward the camp. Why are guards scattered around the area? Are they here to keep us in or out?

SIXTEEN

". . . A rose-red city half as old as Time."   J. W. Burgon, 1845

Petra

Hudson tied back one of the tent flaps, intending to warm up his fingers with a little sketching. The opening faced the Royal Tombs carved out of the distant eastern cliff, still shaded from the morning sun. In the early light the colors were delicate and flowing. It struck him that the genius of the architecture matched the wonder of the coloring. Man had combined artistry with nature to create a masterpiece. This day he would do the same.

The range of color in the rock was enormous—earthy shades of amber, orange, rose, blue and purple. He squeezed the oils onto his palette, blending a little red into the yellow for the amber and savoring the scent of the oils. Most of the mixing would take place on the canvas as the subtle and dramatic bands of the sandstone were layered into place on colonnades, arches, galleries, porticos. A sense of euphoria moved his brush and palette knife as he played with the living colors, teasing them into a subtle harmony. He relished the sensations of sketching in oils, the freedom to express mood and substance with colors and forms, changing with whims and insights. He stopped before he went too far; the *plein air* sketch soared only with intuition, not labor.

Hudson considered the successful sketch a forecast for the day. The only question in his mind that morning concerned the Bedouin. Despite Anne and Mika'il's belief that they were removed from suspicion, he worried about Bedouin being desperate for revenge and striking out again at strangers, especially one who was sketching or painting. The Bedouin in the caravan were now acquainted with his sketching habit, but the events of yesterday signaled that the Huwaitát who lived around Petra would be watching all movements and actions of strangers. He must rely on Mika'il's judgment.

As he left his tent, Hudson noticed the ruins of Qasr al-Bint standing like a sentinel, a stone's throw from his tent. When he arrived the night before, the temple was barely visible. Now the sun highlighted the remaining walls and columns. How amazing, he thought. Unlike the other structures which were carved from the cliffs, this impressive edifice was constructed of blocks of shaped stone. On the north side, facing his tent, cornerstones decorated with large plain circles were stacked to about forty feet. Shading his eyes from the sun, Hudson could see an overhanging cornice strongly carved with a handsome design of alternating triglyphs and rosettes. As he walked closer to the temple, a sweet herbal aroma filled his nose, and he looked down at a green carpet of wild sage, thyme, and camomile. He reached down for a sprig of thyme and rolled it in his fingers. Katharine had planted thyme between the stones leading to their cottage.

At the breakfast table Hudson was pleased to see a platter of omelets, stacks of bread and the usual apricots and dates which would suffice for breakfast and a packed lunch. Anne and Lockwood interrupted their chatting to say good morning. Fowler stared into his half eaten omelet. His left hand propped up his head, and the right hand stabbed halfheartedly at the apricots.

"Are you all right, Fowler? How is your leg?" Hudson asked.

"Good, no pain at all," he replied, his eyes at half-mast. "However, I regret to report that I listened to music most of the night instead of sleeping."

"Music? I thought the music ended early." Lockwood looked amazed. "I slept quite well."

"If you can sleep through your snoring, Lockwood, you can sleep through Bedouin drumming," Anne teased. After the first few days in the caravan, she had made an arrangement with Mika'il about her tent location, as far away from the snorer as possible.

"We need to change your bandage, Fowler. Will you be able

to tour today?" Anne asked.

"As you can see, I am knackered. Thought I would rest after breakfast and join you for the afternoon. Mika'il has arranged a donkey for me, and a half day is probably enough for my leg."

"Hudson, I expect you will be painting today?" Anne asked.

"Already started in my tent this morning and plan to continue in the valley until someone points a gun at me. By the way, Anne, I wanted to speak with you about Amir."

"Oh, yes. He is so keen on his sketching. He carries the little sketchbook and pencil wherever he goes." Her expression changed slightly. "I hope he is not becoming a pest."

"Not at all," Hudson replied. "In fact, he has opened my eyes to the charm of camels. He is making great progress, but I cannot take him with me today. I would like to leave some paints and a canvas board for him to try out, if you are agreeable."

"How very generous of you, Hudson." Anne reached across to the table to squeeze his hand. "I will speak with him about plans for the day and then send him to your tent." Anne turned to Lockwood. "What about you? Would you be interested in exploring the cliffs this morning until Fowler is ready to tour with us?"

"Absolutely Anywhere, anytime you choose."

Hudson called Mika'il to join them. "Did you learn anything last night about the wounded boy's family?"

Mika'il glanced around the area. He spoke quietly. "Faisal's grandfather has set up small camps outside the Siq and in Wadi Thughra, Wadi Turkmaniyya, and Wadi Farasah—the four main entrances to Petra. There is a larger encampment near Elji, which is a mile or so east of the Siq. They think the shooter will be found in the Elji area, but friends and family are watching everywhere. From above the theater, they can see the entire . . ."

"Help!" Fowler shouted and threw up his arms.

"Are you in pain, Fowler?"

"No, I am in the valley of confusion. I am completely lost with all these names—wadis, entrances, buildings."

Mika'il reached into his robe. "I do not have a good map of the Petra Valley, but here is a rough drawing given to me by a

previous traveler. Think of this valley as a male camel in profile—
its head lifted and pointing northwest, its unusually long tail as the
Siq leading to the east." His finger traced the Siq toward the
direction of Elji. "The body is the valley floor. From the Qasr al-
Bint Temple and our camp, which are at the chest of the animal,
you go past the neck to the animal's back where an ancient wall
outlines the spine and hump and descends to the Royal Tombs—
forming the rump of the camel. At the level of the manly parts,
the theater is located and just above the tail branches off to the
ravine, El Khasneh and the Siq." Mika'il paused for a moment
and saw heads nodding their understanding. "Now for the
wadis—think of the four legs in walking position. The advancing
front leg is Wadi Thughra, which you descended yesterday, and
the other front leg is Wadi Nmayr. The first back leg is Wadi
Farasah; the second back leg is the path near the Theater to the
high place of Sacrifice."

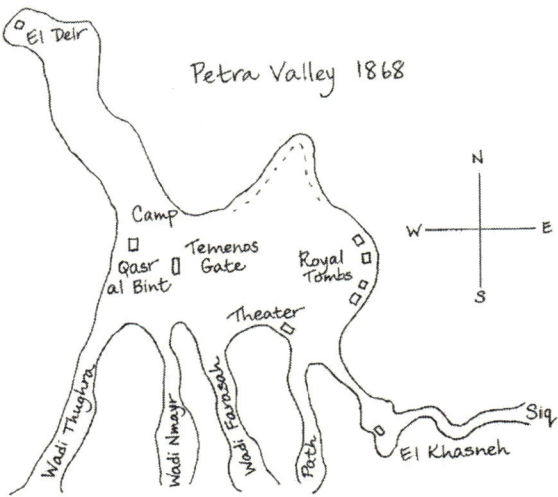

"Bravo, Mika'il," Fowler clapped, a good image to stick in my
mind. What is the mark that looks like the nose of the camel?"

243

"Ah, yes, I forgot the nose," he said. "It is El Deir. The neck and the head lead to the temple structure, usually called The Monastery by foreigners. I think you saw it from the summit of Jebel Haroun."

"Yes, we did, and it is on my list," Hudson added. "Speaking of all these wadi entrances, Mika'il, I forgot to ask if you were stopped by the Huwaitát yesterday when you brought the caravan down Wadi Thughra?"

"We passed a tent before the Bedouin settlement, and the men came out to greet us. It was a fine day so our faces were not covered, and they could see us. We exchanged greetings, nothing more."

Hudson was drumming his fingers on the table and thinking about Mika'il's reply which suggested Bedouin were not looking for Arabs, but admittedly, it was not conclusive. He looked at his pocket watch for the third time since arriving at the table. "Will we be able to move about the valley safely, Mika'il? Will I be able to paint at El Khasneh?" His voice mixed desire with nervous hesitation as if he were not certain how much he would risk for his quest.

"Mr. Hudson, I was told by a member of the family that our caravan is safe, absolutely safe. They know the wife and son of leaders of the Anazeh tribe are among us, and I promised we would not go beyond their checkpoints."

Reassured by the report, Hudson was eager to be on his way. "Any other questions for Mika'il?"

"Last night I went for a walk during the music," Lockwood said. "I wandered into the ravine leading to El Khasneh and the Siq. About halfway through the narrowest part I was stopped by a Bedouin pointing a rifle at me. I turned to walk back to the camp, and as I left the ravine there was another armed Bedouin hiding beside the wall of a tomb. These encounters make me wonder about Bedouin intentions."

"Those were men from our caravan. After I spoke with Faisal's family, I arranged for our men to be stationed on the valley side of each entrance."

"You did not tell us?" Lockwood looked surprised.

"I am sorry if you were frightened by the men, Mr. Lockwood. It did not occur to me that any of you would be walking in the dark after yesterday's problem."

"I suggest none of us move alone at day or night. Agreed?" After a nod from each one, Hudson continued. "Mika'il, my group will be going in different directions this morning. Fowler will stay in camp for a little rest. Anne and Lockwood plan to explore the nearby area. I intend to head off with my sketching equipment and eventually settle into the area surrounding El Khasneh. Can you send one of your men with me?"

"Two of my men are ready to accompany you and help with questions or translations," Mika'il said. "They know about your plans to sketch, and they are prepared to protect you. They will be armed and alert to anyone approaching. I will remain in the camp area until Fowler, Lockwood, and Sitt Mezrab come together in the afternoon. When they start their touring, I will keep them in sight. Does that meet your needs?" Mika'il asked.

"Fine, a good plan, and I expect by the time you reach El Khasneh, I will be ready to join you for a walk through the Siq, if it proves to be possible." Hudson was determined to seize the day for the most important sketching. The weather was excellent, and he would see El Khasneh in several lighting conditions. If he had one more fine day, he would make El Deir the priority.

"By the way, Mika'il, I plan to stop several places before El Khasneh to sketch. My intention is to be open about my work. I am fully aware an artist was shot here several years ago."

Mika'il's face registered his surprise. "That man was here with a guide from Kerak, not a Huwaitát and not with Huwaitát permission. He was foolish and did not stop when he was warned. Luckily, it was a minor wound."

"I understand, Mika'il, and I would not be walking down the valley with my paintbox if I were frightened. Take care, everyone, and I will see you in the afternoon."

"Wait up, Hudson," Fowler called to Hudson who was moving briskly.

"Sorry, Fowler, do you need an arm?"

"No, no. Just a little slow," he replied. "I say, Hudson, did you

245

notice how agreeable Lockwood was at breakfast?"

"Not really."

"Well, he practically leaped in Anne's lap when she invited him to go exploring." Fowler grinned and looked over to Hudson's face, which made him stumble.

Hudson grabbed his arm and slowed his pace.

" . . . and he stared at her constantly. And then the sudden shaving . . . I think he has a bit of a fancy for our Anne."

"Hmm. Well, you are a romantic, old boy. I really must be off, Fowler." Hudson entered his tent to collect his paintbox and sketchbook. When he stepped out of his tent, he found two men armed with rifles, long knives, and clubs with bulging knobs. He looked at the weapons with raised eyebrows and was about to speak, but decided not to comment.

"*As-Salaam Alaikum*, Mr. Hudson. We are ready with your food and water and will follow you." The taller man displayed enough English to convince Hudson he would be useful. The other man offered to carry his supplies. Hudson gave him the paintbox and tucked the large sketchbook under his arm.

Anne and Lockwood climbed the worn steps carved into the cliff near the theater. It was warm, and the steep ascent caused Lockwood to stop frequently to catch his breath. Stopping was slightly unnerving, as it called attention to the vertical angle of the cliff, which appeared more precipitous with each step. He envied Anne's nimbleness as she moved toward the top of the cliff. She must have several years on him, yet she climbed with the certainty of a mountain goat, finding footholds on the narrowest of ledges and leaping over tamarisk bushes growing in impossible places. Her little yellow boots flashed against the rock. He put his head down, watching the path, vowing to continue to the top with no further stops.

Anne waited at the top near the edge of the cliff, perched on a large rock. He saw her in profile as she concentrated on something lower in the wadi. Faint lines radiated from her eyes. Any earlier rosy English complexion had disappeared into a permanent rosy tan. He found her alluring and exotic—a perfect combination of beauty and mystery. He moved quietly to stand beside her. The day could not have been more perfect. The cloudless sky presented a pale blue background for a ballet of hawks sweeping across their stage and rising in grand pirouettes.

"Do you think the hawks find our presence annoying?" Anne looked up at Lockwood, shielding her eyes with her hand. She smiled, an openhearted and trustful smile between friends.

"No doubt we interrupt their hunting." Lockwood placed his hand gently on her shoulder, a small gesture replying to her smile. He felt the softness and warmth of her body. They watched two of the hawks settle onto the portico of a tomb with wings at rest, but heads turning left and right to search for prey.

Lockwood closed his eyes to absorb the pleasure of the moment and drifted into a dream, allowing his imagination to follow his desire. Anne rose, took his hand, and led him away from the cliff through a scattering of wild red poppies and white broom springing up in stony ground. They scrambled up bare ledges stacked into giant steps, ascending toward a still invisible peak. The rock radiated a scorching heat, a golden fire burning bright under a noonday sun, and streams of perspiration penetrated his clothes. Ahead he saw a dark crevice cracked open by a cataclysmic quake of the earth. Close to the entrance, a sweet moisture was seeping from the crevice. They slipped into the darker area and adjusted to the narrowness and shadows. The sudden coolness shuddered through him. Overhead the rock met and overlapped, then opened, creating alternating darkness and light as the path twisted and turned in a pleasant rhythm. Anne laughed with pleasure. Lockwood moved to enclose her in his arms again; then lost his balance and found himself falling against Anne, still sitting at the edge of the cliff.

"Steady, Lockwood, did you hear me? I asked if you wanted to explore before returning to the valley." His expression, shifting from wonder to pain, startled her. "Are you all right? You look as if you are about to faint . . . and you are hurting my shoulder."

Lockwood groaned. Anne grabbed his arm and pulled him

onto the rock, beside her.

"I am sorry, very sorry. I must have been daydreaming. Did I bruise your shoulder?"

"Bloody hell. I thought you were going to sail over the cliff after the hawks! What a fright you gave me."

"Oh, Anne . . . you care." Lockwood encircled her with strong arms, searching her face with soft lips. His hands moved through the folds of her robes; he sensed her body melting into his, until . . . until the moment when he knew he was being pushed away.

Anne stood up and shook her robe, glaring as she moved away. "What has come over you?"

"I thought you . . ." Lockwood stammered. "Yesterday, when you . . ."

"Whatever you thought was wrong! If I gave you any reason to think . . . well, you are just wrong." She swung around to leave, then turned her head. "Perhaps it is the heat . . . ." And this little incident? It never happened."

She thought about whether Lockwood was well enough for the steep descent. "Sit for a moment, and I will look beyond those ledges for a more gradual way down to the valley."

"No, wait, please. I am fine. I want to go with you." He reached out to take her hand.

Anne looked at his hand, gave a little shake of her head, and said, "If you are steady enough to walk on this flat ground, you do not need to hold my hand, Lockwood.

He followed her in silence along the high plateau where they found stone cairns guiding them to a descending path which seemed to be heading toward the valley. "I am guessing this might be Wadi Farasah," Anne said. "Remember? Mika'il described it as the third leg of the camel map, just to the west of the theater?"

After a short scramble and sharp bend, where a lion figure was carved in high relief, they found themselves along an old road slanting downward through the wadi. Straight ahead, a garden of greenery nestled in a corner of the cliff beside a columned tomb. Anne squinted at the shrubs and hanging plants, looking for some sign of a hidden water source and then saw the roughly carved, steep steps beside the tomb. Anne was up the steps in less than a minute and called down to Lockwood. "Seems to be a cistern on top of the tomb."

"I am coming up," Lockwood said somewhat hesitantly.

"I think not, Lockwood. I do not trust you near steep drops, and it is time to get back to camp."

Fowler wrestled with his covers for more than an hour, then gave up on the napping idea. The bandage on his leg felt too tight, and he unwrapped it. The wound was slightly swollen, but not more than normal given the impact of the rock. As he wound the gauze around his leg, he could hear something moving behind his tent. The noise stopped, but the canvas was moving as if someone were trying to enter the tent from the back side. Fowler pulled himself up and limped around the outside of the tent.

Behind the tent, Amir knelt holding the lower edge of the tent off the ground. When he noticed Fowler standing nearby, he placed a finger on his lips, then lifted the tent edge higher and peered into the shaded area. The boy waited patiently, completely still. After a few minutes he dropped the canvas and shrugged his shoulders. "A blue lizard ran under your tent, Mr. Fowler," he whispered.

Fowler nodded and pointed to a smooth rock just beyond Amir, where a lizard with a sky blue head and spotted brown body, no longer than his hand, lay in the sun. Amir turned slowly and cautiously removed the sketchbook and pencil from his pocket. The lizard relaxed into the warmth of the rock, posing for the young artist. He finished the drawing, added some notes, and beamed a smile of satisfaction. When he turned to Fowler, the lizard sensed the motion and disappeared.

"Beautiful?" Amir asked. "Did you see the pattern on the under part of his neck? It is like the honeycomb of bees. You know, it is called an Agama."

"Is that the Arabic word?"

"I do not know the Arabic word—it is the Latin word," he said proudly. "Mr. Hudson told me this morning. I do not know

Latin."

Less than an hour later, Fowler was on a donkey, leading Anne and Lockwood through the valley, an umbrella in one hand and book in the other. "Porter suggests we concentrate on the 'lions,' the tombs that roar with their importance. The group ahead known as the Royal Tombs roars quite loudly."

Ascending a natural ramp up a partially walled cliff, they reached a plateau facing a quartet of princely tombs, each unique in architecture and decoration. Fowler lowered his spectacles to glance at Anne and Lockwood, who appeared to be waiting for guidance.

"I do not intend to lead you around like a stodgy old school master. I will say, my understanding is that the structures were built as tombs, but there is no evidence of burials inside. Starting on the left is the Palace Tomb, then Corinthian, Silk, and Urn Tombs. Have a look around and find me if you have questions."

Anne looked at the facades of each of the tombs before deciding to concentrate on the Urn Tomb. To the right of the tomb, a path zigzagged past the double vaulted base and up to the terrace leading to the tomb entrance. Even before she entered the tomb, she felt the pleasantly cool air drawing her toward the lofty inner chamber. The door and small upper windows brought in enough light to see that other than three shallow recesses and several birds' nests the chamber was bare. The startling aspect was the color embedded in the rock. Waves of blue, purple, red, orange, and white on the walls and ceilings gave the sensation of being underwater. She floated on the feeling of swimming until the diving finches drove her out to the terrace.

Lockwood found Fowler near the Palace Tomb where he was examining traces of paint on the lower level of the densely colonnaded facade. "Look here, Fowler, I have found a treasure." Lockwood displayed a flat, palm-sized rock, covered with inscriptions. He handed it to Fowler.

Fowler took off his spectacles and peered at the etched surface with its elongated script. "It resembles drawings I have seen of the Nabatean script. Where did you find it?"

"I was poking around that pile of stones." Lockwood pointed toward a mound of carved stones which appeared to have fallen from the upper colonnade of the Palace Tomb.

"It is quite an interesting piece. It might be a good idea to make a sketch of the inscription," Fowler remarked. He turned the stone around, looking for the proper orientation of the script.

"I could do it, back at camp tonight."

Fowler tightened his hold of the stone and looked up at Lockwood. "You are not planning to take this artifact, are you?"

"Give it to me. I found it. It is mine." Lockwood took the stone when Fowler opened his hand.

Fowler shook his head wearily and said, "We have talked several times about Bedouin attitudes toward removing artifacts from Petra."

"It is not an artifact—it is just a stone with some scratching. There are dozens more in those piles." Lockwood shoved the stone in his pocket and walked away, descending from the tombs toward the theater.

Fowler was annoyed, but it was a very small object, probably common, and not worth an argument. He called to Anne as she climbed down from the terrace, and they followed Lockwood.

They found him standing on the stage of the theater, looking up at the carved recesses above the tiers of seating chiseled out of the cliff. "What are those openings, Fowler?" Lockwood asked. "They look like box seats at the Opera, but a little too far removed from the stage."

"Porter says they are tombs—seems a strange location for burials, but a good view for the ghosts," said Fowler. "No one seems to know whether the theater was Nabatean or Roman, but Porter estimates it could hold three to four thousand spectators for plays, rituals, music, athletics, symposia—all part of the ancient theater tradition."

They heard the hoofbeats of a fast moving horse before they saw Mika'il, on his way to meet Hudson at El Khasneh. Lockwood shouted, "Wait!" Mika'il stopped and saw the three of them descending from the back wall of the stage.

On their way through the ravine beyond the theater, Mika'il

pointed out remnants of the ancient water system. "Water was brought from the other side of the Siq into the city through these open channels and stored in cisterns and pools throughout the valley."

Lockwood noticed broken clay pipes higher up on the sides of the ravine. "I am realizing Petra was much more than a city of the dead. The theater was the first hint, and now this water supply system suggests a thriving town with houses and agriculture." He found places where water channels split between two pipes, then disappeared underground. Picking up a shard of clay pipe he murmured, "We are surrounded by evidence of Nabatean religion and death, but we know so little about how they lived."

Nodding his head, Fowler added, "Someday scholars will arrive with more knowledge to tease out the secrets. Until then, we stand here wondering about mind-boggling accomplishments in one of the many great cities of the desert to rise, thrive, fall, and almost disappear from history. It is humbling."

When Hudson and his guards left the camp earlier that morning, they walked east from Qasr al-Bint for about a hundred yards toward a triumphal arch with three portals, built after the Romans annexed the Nabatean kingdom. The upper portions of the arch, known as Temenos Gate, laid scattered on the ground, brought down by earthquakes which frequently rearranged the landscape of Petra. The four piers of the arch stood like sentinels guarding a sacred space. Hudson ran his hand over the sculpted edges of the central arch. At one of the corners a stack of squared stones carved with faces, plants, and curious symbols caught his eye. He brushed the sand from one of the low stones, sat, and opened his sketchbook. He sketched the stones bearing acanthus leaves and rosettes, then tried a few of the faces which appeared to depict Roman gods and goddesses. He considered drawing what was left of the entire arch, but decided it would be of little effect. Instead, he turned toward the cliff and made several small sketches of tamarisk trees and thickets of oleander bushes. On the same page, he added views of fig trees hugging the base of the nearby cliffs and several goats teetering on ledges to reach small shrubs on the rock face.

The few Huwaitát who had passed near the arch gave little or no attention to his sketching. Hudson stood up and looked toward the sky—a glorious day. He enjoyed the relative solitude; his guides appeared only to offer water and help carry his materials. After a drink, they continued east on the scattered stones of an old paved road leading from the arch toward the Royal Tombs. As he neared the row of tombs, the Urn Tomb was catching the sunlight reflected from the terrace below. To the left, the smoothly worn sandstone of the Silk Tomb reminded Hudson of marbled papers laid into book bindings—white, blue, and salmon tints swirled with gold, gray, and red.

He barely glanced at the huge theater carved out of the high cliff. He could feel the magnetic force of El Khasneh pulling him out of the valley, drawing him toward the jewel of Petra. Quickening his pace, he hurried by tombs with Egyptian and Assyrian motifs. He entered a wild ravine, worn by time into rounded walls below ragged precipices. Along the path tall oleanders reached for a few rays of sun.

Almost breathless, Hudson turned a corner. Before him the tomb known as El Khasneh waited—an exquisite creature in shades of gold and burnt orange reaching out from the sheltering black cliffs. Late morning shafts of sunlight stroked the facade, releasing light and warmth from the sandstone.

He stood alone before this elegant triumph of artistic genius. His eyes moved slowly over the classical facade. The graceful proportions of the lower portico were accentuated by the six soaring Corinthian columns carrying a frieze and pediment. Only the two central columns were freestanding, and part of one lay at Hudson's feet. The upper story repeated the elements of the lower story on each side, but here the architect had sliced open the pediment and the portico to make room for a cylinder surrounded by four columns. A dome surmounted the columns and cylinder, and as Hudson stepped back for a better angle, he thought he saw an urn just above the dome. Sculptures, reliefs, and intricate details on friezes and cornices gave life to the building, and he imagined stories about the man for whom it was built. Surely this edifice was the last home for a Nabatean king with artistic sensibilities.

Hudson breathed deeply, restraining an urge to begin sketching before more closely examining what he could reach. He ascended the few steps to the portico and followed the lofty columns upward with his eyes. He touched the life size reliefs of headless riders on horses moving across the lower level of the facade toward the ravine. In them, he saw the poise and authority of sons or generals of the great ruler buried within, men now wounded in the battles of time.

Inside the doorway Hudson found himself in a square vestibule startling for its plainness. Ahead and up a few more steps, in a larger chamber, a large niche in the back wall and smaller niches in the side walls appeared to be places for the sarcophagi of a royal family. On the way out he quickly looked at the side rooms off the vestibule, but they were damp and bare, of little interest to him. His hands were itching for the pencils in his pocket.

Outside, he opened the paintbox and removed his telescope. His plan was to examine each sculptural element with the telescope and then sketch, building up a collection of details for the studio painting. Then he would be prepared to paint a sketch of the entire tomb.

He settled on a convenient rock, opened his large sketchbook, and took a breath. Sketching for him was not simply capturing the image; it was the summoning of the creative force to penetrate the essence of his chosen subject, to feel and interpret what was alive, compelling.

In less than an hour, two pages were filled with small, precise drawings and notes on color, shape, and size. Even the quality of the light and the feel of the weather were noted. The first page was devoted to flora—poppies and pine cones from the column capitals, sheafs of wheat, rosettes, and garlands of pomegranates, grapes, ivy, and laurel from the friezes.

On the next page, he sketched the stone eagles perched at the edges of the upper sliced pediment and the dancing women, carved in relief on the rotunda and sides of the upper portico's pavilion. From the lower portico, his renderings were detailed drawings of the high relief sculptures of vague figures on horseback, griffins holding drinking cups, and winged felines. Hudson understood classical architecture and knew these symbols and figures were associated with the royal nature of the tomb. He smiled with slight envy of a king being accompanied to his tomb by a feast of food and drink, everlasting flowers, and a retinue of male friends, dancing girls, and pets.

Behind him, Mika'il's men walked back and forth, glancing over his shoulder at the pages of sketching, watching for other visitors. So far no one else had appeared. He closed his sketchbook, stood up, and walked around the small chasm surrounding El Khasneh. It did not take more than a few minutes to decide on the perspective he wanted for an oil sketch of the entire tomb. He would sit slightly to the left of the tomb, just beyond the entrance from the Siq. The location presented a good angle for the facade and allowed him to see any new arrivals as quickly as they would see him.

Hudson opened the paintbox, replaced his telescope and removed his palette and canvas board. In the few hours he had been with El Khasneh, sunlight had changed the tomb's color from a golden color to a pale salmon color. He chose the few colors he needed and lightly mixed the shades of salmon for the tomb, the greens for the adjacent foliage and the browns and black for the cliff.

His guards drew nearer and held their rifles at a ready position. Hudson nervously searched their faces, causing one man to smile broadly and give a thumbs-up signal which Hudson interpreted as either a comment on his work or an indication of their readiness for action. He drew a few quick pencil lines on the canvas board, selected a brush, and began.

The tomb appeared on the canvas with the suddenness of an apparition. His instincts moved paint into architecture with little apparent effort. With smaller brushes and a palette knife, he added slight detail, texture, emphasis, light, and dark. The cliffs with their dark bulges and overhangs took form in sweeps and globs of brown and black paint. Lastly, Hudson feathered in the green foliage near the steps to the tomb. It was enough for his purposes.

Propping the canvas against a boulder, Hudson stepped back to view his work. It was only a sketch, an impressionistic study of the reality before him. He felt a sense of triumph. He dared to think he had achieved his goal in the Orient. He knew several more sketches, today or tomorrow, of other tombs and temples could fill his portfolio and produce an abundance of studio paintings, more than enough to revive his reputation and purse. He would answer emphatically the critics who were bored with his mountain landscapes and doubted his ability to paint in a more modern fashion. Collectors who fancied the exotic French paintings of Egypt and Syria would be lured again to his studio.

He needed sales to support his family, but even more he craved the affirmation of fame. Fame had come quickly to Hudson, and now he understood it could take wing. He had come to the Orient determined to open his mind and spirit to new, different landscapes. During the journey, there had been hopes, expectations, doubts, even despair, and now he felt close to his goal. His studio paintings of Jerusalem, El Yemen, and Petra would demonstrate his ability to paint in a new vein.

He turned and stared again at El Khasneh—a shining vessel of beauty and truth, conceived and accomplished in a wild ravine, thousands of years ago. It was astonishingly beautiful, a beauty resounding with the architect's dedication to truth and belief in the spirit of his art— the noble vision of a supreme artist.

Hudson brushed away unexpected tears. Then a most unwelcome thought squeezed into his mind.

This glorious building was not his vision. He had simply recorded an earlier artist's vision. Was this the desired path for his art? Would he abandon his belief in the spiritual power of the natural landscape, compromise his artistic integrity? Year after year, powerful emotions about truth and spirituality in nature had driven his creative energy. Why was he now satisfied, even excited to paint beautiful scenes? He shuddered to think about his present motivations. Was he simply chasing fame? Would his final legacy be scene paintings of Palestine and Syria?

The voices of his approaching friends rescued Hudson from a widening vortex of doubt. His thoughts begged for attention, but not right now. He tended to his paints, wiped his brushes, and carefully slid the oil sketch of El Khasneh into the upper portion of the paintbox where the still wet surface was protected and closed the box quietly.

Mika'il was the first to round the corner, and his eyes moved quickly between Hudson and his men before an expression of great relief flooded his face. "All has gone well, Mr. Hudson?" Seeing Hudson nod his agreement, Mika'il exclaimed, "*Alhamdulillah*, thanks be to Allah!"

Anne, Fowler, and Lockwood stood in awe before El Khasneh. They gave their silent attention to the tomb. Anne moved to the lower portico to look carefully at the sculptures of the men on horses. Lockwood borrowed Hudson's telescope to examine the higher level, and Fowler fumbled in his pockets and drew out a paper.

"I think this is an appropriate time to deliver the poetic thoughts of my Oxford colleague, Dean Burgon:

PETRA

It seems no work of Man's creative hand,
By labor wrought as wavering fancy planned;
But from the rock as if by magic grown,
Eternal, silent, beautiful, alone!
Not virgin-white like that old Doric shrine,
Where erst Athena held her rites divine;
Not saintly-grey, like many a minister fane
That crowns the hill and consecrates the plain;
But rose-red as if the blush of dawn
That first beheld them were not yet withdrawn;
The hues of youth upon a brow of woe,
Which Man deemed old two thousand years ago,
Match me such a marvel save in Eastern clime,

A rose-red city half as old as Time.
Dean J. W. Burgon, 1845

"A bit old fashioned, but not bad for someone who at the time of writing had not experienced the reality. Good enough to win the Newdigate Prize," Fowler added.

Anne sighed. "Imagine if all of Petra were as well protected from time and the elements as El Khasneh. Even the earthquakes you mentioned, Fowler, had little impact here. The fallen column might be the only casualty."

"It must be about 130 feet to the top of the tomb," Lockwood guessed. "I wonder if sculptors dropped on ropes from the cliff above to work. There was no tolerance for error as they carved away this cliff."

Fowler explained what little was known about El Khasneh and added, "El Khasneh means the treasury, but now we know it was a tomb. Earlier Bedouin shot at the urn on the top, hoping treasure would rain down on them."

"Mr. Hudson, this might be a good time to enter the Siq. According to your guards, no other travelers are here today, and they have not spotted any of the local Huwaitát tribe." He sent his men ahead to scout and alert them to any danger. Hudson gave his paintbox and sketchpad to Mika'il who carefully strapped them to the saddle of his horse before leading it into the Siq.

Entering the Siq from El Khasneh on a bright afternoon offered little transition from light to the deep shade of the soaring chasm. Overhanging rock blocked light, and twisting cliffs hid what lay ahead. The path was uneven and a streamlet shared the space. They were aware of ascending gradually, as if rising out of a subterranean passage. As they moved forward, the walls of the Siq turned, opened, and closed with infrequent breaks to the sky. When the light grew stronger, they could see curious, carved nooks and crannies with square faces or inscriptions in the sides of the cliff. At one broadening of the path, Mika'il pointed out a carving in low relief of a life-size caravan with camels and men moving toward Petra. All along the course of the mile long Siq, they found remnants of water channels and pipes leading into the valley.

Lockwood marveled at the Nabateans' attention to engineering. "They have left much for me to study here. Beyond the obvious catchment devices and cisterns in the valley and water channels such as this one, there must be hidden systems of connection and distribution . . . my exploring for tomorrow."

Mika'il's men were waiting ahead where the Siq broadened with more consistent light and a steeper grade. Mika'il spoke to the men who had returned from scouting beyond the entry to the Siq. "My men found no one stationed near the entrance. We can go as far as the arch at the entry to the Siq before returning."

Hudson pulled his small sketchbook out of his pocket, and with a nod from Mika'il, made a quick sketch of the constructed arch which spanned the entrance to the Siq at a height of about a hundred feet. From his reading of Laborde, Hudson knew there were other monuments beyond, but it would be risky to show oneself more openly.

The group turned around to retrace their steps, and Hudson stopped frequently for one minute sketches of carvings and cliff sides. Now they were approaching El Khasneh by the traditional route. Even though they were prepared for leaving the Siq and finding El Khasneh, they were startled when they reached the point in the winding, dark chasm where the cliffs parted slightly to reveal only a vertical slice of the tomb facade. It was the moment of discovery lodged in the mind of every traveler.

Hudson knew instantly that his painting was composed for him. In less than a minute, he sketched the contours of the rock opening to overlay on his oil sketch of the facade of the tomb. His painting would portray the drama and poetry of raw nature opening to the creative hand of man. Every traveler dreaming of wandering into hidden splendors would yearn for Petra.

Clouds had replaced a clear blue sky, and the color of El Khasneh had softened to a dusky rose. Soft breezes rattled the dry leaves of the oleanders. They were reluctant to leave the wonder of the place. Would they remember the eagles of the Nabatean god Dushara, the statue of the Egyptian Isis, the sons of Zeus on horseback, garlands of laurels and grapes? Would they recall the privilege of being almost alone in a sacred space?

Mika'il was the first to break away. "I will ride back to camp to organize the evening. The light is fading."

Hudson found his measuring tape, and with the help of Fowler and Lockwood, noted in feet and inches the dimensions of the lower portico, the doorway, the interior chamber and the circumference of the columns.

Anne borrowed Fowler's guidebook to read about the statues in the upper portico. She was visibly affected by Porter's romantic descriptions. "Your man, Porter, deserves the last comment. 'It strikes the eye once, and ever after haunts the memory.' "

A happy and contented group walked beside Fowler's donkey to their encampment, chatting and laughing about all the earlier reports of danger. They had seen the highlights of Petra without untoward incidents, and the next day would be a more relaxed approach to what remained.

Hudson headed toward his tent, but he was followed by his friends. "Do you think we will allow you to disappear into your tent without showing us your oil sketch of El Khasneh?" Fowler announced from his elevated position on the donkey.

"Well, I am flattered by your interest, your confidence. It is only a rough sketch," he said, as he opened the paintbox and removed the painted sketch. He held it in front of him and tried to imagine what they would see in this vague representation of the grandeur they had experienced.

Anne's eyes scanned the image slowly and carefully. "The colors and proportions are perfect perfect, Hudson. Well done!"

"Will the final painting resemble this charming view?" Fowler asked.

Hudson cringed at the word 'charming' and reminded himself that Fowler had the best intentions. "I expect the painting might be strongly influenced by our view of El Khasneh from inside the Siq. One never knows what strange and wonderful revelations will occur in the studio. Perhaps I will add a few Bedouin with rifles to hint at danger!"

Amir's eyes lit up at the mention of Bedouin. "Mr. Hudson, I would like to be in your painting!"

Hudson laughed and crouched down to the boy's level. "And what did you do with your paints today, Amir?"

"Come and see." He led Hudson to Anne's tent, where his picture of two camels was propped against a small table.

Hudson picked up the canvas board by its edges and examined it carefully. Amir had chosen to paint the camels in a resting position, legs tucked under bodies facing in opposite directions. The slim neck and head of one camel rested on the rear quarters of the other, who had that mysterious camel smile on her face. "Amir, in this painting you show me that you know camels well. They are so alive I can almost hear their throats gurgling and their stomachs rumbling. And what is this little blue spot tucked into the curly hair?"

"Oh, it is the blue bead we hide in the camel hair to protect her against the evil eye, Mr. Hudson. You have not seen it before?"

Hudson shook his head. "Amir, you see with the eyes of an artist. I think I must give you another canvas board." Amir followed Hudson out of the tent, marching with head high, back straight, and a slight grin.

Dinner was still a few hours away, and Hudson excused himself to catch up on his much neglected letters to Katharine. The others decided it was time for tea.

The late afternoon shadows of the cliff behind the tent gave a chill to the air inside. Hudson tied open the tent flaps to admit the warmer valley air. He could see Amir sitting on the edge of his seat, his head and hands punctuating his speech. He was sure the boy was describing his camel painting. The boy had talent and enthusiasm, and Hudson hoped Anne would encourage his interest.

He wrapped his paintbox and sketchbook in waterproof sheeting, placed it on his chair, then scanned the interior of the tent. The diary where he wrote his letters to Katharine lay on a metal box which served him as a bedside table and the caravan as a chest for cooking pots. A thick pad covered with striped blankets was his bed. With its simple, spare furnishings, the tent had been his home for two weeks. A sense of weariness flooded his body, and he lay down on his bed to think about what he wanted to tell Katharine. If only she were lying by him. He was alone, with thoughts that should be spoken, but only Katharine would understand their significance.

He linked his hands behind his head to form a cradle and stared at the dusty light streaming though the hole where the tent poles poked through to the sky. The day had teetered between success and doubt, and he needed to examine the arc of his emotions. He was at last in Petra, undisturbed and able to devote himself to sketches for the paintings likely to restore his reputation. The oil sketch of El Khasneh required no imagination; the scene was complete—and therein lay the dilemma. The paint was not dry on his sketch before he began anxiously questioning motives that brought him to the Orient. Would he compromise his search for the spirituality in nature for fame and fortune? He shuddered at the thought of returning home with no worthy paintings.

March 1868 Diary, Petra

Dearest Katharine,

Today I followed ancient paths until I came in sight of the far-famed El Khasneh, the place you had so longed to see. We had hoped to walk these paths together, and I kept you at my side.

For the entire day I felt the excitement of being where an ancient civilization emerged and thrived before Christ taught, before the Romans conquered. Here were people who traveled out of Arabia for a new life, traded the goods of the world, attended the theater with their families, built sophisticated channels and cisterns for water, created a government and network of cities, and carved tombs from living rock to honor their dead.

The written record of their achievements is minuscule, but the architectural record soars in every direction. There were brilliant architects here. The Nabateans who designed these structures combined Assyrian, Greek, and Egyptian forms with their imaginations.

The tombs in the valley are many and varied, large and small. You might remember the Royal Tombs from the lithographs by Roberts and Laborde that we saw at the National Academy. Each of those four adjacent tombs is striking in its grandeur and uniqueness.

But no earlier drawings prepared me for my first glimpse of El Khasneh. It was like the sweet surprise of rounding a bend in the wilderness and finding a waterfall spilling musically onto mossy rocks. I attribute its wonder to the tightness of the ravine, the looming apparition of the tomb, and its near perfection almost two thousand years later.

This magnificent tomb was carved from the face of a tremendous dark precipice. It is like a beautiful woman stepping out of a doorway on a dark night—shining by her own internal light. Sometimes it seems the color of salmon; other times it looks like a sliver of ivory or bracelet of gold. The colors change as the light and weather play with the surface of the rock. No richly embroidered words express the essence of El Khasneh. In its conception and execution it approaches perfection. It is as a dream that is wondrous and elusive.

I found a convenient rock to serve as a stool, opened my sketch book, spread out the paper, sharpened the pencil, took a square look at El Khasneh and a side glance at the Bedouin, and made my first line. The Arabs got a glimmering of what I was about, and later when I worked in color, they were delighted. Now I have an oil sketch which will become a painting for your study at our new home. I will not know if I can convey the grandeur of El Khasneh until I face a canvas in my studio. But it will be a scene painting, not at all like my past work, and I struggle with that thought.

Today, just when I accomplished the major goal of my travels, I confronted the fallacy of my goal. I am a painter of nature, and my sensibility is anchored in the Americas. Here, I am in a landscape alien to my identity, and I simply do not feel I can portray the spirit of this place. I can paint pictures with beauty, structure, precise colors, but I cannot invest those images with meaning.

Katharine, you alone understand the intensity of my feelings about nature and spirit. You have seen my paintings soar with the power of the natural world. Here, I see the beauty, but I am not able to feel the power of the landscape. Only on one day in the mountains of El Yemen did I approach a sense of the sublime that I may be able to convey in a painting.

Please do not worry about me. I do not feel the journey is a loss. More than any other travel it has opened windows beyond painting. I will bring *home many stories for our own Oriental nights.*

By the time you receive this letter, I might be reading it with you. Now that is a delicious thought!

All my love for you and Tommy, always, Your Thomas

SEVENTEEN

There are those whose pleasures in settled lands be, But in us, great men of the desert you see!

Umayr ibn Shuyaym al-Qutami, 8th Century

Petra

Two riders thundered into the encampment and jumped off their horses in front of the sheikh's tent. Sheikh Saud dashed out, his robes flowing and prayer beads flying through his fingers. The riders spoke quietly, only to the sheikh, their arms pointing toward the Siq. An unruly crowd of Huwaitát men ran toward the tent, shrieking and jabbing fists into the air. The sheikh looked back and forth between the riders and the frenzied Bedouin. Behind them, other men gathered guns and saddled horses and camels.

Hudson stuck his head out of his tent and watched the gathering storm. Mika'il stood midway between him and the sheikh, his gun resting in his folded arms. The wild behavior alarmed Hudson; he wavered between remaining in the relative security of his tent and investigating the problem. Finally he called to Mika'il who turned and signaled for him to come.

Anne, Fowler, and Lockwood stayed near their tents, and Anne translated what she could understand from the chaos spreading through the camp. "A large cohort of Huwaitát is escorting a caravan of foreigners into the valley. At least two of the foreigners are under guard, with hands tied behind their backs. These riders were sent ahead to warn others not to interfere."

"It appears our hot-blooded Bedouin have other ideas." Lockwood held his rifle balanced in the crook of his arm.

"Sheikh Saud is the leader of the Petra Huwaitát, and he

must get his men under control." Anne looked worried. "If foreigners have been seized by the Huwaitát, no matter the charges, there could be serious repercussions for the tribe. Here comes Hudson."

"Looks like an ugly incident heading our way. A caravan from Aqaba was surrounded by a group of local Bedouin as they approached a nearby town—six foreigners in the caravan, two were taken captive. The group includes a few Frenchmen, no mention of the nationality of the captives. You can see the caravan in the distance." Hudson chewed his lower lip as he watched the arrival. "We may be . . ."

Mika'il ran in their direction and interrupted. "Excuse me, Mr. Hudson, I want to assure you that Sheikh Saud has guaranteed his protection for our caravan. He has warned the Huwaitát to stay in their camps. Whatever happened pertains only to two men within their caravan, but it must be a serious charge. If necessary we will depart early in the morning, but I hope to negotiate a better arrangement. Sitt Mezrab, I need your assistance, if you are willing."

"*Ma'aluum*, of course, Mika'il, I will help in any way possible."

"It seems," Mika'il said, "the Huwaitát tribal leaders who approved the capture are not among the Bedouin who seized the caravan. Sheikh Saud and I want them involved immediately, before disputes occur, and they will occur. The Huwaitát here know something about the capture. I expect it relates to the shooting of the young boy."

Fowler noticed Anne shiver. "Anne, are you feeling well?" Fowler reached out and placed both hands on her shoulders.

"I am quite worried," Anne said, brushing off Fowler's concern for her. "Even the little we have heard is frightening. What can I do, Mika'il?" Anne sheltered her eyes with her hand to block the setting sun from her view of the approaching caravan of animals and men.

"The tribal leaders must come quickly. One of Sheikh Saud's sons will ride out to their winter camp, just north of Elji, about five miles from here. Anne, would you go with him? I feel I must stay here with Hudson's group."

"When do we leave? I am ready."

"As soon as the horses are saddled," Mika'il said. "Saud's son can be here with Inam in a few minutes. You should find them in less than an hour. Follow the young man." Mika'il left to arrange the departure.

"Anne, do you know anything about these tribal leaders?" Hudson was not comfortable with an Englishwoman riding off into the approaching night even if she was the wife of a Bedouin. He saw the crowd of Huwaitát retreating from the sheikh's tent and forming small clusters where they argued noisily.

Anne was searching her memory even before Hudson spoke. Her eyes focused on the caravan, and her hands massaged the tension out of her neck. "I have never met them; they rarely come to the yearly gathering of tribes in the Hauran, just south of Damascus. The Huwaitát are a small tribe, not considered one of the predatory tribes. They survive on their herds and small gains from travelers to Petra. I remember the leader of the tribe died last year, and leadership passed to the eldest son."

"What could the men have done?" Fowler wondered aloud. "They were taken before they arrived at Petra, so it is not likely it relates to how they were entering."

"I suspect they committed a serious violation of the Bedouin code," Anne said, as she turned and looked directly at the three men. "A minor infraction of the code—hunting gazelle or petty theft—is addressed immediately with foreigners by levying a fine. Here two men have become captives and the tribal leaders are involved. Frankly, it sounds quite serious, and . . ."

Someone was calling her name. She looked up to see Mika'il leading her horse. Saud's son, Abed, made a slight bow, and Anne quickly mounted Inam. "Hudson, will you watch Amir?"

"Of course. Take care, Anne."

The two riders left at a gallop, passing close to the caravan which was nearing the edge of the encampment.

A heavyset, elderly Bedouin sheikh on a dark bay stallion led the caravan into camp. He carried a spear, and a rifle lay across his lap. A dark scowl disfigured his face. Behind him were two men on foot, roped to men on horseback armed with rifles. Next came a single file of foreigners on camels followed by a long line of camels and horses with men and packs. At the rear was a howling pack of dogs, leashed to several handlers.

Hudson recognized Vesoul immediately, despite the large canvas hat drooping over his face. He was the first of the foreigners to dismount and needed no assistance to bring the camel to kneel. "I know that man," Hudson said pointing to the Frenchman.

"No, really?" Fowler's eyes widened.

"He is a French painter, Jacques Vesoul. I met him several months ago in Paris. We talked about Petra. I knew he was traveling in this direction, but we thought there was little chance of meeting. I will speak with him."

Hudson began walking, and Mika'il grabbed his arm. "Mr. Hudson, you do not understand. We are on Bedouin land, a breach of tribal law occurred, and until resolved, I must ask permission for anything we want to do, anywhere we want to go, and definitely for any contact with that caravan."

For a moment Hudson felt his hands forming fists. He looked at Fowler who shook his head. Turning back to Mika'il, he said, "I insist you speak with the sheikh in charge right away, tell them I know Vesoul, I will vouch for him, and I want to speak with him now."

"Of course, I will ask." He hurried to the sheikh's tent where he found Saud listening to Vesoul yelling and pointing without understanding a word of French.

The Huwaitát guards pushed and dragged the captives into a newly erected tent on the fringe of the encampment. The captives' ropes were secured to a camel peg outside the tent flaps, and two guards remained beside the tent.

Fowler watched with some amusement as the group of Frenchmen engaged in a heated exchange, gesticulating frantically in the French manner. "Hudson, do you know the men with your friend?"

"No. Vesoul mentioned his travel companions were good friends—artists and a journalist, I believe. They left Paris at about the same time I did, but took a quite different route, through

Egypt and the Sinai. He planned to approach Petra by way of Aqaba."

Hudson's impatience grew as he watched Mika'il move from Saud to the Huwaitát sheikh who had been on the lead horse. The hostility of the sheikh heated the air around him, and Mika'il behaved in a way too obsequious for Hudson, bowing and salaaming. In the end, he succeeded in persuading the belligerent man to allow Vesoul and Hudson to meet.

"Vesoul, my friend, are you all right?" Hudson embraced Vesoul whose mouth was gaping open with disbelief.

"*Mon Dieu!* Hudson! What a surprise. What a relief to find you! I am not sure if we are all right."

"We heard you were attacked by Bedouin."

"Yes, just today!" Vesoul exclaimed. "We were overtaken and surrounded by these ruffian Huwaitáts, just south of here. Their behavior was outlandish. Our Bedouin guides were sent back to Aqaba, the Germans were arrested by the Huwaitát, and a Bedouin sheikh from Aqaba is around here someplace." Vesoul looked around for Sheikh Makboul, but did not see him. "Have you had any problems here in Petra?" Vesoul asked.

"There was a peculiar incident yesterday as we were approaching the valley," Hudson said. "We arrived from the west. As we came down the last wadi before the valley, a gang of Bedouin boys rolled large rocks off a cliff into our path, slightly injured an Englishman in our group."

"Did you catch the boys?"

"No. But we did learn the incident was related to some crisis among the Huwaitát." Hudson told Vesoul about the shooting of Faisal and the guarding of entrances to the Petra Valley.

"*Mon Dieu*, I expect they were looking for us," Vesoul said. "The Huwaitát clearly had a warning of our arrival and they knew what they wanted—the two young Germans.

"Do you know why?"

"*Non, non.* I was slightly suspicious when we were in Aqaba. It seemed we were under constant surveillance by Turkish officials and the local Bedouin. For no good reason, the Governor delayed our departure for several days. It was a ridiculous mistake on my part to allow the Germans to join us." Vesoul looked discouraged and tired. He had been crossing deserts and mountains on a camel for weeks. His skin was the color of tea stains, and his entire body sagged in dusty clothes. His usually well-clipped mustache now crept down into a wiry brown and gray beard.

"Look, Vesoul, we all need food this evening, and I have told my dragoman that you and your friends will join us at dinner. How does it sound?"

"Grand. I can add a few bottles of red wine to the gathering, our last bottles, saved for a celebratory dinner in Petra. I fear there is nothing to celebrate. Those young Germans are in trouble."

"We will find a way to help them." Hudson shook hands with Vesoul, and then stood stiffly as Vesoul kissed him on both cheeks. "Come when you are ready."

The four Frenchmen arrived at the dinner tent with bottles of wine and expressions of men anticipating punishment, not pleasure. Even the sight of a table covered with cloth, china, and candelabra failed to cheer them.

Hudson introduced Fowler and Lockwood with brief remarks, and then mentioned Anne and Amir. "There are two other members of our group—a woman known as Sitt Mezrab and her young nephew. You will be intrigued, and maybe relieved, by the presence of a woman, who may prove to be as helpful as she is charming. She is an Englishwoman, the wife of a Bedouin sheikh from a Syrian tribe. I gather it is a rather large and important tribe in the area north of Damascus."

Vesoul looked toward the nearby tents. "Will she join us for dinner?"

"Mika'il has sent her and one of the Bedouin from our caravan to find the Huwaitát tribal leaders and bring them to Petra," Hudson replied. "They should return in about an hour."

"Of course, I remember," Vesoul said. "They were the riders who passed us as we approached the camp. It struck me the figure might be a woman; no Bedouin man would be wearing a blue abaya. Why is she in your caravan?" He could not recall Hudson mentioning a woman when they spoke in Paris.

As they took their seats at the table, Hudson briefly explained the incident near Semua which brought Anne and Amir into their group. Meanwhile, Fowler shook hands with each of the Frenchmen before he sat. Vesoul reacted quickly to the welcoming gesture.

"*Pardonnez-moi, Messieurs*," Vesoul said. "I have neglected my duty as leader. Here you see my rogues' gallery, a little worse for wear, a little more subdued than usual." He appeared more relaxed with the news of tribal leaders arriving and an Englishwoman with Bedouin influence.

"On my left, my brother-in-law, Albert Goupil, is both official photographer and confidant. He has photographed the world's most extensive portfolio of camels." Vesoul attempted to tease a smile out of Albert, who perched his short, rotund body on the highest chair at the table. Everything about him was round from his head to his shoes, and when he grinned, his small, black eyes and arched eyebrows emphasized the roundness.

"My right hand man is Paul Leon, an immature art student and clown from my Paris atelier. He spends too much time on his journal of foolish hyperbole and neglects his sketching." Leon managed a faint smile and slight bow. He was wickedly handsome with fashionably long black hair and a well-trimmed goatee, the very image of a young Parisian rogue.

"And lastly, Frédéric Moreau. He enlisted with a double mission—as a journalist on assignment with *Le Figaro* and in pursuit of a French-Egyptian beauty living in Cairo. He is always willing to report on the beauty." Moreau was more seasoned, older than Leon and Goupil, with a swarthy complexion and dark chocolate eyes. Moreau tipped his head, "*Bonsoir, Messieurs.*"

Vesoul and Hudson attempted to steer the dinner table conversation away from the tension of the afternoon confrontation, but Leon consistently interrupted with his concerns about the seizure of the Germans. The bottles of wine did their job of lifting spirits and were empty before dessert arrived. Lockwood returned to his tent for another bottle of brandy from his private hoard.

On his way back to the dinner tent, Lockwood stopped to

watch the raising of an enormous tent—more than sixty feet in length—on the edge of the camp near the stream. Four men struggled to erect tent poles attached to a woven goat-hair roof which had to have been a considerable weight. The tent sides were unfolded, fastened, and pegged to the ground. Inside, the tent was divided into three spaces by curtains attached to the interior poles. The men carried carpets and bedding into each of the two side sections and then added kitchen equipment and saddles with sheepskin covers to the central section.

As Lockwood started back toward the dinner tent, he found himself facing a hostile crowd heading toward the captives' tent. Men chanted and carried torches. Women, Jamal and Faisal's mother among them, stood to the side, ululating and waving their arms. He searched anxiously for anyone coming to control the unruly mob and found Mika'il almost at his elbow. "What the devil . . ."

"Control yourself, Mr. Lockwood. Sheikh Saud will be here in a moment."

Lockwood growled, "In a moment might be too late. Those men may light the tent with the Germans inside! We need to help them!" Lockwood dropped the bottle of brandy and ran toward the tent.

Mika'il signaled to his men to stop the American, and Lockwood found himself pinioned between two Bedouin who pushed him back to where Mika'il stood.

"It is foolish to think you can interfere. You will only make it worse." Mika'il spoke in a tone heavy with threat.

Lockwood struggled to free himself of the restraining arms and growled, "I will not stand by and allow these boys to be harmed or killed because we are too afraid to rescue them."

His tantrum was drawing attention. Mika'il raised his fist to Lockwood's face and spoke, "You will stop now before this mob attacks you."

Lockwood saw some of the Bedouin pointing at him and waving the torches in his direction. Fear replaced bravado. As Mika'il turned to shield him from the mob, Lockwood seemed to shrink in size. At the same time, Sheikh Saud appeared and fired his rifle in the air. Within minutes, the mob was dispersed, and Mika'il and his men led Lockwood back to the dinner tent where no one had noticed the uproar. Lockwood slid into his seat at the table, and Mika'il placed the bottle of brandy in front of him.

"Quite an elaborate tent for a gang of Bedouin, Mika'il," Hudson said. "I would guess about seventy feet long . . ."

"Yes, as soon as I saw it unpacked, I realized I had misread the situation. The tent was sent ahead for the Huwaitát tribal leaders. I expect the cloud of dust in the distance, near the theater, is Anne and Abed returning with the leaders and their entourage. They must have intersected at just about halfway."

Darkness prevented a glimpse of the faces of the Huwaitát leaders. Two men in white robes and kafiyas dismounted and entered the large tent. Another man, similarly dressed, waited on his horse until a smaller tent was erected. The remainder of the Bedouin accompanying the leaders escorted Anne to the dinner tent and continued on to the camp of the Huwaitát.

Anne dismounted and called to Mika'il. "Would you have one of your men see to Inam? I am famished. Is there anything to eat?"

All the men were standing to greet Anne, but Vesoul stepped forward first. He extended his hand at just the angle that suggested a desire to kiss her hand. As Anne raised her hand with a tired smile, the sleeve of her abaya fell down her arm, revealing the wide gold bracelets and tattoos of a Bedouin sheikh's wife who lived far beyond drawing rooms and hand kissing.

"Madame Mezrab, I am honored to meet you, and I think you may have news for us?"

"I can tell you the leader of the Huwaitát and his brother are here to conduct a legal inquiry tomorrow."

"Mon dieu!" "Sacré bleu!"

Anne paused to listen to the murmurs of concern. "They have asked me to be a translator and an impartial intermediary. It is late, we are all exhausted, but I really must know about your relationship with the Germans, now, before we meet with the sheikhs in the morning. Please sit, gentlemen." Anne ate her rice and pigeon dinner with her fingers and sipped Lockwood's brandy while she waited for Vesoul's story.

Vesoul was sitting at the far end of the tent, drumming his fingers on the table. He thought back over the last week of travel with Karl and Johann Berg. It was difficult to know where to begin describing their relationship. They were simply travelers together for a few days, Vesoul's gesture of kindness to two young Germans who appeared to be sick and mistreated. There had been hints of deceit on several occasions, but Vesoul knew young men were often careless in their speech and actions.

"On the morning before our caravan left the Sinai Mountains, two young men with a pack camel stumbled into our camp below the Monastery of Saint Catherine. They were slightly delirious, severely dehydrated. They babbled about camel drivers who robbed and deserted them on their way through the Sinai Mountains.

"After they bathed and were given food and water, I took them to the monastery for medical attention—they were complaining about severe stomach problems. Karl and Johann were examined by a monk with some medical knowledge. The monk decided they had eaten bad food and offered to prepare medicine for them. We were taken to the courtyard of the monastery to wait for the medicine, and it was then that I asked the young men about their travel."

Vesoul stopped to sip his brandy and watch Anne forming and eating the balls of rice and pigeon in the Bedouin style. Something about Hudson's description of her was familiar. Years ago, while visiting in Damascus, a friend in the French Consulate had told him of a Englishwoman who had sheltered both Christians and Muhammadans during the massacres of 1860. He placed his glass on the table and continued.

"Their travel account was vague, and I attributed it to their poor health. They were weak and confused." Vesoul passed his glass over to Lockwood for a little more brandy. His weariness was apparent. "I have had similar difficulties while traveling in the Ottoman Empire, and I wanted to be helpful."

"Did they mention coming from Aqaba?" Anne asked.

"No, I believe from Suez. They identified themselves as scholars from Nuremberg University, researching classical archaeology in Egypt and Syria. They asked if they could stay at our camp for an overnight. In a spirit of hospitality, I agreed and mentioned we would be leaving for Aqaba and Petra the next day. They were very eager to know my plans for Petra and offered to pay generously if they could join the caravan."

"And you agreed right away?" Anne seemed surprised.

"Yes. I looked at Karl and Johann as two young men on a scholarly quest. Once they had cleaned up, they looked perfectly respectable and seemed knowledgeable. I said they could join us and use two of our camels."

Moreau leaned forward and said, "Jacques, remember to tell them about the wound . . ."

"Yes, of course. The medicine was not delivered by the monk who had examined Karl; instead, an older, more imposing figure came down the steps into the courtyard. He wore the vestments of a Greek Orthodox high priest—a white cassock belted at the waist with a scarlet sash. I remember being impressed by his presence and wondered why a high priest would be carrying the medicine. He introduced himself as Archimandrite Gregory and said he would keep the Germans in his prayers. He asked to speak privately with me about the restoration of an icon in the Chapel of the Transfiguration."

Paul Leon interrupted here. "Vesoul and I had visited the monastery earlier and offered advice about a fresco which was being badly restored with poor quality paint. The Monastery of St. Catherine has the finest Byzantine frescoes in . . ."

"Leon," Anne said, "we need to concentrate on the Bergs. I would like to hear about the monastery another time. Please continue, Vesoul."

"I followed the Archimandrite into the chapel where he told me the monk who examined Karl had found a jagged knife wound. The German would not give an explanation when asked about it. The monk felt I should be advised."

Leon spoke up again. "I saw the wound. It was fairly recent, still raw and swollen. Karl said he fell on a sharp rock."

Vesoul appeared annoyed by the interruption; he shook his finger at Leon before resuming his account. "The Germans were waiting for us in the courtyard. They asked the high priest several questions about the monastery and gave a small donation. On the hike back to camp I was still thinking about the implications of the monk's story. I wondered how the Germans had managed to escape with one of the camels. When I asked that question, Karl, the older and more assertive of the brothers, stated firmly they had paid a large sum to the camel drivers who had deserted them, and had the right to keep one of the camels for their baggage."

Anne stopped Vesoul. "And who would return their camel to its owner?"

"Karl did not care. Ultimately, I felt the questions of the camel and the wound were not important and none of my concern. We would share only a few days together."

Vesoul stood and pushed back his chair. "Leon, would you take over for a few minutes, while I tend to an old man's bladder? Maybe you can give Sitt Mezrab a sense of your friendship with Karl and Johann, a brief account, *d'accord?*"

"Leon does not do brief accounts," mumbled Goupil.

"*Exactement!* Think about his journal, filled with excruciating detail and exaggerated drama," laughed Moreau.

Ignoring his friends, Leon positioned himself at the center of the table. "I was surprised, but pleased, by the news that the Bergs would join the caravan. It seemed out of character for Vesoul to allow strangers in our travel entourage which he limited to his inner circle—fine fellows, as you see before you."

"*Excusez-moi,*" said Moreau, "Goupil and I knew Vesoul had been worn down by the antics of Leon, and he thought two young men would divert Leon. Indeed, the three did form a bond and became known as the Trois Juvéniles on the first night."

Leon knocked on the table for attention. "I will tell them," Leon said rubbing his hands together, eyes gleaming above the candlelight. "That night was terribly cold; the frigid rock of the Sinai massif was wrapped around us. We heaped everything expendable and flammable on the bonfire, creating flames that leaped above the tents and cast fantastic shadows on the side of

Mount Sinai. The shadows inspired Karl, Johann, and myself to present a pre-dinner cabaret with singing, dancing, and the lighting effects of a fiery stage. Our shadows flew hundreds of feet up the mountain . . ."

"Enough, Leon." Vesoul took his seat and continued his story. "In the morning I was relieved to find Karl and Johann were ready early—unlike my men. We were all intrigued by their unusual dome-shaped hats which were as effective as a Bedouin's kafiya in protecting their entire heads. Leon playfully knocked Johann's to the ground. He wanted to see if it would crawl away like a turtle. Karl became very angry, complaining about Leon ruining his hat. Johann quickly stepped between them and jested about needing to preserve their fair skin for the fräuleins.

"Over the next four days we passed from mountains down to immense wadis, and back up to terraces of giant steps. The Germans seemed to know the route, but hung back in the line of camels. One night, in a discussion about Aqaba, Johann said it was full of pilgrims going to Mecca. Karl contradicted him, saying, they had heard about the pilgrims in Cairo.

"On the fourth day we sighted the aquamarine waters of the gulf of Aqaba. We raced our camels across the sand down to the sea, where we stripped off our clothes. The *Trois Juvéniles* were first to charge into the water—Johann warning us against going too deep, telling us of sharks chasing fish toward shore and occasionally feasting on human flesh." Vesoul laughed and pointed to Leon. "I am certain that without his advice, Leon would be lining the stomachs of those meat grinders."

Anne interrupted. "It sounds like the Germans had been in Aqaba earlier. Is that right?"

"I questioned them after the swim," Vesoul said. "Karl was quick to reply, saying, '*Ja, ja*. We sailed from Suez to Aqaba. There we learned of the Monastery of St. Catherine below Mount Sinai—it sounded like a good adventure to add before Petra, so we hired camel drivers to guide us through the Sinai Mountains. Every day they wanted more baksheesh.' Karl was convincing with his wide smile and rosy cheeks. As we made our way along the sea toward Aqaba, I was nagged by the fact that

Karl had deliberately misled me about their travels, and I began watching the Bergs more closely.

"The town of Aqaba is noted for its greenery, and we could see large groves of palm trees which looked like a good camping ground. But, to our amazement, a group of Arabs rode out to greet and escort us to the fortress area where we were invited to camp and . . ."

Moreau raised a finger. "Excuse me, Vesoul, it felt more like a command than an invitation.

"At the time I disagreed with Moreau's interpretation," Vesoul admitted. He stood and paced back and forth at the end of the table. "I thought it was the usual Bedouin hospitality. The very first evening the Governor of Aqaba paid a visit to our camp, which seemed to confirm a welcoming reception. He was a Turk, a young man, not delighted with his assignment in this remote outpost where his authority was trifling. I handed him the letter of introduction given to me by an Egyptian Minister of State. He barely looked at it before passing it to one of his guards. I was disturbed that the Governor was not impressed by the official letter with an elaborate seal and ribbon.

"Within an hour, an army of sheikhs with their Bedouin guards, all hungry and thirsty, appeared from every direction. We invited them to join us for coffee and cigars, and everyone enjoyed the evening—except for the Bergs."

Vesoul nodded to Leon, and he explained. "Johann told me their stomachs were aching again, and they would retire early. I understood their problem; I had been sick in Cairo for weeks. I took some rice and tea to their tent."

"Just before the fireworks in our honor, the grandest sheikh of all, Sheikh Muhammad Gaad, graced our . . ."

"Monsieur Vesoul," Anne said, "it is difficult to hear you at this end of the table with all that walking."

"*Pardon, madame.*" Vesoul took his seat and continued. "Oh, yes, the arrival of Sheikh Gaad—a portly and unattractive man, who was somewhat improved by being mounted on a handsome mare wearing a saddle fringed with silk and gold. An immense pistol was attached to a leather strap around his wide girth, and he carried a lance adorned with bunches of ostrich plumes in his left hand, saving his right hand for scratching himself in places hidden by his red silk robes. To him, I gave the letter of introduction from Monsieur Linant-Bey, his good friend in Cairo. He read the letter, smiled slyly, and said, 'The letter only mentions four Frenchmen, but I believe you have two other men in your group.' I confirmed that two young Germans had joined us in the Sinai, but they were not feeling well.

"Sheikh Gaad rocked back and forth with laughter, until I feared he would fall from his horse. It was a strange reaction to illness. Then he said, 'I trust I will have the pleasure of meeting them on another occasion.'

"The next morning I received a distressing message from the Turkish Governor of Aqaba. It said the letter I had given to the Governor stated that the Egyptian Viceroy's camels in our caravan could not go beyond Aqaba. This instruction was entirely contrary to what we had been told in Cairo and Suez." Vesoul tapped the table with his hand.

"Why would the Governor lie about the letter?" Hudson asked.

"Now I understand it was to suit Sheikh Gaad's purpose— he wanted to delay us in Aqaba to get word to the Huwaitát about the Germans being in our caravan. Needing to find camels would delay us."

"And you think Gaad was working for the Huwaitát?" Anne asked.

"At the very least, in sympathy with them," Vesoul replied. "I recall the Egyptian minister remarking that Sheikh Gaad was a notorious spy for anyone with gold in his pocket or a sheep to offer for dinner. For three days we waited for a caravan being arranged by Gaad. On the fourth day our new caravan of camels and camel drivers, led by Gaad's brother, Sheikh Makboul, was waiting for us. After the usual hassle of camel loading, we were astonished to see Gaad appear with lance in hand on a different, smaller horse, looking for all the world like Sancho Panza. He wanted to surprise and honor us with his presence for a few hours of the journey before he turned east into Wadi Rum. Looking back on the delay in Aqaba, I expect he was sending messages ahead to the Petra Bedouin.

"After four exhausting travel days with one interruption on the third day to shoot desert partridges, we arrived at Elji and stopped for lunch before entering the Siq. No sooner had our picnic been spread before us than a thick swarm of Bedouin surrounded us with guns pointing and jabbing at our bodies. We were trapped in the center of their circle, unable to understand what they wanted from us. I could hear our dragoman shouting, but he could not break through the crowd."

"Johann begged me to hide him," Leon interrupted again. "I tried to calm him, but he fell to his knees, crying for help!"

Vesoul stood again and motioned Leon to his seat. "Into this chaos rode the Huwaitát Sheikh who tonight led our caravan into Petra. The Bergs were seized roughly and dragged out of the crowd. I immediately went to Sheikh Makboul with questions, but he ignored me. I pleaded with him to protect the young men from the crowd, but he did not answer. *Mon Dieu*, I was frantic. The next time we saw the Berg brothers, they were shackled and pushed into our caravan, walking as prisoners in front of me. And that is the extent of our relationship with Karl and Johann Berg."

Silence thickened the air around the foreigners. For weeks, months, they had moved through the Orient feeling superior and invulnerable, living in a stratum above the natives, mostly oblivious to their lives and concerns. Now their immunity was challenged. They were no longer in control of their fate, if they had ever been. They felt foolish, vulnerable, and afraid. The Bedouin, who had been peripheral to their lives, were now central to their survival.

Anne spoke. "I can tell you the Germans are in serious trouble. They are accused of theft of antiquities from Petra and the shooting of a young Huwaitát who may have attempted to stop them." Anne paused as shock swept around the table. "The tribal leaders who arrived with me this evening, Sheikh Ahmed and Sheikh Rami, will begin the inquiry tomorrow morning. They intend to handle the matter according to the Bedouin Code.

They require a few of us to attend—Monsieur Vesoul, Mr. Hudson, and myself as translator because I speak Arabic, German, French, and English. The family of the injured boy will be present. At some point in the inquiry, Karl and Johann Berg will be questioned. If you have questions, I will address them in the morning." On some faces Anne saw disbelief, on others outrage.

EIGHTEEN

"Even he with the long sword must submit to the law."
Bedouin proverb

Petra

During the night, the barking of the dogs guarding the Bergs' tent awoke Hudson several times, their sharp cries a chilling sound filling him with dread. He worried the boys might be attacked during the night, or they might try to escape—either would result in a beating or killing. They were young and must be afraid and wondering why we foreigners were not helping them. Hudson slipped out of his tent around midnight, wrapped in his blanket against the frigid air. Only one small campfire, near the captive's tent, was still smoldering; the two guards were awake, huddled together and sharing a hookah pipe. When a cold wind blew up the sand, he returned to his bed.

Storms moved through the valley before dawn, and Hudson heard the roar of full streams at daybreak. Immediately, thoughts about the Bergs swirled through his mind. Were they safe, cold, frightened? Did they know about the Sheikh's inquiry? Were they falsely accused? He decided a few sketches would distract him from concerns about the day ahead. Propping up the back side of his tent and leaning out slightly gave him a good view of the Qasr al-Bint temple. The rains had washed the structure and the wetness highlighted the rich color of the yellowish-beige stone blocks. The sun had not risen over the eastern mountains, but a glow from the unseen horizon provided a soft light. He sat on the ground and mixed his colors.

That morning a tired, nervous group gathered at the table. Leon was especially anxious about Karl and Johann. The bond of the *Trois Juvéniles* seemed even more vital to Leon now that the Bergs needed allies. He announced, "I plan to take food and drink to Johann and Karl."

"I was told they would be provided with food, water, and bedding. I am sure it is minimal, but they will not be mistreated. No contact with them is allowed until after the inquiry is completed." Anne surveyed the faces at the table. "Are there other questions for me?"

Leon stood up and leaned across the table toward Vesoul. "Are we accepting all these restrictions?"

"Have you not understood?" Vesoul spoke slowly and firmly. "The Bergs are accused of crimes. We have no control over these proceedings."

"Anne, last night you mentioned a Bedouin Code. What is it?" Hudson asked.

"Basically, our law," Anne said, as she pushed her plate to the side and signaled for more coffee. "In the Ottoman lands, there are two legal paths. One is Bedouin law; the other is Shari'ah, the law of Qur'an, the holy book of Muhammadans. The latter is written law, like western legal systems. If we were in a city or town, Shari'ah would be applied."

"Excuse me, Anne," Vesoul interrupted. "Could we not ask for the inquiry to be held in a town by Ottoman officials?"

"*La*, no," Anne clicked her tongue. "We cannot ask, and, in fact, it would not be advantageous for the Germans."

"Why?"

"It is complicated," Anne said. "For example, in the area of criminal activities, Shari'ah reads like the Bible—'an eye for an eye and a tooth for a tooth.' It can be harsh. If a thief steals something valuable, his right hand may be amputated."

"*Mon Dieu*, that is barbaric!" Leon shivered, his voice trembling.

"I am not saying it will happen here," Anne spoke directly to Leon. As she turned to face him, she noticed Amir sitting nearby and wondered if he were listening. She called to him. "Amir, please ask Mika'il to come. Then you need to groom our horses." Amir looked disappointed, but ran off to find the dragoman.

When Mika'il arrived, Anne pushed back her chair to make room for him in the circle, then tilted her head to see his face. "I have only a few experiences with Bedouin justice. Could you explain how the Code works?"

Mika'il thought for a moment. "It is the difference between custom and law. Law comes from outside and requires us to take or not take certain actions. Custom arises from within each tribe and requires us to behave with honor and loyalty to the tribe."

"Is that clear?" Anne asked. "Think of the tribes and sub-tribes as large families who live together every day and depend on each other for survival. They must cooperate, or they endanger the entire group."

"And when they do not cooperate . . . ?"

"In the case of a serious offense such as murder, the injured party has the right to take blood-revenge or ask for mediation," Mika'il said.

Blood-revenge!" Leon's voice cracked as he asked, "What does it mean?"

"It means," Anne replied softly, firmly, looking directly at Leon, "the family has the right to use violence against the Bergs for shooting Faisal. But, here they have chosen mediation, and that is a good sign for Johann and Karl."

"Anne," Hudson said, "here we have foreigners accused. What difference will it make?"

"Probably none," she said. "What they have done are offenses within their own society, and the Huwaitát know that."

"I find it ironic—the Bedouin punishing thievery," Lockwood remarked. "According to you, Anne, camels are constantly being stolen by one tribe or another, and certainly they are more valuable to tribes than antiquities."

"Ah, that is *ghazzu*, an honorable raid, a tradition, not theft," Anne explained. "It is part of our culture, and *ghazzu* permits retaliation."

"Maybe the Bedouin have the wrong men!" Leon stood, gripping the edge of the table and searching faces for any hint of an ally. "They must be terrified. They must think the only people they know have deserted them, and the rest of us do not care. We must rescue them, even if they are guilty, send them back to Germany for trial."

"Rescue is out of the question, Leon!" Anne stood up beside Mika'il. "An attempt at rescue would be an attack on the Huwaitát—it could bring down the force of the tribe on all of you. If you behave irrationally, they will return the insult." Anne waited for that to sink into the group. "I know they are your friends, Leon, but there is evidence for the accusations."

Vesoul spoke up. "Madame, you mentioned the shooting of a young Bedouin. How serious was the injury?"

"The boy survives," Anne said, "but he is paralyzed below the neck. He was shot in the back at the upper section of the spine. He is the eldest grandson of one of the lesser Huwaitát sheikhs. It was his grandfather who led your caravan into Petra."

Fowler dropped his fork, then leaned toward Hudson and whispered, "The man who led the caravan. Did you see his face? He will crucify those boys." He looked over his spectacles at Anne and Mika'il. "What is likely to come out of this mediation?"

Anne nodded to Mika'il. "Compensation, in money or camels, is the usual result."

"And the unusual results?"

"It is not worth speculating," Anne replied firmly. "For now, we need to show respect for their inquiry in every possible way. Vesoul and Hudson, you will be present as observers, to witness that it is a fair hearing of the accusations and the responses by the accused. Vesoul you will also be asked to briefly summarize your association with the Bergs, and I will translate."

"And if we have questions. . . ?"

"I must stress—we are there as observers, not participants. By the way, I think it would be wise to remember anything we say in our languages may be understood by someone among the Bedouin."

"Madame, will you be able to translate for us during the inquiry?" Vesoul asked. "I would prefer to understand the event as it occurs."

"Yes, *Monsieur*. We will be seated to the side where my whispering will not disturb others, but we will be in full view of all participants. I should emphasize that Sheikh Ahmed and Sheikh Rami have anticipated our concerns. They are determined to conduct a fair inquiry, both for our benefit and to avoid questions or retribution from foreign governments. It will be fair, but according to their law, not our law."

Lockwood smashed his fist on the table. "I will not accept your Bedouin Code for these boys!" He looked around the table. "What is the matter with you people? We are from the most powerful countries in the world. There is no need to accept the law of these barbarians."

"What would you have us do, Lockwood?" Hudson asked. "Cable the Navy?"

"Certainly not. All of our countries have consular officers in Jerusalem. They should conduct any inquiry, not these local two-bit sheikhs."

Hudson looked at Anne's face, stained by anger. "What do you say, Anne?"

Anne stood, placed her hands on the table, and leaned toward the group. "Under Ottoman rule, I repeat—Ottoman rule—certain foreigners are granted immunity from our law and can be returned to their homeland for trial. Immunity applies to registered foreign traders and foreign residents in the empire, not to travelers, certainly not to travelers who shoot at children and steal from the Bedouin." Anne turned and walked in the direction of her tent.

Hudson was tempted to follow her, but he knew there were other matters to discuss before leaving for the inquiry. So many thoughts were ricocheting in his mind. Lockwood, an unpredictable man, needed to be watched. He worried about Fowler's reaction to the fact that the grandfather of Faisal had led the captured caravan into Petra. He feared Leon's friendship for the Germans might lead to reckless behavior. As guiltless foreigners, were they truly safe from retribution? Since violations were now under discussion, would someone in their caravan mention his sketches as a violation of acceptable behavior? He needed to talk to Mika'il before they left for the inquiry.

"Forgive me, Hudson," Moreau said, "I know this is trivial

compared to the matter at hand, but what will the rest of us be allowed to do today?"

"I will ask Mika'il to find out, and he will advise you. You can count on his judgment."

Mika'il listened attentively to Hudson's concerns about the sketches. He immediately offered a plan. "It is possible the Sheikhs will decide the tents should be searched. How large is your material?"

With his hands, Hudson shaped a rectangle about the size of a bed pillow.

"I have a good place. In the trunk that carries our china and linen, there is a false bottom where I often hide money. Wrap your sketches in your bedding, and bring it to the cook's tent. I will handle it from there. We should be quick about it."

"Another question, Mika'il. Could you assign one of your men to watch Lockwood? If he knows someone is following him, maybe he will stay out of trouble."

Mika'il was quiet. Then he raised his arm and swept it through the air above. "All around this valley, Mr. Hudson, Bedouin are watching. From little children to old women, they know what happened and are watching. I will put one of my best men at Mr. Lockwood's back."

Hudson and Vesoul waited outside Anne's tent. The Frenchman peered at the tombs rising out of a morning mist. "I expect the lost city of the Nabateans may be lost to me." He folded his arms with a sigh. "And you, Hudson, did you accomplish . . . ?"

Anne stepped out of her tent. She had put aside her light blue robes, replacing them with a black abaya and head covering, both edged in red embroidery. A heavy layer of kohl around her eyes electrified their blueness. Altogether the effect was elegant.

A messenger arrived from the Huwaitát Sheikhs, and the solemn group walked toward the large tent. The approach led them by the tent where Karl and Johann were being held. The tent flaps were closed and tied, and two Bedouin with rifles over their shoulders and knives in their belts struggled to restrain the barking dogs.

The three entered the center portion of the Bedouin tent, pausing a moment to adjust their eyes from the glare of day to the darkness of the tent. Then Anne moved straight ahead to where the Sheikhs were sitting. They rose to greet her.

"*As-Salaam Alaikum*, Sitt Mezrab." The Sheikhs spoke almost in unison.

"*Wa Alaikum as-salaam. Bi'smi'llah al Rahmán al Rahím.*" Anne stepped aside so Hudson and Vesoul could approach the Sheikhs. Vesoul stared at the falcon sitting on Sheikh Ahmed's wrist. Polite greetings were exchanged, and the foreigners joined the group seated on folded, striped carpets, arranged in a large semicircle facing the open side of the tent.

Sheikh Rami picked up a sword lying beside the camel saddle on which he sat and recited from memory the Holy Qur'an:

> "*O, YOU who have attained to faith! Be ever steadfast in your devotion to God, bearing witness to the truth in all equity; and never let hatred of anyone lead you into the sin of deviating from justice. Be just: this is closest to being God conscious. And remain conscious of God: verily, God is aware of all that you do.*" Qur'an 5:8 (Asad)

Anne whispered to Hudson and Vesoul, seated on either side of her, telling them it was a recitation from the Qur'an, reminding those present of the need for truth and fairness.

During the recitation, Hudson studied the assembled Bedouin and their surroundings. The men varied in age from quite old to a young boy whom he recognized as Jamal, the brother of the wounded boy. Sheikh Ahmed and Sheikh Rami were mature men, but not elders. Anne had told him the Sheikhs were brothers, Ahmed being the eldest and the leader of the tribe. Their appearance was striking—tall and slender in long, flowing robes. Their white kafiyas accentuated the boldness of their stern, manly countenances. Their hooded black eyes and hooked noses reminded Hudson of the falcon. They sat on camel saddles giving them a slightly elevated position among those gathered.

Hudson considered the tent interior attractive, even comfortable. Handsome carpets striped in red, yellow and black covered the ground, and woven curtains separated the central section from the two side rooms. Oil lamps of filigreed brass cast arabesque patterns on the walls and ceiling on this dark morning, and a glowing incense burner masked unpleasant odors. Behind the Sheikhs, rifles and spears hung from tent poles. In the far corner, Hudson saw an elderly man bent over the rocks of a fireplace, busying himself with cleaning coffeepots, then grinding coffee beans with mortar and pestle.

Vesoul's attention was absorbed by the magnificent falcon now perched on an elaborate brass stand beside Sheikh Ahmed. The bird's foot was tethered to the stand by a chain, and its hood dangled from the chain. Its head was mostly white accented with a few brown streaks and dominated by large, bulging black eyes. The beak was small; the talons were the deadlier weapons—perfect for snatching prey from the sky or clawing gazelles until they were blind. The folded wings, marbled with brown and gray tones, betrayed none of their power.

When Rami finished the recitation, he passed the sword to Ahmed who identified the Bedouin men seated in the circle. To the left of Rami was the eldest man, frail and struggling with a shaking palsy; he saw the world through eyes glazed by cataracts. Beside him was Sheikh Abdullah, his brother, a younger, stronger man with an exceptionally large head and thick neck, deeply furrowed forehead and a perpetual frown pulling down the sides of his mouth. He was the grandfather of Faisal, the injured boy, and he had led Vesoul's caravan into camp. Next, Faisal's father sat beside his younger son, Jamal. The father rocked back and forth, eyes closed and prayer beads moving through his fingers. Jamal, freshly combed and dressed in a clean brown tunic, maintained a serious expression and held his father's upper arm. The men of the family all had tangled beards and dressed in almost identical tattered brown robes and black kafiyas. Sheikh Ahmed turned to his right to introduce Sheikh Alim, who had accompanied the tribal leaders to Petra. Alim was described as well-versed in Shari'ah Law and history of the tribe. Next to him were the foreigners. Last was Sheikh Makboul from Aqaba.

Vesoul thought he detected a little nod by Sheikh Alim in

Anne's direction. "Do you know the man next to me?"

"There is something familiar about him." Anne looked toward him again and this time clearly saw a look of recognition in his eyes.

Two men arrived to pass coffee, and during this small interruption, Hudson whispered to Anne. "Why are the Germans not here?"

"It is not entirely clear to me. Possibly, Ahmed and Rami want us to hear what the family of the injured boy has to say before the Germans arrive."

Sheikh Ahmed began the inquiry by addressing the only witness to the shooting and theft, the younger brother. "Jamal, you must stand, and tell everyone, speaking loudly and clearly, about the day your brother, Faisal, was shot." A Bedouin standing behind Ahmed moved the sword to the ground in front of the boy.

The boy jumped to his feet and bowed to the Sheikhs. "*Humdillah*, your gracious ones. Faisal and I herd many goats in high land, up over the building of many steps. That day we heard men talking below, not in Arabic. We went to the edge of the cliff and looked down. Two men with yellow hair were picking up stones. We laid down and watched. The men laughed and shouted many times. Each time they found a carved stone, they wrapped it in cloth. Then they brought two camels from the shade and put the stones in saddle bags and rode up Wadi Farasah. They dug holes near the broken tombs and put the stones in the holes.

"*Wallahi*, our goats started running down Wadi al Farasah. I called for the goats, and the men saw me and shouted. Faisal told me to run, and I ran fast. Faisal ran slower with the goats. One man ran after him and shot his gun, many shots." The boy was sobbing now, and he talked faster. "I ran and ran. Then the noise from the gun stopped. I thought, where is Faisal, maybe hiding. I waited for Faisal. I saw the men ride their camels back toward the Siq. I ran back to look for Faisal. Faisal looked dead, not moving. His eyes moved a little, but no talking, no moving . . ." The boy was unable to continue. He bent over, trying to hide his tears. The sword was passed back to Ahmed.

"*Shukran*, thank you, Jamal, you are a brave boy. Sit down now with your father." Ahmed waited until the boy was almost quiet. "Three shepherds, herding above on Jebel al Madhbah, heard the shots and ran down until they found the boys and their goats. Faisal was not conscious. They carried him to their tent, and then Jamal went for his father."

Ahmed stood with the sword in both hands. "I have one question to ask of everyone here. Is anyone able to say Jamal's story is not true?" Ahmed walked around the inner circle and looked into the eyes of each man and the woman. Silence.

Returning to his place, he said, "Rami and I have seen Faisal on two occasions—shortly after this happened several weeks ago and last night. The boy is paralyzed from the neck down. He cannot speak and does not remember anything about the day."

The sword was passed back to Rami. "We know the Germans captured yesterday are responsible for this crime. We know because Faisal's grandfather who sits among us was the dragoman hired by the Germans on their first trip to Petra. Sheikh Abdullah, you will speak now."

Again the sword was passed, and Abdullah stood, holding the sword in his right hand.

Abdullah jabbed the air with the sword and bellowed like a camel. "The Germans must be punished. A life for a life. Faisal is as dead. They shot him as if he mattered less than a goat!" The grandfather's eyes flashed with anger; his frown was now a grimace. Sweat dripped from his forehead on the cool day.

"Sheikh Abdullah, I warn you to control yourself," Rami insisted.

Abdullah dropped the sword at his feet with a few muttered words. "About a month ago, the Germans hired me and my camel drivers in Aqaba because I know a few words of German." He reached into his robe and withdrew a piece of paper. "This paper was written by a Turkish man in Aqaba who knows German. It is a contract for eight days of service, signed by the Germans and by me. You have seen it." Abdullah moved to hand the paper to Sheikh Rami.

"They wanted to move very fast—three days to Elji, two days

in Petra, then back to Aqaba. They were experienced riders so it could be done. On the first day in Elji, I took them to Wadi Musa and through the Siq. We got to El Khasneh, and they told me to go back to Elji. They wanted to have the day alone with their maps and books, and they did not need a guide. Some foreigners are like that. We are only servants to them, not smart enough to guide. I rode back to Elji.

"The men returned in early afternoon. I noticed the camels had been racing. The Germans said they were finished, not much to see in Petra. They wanted to start right away, to return early to Aqaba. We left and camped four hours south of Elji. Two days later we were back in Aqaba, and the Germans disappeared.

"The next day, my relatives found me and told me about Faisal. Everyone in Aqaba looked for the Germans. Sheikh Gaad's men warned every Bedouin camel driver to watch for them. Every caravan that went in and out of Aqaba was searched. When they returned with the Frenchmen, we were ready. We were not fooled by their big hats. We want revenge!" The man was vibrating with hatred and shaking his fists toward the heavens.

Sheikh Rami reached across Abdullah's brother and grabbed the sword. Abdullah was forced to sit.

Anne looked at Hudson and Vesoul. Vesoul shook his head and groaned. Then he whispered to Anne, "I expect I am the next part of the story, no?"

Anne patted his hand and waited for Ahmed and Rami who were talking quietly and looking in her direction. Anne whispered again to Vesoul. "Remember, give them a summary of what you told us last night. I will translate precisely what you say."

Suddenly Karl and Johann were pushed into the tent, shackled at the wrists and ankles.

Hudson wondered what they were thinking. They looked so naive, so young, surely less than twenty years old. Like all young men they believed no harm ever would come to them. Did they know how severely they had injured the boy? Did they think he was dead with no witnesses to the shooting? Did they believe his life had no value? They would be lucky to escape with their lives. The saving grace was the fact that Faisal was not dead, at least not yet. How could they be so foolish, so arrogant?

The Bergs were left standing, just inside the break in the circle. Each member of the circle sat silently, watching the Germans, emotions running from anger to pity. The evidence against these young men was persuasive; it was difficult to doubt their guilt.

Sheikh Ahmed did not deal in a shred of doubt. He wanted a confession from the Germans and assurance that the Frenchmen were not involved. "Sitt Mezrab, we want first to hear from the Frenchman about his relationship to the Germans."

Anne knew from Vesoul that the Germans understood French quite well, although their speaking was limited. The sword was passed to Vesoul. He started to rise, and then hesitated until he saw Sheikh Ahmed nod in his direction. He rose somewhat shakily from the carpet, cleared his throat, and began again the story he had told the previous night, speaking slowly and stopping frequently for Anne to translate. He looked directly at the Sheikhs until he was finished. Only then did he look sadly at the Germans.

Again, the sword was passed to the place in front of Sheikh Ahmed. He placed his fingers on the hilt and traced the engraving, moving his index finger along the elongated Kufic script. After an uneasy silence, he raised his head and spoke to Karl and Johann. "The charges against you are serious—shooting to kill a boy and theft of antiquities."

Karl stood erect with an arrogant expression. Johann breathed heavily, looking left and right and shuffling his feet.

Sheikh Alim placed the sword at Anne's feet. She rose slowly, remaining within the circle. She spoke in German. "Karl and Johann, my name is Anne Mezrab. I am from the Anazeh tribe of Bedouin. My husband is Sheikh Medjuel Mezrab of Homs and Damascus in northern Syria. I will translate for you because I speak Arabic, German, English, and French, the languages of people in this circle. What I say will be only what I hear. I am not permitted to answer any questions. You should answer and address only the leaders of the Huwaitát tribe sitting in the center of the circle, Sheikh Ahmed on your left and Sheikh Rami on your right." She turned to the Sheiks and nodded to indicate she had finished their instructions.

Suddenly, Karl took several steps forward toward the Sheikhs. A gasp escaped from several members of the circle. "We reject the authority of these savages and demand the presence of the German consul from Jerusalem."

Abdullah surged forward. "*Shaitan*, devil! *Khanzeer*, pig! The German called us savages! I will kill him with my hands. I will pluck out his eyes and . . ." Two guards rushed to restrain the grandfather and forced him to sit.

"Herr Berg, stand back," Anne spoke firmly. "You are not in Germany. The German Consul is fully aware of the limitations of his authority in Bedouin lands."

"Sitt Mezrab, I remind you of the need for careful translations. Take the time you need to be accurate." Sheikh Ahmed looked at Anne with understanding for her quickness to correct Karl.

Ahmed again addressed the Bergs. "Have you decided which of you will answer our questions?"

Karl moved back beside Johann before speaking. "I am the older one, and I am responsible for our talk and actions." He spit out his words and raised his chin as if looking down with contempt for the Sheikh.

Ahmed showed his displeasure with Karl's rudeness. He leaned forward and grasped the sword. "Did you shoot a Bedouin boy and steal artifacts from the Petra Valley?"

There was a long silence before Karl spoke. Hudson watched the boy and wondered if he would further insult the sheikhs, lie about being in Petra, not remember his contract with Abdullah. Civility would be a better strategy for Karl.

"My brother and I collected a few old stones. We decided it would be too much weight for the camels to carry us and the stones, so we secured them to pick up the next day. When we were leaving, a large herd of goats came down the hill and got in our way. So I shot my pistol to scare them away. Then we left the valley for our camp."

Ahmed smacked the sword with the palm of his hand, announcing his anger at the lies spoken by Karl. "Did you shoot a young Bedouin in the back—like a coward? Did you insist on leaving for Aqaba immediately, without returning for your hidden stones? Did you later leave a package with the Master of the Port to be sent to Jerusalem?"

"We, we did not . . . I wanted . . . the goats . . ." Karl stammered, raising his shackled hands toward his face. He sucked in a deep breath, lowered his arms and began again. "My brother was sick. We needed to get to Aqaba for help. I decided to send our . . . " Karl's composure unraveled with every sentence until his body sagged with naked defeat. Johann's head fell to his chest.

Sheikh Ahmed signaled to the Bedouin guarding the entrance. The shadow of a robed man outside the tent became visible. The shadow slowly grew larger as he approached the tent, until it loomed over the two German boys.

Under his breath, Vesoul murmured, "*Sacre bleu!*"

Ahmed and Rami stood up to welcome Sheikh Gaad with kisses on both cheeks and embraces. Gaad was wrapped in a broad striped galabiya which further emphasized his height and the rotundity of his figure. He handed a small package to Sheikh Ahmed. "This is the box which the Germans tried to send to Jerusalem. It was still sitting in the office of the Master of the Port when we learned of the tragedy in Petra." He turned to face the Bergs, a cruel smile briefly visible.

Ahmed opened the box, pulled back a cloth covering, and lifted a sculpted eagle's head for everyone to see. The eagle was handsomely carved from limestone and well preserved with fine details in the head and neck feathers, about the size of a baby's head. Ahmed eyed the Germans with disgust. Karl had fed them lie after lie, never thinking to ask about the condition of the boy he had shot to protect their stolen treasures. "Is this more important than the life of a young Bedouin boy? Is it worth your life?"

Ahmed looked closely at the eagle head, turning it in his hands. Raising it above his head, he spoke slowly, "I would smash this into a thousand pieces if it would restore Faisal—but it will not. I would be no better than you—a destroyer of the heritage which we have sworn to protect. We do not believe any of your words. They are as sand blowing in the wind, hurtful but without substance."

Ahmed turned away and signaled for Karl and Johann to be removed. Karl attempted to break away and speak, and the guard knocked his head with the muzzle of his gun. The Germans were dragged from the tent.

Anne sank into her place within the circle. She looked exhausted, and Vesoul touched her drooping shoulder and watched her wipe away tears.

Hudson sat silently, staring into the darker recesses of the tent, watching the play of light entering the tent through small openings. The dust in the light veiled the scene. Shadowy figures moved together and apart. What had he witnessed? Was it real? Was it a mirage already dissolving, or a dream not fully grasped after awakening? Was there an ending? He did not remember an ending.

As most of the group began leaving the tent, Sheikh Ahmed and Sheikh Rami stood and thanked Anne for her vital role in helping everyone to understand the course of events.

"Monsieur Vesoul," Ahmed said, "we have no reason to doubt your explanation of your association with the Berg brothers. I know you and Mr. Hudson will understand our search of your caravan's belongings which occurred this morning while you were here. It was necessary to make certain the Bergs did not hide items in your group's baggage."

"Of course, I understand." Vesoul felt sweat forming on his forehead. "I trust my sketches will not be a problem."

Sheikh Rami gave him a somewhat bemused glance. "Paper should not be a problem."

"Sitt Mezrab, after the family has made their decisions, would you be willing to help us communicate the information to the Bergs? I expect it will be in the late afternoon. We intend to complete the inquiry today and depart for our camp in Wadi Rum tonight or early in the morning."

"Yes, of course, I am at your service."

On their walk back to their tents, Hudson and Vesoul peppered Anne with questions.

"Is a Bedouin inquiry usually so calm? Only the grandfather and Karl injected any fire. Of course, I don't know what they were saying, but it looked mostly calm." Hudson had been expecting more argument and drama, something more like a feisty New England town meeting.

"The Sheikhs demonstrated remarkable control." Anne said. "I have never attended such a restrained event in a Bedouin tent. Bedouin are very excitable, more like Abdullah. I expect Ahmed and Rami were determined to conduct an inquiry that would not be criticized by foreigners as a travesty of justice or a circus of wild behavior. There is always concern about foreign reprisals."

"What will happen next? Do you know?" Vesoul asked.

Anne glanced around the area. "Over there, by Temenos Gate," she pointed. "It would be a good place to sit and talk about the next step before we get back to all the questions of the group."

Hudson steered them to a place just beside one of the arches. It was hard to believe that only yesterday he had sat there drawing rosettes with his only concern being whether he would be able to sketch El Khasneh. He brushed off a fallen block of stone for Anne to sit.

"Sheikh Ahmed and Sheikh Rami will discuss the range of possible punishments with Sheikh Alim who must be well versed in the code and tribal custom," Anne said. "They will look to the past for precedents and strive for consistency. Later in the afternoon, Ahmed and Rami will meet with Faisal's family, and the father of the boys will choose from the options presented by the Sheikhs."

Vesoul's eyebrows raised toward his hairline. "I am surprised the Sheiks do not make the decision. If the family decides, there is little chance the boys will not be killed or maimed, *non?*"

Hudson thought about the implications behind Vesoul's question. He had already decided the Bedouin would choose violence over reason. He waited for Anne's explanation.

"Foreigners assume they should be privileged in societies they consider less civilized. They should be excused from laws, exempt from punishment. Is it not so?" she asked.

Hudson nodded, but Vesoul sat quietly looking at his hands.

"One has to live within a culture to appreciate the intricacies that make it work, to accept the differences they value." She traced the tattoo on her wrist. "Despite what you may have heard or read, Monsieur Vesoul, the Bedouin are not barbarians. They do not chop off the heads of their royalty or slaughter women and children in war."

"*Pardon, Madame,*" Vesoul said and bowed his head, "I was careless in my question."

"I believe the Sheikhs will urge Faisal's family to accept compensation, perhaps some combination of animals, weapons, and money. It is a more modern approach, avoiding physical violence. But violent revenge is still there for the family to choose, just as gruesome punishments still exist in England. What would happen to a Bedouin in London who stole a statue from Westminster Abbey and then shot a child who was a witness to his crime?"

"Anne, you know that is not likely."

"Likely or not, you know the Bedouin would be hanging from a gallows before long."

Hudson looked toward the black Bedouin tents scattered nearby, and he thought about his few insights into Faisal's family. The father was grieving about his severely injured son. He might accept the Sheikhs' recommendation of compensation—thinking the money could make the boy more comfortable. But the grandfather was seething with rage, hungering for vengeance. His state of mind might be compounded by years of insults from foreigners. Jamal would want the best resolution for his brother, but he would have little say, except perhaps some influence with his father.

"I was surprised the Germans did not plead for mercy. Were you, Anne?" In their shoes, Hudson would have begged.

"I agree," Anne said. "Karl's pride trumps his intelligence, a definite sign of immaturity, I would say."

"Maybe it is too soon to speculate, but if a harsh physical punishment is chosen, could we have any influence?"

"No. I am afraid not," Anne replied, as she looked at both Hudson and Vesoul with narrowing eyes. "It is far beyond our control, and offenders are punished quickly."

"As the wife of a leader of one of the most powerful Bedouin tribes, could you not ask for lenience?"

Anne shook her head and laughed nervously. "Vesoul, even in France or England women have little status. Women in Bedouin society have no status. Medjuel would be horrified if I attempted to interfere. While I believe I hold a special position in our tribe, neither Medjuel or his brother would support any further involvement on my part in the affairs of another tribe."

Hudson saw Amir sprinting in their direction. "We should return, Anne. Back at camp, how should we handle questions?"

Anne thought for a moment. "Among the foreigners I think we should be frank about our observations. At the same time, we should caution them, especially Leon, to avoid any actions that could further jeopardize the fate of the Germans."

NINETEEN

The wonderful flight of the proud falcon
As he breasts the wind,
And how his golden eyes hold
The prey which his strong talons shall seize.
"The Falconer's Song"

Petra, March 1868

During the hours Anne, Hudson, and Vesoul attended the Bedouin inquiry, the other foreigners moved around the valley floor, keeping an eye toward the Sheikh's tent. Except for the grunting and snorting of camels plundering the foliage along the stream, the valley was quiet—a quiet that spoke ominously of anger, hatred, revenge, of desperate people seeking an indefinable justice. No other caravans entered, and the Huwaitát stayed close to the encampment.

With Leon's assistance, Goupil lugged his camera, camera stand, and case of glass plates and painstakingly set up his operation wherever Leon and Moreau suggested. Vesoul wanted photographs of the Royal Tombs, but the midmorning light did not show them to best advantage, so Goupil constantly changed angles and fiddled with focus before opening the shutter for each photograph.

Lockwood walked beside Fowler who again rode a donkey to rest his leg. When they passed the Palace Tomb, Lockwood reached into his pocket and slyly dropped the inscribed stone on the pile of tomb fragments. From his elevated position on the donkey, Fowler noticed the quick hand movement but did not comment.

The Frenchman stopped to photograph the theater; Fowler

and Lockwood lost interest in archaeology and continued toward Temenos Gate where they heard voices in the distance. Outside the large tent, Faisal's grandfather was arguing with another Bedouin.

"Sounds like old Sheikh Abdullah is mad enough to chew nails," Lockwood said. "He is waving a knife at the fat fellow in fancy striped dress who passed us this morning."

"Should we . . . ?"

"Head back to camp, Fowler. I will collect the Frenchmen and meet you there." Lockwood jogged back to the theater.

Anne, Hudson and Vesoul were waiting in front of Qasr al-Bint. Leon pushed to the front. "What happened? Where are Karl and Johann? What did they do to them?"

Anne moved toward him and took both of his hands. "Paul, calm yourself. There are eyes and ears all around, my dear, and we must be careful."

Mika'il arranged lunch in the large tent belonging to the Frenchmen. Hudson looked around the group of nine people settling into their chairs. Four Frenchmen, two Americans, one Englishman, the English wife of a Bedouin sheikh, and a dragoman. An odd group, he thought, brought together by the desire to enjoy an ancient site, now thoroughly distracted by a violation of the human code. The gods and goddesses of the Nabateans looking down on the continuing folly of mortals must be enjoying the drama.

Hudson suggested Anne give a brief review of their morning as it might answer most questions in a more logical manner. With her usual thoroughness, she repeated what was said by the Bedouin and the Germans, including descriptions of the speakers.

Everyone expressed their surprise at the poise of young Jamal and the foolish arrogance of Karl Berg. Fowler interpreted the anger of the grandfather as the grief of a patriarch. Vesoul saw it as a loss of face for his tribe—Abdullah had been fooled by the Bergs. The Frenchmen considered the appearance of Sheikh Gaad an intriguing climax, especially since in Aqaba they had viewed him as a buffoon.

"Anne," Lockwood said, "I have a hard time believing what

you say about the civility of the event. Bedouin always argue and interrupt. Abdullah was waving a knife at Sheikh Gaad after they left the tent."

"Oh, excuse me, Lockwood, I had forgotten how much Arabic you know," Anne iced her reply with sarcasm, showing no patience with Lockwood's quickness to disparage the Bedouin. "Might you be mistaking mannerisms for language?"

Vesoul mentioned the sword. "It was interesting to me that speaking was controlled by the possession of the sword. When the sword was in your hand or by your feet, you were allowed to speak. It was a common understanding and was only broken once when Abdullah lost his temper. The guards restrained him immediately."

"What is next?" Leon asked impatiently.

"The Sheikhs will discuss the possible punishments and present them to the family for their decision," Anne said. "We should know the result this afternoon."

Leon looked around the table, his distress turning into fury. "No, no, it is impossible! The family will hurt them. They might even be killed. We cannot allow . . ."

"I am a betting man," Lockwood said. "I will wager the father will choose money. Bedouin are as greedy as wild beasts tracking travelers as their prey."

"Lockwood," Hudson said, "you have an uncanny knack for inflaming an entire table with one remark!"

"What makes you think he will choose money over revenge?" Vesoul asked.

Fowler shook his pipestem toward Lockwood. "Your cynicism knows no bounds, Mr. Lockwood. The Bedouin see our wealth— our trunks of clothes, fancy guns, and tables overflowing with food and drink served in china and crystal. Would not all the poor of the world want to sit at that table? Are the Bedouin less human to want a thin slice of that pie?"

"Hold on! Call off the dogs." Lockwood held up his arms to deflect the criticism.

"What bothers me, Lockwood," Anne countered, "is your sweeping statement—'Bedouin . . . greedy as wild beasts, tracking travelers.' I think you know it is nonsense to judge dozens of tribes, thousands of people by the behavior of the few who hassle travelers. Most Bedouin never have contact with travelers. In places like Petra and Palmyra where there is contact, I agree the traveler may become prey, but sometimes it is due to the traveler's behavior."

"Hmm. What do you mean—the traveler's behavior?" Hudson asked.

Anne paused and then decided to go ahead with a favorite parody for entertaining her foreign friends in Damascus. "Let us look at the genus 'travelerus vulgarus.' There is the arrogant traveler who treats the natives with contempt. The naive traveler who is so ill informed he believes every ridiculous thing the guide says. The sly traveler who cheats the native out of his due and is surprised when the native knows it. The bandit traveler who steals from classical ruins and brags about the sculpture he saved for posterity . . ." Anne had not finished her roasting of travelers before the laughter began.

"*Touché*, Anne," Lockwood held up his arms to deflect the criticism, "I misspoke again. But think about the situation at hand. It seems to me we would want them to take the money rather than inflict some other punishment."

"You are learning, Lockwood," Anne said, restraining her grin.

The group dispersed in different directions. Anne went to her tent for a rest before the sentencing. Fowler wrote and sketched in his Book of Wonders until Amir sat in front of him, begging for a story. Lockwood, Leon, Goupil, and Moreau decided to hike the mile up to El Deir, the monastery, the nose on the camel map.

Vesoul and Hudson looked for Mika'il to ask about the search conducted by the Sheikh's men. On their way, Vesoul said, "My sketchbook is voluminous, including about a dozen sketches of women dancing in Cairo and Suez. They are not nude, but they might as well be."

Hudson had not mentioned to Vesoul that he had anticipated the possibility of a search, an oversight which now troubled him.

They found Mika'il outside his tent, studying maps. He described the opening and closing of each trunk and bag. They searched carefully for antiquities, but did not even open Vesoul's sketchbook.

"What a relief," Vesoul said as he scratched his neck. "Will you join me for coffee, my friend?"

Hudson laughed. "Will it be a repeat of our first meeting in Paris?"

"It seems years ago," Vesoul said. "The surroundings are not as elegant as the Galerie Goupil, but they are impressive."

Hudson heard the resignation in Vesoul's voice. The Frenchman would have little or no chance to sketch or paint under present circumstances. He wondered if Vesoul was disappointed. Vesoul collected two cups of Bedouin coffee from the kitchen, while Hudson dragged chairs from the table to a shady spot by the portico of the Qasr al-Bint temple.

"Well, *mon ami,* has the Orient reached up to your imagination?" Vesoul asked.

"The Orient has vastly exceeded my imagination, both in splendor and in complexity." Hudson's eyes moved slightly from the distant Royal Tombs to the Sheikhs' tent. Only yesterday, he had started his morning with a lighthearted oil sketch of those tombs. Today he witnessed a trial conducted by Bedouin leaders under their legal system.

"Complexity? Are you referring to the German boys?"

"Their arrogant behavior is part of it." Hudson hesitated to introduce a political topic when he really wanted to talk with Vesoul about painting, but he was thinking back to a comment Vesoul had made in Paris. "Do you remember mentioning your lack of sympathy with your countrymen's economic and political purposes in the Orient and saying you preferred the Orient the way it is?"

"Not precisely, but it sounds like a remark I would make."

"At the time," Hudson said, "I interpreted your sentiments as being opposed to progress, and from my reading I had thought it a place much in need of progress. However, in two short months, I have been made much aware of the designs of foreigners to change the Ottoman Empire under the flag of progress, and I have come to question their motives and the possible results.

"For example, in Lebanon, Christian missionaries are certain the Muhammadans should be brought to Christianity. In Palestine, foreigners are buying land for large farming communities, creating divisions among families and neighbors that never existed. Everywhere, European businessmen are setting up markets and banks for the export of goods and resources.

"*Mon Dieu*, Hudson, are you painting or investigating?" Vesoul leaned back in his chair and crossed his legs. "*Mais je vous taquine*. How do you say '*taquine*?'"

"Tease—you are teasing me about my ideas?" Hudson asked.

"I am amused you have been distracted from your artistic objectives. Beware, Hudson, the Orient can lure you into its mysteries and toss you out into confusion."

Hudson wondered if Vesoul was being witty or serious. "You are right, Vesoul, I am more than a little confused. The truth is I am questioning my own motives, my reason for being here, my choices when I sit down to paint. I find myself painting cities with buildings and deserts with ruins, and I have little feeling for these landscapes." Hudson was becoming agitated. He stood up and patted his chest. "I can do it, but it is not me. It is a different person who is willing to bend to critics and patrons in order to . . . ," he paused, ". . . to hold onto fame." Hudson surprised himself. Until this flood of thought rushed out, he had not spoken the last word—fame.

"Ah, Hudson, *mon ami*. Fame is elusive, held too tight it becomes a chain."

Hudson laughed, and the laughter relieved his tension. "Right, absolutely right. The American critics are sculpting a chain around my neck, and I am helping them."

Vesoul rose to his feet and suggested they walk along the stream. "I never worry about the critics. I befriend them, drink with them, persuade them, but never bend to them. They are as fickle as the coquette." Vesoul placed his hand on Hudson's shoulder. "The Parisian critics bounce between demanding works to be 'finished' in the manner of Manet and praising the more natural, sketchy approach of Corot. To some I am a radical realist, displaying the harshness of life; to others, I am an opportunist, pandering the erotic Orient to the rich; and still others see me as an agent of imperialism. I am generous, I try to please all of them!"

"Your clients? Do you paint to please them?" Hudson asked.

"*Mais oui, certainement.* I paint because I enjoy painting, but I must sell my art to live a good life. It is my profession as well as passion."

"And if your paintings stopped selling, what would you do?"

Vesoul stopped and leaned toward Hudson with a puzzled expression. "Ah, yes. You are referring to the changing art trends in France, *oui?*"

"Yes."

"I am quite aware of the new movements. I know the work of many of the youngsters—Bazille, Renoir, Pissaro. It is not to my taste. It is not finished work." Vesoul shook his head slowly and deliberately. "I will never change my style of painting, only vary the subjects. Now I am enjoying painting scenes of the Orient— rug merchants, soldiers, dancers, women of the harem. And happily, it is what my public wants."

Hudson listened quietly, with his eyes fixed on the distant mountains of ash-Shara. Would his public want the mountains of the Orient sown with a few relics of civilization? Perhaps they would, but he doubted such paintings would restore his self-esteem.

During the late hours of the afternoon, Anne was called to the Sheikh's tent. She entered and found only a small group, sitting solemnly. A row of four camel saddles was on her left. Sheikh Ahmed and Sheikh Rami sat on the center saddles, with Sheikh Alim on their left and an empty saddle for Anne on their right. On the opposite side, Faisal's father and grandfather sat on a carpet.

Anne breathed deeply, exhaling slowly. The expressions of the family members did not promise a favorable outcome. She reminded herself they would be stern no matter what the decision. The grandfather stared at her, his eyes questioning everything about her. She stood still, returning his stare, until Sheikh Rami motioned her to the empty saddle. Sheikh Ahmed signaled to the guard to bring the Berg brothers.

Karl and Johann now looked like frightened boys, disheveled and dirty, their eyes pleading for mercy. Karl had abandoned his arrogant demeanor. He bowed to the Sheikhs and asked if he might speak. Anne translated and watched the boys as the two Sheikhs deliberated.

"Herr Berg, speak briefly," Rami said.

Karl cleared his throat and straightened his body. "I confess my guilt. I planned the theft of the sculpture. Johann argued against it, but I insisted. I was the person with the rifle, and I shot at the Bedouin boy. I take full responsibility." Karl bowed his head.

Anne glanced at the Sheikhs. She opened her mouth, but Sheikh Rami placed his hand on her arm and shook his head.

"Karl and Johann, your punishment has been decided." Sheikh Ahmed spoke slowly with Anne translating each sentence for the Germans.

"For the shooting of Faisal ibn Kharúf, you will pay one thousand piastres to his father.

"For the theft of antiquities from Petra, Karl Berg will suffer one hundred lashes."

Anne gasped—the pain, the wounds from a hundred strikes of a camel whip. Her hand reached instinctively to cover her mouth. No one else reacted, and she took another deep breath. As she translated the last words into German, Johann fell to his knees. Karl reached to help his brother to his feet, and they were escorted from the tent. Anne knew she should be relieved; the punishment could have been so much worse. The confession made her hope for leniency, but it had come too late. She leaned slightly forward to look at the men. Alim closed his eyes and moved the prayer beads in his lap. Rami stared at the space where the boys had stood. Faisal's father slipped into his rocking motion. The grandfather threw back his head and an unearthly moan escaped.

Sheikh Ahmed rose swiftly to stand above Abdullah. "Sheikh Abdullah, be warned!" He spoke harshly. "*Wallahi*, I have thrown my face on behalf of your family. You know, better than most, what that means. I will consider any action interfering with the decision for the Bergs to be a stain on my honor and an attack on me!"

Abdullah bowed several times. When he and Faisal's father got up to leave, only the standard farewell was exchanged.

Ahmed and Rami approached Anne and helped her to rise. "Would you join us for a few moments, Sitt Mezrab?" Anne followed them as they held aside the curtain leading to one of the smaller sections of the tent where carpets and pillows were arranged for sitting. Before he sat down, Ahmed removed his falcon from its perch and pulled off his hood. Two hookah pipes were ready with glowing coals.

Sheikh Rami sat and reached for the hookah tube. He inhaled and slowly exhaled the smoke. "It was difficult, extremely difficult to mediate the punishment. After much argument, it was agreed that Karl, as the elder, should be primarily responsible. As we heard, he confirmed his responsibility with the confession. Ahmed, Alim, and I tried to persuade them to accept a larger sum as full compensation, but the grandfather would have none of it. He demanded blood. Because he feels Faisal is dead to them, he wanted Karl executed. We persuaded the father to accept lashes, a traditional punishment for theft, and that satisfied Abdullah's thirst for blood."

Sheikh Ahmed continued, "I know you are disturbed, Sitt Mezrab, but you must help the foreigners understand our ways. This is not the first time a foreigner has paid a price for thievery in the Ottoman Empire, but we are aware the European governments are exerting more influence on the Empire as the Sultan's power weakens. It would not benefit anyone for there to be retaliation."

Anne nodded sadly, in agreement. She would have given a thousand camels to have Medjuel beside her. "I grieve for Faisal and his family, and I am sorry for Karl and Johann. All their lives will be marked by this tragedy. I hope the compensation will improve Faisal's life. It is unlikely to relieve the father's pain. The grandfather—perhaps he will find satisfaction in spilled blood."

"There are arrangements to be made," Ahmed said. "Alim will tell you when the punishment will be inflicted. If the Germans are to leave with the Frenchmen or with your caravan, we will need the Anazeh tribe to guarantee the payment to the father."

Anne was quick to respond. "I guarantee the payment to be delivered by our Damascus banker in less than three weeks."

"Is there anything else to be discussed?" Ahmed asked.

"Will the boys remain in seclusion?"

"Yes, they will be guarded until they leave Petra."

"May we visit them?"

"What do you think, Rami? I would say yes, but only the Sitt."

"Yes, and I will tell the guards you may enter whenever you wish. Our sincere greetings to Sheikh Medjuel and his brother. *Ma'asalama. Bi'smi'llah al Rahmán al Rahím.*"

When Anne left the tent, she found Alim waiting for her along the path. "*Ya*, Sitt Mezrab, I am sorry for your troubles— such an unfortunate day. We met years ago in Damascus. There was a meeting of tribes, and I attended for the Huwaitát. I remember your beautiful garden and your interest in the history of the Bedouin tribes."

"Yes. Yes, of course, I thought I recognized you this morning, Sheikh Alim."

"I wanted you to know that I will supervise the lashes. I have a collection of herbs to give to the German to lessen the pain. It would help if you were present as a witness. Will you do that?"

"Yes, I will be there. Is there anything else?"

Alim paused. "I trust you will help the foreigners to understand our ways, Sitt Mezrab. If a Bedouin had committed this crime, he might be killed tonight."

"I know it is true." Anne was both sad and grateful, and the tension caused her voice to shake. "I have been telling them about the Bedouin code and reminding them of the harshness of Western justice."

"The Huwaitát are grateful to you." Sheikh Alim placed his hand on his heart.

"I must go now to prepare my friends," Anne said. "We should discuss plans for leaving quickly to get Karl to the German hospital in Jerusalem. I will meet you tomorrow, when you are ready, Sheikh Alim."

When Anne returned to camp, she saw Hudson and Vesoul sitting near the temple ruins and Amir near the kitchen tent. The others were probably still on the hike to El Deir. A discussion about the sentence and departure arrangements could wait. For now, she needed to get away from people. She found one of Mika'il's men and asked him to saddle Inam. She mounted her mare and galloped toward El Khasneh. The speed and sureness of her horse focused her energy. The thundering of the hoofs was the only sound, and it vibrated in her body. She felt every movement, every moment, until she became oblivious of all but the unity of their instincts, the synergy of their flesh.

At the tomb, Anne slowed Inam and stroked her neck as they entered the twisting and turning rock walls of the Siq. Anne spoke softly to Inam, her words rising and falling gently like the songs of small birds fluttering through the chasm. She rode peacefully, past the sculpture of the camel caravan, under the arch, and beyond to some of the early tombs, until she stopped Inam in front of a high tomb carved from an upper part of the cliff. The first level of the tomb was quite eroded, but still bore fragments of decoration around the central opening. On the second level, four large obelisks reached toward the sky. The plainness and geometry of the tomb appealed to Anne. Two thousand years had elapsed since the burials in this tomb. So much time, so much human presence erased. In time these days would be erased, but they would not be forgotten by those who were here today. Karl and Johann would survive, Karl better than Faisal. Anne sighed and stroked Inam's neck, then turned her toward the Siq.

On the way back to camp, she stopped briefly at El Khasneh for one last glance at the silent, sheltered tomb. Inam turned her head and Anne looked into her large liquid eyes. She remembered

Medjuel's favorite proverb. 'The air of heaven is that which blows between a horse's ears.' She kissed Inam's ears and turned her into the ravine.

As she approached the camp, Sheikh Gaad was heading in her direction—the enormous man balanced on the small horse ended her solitude.

"Good afternoon, Sitt Mezrab, you have enjoyed your ride?"

"A pleasure to be alone for a while, Sheikh Gaad."

"Alone? I am never alone. Who would I talk to if I am alone?" The stripes over his belly bounced with his feeble joke.

"May I interrupt your aloneness with a request?"

"You already have. What can I do for you?"

"I believe there is an American, Mr. Lockwood, in your caravan?"

Anne was startled to hear Sheikh Gaad knew of Lockwood, and wondered if it meant Lockwood was under surveillance. She hesitated and then answered, "Yes, he is with us. Do you know him?"

"Not yet, but I would like to know him, and I think he would like to know me." More laughter erupted from the Sheikh. "Would you ask him if he would like to discuss his travel to Kerak at around nine tomorrow morning? He can send a message to me at Sheik Alim's tent. *Ma'asalama*, Sitt Mezrab."

Anne found her foreign friends waiting for her at the Temenos Gate. The late afternoon sun cast a long shadow from the remaining pylons of the gate. A good location to talk, since anyone in listening distance was visible. She spoke quietly. "It is beginning to feel like Macbeth—all these meetings and reports." Anne was not smiling, and neither was anyone in the group.

"Is it a tragedy?" Hudson asked.

"It is neither the best, nor the worst result we could have expected." Anne described the meeting and sentencing, including her later discussion with the Sheiks. She spoke of the reactions of the family and the Bergs.

"There must be something we can do for Karl." Leon was

pacing with the determination of a caged tiger.

"Sit down and calm yourself, Leon," Vesoul said forcefully.

"Unfortunately, my young friend," Fowler said softly, "we could place everyone in jeopardy by interfering. We will use our energy and time better by planning how to get Karl to the German hospital in Jerusalem quickly. "

Anne noticed Lockwood chewing at his thumb, in deep thought. When he looked up and saw her watching, he moved closer. "I have little sympathy for Karl, a man who shot an unarmed boy in the back. Even so, I loathe the idea of his being lashed. I know the risks under similar circumstances."

"I believe you," Anne said, "but there is nothing we can do. It is now up to Sheikh Alim, and I will be there to help him. I am certain he will do the minimum. Would you help afterward, Lockwood?"

"Of course, Anne. And what about the compensation? How will it be paid?" Lockwood asked.

"I have guaranteed the amount to be delivered in three weeks."

"Do you need help?"

"It is not necessary, but it would be appreciated. Our tribe has only a little money for emergencies. It is most generous of you to offer." Anne had not really given thought to how she would find the money. Somehow it would be raised. She had a small stipend from England and friends with money who would help.

Hudson and Fowler also stepped forward with offers to help, and Vesoul promised the Frenchmen would make a donation.

As the group dispersed, Anne remembered Sheikh Gaad. "Lockwood, there is something else. There is a man here from Aqaba, Sheikh Gaad, a very powerful man in this area . . ."

"Muhammad Gaad? Yes, I heard his name mentioned in Jerusalem."

"He asked me to invite you to his tent tomorrow at nine in the morning. Something about Kerak."

"I wonder what he knows?" Lockwood almost smiled. "I mean, it is curious he knows I am going to Kerak when I leave here."

Hudson overheard the remark, and his eyes flashed in Lockwood's direction. "I trust you have not overstepped our agreement. There is enough turmoil already. I don't want to hear that Turkish officials in Aqaba are asking questions about mapping and surveying."

"There is nothing for them to question," Lockwood replied sharply. "It is time for you to back off, Hudson. We made our way to Petra without any interference. What I do after Petra is not your business."

As Lockwood strode to his tent, Anne whispered to Hudson. "He is the oddest of men in my experience. At one moment he is congenial and generous; the next moment, he is bound to be obstinate. Why are you grinning, Hudson?"

Hudson had reacted to Anne's addition of "in my experience." He was thinking back to Fowler's comments about her vast experience with men. "Oh, I am just happy to know I have only a few more days in his company."

By the time everyone drifted back to camp from Temenos Gate, the table was being readied for dinner beside the campfire. The sky was clear and bright—a hint of the full moon that would rise above the mountains opposite their camp.

Not everyone appeared for the evening meal; both Leon and Lockwood were absent, and Goupil was late. There was little conversation or eating, but the dogs ate well that night.

After dinner, Anne found Mika'il waiting for her at her tent. "A messenger came from the Sheikh's tent. One of the Berg brothers is very ill with stomach problems. They asked for you, Sitt Mezrab. Will you go to them?"

"Yes, yes. I will collect my medicines and go right away. Could you get a lantern for me?" Within minutes she was walking the short distance to the white tent with one of Mika'il's men holding the lantern. The guards pulled the barking dogs back from the entry to the tent.

Even before she entered, the smell emerging from the tent caused her to gag. Anne pulled her head scarf across the lower part of her face. She lifted the tent flap and entered to find Karl vomiting in a hole they had dug at a back corner of the tent. She raised the lantern and attached it to the center pole. Then she saw Johann, using his hands to sweep dirt into another hole used for excrement. Anne glanced around the tent—two sleeping pallets, clothes, rags, cups, and an earthen jug.

"Do you have water?"

Johann looked up, his face filthy and tear stained, his lips cracked. "Only a little now. But Karl, he cannot keep it down."

Anne gave the jug to one of the guards and sent him to their camp for boiled water. No doubt the Bedouin had not thought to boil water for the Germans. When she reentered the tent, Karl was wiping his hands and face with the rags, huddled against the tent wall like a trapped, wounded animal searching for a place to hide. She was not sure Karl knew who she was.

"Karl, I am Anne, Sitt Mezrab. Do you recognize me?" Anne pushed back her head scarf and crouched down to his level.

"Translating . . . Good German . . ."

Anne smiled and asked, "What have you been eating and drinking since you arrived here?"

Karl began retching again and crawled quickly toward his hole. Johann moved beside Anne. "We have had bread and water. That is all. After we were at the Sheikh's tent this afternoon, they brought coffee for Karl."

"Not for you?" Anne asked.

"I do not drink coffee," Johann replied. He lowered his voice to a whisper. "Karl is very weak. I am afraid the lashes will kill him!"

Anne was searching through her bag of medicines while Johann was speaking, but she looked up when Johann said 'kill him.' "You must not think it, Johann; you must be strong for your brother. I have medicine for him. See, here it is!" The laudanum would be useful, but if Karl could not keep water down, he might be beyond medicines. She poured a little into his mouth, and Karl immediately vomited it. Anne took the water jug from the guard and sent him back to the camp for tea and boiled rice. She removed her scarf and tore it into two pieces. One of the pieces she dipped into the water jug and handed to Karl.

"You must suck on this cloth to get some moisture into your body. You are severely dehydrated which is why you are so weak."

Karl stared at the wet cloth in his hand and then at Anne. "Tomorrow I will be disfigured by the lashes. I have no use for life . . ."

A fury arose in Anne. "You have no right to choose death. Every day I see people scarred in worse ways—blinded by disease, deformed at birth, crippled by accidents and amputations of noses, ears, legs. You will atone for your crime bravely and you will survive."

The despair on Karl's face dissolved in a groan of pain.

Johann moved even closer to his brother, using his body to support Karl and alternating the wet cloth, tea, and a few grains of rice until the retching stopped. Karl asked for more coffee.

"Are you sure, Karl?" Anne did not think it was a good choice for an almost empty stomach.

"Yes, it settles my stomach," Karl replied firmly.

A Bedouin arrived with cups and the steaming pot and bent down to pour the coffee for Karl. Anne looked at the man's filthy hands; no wonder Karl was sick. As the man poured, his hand trembled and the coffee dripped on his dirty thumb before falling into the cup. The Bedouin shouted with the pain of the hot liquid but regained control of the cup and pot, murmuring a few prayers to Allah. He handed the cup to Karl, then placed two cups on the ground and poured coffee for Anne but Johann covered his cup with his hand.

When the man left, Anne tied open the flaps to freshen the air in the tent. She could hear strains of Bedouin songs from the area of the campfire. As she stood listening to the familiar melodies, she glanced at the boys. They were just boys, just beyond childhood. Not so long ago, they mapped an adventure in distant lands with the bravado of youthful invulnerability, oblivious of dangers or consequences. Now they suffered the bite of reckless deeds. Anne gathered her robes and sat down with Karl and Johann. She gave voice to the stories of the songs—a young woman unbraiding her hair for her husband, travelers arriving in the night before hope was lost, camels stolen by day and sheep by night, lovers consoling each other.

Then silence and a different sound arose. Someone was playing a *rababah*. Anne liked the aching tone of the simple instrument which was little more than a sound box affixed to a neck with a single string. It was played with a slender bow. The sounds and rhythms mimicked the human voice in lyrics which spoke of the human yearning for love. Sometimes in the desert at night, Medjuel would play the *rababah* and his brother would sing, each trying to make their instrument sound like the other, reaching to close the distance between voice and string.

Karl and Johann huddled together, struggling with tears brought on by the haunting melody and their own longings. Anne left, whispering to Johann to send for her if there were problems during the night.

TWENTY

Petra, March 1868

At dawn Anne heard voices outside her tent. She rose quickly, recognizing Hudson's voice. She lifted the tent flap and saw Hudson shaking his head as Mika'il spoke quietly.

Hudson came toward her, arms outstretched to enfold her. "Something terrible has happened. Karl is dead. We should go to Johann."

Anne melted into Hudson's arms, weeping softly. "Now. I can go now. Do you know anything more?"

"No. One of the guards from the tent came to tell Mika'il of the death, but he said nothing more. Mika'il awakened me."

When the three of them arrived at the Berg's tent, Johann was sitting beside Karl's body. He did not look up or respond to their questions. He simply stared at his hands. Anne gathered her robe and sat beside him, placing her arm around his shoulder. Gradually, he relaxed, softened, and turned to look at Anne.

"I do not . . . I do not know what happened. He was very tired, very quiet. We went to sleep. Now he is gone, gone forever."

"May we look at him, Johann?" With Johann's permission, Anne and Mika'il examined the head and chest, lifting each piece of clothing gently. There were no new wounds, only a scab on the knife wound.

"Johann, I am sorry, very sorry," Anne whispered as she sat beside him again. "You did everything possible for your brother. He was extremely ill last night. It is difficult to recover from such severe vomiting and diarrhea."

Johann had no words to give them.

After a time of silence, Anne removed her shawl. "Johann,

317

may I cover Karl with this?"

Johann took the cloth and placed it over his brother like a blanket and tucked it around his neck and hips. He was not ready to cover Karl's face.

Anne motioned to the others to follow her outside. She walked toward the stream, and then turned to Hudson and Mika'il. "We will need to make decisions for Johann. Mika'il, will you advise Sheikh Ahmed now, before he leaves for Wadi Rum? He will want to confirm the death."

After Mika'il left, Anne thought about the next steps. Karl must be cleaned and prepared for burial. Anne asked Hudson to find Vesoul and ask him to get clothing from Karl's baggage.

Sheikh Alim returned with Mika'il. He entered the tent with Anne and saw the body and the grieving brother. He looked around the filthy tent with its distasteful odors and shook his head sadly. He signaled to Anne to come outside with him and Mika'il.

"*Wallahi*, it is sad, very sad. What was unfortunate has become tragic. Mika'il found me saying my prayers, preparing for the difficult day ahead. I could hardly believe what he told me. The Sheikhs left at daybreak, but I will help you, Sitt Mezrab, if I can."

Anne bowed her head and expressed her gratitude. "We need to arrange the burial. Will you ask the Petra Sheikhs where they will allow it?"

"Given the circumstances, they will not want him buried in Petra. I will suggest Jebel Haroun. It is a place holy to Christians and Muhammadans," Sheikh Alim said.

Mika'il quickly added, "We could have a gravesite ready before sundown, Sitt Mezrab."

The campground quickened with activity. The Bedouin took down the large tent and saddled camels to follow the Sheikhs to Wadi Rum. All but the Petra Huwaitát would depart. Anne constructed a mental list. Ask Hudson to speak with Fowler and Lockwood. Talk to Vesoul about Karl and discuss burial and departure plans. Take care of Johann. Explain to Amir. Decide on their departure. These were the priorities.

Anne returned to the tent and sat beside Johann. "Your brother will be cared for by our men. We will bury him on Jebel Haroun, a mountain top where Moses buried his brother, Aaron, on his return from Egypt. It is a high place, a holy place for Christians. Please come with me now, Johann."

Her gentleness persuaded Johann. He bent to kiss his brother's forehead and moved the shawl over his face. She held his hand as they walked back to the camp, avoiding everyone.

Anne settled Johann in her tent, urging him to rest in Amir's bed. She sat with him for a while. Something about the previous evening was troubling her, but she could not retrieve it from the myriad of scenes. With a few deep breaths, she concentrated her memory on the tent where the Bergs were held. She visualized the pallets, the rags, the jug, water cups, and the coffee cups . . . the coffee? Why did they give Karl coffee in the afternoon? The Bedouin were usually not so generous with their coffee.

Later Karl asked for more coffee; we both had coffee from the same pot. There was the clumsiness of the Bedouin who poured the coffee, but he hurt only himself. Or did he?

She remembered a story Medjuel told one night in Homs when some of her English friends were visiting. A Bedouin was angry with an acquaintance for killing several of his sheep without permission. He bribed the coffee man to poison the man. The coffee man would need to serve several people from the same pot to avoid suspicion. He mixed the thick black residue of old coffee with arsenic, applied the paste to his thumb, and waited for it to dry. When he served the coffee to the man who was meant to die, he placed his thumb over the edge and poured the coffee onto his thumb; the poison and coffee falling into the cup.

Anne shivered. It was exactly what happened in the Bergs' tent. The symptoms of arsenic poisoning are the same as cholera or severe dysentery—vomiting and diarrhea, followed by dehydration and death.

There was no way to prove it—a perfect crime. Anne was convinced it had been arranged by the grandfather, and she was also convinced that no good would come of revealing it. An accusation would bring more grief to Johann, anger from the foreigners, and denial by the Bedouin. She hated the thought of the grandfather having his revenge unpunished, but she understood his vindictiveness. The cruel hunting down of his innocent grandson was unforgivable.

Anne rubbed her neck and shoulders. It was almost noon, and there was still much to be done. Mika'il had placed a tub of warm water in an empty tent; she quickly bathed to remove the filth of the Bergs' tent. The clean, cotton robe felt good against her skin. She peered out of the tent and saw the others at the lunch table. She was hungry, very hungry.

"Come, join us, Anne," Fowler called out. "Hudson has briefed us on what we need to know, and we have declared a moratorium on questions for you, at least until after a decent lunch!"

"Yes, a break would be welcome. And what is the lovely aroma heading our way from the cook tent?"

"Pigeons, masses of pigeons," Lockwood announced. "Sheikh Gaad and I did a bit of hunting this morning."

With a faint grin, Anne said, "Oh, was hunting what he wanted to discuss with you?"

"The Sheikh is a man of many interests." Lockwood winked at Anne.

Anne sat beside him for lunch and needled him for a full report. "How did Gaad know you were here, Lockwood?"

Lockwood moved the remaining rice into a pile on his plate and considered his reply. "When I was in Jerusalem, I met with a Turkish bey who is a friend of Gaad's. Omar Bey notified Gaad that I would be in Petra around this time. Gaad came to Petra because of the French and German group, and our visits happened to coincide."

"And Kerak? Why did Gaad mention Kerak?"

Lowering his voice, Lockwood turned to face Anne. "Gaad is a cagey old fellow with pockets that want lining. Omar Bey mentioned I was interested in bitumen from the Dead Sea, and Gaad decided bitumen sounded like black gold. He told me there are few people between Kerak and Aqaba who are not indebted to him, including the sheikh in Kerak whom Omar Bey recommended."

"Will Gaad accompany you to Kerak?"

Lockwood pushed his chair back from the table and picked at his teeth. "It seems I have no choice about it. He marched over me like Sherman going through Atlanta."

"What?"

Lockwood laughed. "That is what we say in the South when someone is determined to have his way—General Sherman laid waste to Atlanta, Anne."

"Is your bitumen project a secret?"

"Are there any secrets in the Orient? Word travels from Constantinople to Jerusalem to Aqaba to Petra faster than I do!" he exclaimed, then lowered his voice. "My aim is to limit the number of Turks and Arabs who feel entitled to trade a signature for a share."

Leon, usually the extrovert at the table, sat enveloped in gloom. Letting go of the subject of Karl and Johann was not easy for him. It annoyed him to see the others lighten their moods and chat about what now seemed like trivia to him. A horrible event had occurred; the aftermath was smothering him. He saw himself as very much like Johann, easily led, inexperienced, often thoughtless about his actions. He imagined himself joining into their scheme for the hell of it. Not the shooting, he would never go that far. Of course, the shooting was not part of the plan, it was an accident, a dishonorable choice in a moment of panic. The kind of moment that tests the mettle, and Karl failed miserably. Leon thought of Johann grieving for his brother. Coming to terms with the event would be left to the future. Johann needed company and solace. He could pity Johann; nothing else was of value.

He excused himself from the table, taking food and water for his friend. He found Johann sitting on Amir's bed like a puppet waiting for someone to pull his strings. He did not want to be asked anything, simply moved to the next place on his journey home.

"Excuse me, Sitt Mezrab, I am sorry to interrupt your lunch," said Alim. "I have only a few minutes; the last of our caravan is leaving. The arrangements for the burial are completed. Mika'il was part of the discussions and knows everything. His men are preparing the grave for Karl. Your group may build a small cairn to mark the spot."

"We are grateful for your help." Anne rose to bid him farewell. "I hope we will meet again under better circumstances, Sheikh Alim. *Ma'asalama.*"

"*Inshallah. Ma'asalama.*"

Mika'il laid out scenarios about timing and departure for the group to consider. Hudson and Fowler planned to leave the next morning with him to travel toward Gaza. Anne, Amir, and Lockwood would depart in the morning for Kerak with a caravan arranged by Sheikh Gaad. Anne and Amir would continue on to Damascus the following day. The caravan bringing Vesoul's group and the Germans to Petra had returned to Aqaba, but Mika'il's caravan was available to escort the Frenchmen and Johann to Hebron where they could hire horses to take them to Jerusalem. Vesoul accepted his offer and talked to his men about timing.

"I suggest we pack and leave quickly, this afternoon," Vesoul said. "We can make Jebel Haroun in four hours and bury Karl before sunset. Camp there, and start the journey toward Hebron in the morning." Vesoul called it a suggestion, but his group knew he was announcing the plan. They all agreed. For them, Petra was finished before they entered the valley.

Hudson and Vesoul remained at the table. Both were thinking, just as they did months ago, that it was too soon to part. Hudson noticed the Frenchman was staring at the Royal Tombs with a somewhat melancholy expression. The afternoon sunlight heated their facades, causing the muted colors to dance on the warmth of the stone. "My friend, you have not had much time for your sketchbook, have you?"

Vesoul shook his head. "A few sketches of the Urn Tomb this morning."

"Are you discouraged?"

"Yes and no," Vesoul replied. "I regret I had only the few hours this morning to see the tombs and do a little sketching. However, I have seen enough to know Petra does not appeal to my painterly instincts."

"No?" Hudson was surprised.

Vesoul laughed and slapped Hudson on the shoulder. "Where are the sultans and dancing girls?" His bushy eyebrows inched upward. "Seriously, Hudson, I have drunk often from the wellsprings of the exotic, and there is no such liquid here. Here, one is surrounded by death, and we have added more. Petra is a necropolis, so distant from the living, breathing Orient that arouses my creative energy."

"Frankly, Vesoul, I find myself mystified by the layers and contradictions of the Orient which you find so entertaining." Hudson placed his hands squarely on the table. "I even find myself questioning your motives."

"What do you mean, *mon ami?*"

Hudson chose his words carefully. "Vesoul, one thing I have not found in this Orient is the source of your erotic paintings. Where do you find all those enticing young nudes? Are they only in Cairo? Or do you invent them to sell paintings?"

Vesoul's mustache twitched at the sting of Hudson's comment. "In all my work, I am infusing reality with my imagination. I believe that is what you and I do as painters. I am not here to simply portray a scene as it is—I leave that to Albert's camera."

Hudson now felt embarrassed by his caustic remark. "Please forgive my questioning of your motives. It was unconscionable on my part. I attribute it to agonizing about my own motives."

Vesoul recognized the confusion in Hudson's face and leaned toward him. "Life is entertaining because of the variety of choices and motives. There are times for gravity and times for enjoyment—both in art and life." Vesoul placed his coffee cup on the table and yawned. "Would you like to walk? I need a little exercise."

The two men strolled beside the stream flowing through the wadi. The water coursed around rocks and over pebbles, deepening the colors of the sandstone. Clusters of dull green plants reached visible roots toward the water. Water, the essential element, the elixir to revive these barren lands. Hudson wondered about reviving the human spirit in a landscape impoverished by a sparse, fragile nature. His identity resided in a diverse and bountiful land, and he suspected lands so foreign to his experience would never allow him to find their spirit.

"And you, Hudson, how do you imagine painting the rose red city, lost in time?"

Hudson regretted there was not a long evening ahead to sit with Vesoul under the umbrella of a starry night sky and describe his feelings about painting in these lands. He stopped and looked at his hands, then turned to face Vesoul. "For me, the desert landscape is alluring but elusive. The architecture is more intelligible—it speaks with beauty and power about a nearly unknown people who were once central to civilization, a visible reminder of the transitory nature of human efforts."

"And why not paint that conundrum?" Vesoul asked as he clasped his hands behind his back.

The image of a painting by Vesoul at the Galerie Goupil arose from Hudson's memory. Napoleon sat on his horse gazing at the Sphinx, a survivor of forty centuries of history. Hudson appreciated the comment, but knew such paintings were not his talent. "I will paint El Khasneh for my wife. She longed to walk through the Siq and find the tomb rising above her . . . there could be a few other small paintings."

"I hear no enthusiasm in your voice, Hudson," said Vesoul.

Hudson picked up a few stones and thought about skimming them across the stream. Instead, he placed them in his pocket. As he looked across the valley toward the Royal Tombs, he searched for a reply. "Before I arrived in the Orient, I imagined it would be enough to explore; understanding and inspiration would follow.

Now I know this is the wrong landscape for me. It is either too profound or too simple. While I find a certain beauty, I do not find the essence."

"I am not certain I understand you, Hudson, but maybe I understand the difference between us." Vesoul linked his arms behind his back and looked up at his American friend. "I enjoy painting scenes of people living in the Orient in splendid or dreadful circumstances, and I trust the patrons who buy them enjoy looking at the scenes. You search for a high moral purpose to infuse your art. It is an expectation that may not transfer in a culture where survival is so precarious."

A call announced the departure of Vesoul's caravan. The two men embraced and promised to meet again in Paris or New York.

In the late afternoon Hudson could see Vesoul's caravan ascending the wadi toward Jebel Haroun. He sat with his paintbox near Temenos Gate, gazing at one particular rock about the size of a steamer trunk. Its colors mesmerized him—vibrant shades of red and ochre, purple and brown, a rock not just warm, but burning with color. The broken surface emphasized the tension in the colors, folding and unfolding in a harsh dissonance. It would be his last oil sketch in Petra, a completely abstract vision of the forces of nature, stacked by ancient cataclysms.

TWENTY-ONE

Think, in this batter'd Caravanserai
Whose Portals are alternate Night and Day, How
Sultan after Sultan with his Pomp
Abode his destined Hour, and went his way . . .
Omar Khayyam, 11th Century

Petra, March 1868

Sunlight slipped softly toward twilight as Hudson ambled back to the camp. Clouds edged with a golden halo moved across the last rays of the sun, reminding him of summer evenings in the Catskills. He inhaled the eloquent poetry of the heavens filling his senses with the glory of a sky painted by the unseen hand. Tomorrow, the journey home would begin, and the thought lightened his step.

"I thought Vesoul had a military background," Lockwood remarked as Hudson took his seat at the table. "The way he gives orders and stands like he has a rod up his back. When I asked him if he had served in the French army, he looked as if I had insulted him. He mumbled something about unknowing lackeys in the service of politicians."

"You struck a sensitive spot in Monsieur Vesoul," Hudson said. "He deplores the current French tendency to use the military as an advance group for politicians and businessmen—imperialism on the march, according to him."

"One person's imperialism is another's international trade," Lockwood quipped. "I have sat in the cafés of Montmartre during the midnight hours, listening to the debates of inebriated Parisian intellectuals and their journalist friends. They complain about politicians who have inhaled the intoxicant of imperialism supplied by their merchant friends. A few journalists write about artists who nurture imperialism."

"Nurture? What do you mean by nurture?" Hudson asked.

"If an artist creates paintings of Christians slaughtered by Turkish soldiers or nude women in chains enslaved by Arab traders, does that not portray the Orient as a backward and corrupt society in need of European civilization?" Lockwood repeated arguments he had heard from French writers on several occasions.

"One needs to be careful in assigning motives to artists. I can assure you Vesoul's sentiments are entirely opposed to imperialism." Hudson said.

"Of course, there is a vast difference between motive and interpretation," Fowler said. "Historically speaking, art has often served politics and just as often has been kidnapped by politics. Perhaps, Lockwood, that is the dichotomy you are addressing?"

Lockwood looked puzzled, as if he did not understand what dichotomy meant, but he nodded in agreement.

"The Bedouin woman needs some enlightenment here," Anne said cheerfully. "My appetite for art is rarely nourished by gallery visits. I am familiar with the English Orientalist painters but have never seen Vesoul's work. Can you describe his art for me?"

Hudson leaned back as the cook's son removed his soup plate. He smoothed the cloth and thought about Vesoul's exacting technical skill—every detail pursued to perfection, each surface finished to smoothness and brilliance, the nude women with skin polished like white marble, street scenes dazzling the senses with colors and the variety of the human species.

"Vesoul's style is realistic," Hudson began. "He portrays the Orient in stunning moments frozen in time and place. The rug merchant displays his woven treasures in an old palace. Street urchins sell meat dripping with blood. Dancers entertain soldiers in a café, and the sultan watches the bathing of the harem. Men rise to the prayer call of the imam and the battle cry of the Sultan. And, as Lockwood mentioned, Arab dealers sell slaves in the market. He paints an exotic world, a multitude of races and societies—one with great appeal on both sides of the Atlantic."

"Upon my word, people are hanging paintings of slave dealers and street urchins in their parlors?" Fowler looked shocked, then amused. "Do you know the Americans who buy this art, Hudson?"

"Yes, I have seen Vesoul's paintings in the drawing rooms of sumptuous mansions on Fifth Avenue." Hudson and Vesoul had shared their amusement about the contradictory behavior of their patrons. "Wealthy American industrialists collect his erotic paintings of the Orient at the same time they repress sexuality in our culture. Similarly, as Lockwood mentioned, railroad barons buy my paintings of the unspoiled American landscape while they lay down tracks destroying huge forests." Hudson threw up his hands and shrugged.

Dinner was finished; the cook's son cleared the last plates from the table. "It feels like the last supper," Fowler remarked as he filled his pipe, "and I see you did not eat your last pudding, Anne."

Anne frowned at the glutinous white mass. "The puddings are the only part of this journey I will not miss."

A full moon was rising over the eastern mountains—a moon like a giant sponge, squeezing light into darkness, reversing night into twilight. Moonshine plunged into the stream flowing through the wadi, and the dark water glittered with flakes of white light among a thousand shades of blue and black. Beyond, the exposed rock held the shape of tombs retreating into the cliffs at a millennial pace as wind, rain and earthquakes slowly erased the hand of man. They would miss these moments.

When coffee arrived, Hudson inhaled deeply and audibly the scent of coffee and cardamom. "I will miss this coffee back in New York. Do you think I might find a Bedouin coffee pot in Beirut, Anne?"

"*Ma'lum*, of course. There is a market near the al-Omari Mosque with new and old coffee pots and many varieties of Arabian coffee." Anne swirled her coffee cup, and showed them the patterns formed by the thick residue of the Bedouin brew. "Women in our camps turn over the cups, allow the residue to dry, and then predict the future." Anne turned over her cup, placed her chin on her hand, and thought about the secret in the residue of Karl's coffee cup.

"A piastre for your thoughts, Anne." Hudson smiled as he echoed an earlier request from her many days ago.

Anne looked around the valley, at peace again. The campfire flamed and snapped in the cold night air; only a small group of Bedouin remained. "I was thinking about the Orient depicted by Vesoul, especially what you said about the mixture of races. For me, the people you describe in his paintings conjure up a human map of the Orient—a map of intermingled races, languages, and religions with vague or nonexistent boundaries. It is a map of layers rather than a map of boundaries. It is the image I have of the Ottoman Empire. Does it make sense to you?"

"I think I know what you mean," Hudson said. "On my map I could not find where we would cross from Palestine into Syria or Arabia . . . "

'Yes, yes," Anne interrupted, "it is exactly what I mean. When I was a child, a map of the Ottoman Empire hung in our library. I remember asking my tutor why there were so many place names in Europe and so few in Asia and Africa. I have forgotten his answer." Anne stopped for a moment.

"Even now," she continued, "European maps have almost bare, open spaces for the lands east of the Mediterranean. A few towns along the coast are designated, a few cities—like Aleppo, Damascus, Beirut, Jaffa, Jerusalem—and then large words for Syria and Arabia. Do they know or care that people have lived for millennia in these vast areas and given names to every feature?"

"No reason to worry there." Lockwood pushed back his chair and crossed his legs. "In the next few decades there will be sheaves of new maps with neatly drawn, accurate borders and many new names."

"That is what the Bedouin fear." Anne replied with a sharp edge of sadness.

"They have good reason to fear." Fowler removed his pipe

and used a stone to cover the bowl and increase the fire. "Those enormous areas of wide open space tempt ministers sitting in foreign capitals to draw borders for states or colonies as if the human map does not exist."

"There will be maps whether you like it or not," Lockwood said. "When Turks or tribes ignore mapping, others will do it for them."

"How can you be so arrogant?" Anne spit out the words, glowering at Lockwood. "What gives foreigners the right to put down names and boundaries?"

No one answered Anne's question, and she continued. "The Bedouin have maps, maps in their minds—maps alive with people and animals, wadis and streams, mountains and deserts, plains and oases. They do not need a road or path to guide them over hundreds of miles to their winter and summer camps, to locate the open plains watered and fertilized by winter rains. They know exactly where to graze their sheep and water their camels, and they know when they trespass into another tribe's lands. They know their way to the caravanserais in Aleppo and Resafa and the markets in Homs and Raqqa. They know the Darb al- Shami track for the Hajj caravans, leading safely from Damascus through the desert forts of Qatrana, Ma'an, and Dhat al-Hajii to Mecca and Medina. Every year, Bedouin women find and pray beside the stone of the pregnant woman in the Beka'a Valley, and young boys pluck the greenish black eggs of the kattas from the cliffs of el Szafa. They have known these places forever, and they do not forget."

Fowler puffed on his pipe in the silence that followed. "Lockwood, have you considered Anne's argument against your maps? You know she is defending the Bedouin way of life, their freedom to . . ."

Anne interrupted again. "The Bedouin know that maps inevitably change land into property. One has a different understanding of the world when the land around you is not divided into property."

"Anne, the empire is falling apart," said Hudson. "Borders will be established in this region. Are you worried about the

330

borders or the changes they will bring?"

"The borders and the changes are two sides of the same coin," Anne argued. "As Fowler said, the borders are drawn by people who do not recognize the human map. What will happen when they divide our tribal grazing lands, place us in a region where our enemies predominate, separate us from our markets and oases? Mapmakers draw lines which fit their purposes, not our needs to preserve our livelihoods and traditions."

"None of us can avoid the changes progress brings. The Bedouin will adjust and benefit from it." Lockwood spoke as if progress were a medicine to cure all human desires.

Anne was tired, too tired to continue, but she was too annoyed to allow Lockwood the last word. "The Bedouin have always traded what you call progress for their idea of freedom. To be acceptable, change must be according to their timetable not yours, Lockwood." She rose and bid everyone good night.

Before she entered her tent, she skirted the edge of the campfire and went in search of Inam. The mare was standing in the moonlight, waiting for her. She stroked her forehead and scratched her ears, and the horse nickered softly. "In three or four days, we will be home, my beauty. Medjuel will be waiting for us, *Inshallah*."

Hudson lingered by the campfire after everyone had retired to their tents. The fire burned bright and hot with sparks shooting like fireworks into the night. Alone with the last fire of the last night, he already missed the company of the others. They were four strangers, tentative at first, only gradually revealing their thoughts and lives. Fowler had appealed to him immediately, no doubt because they shared a calm, reserved nature. He admired Fowler's empathetic responses to people and enjoyed his intellect. Only Lockwood managed to ruffle his feathers, a nuisance from the beginning, though occasionally his quirky candor redeemed him. Then there was Anne, the unexpected, invaluable member of the group. Without her patient guidance, he would be departing with little or no understanding of these lands and people. And lastly, Amir, whose tender ways had massaged his heart. Being in the Orient might not have changed his art, but it had altered his sense of humanity. He smiled and wondered what his fellow travelers would say about him.

He stood and turned around slowly for one last circular glimpse of Petra under a night sky. The bright moonlight played on the walls of the Qasr al-Bint, casting sharp shadows which crept up from the fig trees. Two birds flew from the cornice of the temple and glided over the cook tent. He could see wisps of smoke drifting from the mouths of caves nearby. To the south, the dome-shaped mountain of Umm al-Biyara guarded the entrance to Wadi Thughra where the Huwaitát lived. He thought about Faisal and the family gathered around him.

As he walked toward his tent, he noticed that one of the camels stood, chewing his cud, nodding and watching. The other camels were lying down in a circle around Mika'il and his men asleep under lumps of camel blankets. What queer animals the camels were. Never failing to register their displeasure by spitting and screeching, then guarding their masters instead of sleeping.

No one saw the last embers of the fire, the closing of the eyes of the camel, the birds folding their wings. In the night a light snow fell, laying a silent, profound sleep on man and beast. Even the light of dawn did not arouse the sleepers. They turned and dug deeper into their burrow of blankets.

The last breakfast was a standing meal of egg sandwiches and tea. They chatted and watched the men take down the tents, shaking the snow from the canvas before folding and packing them onto the camels which would move west for their evening camp at the edge of Wadi Arabah. When the horses and camels were saddled, it was time for farewells.

Hudson, Fowler, and Lockwood shook hands and clapped backs with wishes for a safe journey.

Fowler reached for Anne's hands. "I will miss you, Anne Mezrab. Bridging cultures is a delicate balance, and you taught us invaluable lessons in looking through the eyes of others. *Inshallah*, we will meet again in England."

Anne kissed him on both cheeks before she brushed a little

snow from his shoulder. Words stuck in her throat.

Hudson stepped forward to embrace her. "You have enriched my life in so many ways, Anne. I find it hard to say goodbye."

Anne whispered in his ear, "Do not say goodbye. Say, *ma' as salama*, go in peace." Then she reached a hand to each man. "Come and visit us in Damascus, before you leave Beirut for home."

Amir stood quietly beside Anne, looking sadly from face to face until his eyes settled on Hudson.

"Amir, could you help me with something?" Hudson asked.

"*Ma'lum*, of course!" The boy's eyes brightened. "I was afraid you would forget to say goodbye to me," he grinned.

"Follow me." Hudson led Amir toward the temple where he had placed his paintbox on one of the fallen columns. "I would like you to keep this box, my friend, and someday paint one of your camels for me."

"But what will you do without it, Mr. Hudson?"

"*Maalesh*, never mind, I have more paints and brushes in Beirut."

Amir's eyes were shining; he reached for Hudson's hand and covered it in kisses. "For you, I will paint Amma's camel!" He grabbed the box and ran to Anne to show his prize.

Anne, Amir, and Lockwood rode east toward El Khasneh, through the Siq, to Elji where they would join Sheikh Gaad for the two days of travel to Kerak.

Mika'il led Hudson and Fowler on a hike up to El Deir, a last excursion in the world of the Nabateans before mounting horses and heading west to Gaza. As they climbed out of the valley, they stopped for a last view.

A Bedouin caravan was entering from the east, traveling slowly from the ravine, past the theater, and toward Wadi al-Farasah where Jamal and Faisal had grazed their goats. The elongated string of camels bearing men and goods and moving across the landscape filled him with yearning. It stirred a desire for the simplicity of a life following the rhythms of the land, the day and the night, the seasons to plant, reap, hibernate. He thought of his farm north of the city and the quiet and safe shelter it offered his family. His eyes softened with tears as he felt the pull of home.

In less than an hour they reached El Deir, the large classical temple projecting from a high plateau. One more brief climb alongside the temple brought them level with the urn at the top. From that great height they surveyed the vast landscape of mountains and wadis they had traversed during the past weeks. In the distance, drifts of snow sat in high mountain pockets. Nearby, acacia trees, denuded by goats in the winter, leafed out again.

Fowler pointed to the tiny leaves on the withered branches. "Amazing the way nature regenerates in an unlikely environment, is it not?"

"There are times, Fowler, when I think you are wandering inside my mind." Hudson grinned at the similarity of their present thoughts. "I feel I have regenerated in an unlikely landscape."

"Does that mean you are feeling more optimistic about your artistic efforts in Petra?"

Hudson looked down to shield his emotions and pushed some pebbles around with his foot. "I believe I have renewed my faith in myself and my art. Any paintings arising from this journey will pale beside that achievement." He paused before raising his head. "Lying in bed last night, I kept returning to Anne's remarks about the Bedouin, and the question of how we choose to live our lives. For the Bedouin, life is an enduring circle of actions, repeating through generations, and a belief in the value of continuing the pattern. Our western lives are more linear than circular. We move forward on a continuum of rising expectations, looking toward some distant satisfaction. Somewhere there is an equilibrium, my friend, and the trick is to know when you have arrived."

March, 1868 Hudson Diary, Petra to Gaza
Dearest Katharine,
Today brings a rich feeling of anticipation—my return journey has begun. While it will still be almost a month before we will be together, at least I am now heading in your direction.

I leave Petra with a jumble of sketches, but I expect there will be only one painting from the valley—the view of El Khasneh for you. Sometimes we artists fall in love with landscapes of our imaginations. We seek those places, and when we find them, they are empty of meaning for us. I have journeyed across endless deserts and through ancient ruins, collecting images and sensations, sketching a nature God and man shaped to speak a language of time and memory. It is not my language, but it is a language of enlightenment. The Orient is not a new direction for me, rather a detour illuminating my way.

While coming here will not result in a treasure chest of paintings, much was found and redeemed within me. I hope you will recognize your loving Thomas when I return to your arms. While my exterior may be slightly worn, my inner being is greatly restored.

Your adoring Thomas

EPILOGUE

May 1870, Letter From Thomas Hudson, New York City

Dear Fowler,

It has been two years since we parted on the dock in Beirut. If I had written every time I thought of you or mentioned your name in conversations, you would be drowning in letters. I think of you settled into the Oxford community—delivering brilliant lectures, herding your students toward wisdom, reading in your study by the fireplace, and traveling now and again.

You will know I have been busy when you read that Katharine and I have two more sons to join Tommy. One born in March 1869, and another born in April of this year. Katharine still yearns for a daughter, but we will take a small break from the baby-making business.

Before I left Beirut, I made a small excursion to Damascus to visit Anne and Medjuel. Medjuel is a gracious, attractive man, but reserved in his conversation. Anne was demure in his presence, but when he left the house on business, she was as lively and charming as ever. Their home is just beyond the old walls of Damascus, and is built in a style most appealing to me. Following the Oriental custom, there is a courtyard inside the main gate, but Anne replaced the usual marble paving with an English country garden. In April, roses and trumpet vines were in bloom, watered by a large oblong pool fed by water from the nearby river. Four fountains bubbled gently, and doves fluttered from a dovecote. The main room of the house, beyond the courtyard, is used for receiving visitors, and consists of a spacious atrium which opens onto a raised divan strewn with carpets and cushions.

Oriental architecture settled into my brain, and Katharine and I have now discarded earlier drawings for a French chateau in favor of a Persian style mansion on top of our hill north of New York City. It will be finished in two years, and I hope memories of the East will tempt you to visit us.

As for my painting, my easel has been fully occupied since returning home. For unknown reasons, the appeal of eastern Mediterranean landscapes grew stronger after I left Syria and Palestine. At a distance, I am more affected by the poetry of the land. I continue to feel that painting the American landscape is my natural gift, but I have grown as an artist by painting a few interpretations of Oriental sentiments. Recently, I completed a large landscape of classical ruins among mountains reaching down to the coast of Syria. The tone of the painting is melancholy, evocative of past glory and present uncertainty. I believe it expresses all the thoughts I am unable to translate into words.

In the night, in the time between sentience and sleep, I often travel again to the barren mountains and parched valleys of El Yemen, the lonely ruins of Petra, the warmth of friends around a campfire. I weave these visions as silken threads into the tapestry of my life.

Yours with friendship and affection, Thomas

AUTHOR'S NOTE

Petra is a work of fiction inspired by people and ideas of the mid-nineteenth century. The three main characters are based on prominent figures who existed in the time and place of the events. The story is a stew of three cups wild imagination, one cup meaty fact, and several tablespoons of spice.

Thomas Hudson resembles the Hudson River School painter, Frederic Edwin Church, and he has 'borrowed' several of Church's paintings and experiences for his portfolio. Church traveled in Syria and Palestine during 1868, and his painting of El Khasneh hangs in Olana, his Oriental style mansion near Hudson, New York.

The great French Orientalist painter, Jean-Léon Gérôme, enters the story in the transparent guise of Jacques Vesoul. The author has shamelessly stolen his physical appearance, personality, and several of his stunning canvases for Vesoul.

Anne Hardy Mezrab embodies the spirit of the adventurous Jane Digby Mezrab, a woman who fascinates at every moment of her European and Oriental adventures. Her life among the Bedouin of Syria gives weight to her vital role in the caravan.

The letters are inventions, but include a few remarks from actual diaries and letters of Frederic Church and his wife, Isabel, written during their months in Syria and Palestine.

Shelves of books were helpful in creating the journey. For the artists, excellent studies exist. *The Paintings of Frederic Edwin Church* by Franklin Kelly. *In Search of the Promised Land* by Gerald L. Carr.

Frederic Church by John K. Howat. The Middle East diaries and letters of Frederic and Isabel Church are located in the archives of the Olana State Historic Site Hudson New York. *The Life and Work of Jean-Léon Gérôme: with a catalogue raisonné* by Gerald M. Ackerman. *The Spectacular Art of Jean-Léon Gérôme* edited by Laurence des Cars, Dominique de Font-Réaulx, and Édouard Papet. A lively telling of the exploits of Jane Digby Mezrab is *Rebel Heart: the scandalous life of Jane Digby* by Mary S. Lovell.

Many historical works and travel narratives were essential for historical detail, and the author owes a particular debt to the following nineteenth and twentieth century works. Excerpts of *Personal Diary of Jean-Léon Gérôme*, 1868, translated for me by Caroline B. Young. *Notes on the Bedouins and Wahabys* by Johann Burckhardt. *The Desert of the Exodus* by Edward Henry Palmer. *Travels in Arabia Deserta* by Charles M. Doughty. *The Fayoum or Artists in Egypt* by Paul Lenoir. *Black Tents of Arabia: my life among the Bedouins* by Carl R. Raswan. *The Arab of the Desert* by H. R. P. Dickson. *Bedouin Law from Sinai and the Negev: justice without government* by Clinton Bailey.

The writing of Petra draws from my life experiences. The themes and characters are based on eight years of international development work and life in Washington, Jordan and South Asia; ten years of foreign affairs research and writing for the Congressional Research Service at the Library of Congress; eleven years of helping students with research at Middlebury College; and many, years of researching and writing about the life and work of Frederic Edwin Church, a leading figure among the Hudson River School painters. In creating friendships that did not exist and incidents that did not occur, I have tried to steer my camel very close to the terrain I traveled in this fictional work.

My journey to Petra was nourished by family and friends willing to read and offer comments or simply express welcome words of interest and encouragement.

Close readings by my daughter, Laura Rose, helped me question and clarify ideas and language. My son, Brian Schwarzwalder, and his wife, Nashra Rahman, encouraged me from their distant shores. Bob and Donna Kanich waded through the confusions of an early draft and set me on a better path. I thank Virginia Kanich and Joanne Young for their continuing interest and encouragement.

No influence compares with that of Sally Stiles, my writing mentor. She welcomed me into her writing class and writers' group, connected me with her generous editor, Phyllis Barber, and commented with patient intelligence on endless revisions. John Conlee formatted the book more times than I want to remember and rescued me from stumbles, as did the other members of my writers' group, Katharine Fournier and Mac Laird.

I am grateful to Ellen Lesser for welcoming me into the Postgraduate Writers' Conference of the Vermont College of Fine Arts and to all the faculty and participants of the conference who sharpened my creative instincts, especially Lee Martin.

Other friends donated insightful comments and sustaining encouragement, and I am grateful to them: Caroline and Richard Young, Caroline H. Williams, Richard Cronin, Jack Van Horn, Anne and Larry Heilman, Ursula Darrah, Jurij Dobczansky, Fleur and Russell Laslocky, Bland Blackford, Chris Llewellyn, Marjorie Robbins, Dinah Smith, Suzy Slavin, Paula Scott, Simone Whittemore, and Joanne Schneider. Special thanks to Éva Borsody Das for joining my journey to rediscover Jordan and Petra. In Jordan, Barbara Porter, Director of the American Center of Oriental Research, shared thoughts and contacts for Petra and Wadi Arabah and offered valuable comments on the book. Over several years, Evelyn Trebilcock, Valerie Balint, and Ida Brier, staff members of Olana, have graciously provided important research materials. Olana was the home of Frederic and Isabel Church in Hudson, New York, and it is now a State Historic Site open to the public.

33549764R00211

Made in the USA
Charleston, SC
18 September 2014